THE RANGE
DETECTIVES

THE RANGE DETECTIVES

WILLIAM W. JOHNSTONE

with J. A. Johnstone

PINNACLE BOOKS
Kensington Publishing Corp.
www.kensingtonbooks.com

PINNACLE BOOKS are published by

Kensington Publishing Corp.
119 West 40th Street
New York, NY 10018

PUBLISHER'S NOTE
Following the death of William W. Johnstone, the Johnstone family is working with a carefully selected writer to organize and complete Mr. Johnstone's outlines and many unfinished manuscripts to create additional novels in all of his series like The Last Gunfighter, Mountain Man, and Eagles, among others. This novel was inspired by Mr. Johnstone's superb storytelling.

All Kensington titles, imprints, and distributed lines are available at special quantity discounts for bulk purchases for sales promotions, premiums, fund-raising, educational, or institutional use. Special book excerpts or customized printings can also be created to fit specific needs. For details, write or phone the office of the Kensington sales manager: Kensington Publishing Corp., 119 West 40th Street, New York, NY 10018, attn: Sales Department; phone 1-800-221-2647.

PINNACLE BOOKS, the Pinnacle logo, and the WWJ steer head logo, are Reg. U.S. Pat. & TM Off.

ISBN-13: 978-0-7860-4491-7
ISBN-10: 0-7860-4491-8

First printing: April 2016

10 9 8 7 6 5 4

Printed in the United States of America

An electronic edition is available:

ISBN-13: 978-0-7860-3814-5
ISBN-10: 0-7860-3814-4

CHAPTER ONE

The rider who brought his horse to a stop at the edge of a pine-covered bluff so he could look out over the verdant Tonto Basin country was young, with clean-cut features and dark hair under a thumbed-back Stetson. He sat his saddle with the easy grace of a born horseman, but a certain tenseness gripped him as well, a readiness for trouble.

Lord knew he had ridden into plenty of it here in this corner of Arizona Territory.

The basin rolled away to the northeast. On the far side of it was a dark line marking the Mogollon Rim. The country below the rim was good rangeland for the most part, although in some areas the grass was a little sparse. There were a number of successful ranches in the basin, including the Box D, the spread Dan Hartford rode for.

He was on Box D range now and was supposed to be looking for some cattle that might have strayed in this direction. The herd was bunched in the higher pastures, but for some reason a few cows always got it into their heads to drift back down to the lower reaches of the basin where they had spent the winter.

Dan's eyes searched the landscape below him but didn't spot any of the stock he was looking for. He stiffened in his saddle and turned his horse as he heard hoofbeats approaching from behind him.

A rider emerged from the pines and headed for the edge of the rocky bluff. Dan recognized her instantly. She sat a saddle with the ease and grace of a Western gal, born and bred. Her long brown hair was pulled into a ponytail that hung down her back. She wore a soft flannel shirt, a split riding skirt, and a flat-crowned black hat with a cord pulled snug under her chin.

A sheath strapped to the young woman's saddle carried a short-barreled Winchester carbine. It had been a good while since there had been any Indian trouble around here, but there were always four-legged varmints to think about—and plenty of two-legged ones as well.

The young woman rode up to Dan and reined in. He gave her a curt nod and said, "Mrs. Dempsey."

"Hello, Mr. Hartford," the wife of his employer said, her voice cool but not unfriendly. "What are you doing up here this morning?"

"Looking for stray stock, as usual."

"Have you found any?"

"Not yet. The day's young, though."

Dan heard other horses moving through the trees. Three men rode into view and came straight toward Dan and Mrs. Dempsey.

The rider in the lead had a crisp, military bearing, an impression that his neatly trimmed gray mustache reinforced. His clothes weren't fancy, but they were functional and of high quality, from the boots to the gray Stetson that matched his hair and mustache.

The other two men were clearly ranch hands, one of them lean and middle-aged, the other younger and burlier, with a thatch of blond hair under his sweat-stained hat. His face was either flushed or had a permanent sunburn.

The leader of the group said to the young woman in an annoyed voice, "You shouldn't have galloped off from us like that, Laura. You know there's no telling what you might run into out here."

"I didn't run into anything except Mr. Hartford," Laura Dempsey said. "I don't think he represents any sort of threat, Abel."

Dempsey grunted and seemed unconvinced of that. He said, "What are you doing over here, Hartford?"

Dan was getting a little tired of people asking him that question, but he said, "Just looking for some cows that might have strayed down from the higher pastures."

"I told Dan to do that, Mr. Dempsey," the older of the two cowhands said. "Figured I could spare him from any other chores this mornin'."

Dempsey nodded and said, "All right, then, that's fine. You know I trust your judgment, Lew. That's why you're my foreman." The rancher looked at Dan and made a brusque motion with his head. "Get on with your work, Hartford."

"Sure, boss," Dan said, even though the words tasted a little bitter in his mouth. He lifted his reins and nudged his horse into motion toward the head of the trail that led down into the basin.

He heard Dempsey say behind him, "Come along,

Laura, and don't run off like that again. I know you're young and impulsive, but you're too reckless. You're going to ride right into trouble one of these days."

"I'm sure I won't as long as I have you around to look after me, Abel," Laura said.

Dan looked back to see her turning her horse and falling in alongside her husband as Dempsey rode away. Lew Martin, who ramrodded the Box D for Dempsey, and the stocky cowboy, Jube Connolly, followed them back into the trees.

They had been quick to ask him what he was doing, thought Dan, but none of them had offered any explanations for their presence here. Of course, that wasn't surprising. This was Dempsey's range, and he had a right to go wherever he wanted. And as a rich man, he wasn't in the habit of explaining himself to any of the hombres who worked for him.

As a rich man's wife, Laura was the same way, Dan supposed. Martin and Connolly were employees, and it wasn't their place to speak up.

Dan told himself to concentrate on the chore that had brought him to this part of the ranch and not waste time brooding over situations he couldn't do anything about.

He had been riding through the basin for another fifteen minutes or so, still without spotting any strays, when he heard hoofbeats drumming rapidly behind him. He reined in and turned his horse, moving his hand to the well-worn butt of the gun on his hip as he did so.

Even though this was a basin, the elevation was still high enough that the air didn't get as hot as it did farther south, closer to the border, but the day was still warm enough that no Westerner worth his salt would run a horse that hard unless there was a good reason.

Dan spotted the rider and recognized him, but that didn't make him relax. If anything, the tension inside him increased. He didn't particularly like Jube Connolly, and since Jube had been with Dempsey, Laura, and Lew Martin just a short time earlier, his presence here made Dan think something might have happened to one of those three.

"Something wrong, Jube?" Dan called to the florid-faced puncher as Connolly reined in.

"The boss sent me to talk to you," Connolly replied. He swung down from the saddle and added, "Light down from that horse."

A puzzled frown creased Dan's face, but he did as Connolly said. As he stood there holding his mount's reins, he asked, "When you say the boss, do you mean Lew or Mr. Dempsey?"

"Mr. Dempsey," Connolly replied. He moved closer. "He's got a message he wants me to give you."

Dan was more confused than ever. He said, "What sort of message?"

"This," Connolly said.

He uncorked a sudden punch that took Dan by surprise. Connolly's blocky fist crashed into Dan's jaw and sent him reeling back as his hat flew off his head. He lost his balance and sat down hard, thankfully not landing on any of the cactus plants that were scattered around here.

He was stunned, and pain from the blow filled his head, but he was able to exclaim, "What the hell!"

Instinctively, his hand went to his gun again. Connolly rushed him, and just as Dan cleared leather, the toe of Connolly's boot smacked into the wrist of his gun hand. The revolver went flying from Dan's fingers and landed in the dirt several yards away.

"Damn it! Jube, what—"

Connolly reached down, grabbed hold of Dan's shirt, and hauled him to his feet. Connolly's fist sunk into his gut. Dan doubled over as sickness filled his belly.

"Mr. Dempsey don't like you hangin' around his wife," Connolly said. "It ain't fittin' for the two of you to be out here alone together, talkin'."

Dan was able to straighten up some as he pressed his hands to his aching belly. He said angrily, "It wasn't my idea! I was just doing my job when she rode up. And talking is *all* we were doing. Not much of that, either. She'd been there less than a minute when the rest of you rode up."

That much talking exhausted him, as bad as he felt at the moment. He stood there gasping for breath while Connolly leered at him.

"Mr. Dempsey saw the way you was lookin' at her. You can't blame him for gettin' a mite hot under the collar. Fella his age, married to a gal as young and easy on the eyes as Mrs. Dempsey, he's gotta be worried all the time about no-account saddle tramps sniffin' around her, makin' eyes at her—"

"I wasn't doing any of that!" Dan protested. "And I'm not a damned saddle tramp, either."

"No? You was ridin' the grub line, that's for sure, when you drifted in and talked Lew into hirin' you. I thought it was a bad idea then, and I still do. I don't trust you, Hartford. Might be a good idea for you to just draw your time and ride on. Then you wouldn't be tempted to bother Mrs. Dempsey again."

"I wasn't—" Dan stopped short and glared at Connolly. He said through clenched teeth, "You can go back to Mr. Dempsey and tell him I'm not going anywhere, Jube. Or you can just go to hell. I don't care."

That leering grin spread even wider across Connolly's beefy face. He balled his hands into fists and stepped closer as he said, "I was hopin' you'd take more convincin'—"

Dan didn't let him get any farther than that. The young cowboy lowered his head and launched himself into a diving tackle.

CHAPTER TWO

The counterattack seemed to surprise Connolly as much as Dan had been surprised by that sucker punch. Dan rammed a shoulder into the bigger man's solar plexus and pushed hard with his legs, forcing Connolly backward. Even though Connolly outweighed him, Dan was muscular and possessed plenty of wiry strength. He drove Connolly off his feet.

Dan landed on top of him and hooked a right and a left into Connolly's midsection. Connolly might look a little soft, but he wasn't. Hitting him in the belly was like punching a side of beef. He didn't even grunt in pain.

Instead he grabbed Dan's bib-front shirt and slung him off. Dan rolled over a couple of times before he came to a stop on his stomach. He looked up to see Connolly scrambling to his feet.

"This ain't just a chore for the boss anymore," Connolly said. "I'm gonna stomp the guts outta you and enjoy it!"

He charged like a maddened bull. Desperately, Dan flung himself out of the way as Connolly's boots pounded the ground where he had been a heartbeat earlier. Dan rolled again, came up and wrapped both arms around one of Connolly's legs, and heaved. Once again the big man came crashing to earth.

This time when Dan went after him, he swung his fists at Connolly's face. He connected with the cowboy's squarish jaw and rocked Connolly's head to the side. That seemed to have a little more effect than punching him in the belly, but not much. Connolly roared and lashed out with an arm. It slammed into Dan's chest and knocked him away.

Both men made it to their feet at the same time. Connolly fumbled at the holster on his hip, but it was empty, the gun he normally carried there having fallen out during the fracas. Dan thought about making a diving leap for his gun, but Connolly didn't give him time. The big man charged again, windmilling punches.

Dan was quick enough to block most of the blows, but a few of them got through and jolted him to his core. At the same time, Connolly was attacking, not trying to defend himself, so Dan was able to land some punches of his own, mostly jabs that landed cleanly on his opponent's face. Connolly's head rocked back with each punch. Blood began trailing from his nostrils as his nose swelled.

More blood spurted when Dan smashed a hard left to Connolly's mouth. Connolly bellowed in pain and rage and renewed his attack, flailing even more wildly than before. He was big and strong and could take a lot of punishment, but he was stupid, thought Dan. Connolly was out of control now, and he proved it with another ill-advised charge.

Dan ducked out of the way, thrust out his leg, and

swept Connolly's legs from under him. Connolly pitched forward and yelled as he realized he was about to land face-first in a clump of cactus. He got his hands down enough to partially catch himself, but dozens of the wicked spines lanced into his palms and some stuck in his face despite his best efforts.

Connolly bucked and twisted away from the cactus. His bellows turned into screams as he writhed on the ground. Dan almost felt sorry for the brute—almost.

"Stop squirming around, Jube," he said. "I'll help you. Lord knows, you don't deserve it after the way you sucker-punched me like that, but—"

Connolly interrupted by spewing curses at him. As the profanity became even more vile, Dan turned away and scooped up his fallen gun. A quick glance down the barrel told him it wasn't fouled. He swung back toward Connolly, raised the gun, and eared back the hammer.

The metallic ratcheting of a gun being cocked was enough to shut up most men, no matter how they were carrying on. It worked on Connolly, who fell silent and lay there glaring up at Dan. His face and hands were already swelling from the cactus needles embedded in them.

"Just settle down," Dan told him. "I'll get those needles out of you, but you've got to give me your word this fight is over."

"I'll kill you," Connolly grated. "You don't know how bad an enemy you made today, Hartford."

"This is ridiculous," Dan snapped. "You attacked me for no reason. I didn't do a damned thing to act improperly toward Mrs. Dempsey. She's the boss's wife, for God's sake! You think I'd risk my job that way?"

Connolly didn't answer. Instead he started cursing

again. Dan blew out his breath in an exasperated sigh and shook his head.

"All right, I'll just ride away and leave you like this," he said. "How about that?"

"No! . . . Damn it, all right. I won't try anything else."

"Do I need to bend a gun barrel over your head to make sure of that?"

Connolly shook his head, grimacing because evidently that made his face hurt even more.

"No. Just get the blasted things outta me."

Dan holstered his gun and said, "Sit up where I can reach you."

He hunkered on his heels in front of Connolly, off to the side a little so it would be more difficult for the man to attack him if Connolly changed his mind. Dan was alert for trouble, but Connolly didn't do anything except cuss a blue streak as Dan plucked the cactus needles from his cheeks, chin, and forehead. Connolly couldn't very well throw any punches when his hands looked like pincushions.

"You look a little like a porcupine," Dan said with a wry smile.

"Shut up and get on with it," Connolly growled.

When Dan had all the spines out of the burly puncher's face, he straightened to his feet and backed off.

"You can pull the ones out of your hands yourself," he said. "Use your teeth if you have to. Just be careful you don't get any stuck in your tongue."

"That'll take a long time," Connolly protested.

"Yeah, I know, and I plan to be a long way from here by the time you finish. Don't try and jump me when we're both back in the bunkhouse tonight, either."

"You're gonna be sorry you ever met me, mister."

"I already am," Dan said.

He picked up his hat, slapped it against his thigh to knock some of the dust off it, and swung up into the saddle. He turned his horse and rode off, leaving Jube Connolly sitting there carefully picking cactus needles out of his palms.

Anger and disgust filled Dan, and a good chunk of those emotions was directed at himself. He was mad at Abel Dempsey for sending Connolly to give him a thrashing, and he was mad at Connolly for following that order so eagerly. But a lot of the trouble was his own fault because he should have known better than to come here to the Tonto Basin, to the Box D, where Abel Dempsey lived with his beautiful young wife.

Dan shoved those thoughts out of his head. Despite everything that had happened, he still had work to do, so he set about scouring the rangeland for those strays.

He found the wandering cattle, but working alone, it took him most of the day to do it. It was late afternoon before he was satisfied he had located all the missing stock and started driving the jag back toward the higher pastures.

His muscles were stiff and sore from the fight with Connolly, and his belly growled. He'd had a couple of biscuits left over from breakfast wrapped up in a cloth in one of his saddlebags, along with some jerky, so he'd made a midday meal out of that and washed it down with water from his canteen. He was looking forward to getting back to the bunkhouse and putting himself on the outside of some real grub as well as a few cups of coffee.

When Dan reached the higher pastures, he turned the cattle over to Hamp Jones and Charley Bartlett, the cowboys who were staying in the line shack up here.

"Don't lose 'em this time," Dan told them with a smile that took any sting out of the words.

"We'll try not to, but you know how damn mule-headed these critters can be," Hamp said.

"They're cows," Charley pointed out. "I don't see how they can be muleheaded."

"Yeah, well, *cowheaded* ain't a word, as far as I know," Hamp responded.

Dan left them to their good-hearted wrangling and headed for the ranch headquarters.

Night had fallen by the time he got there. By now supper was over, but he knew the stove-up old cowboy turned cook Willie Hill would have saved him some. He rode into the barn and started to unsaddle his horse in the dark, not needing a light to carry out a task he had performed thousands of times.

He wondered as he did so how Jube Connolly had explained the scores of little puncture wounds on his hands and face. Any seasoned range rider could guess that Connolly had landed in some cactus, but he wouldn't know the reason why.

Dan had just slung his saddle on one of the stands when he heard a soft step behind him. He turned quickly, his hand going to his gun, in case Connolly was about to try settling that score.

Instead he heard a gasp in the darkness of the barn and knew it wasn't Connolly sneaking up on him.

"Dan, don't . . . It's me . . ."

A lantern was burning on the front porch of the main house. Dan saw her silhouetted against the glow from it as she moved deeper into the barn.

"Hello, Mrs. Dempsey," he said stiffly.

"You don't have to be like that," Laura said. "Not now."

As if he hadn't heard her, he said, "You probably shouldn't be wandering around out here in the dark. There might be a rattler—"

"You're not worried about snakes. You're worried that somebody might see us." She was close enough now that he could smell the faint scent of lilac water that clung to her. "But it's all right. No one's around. I made sure of that. Abel is in his office, going over the books. He won't come out for hours. Lew has gone to his cabin, Willie is in the cook shack, and all the other hands are in the bunkhouse. There's nothing to worry about."

"Damn it, Laura . . ." The name came out of his mouth before he could stop it. "It was a mistake me ever coming here. We both know that. If I had a lick of sense, I'd put that saddle back on my horse, ride out, and never look back."

She reached out with her right hand, rested the fingertips on his chest, and whispered, "Is that what you're going to do, Dan?"

"You know good and well it's not," he rasped, then he closed his hands around her upper arms, pulled her tight against him, and brought his mouth down on hers in a kiss with enough hunger in it to jolt him more than Jube Connolly's fists ever could.

CHAPTER THREE

A week later, buggies, buckboards, and wagons began converging on the Box D from the other ranches in the Tonto Basin as well as from the town of Hat Creek, the only major settlement in the area. It was Laura Dempsey's birthday, and her husband was throwing her a party.

Dan would have just as soon avoided the celebration. In fact, he had approached Lew Martin the day before and asked the foreman if he could ride up to the line shack and let either Hamp or Charley come back in for a few days.

"No, those two old pelicans are fine right where they are," Lew had said. "They got no use for fancy parties."

"Well, neither do I," Dan had insisted.

Lew had been adamant, though. Abel Dempsey had declared the occasion a holiday, and everybody would participate, no exceptions.

"So I reckon you're just gonna have to drink punch, eat barbecue, and dance to the fiddle-playin' like the rest of us," Lew had decreed. "Just don't go startin' any more trouble with Jube Connolly."

This was the first time Dan had had a chance to talk to the foreman alone since the fracas with Connolly. He said sharply, "I didn't start the trouble last time. Jube jumped me without any warning. Did you know the boss set him on me like that?"

Lew looked like the question made him uncomfortable. He scratched at his grizzled jaw, then said, "Not exactly. Mr. Dempsey got Jube aside and said somethin' to him that I couldn't hear. Then Jube rode off. When I asked the boss about it, he just said he sent Jube on an errand. You know the boss. He ain't one for explainin' himself." Lew shrugged. "But when Jube come back lookin' like he'd run into a buzz saw and you showed up that night with some scrapes and bruises of your own, it was pretty obvious what'd happened. You want to tell me about it?"

"No," Dan had replied, his voice flat and hard.

"I've noticed the way you and Jube been avoidin' each other. My advice'd be to keep on doin' it."

"That's my plan," Dan had said.

He wasn't sure that was going to be possible today, though, he thought as he stood in the open door of the bunkhouse with a shoulder propped against the jamb and watched the visitors arrive. All the cowboys would be on hand for the party. Liquor would flow, even though the punch wasn't supposed to be spiked. Willie Hill had given strict orders about that, and no puncher with any sense crossed the cook. The men would leave the punch alone and instead sneak drinks from the flasks they carried.

Dan wouldn't be a bit surprised if Connolly came

looking for him before the day was over, eager to resume their battle.

Abel and Laura Dempsey were on the covered porch of the big house, greeting their guests. A buggy with silver trim, being pulled by a pair of magnificent black horses, stopped in front of the house, and a craggy-faced man with a thick mane of white hair under his black hat climbed down from the seat.

He turned back to the vehicle to help the woman who had been beside him climb down. She was considerably younger than he was, probably around thirty, with honey blond hair artfully arranged under a blue hat. The hat matched the dress that managed to reveal the fine lines of her body without being too blatant about it.

The gap between the ages of this couple was similar to that of the Dempseys', although Dan figured the difference wasn't as great since this woman was obviously older than Laura. The white-haired man took the blonde's arm and they went up onto the porch, where the man shook hands with Dempsey, and the blonde and Laura embraced like old friends.

It wasn't surprising that Laura had formed a friendship with the woman. They had something in common, after all.

The two couples were still talking in an animated fashion on the porch when Lew Martin walked up to where Dan was standing. Dan nodded toward the house and asked, "Who's that?"

Lew looked at the visitors and then said, "Yeah, I reckon they haven't been around since you rode in and signed on with us. That's Henry Stafford and his wife. Stafford owns the HS Bar spread, up at the north end of the basin."

"They look mighty friendly," Dan commented.

"Well, sure," the foreman said. "The boss and Mr. Stafford were some of the first cattlemen here in the basin. They fought the Utes and the Apaches together, as well as rustlers and the weather."

"That was before either of them was married, I guess."

"Well, not exactly. Stafford had a wife then, just not this one. She died of a fever about fifteen years back. The boss, now, he was an old bachelor until Miss Laura come along. To be honest, I figured he'd stay that way, but shoot, you can't blame a fella for fallin' for a gal like her."

"No," Dan said quietly, "you can't." He paused. "How did they meet. Do you know?"

"Mr. Dempsey and Miss Laura, you mean? I ain't exactly sure. The boss had gone to Saint Louis on business. Reckon that's where he met her, because she came back to the ranch with him to visit. They wasn't married yet, but she brung an old maid aunt with her, so ever'thing was plumb proper. They stayed awhile, then went back to Saint Louis. The boss, he moped around for a spell, then left again, and when he came back, he had Miss Laura with him and they was married. That's all I know." The foreman gave Dan a stern look. "And we hadn't ought to be standin' around, gossipin' and cluckin' like a pair o' old hens, when there's a party to go to. Willie's got damn near a whole cow roastin' on a spit, and as big a pot o' beans as you ever seen on the fire. Come on. Let's go see how it's comin' along."

"You go ahead, Lew," Dan said. "I don't have much of an appetite right now."

* * *

Even though this party was in celebration of her birthday, Laura didn't join in wholeheartedly. She had too much on her mind and had been in that condition for more than a month now, ever since Dan Hartford had ridden up to the Box D looking for a riding job.

During that time she had gotten good at hiding the turmoil in her mind and heart. Abel might be suspicious, but Abel was *always* suspicious. Laura was confident that she hadn't given him any specific reason to feel that way. She'd been careful, so careful, even though what she really wanted more than anything else in the world was to go to Dan, throw herself in his arms, and ride away with him . . .

"My goodness, Laura, you look like your thoughts are a million miles away from here."

The voice broke into Laura's reverie. She looked over at her friend Jessica Stafford, who wore an expression of concern on her face. The two women were sitting side by side in rocking chairs on the porch of the big house. Their husbands were standing in the shade of a nearby tree, smoking their pipes and talking about the ranching business, more than likely.

Dusk was settling over the basin. The party had been going on all afternoon. Laura had eaten more than she should have, drunk enough punch to last her for a long time, and smiled and thanked people for their good wishes until it seemed like her face would crack wide open. Now colored lanterns glowed in the trees, and the fiddlers were tuning up their instruments. The dancing would start soon.

"What in the world are you thinking about?" Jessica went on.

"Oh, just the strange twists and turns that life can take, I suppose."

Jessica laughed and said, "Those are pretty weighty thoughts for a girl on her birthday."

She had taken off her hat and unpinned her hair, which now fell in honey-colored waves around her shoulders. Laura thought she was beautiful in an elegant, worldly way that Laura herself would never be able to manage. Jessica made several trips a year to San Francisco and came back with the latest fashions, including the silk dress she wore now and looked stunning in.

Still, Laura was very glad to have Jessica for a friend. Jessica was a few years older, but she knew the challenges of being married to a man nearly twice her age. She seemed to be very happy with Henry Stafford. The two of them were a good match.

That was something she and Abel might never be, thought Laura.

"It would have been all right with me if Abel hadn't decided to throw this party," she said. "At my age, I'm not sure I should be celebrating a birthday."

"Nonsense," Jessica said without hesitation. "You're still young."

Over in the clearing next to the trees, the musicians began to play a sprightly tune. Folks young and old paired up and started to dance.

"In fact," Jessica went on, "we should march out there, grab hold of our husbands, and make them dance with us."

"Maybe you should, but Abel's not much for dancing. His right knee is still a little stiff, you know. It has been ever since he was wounded at Chancellorsville during the war."

The war in which Abel Dempsey had served with her father, Laura mused. Both men had commanded Union cavalry units and had become great friends during the epic clash with the Confederacy.

If not for that friendship, she wouldn't be here in Arizona Territory tonight, and she couldn't stop a trace of bitterness from creeping into her mind along with that thought.

"If Abel won't dance with you, there are a lot of handsome young cowboys here this evening who'd be happy to," Jessica pointed out.

Laura felt her face growing warm as she said, "I couldn't do that. It . . . it wouldn't be right."

"Well, that's just crazy. Dancing doesn't mean anything. It's just for fun."

"You really think so?"

"I *know* so. I'll dance with Henry tonight, sure, but I intend to dance with as many other men as I can, too."

"You're more daring than I am."

Jessica laughed and said, "Honey, you've got to have a little bit of daring in your life or you might as well already be dead and buried."

What her friend said made sense, Laura thought. She nodded and said, "All right. But I should probably ask Abel about it first."

"No, you shouldn't. Look at those two. They're complaining about the price of beef and about what all the politicians are doing in the territorial capital and anything else they can think of. When men get to be that age, complaining is their main leisure-time activity. Don't spoil their fun." Jessica stood up and held out a hand to Laura. "Come on."

Laura hesitated, but only for a second. Then she took Jessica's hand and stood up.

The two women went down the steps and started toward the area where the dancing was taking place. Laura glanced toward her husband and Henry Stafford. As Jessica had said, the two men were engrossed in their discussion, and neither of them seemed to have noticed that their wives had left the porch.

The fiddlers had launched into a second tune as merry as the first. Laura and Jessica paused at the edge of the clearing, and Jessica said, "It's not proper for ladies to cut in, so I guess we'll have to wait until the next song. I'm sure someone will ask us to dance."

Laura surprised herself by saying, "I don't think I want to wait." She headed for a cottonwood where a man stood leaning against the trunk with his back to her. Behind her, Jessica laughed in approval of Laura's boldness.

Laura stopped behind the man, touched him lightly on the shoulder, and as he started to turn toward her in obvious surprise, she said, "You're going to dance with me, Dan Hartford."

CHAPTER FOUR

Dan drew his breath in sharply as he saw Laura standing there. She looked beautiful, of course, in the light of the colored lanterns in the trees, but she had looked beautiful all day, so much so that he'd barely been able to keep his eyes off her. She wore a green dress that went well with her brown hair and eyes, and an emerald necklace sparkled at her throat.

He could never afford to give her something like that, he thought. Not on the wages a cowboy made. Not even on what he could earn from a spread of his own. That was his other dream, and neither of them were likely to ever come true.

Without thinking, he said, "Laura, you'd better go back—"

"Go and sit on the porch like a good little wife, you mean?" she broke in. "I'm tired of that, Dan. That's why I want you to dance with me."

"You're my boss's wife, Mrs. Dempsey." He emphasized the title. "I don't reckon it would be proper."

"And right now I don't care what's proper. If you work for my husband, that means you work for me, too, *Mr.* Hartford. And I'm ordering you to dance with me."

Anger welled up inside him. No matter how he felt about her, she had no right to talk to him like that. Something had her stirred up—no doubt the resentment she felt toward Dempsey, who was ignoring her as usual and talking to Henry Stafford—and she was letting that out.

"Don't do this, Laura," Dan said quietly.

"It's high time that I did," she said.

He sensed the determination in her and knew she wasn't going to give up, now that she had her mind set on this. He said, "All right, I'll dance with you, but you have to dance with some of the other fellas first. That way there won't be anything that looks unusual about it."

"I don't want to dance with anybody else. And you don't want me to make a scene, do you, Dan?"

"Damn it . . ." He grimaced and took her hand. "Let's get this over with."

"You could at least look happy about it," she said as she faced him and put her other hand on his shoulder. He slid his free arm around her waist, and they began stepping and turning in time to the music.

The problem was, he was *too* happy to have her in his arms like this, he thought as they twirled. He was careful to keep some distance between them, but he felt the soft warmth of her body through their clothes and it made him want to pull her against him. He wanted the music to slow down, so they could dance close and she could rest her head against his chest and the tantalizing fragrance of her hair would fill his senses . . .

"By God!" an angry voice said loudly. The music

came to an abrupt stop. A hard hand gripped Dan's shoulder, pulled him away from Laura, and hauled him around. As the people around them stared, Abel Dempsey went on, "Get your hands off my wife."

That was bad enough, but then Dempsey did something worse.

He slapped Dan across the face.

Dan's first instinct was to strike back, to bring up a fist and crash it into the older man's jaw. He reined in that impulse for a couple of reasons: for one thing, Dempsey was his boss, and for another, the rancher was twenty years older than he was. Dan had been raised to respect his elders—even when they sometimes didn't deserve it.

Standing there with the imprint of Dempsey's hand hot on his cheek, Dan said tightly, "I'm going to let that slide—"

Dempsey slapped him again, this time with the left hand.

"Abel, no!" Laura cried. "What are you doing?"

"Defending your honor from this boorish cowboy," Dempsey snapped. "He should have known better than to ask you to dance with him."

"But he didn't—"

Dempsey ignored her, balled his hands into fists, and moved toward Dan.

"Now I'm going to give him a thrashing before I throw him off this ranch for good."

Dan could stand a lot when he had to, but damned if he was going to let Dempsey attack him again without fighting back. He had turned the other cheek, like it said in the Good Book, and wound up with both of them slapped.

Dempsey wasn't going to hit him again. Dan swore that to himself.

Laura must have seen the light of battle in his eyes. She moved quickly, trying to get between the two men and forestall any fighting. Dan didn't figure it would do any good, though. Dempsey had his heart set on a ruckus.

"Abel, please—" Laura began.

A man yelled, "I'll get him, boss!"

Dan's head whipped toward the sound of the shout. He was just in time to see Jube Connolly leaping toward him with a savage snarl on the flushed, round face.

Connolly crashed into him and drove him to the side, scattering the guests who had been dancing but had stopped to watch the confrontation between Dan and Abel Dempsey.

"Watch out for my fiddle, gol dang it!" one of the musicians yelled as the crowd jostled him.

Dan heard Laura cry out, then he slammed into the ground with Connolly on top of him. The impact drove the air from his lungs and stunned him.

Connolly's fists pounded into Dan's head and body. He could tell that he was about to pass out and knew that if he didn't fight back right now, he wasn't going to get the chance to.

He struck desperately with a left that connected with the side of Connolly's head. That made the big man pause for a second. Dan took advantage of that to rocket his right fist straight up under Connolly's chin.

Hitting that rocklike wedge might not have done any good if the tip of Connolly's tongue hadn't been sticking out between his teeth. Connolly howled in pain as he bit deeply into it. Blood sprayed from his mouth and splattered over Dan's face.

Dan grabbed Connolly by the throat with both hands and rolled over, forcing Connolly off him. With that weight gone, Dan could finally gasp for breath again. He bore down with his grip on Connolly's throat, digging in with his thumbs as in his rage he sought to crush the man's windpipe.

Blood roared in Dan's head like a raging river. He barely heard the order Dempsey shouted.

"Get him! He's going to kill Jube!"

Maybe, maybe not, but a second after Dempsey yelled that command, the toe of a boot caught Dan in the ribs. The vicious kick knocked him to the side and made him let go of Connolly.

Strong hands clamped around his arms and jerked him to his feet. His dark hair fell over his eyes. Through it he saw a couple of men closing in on him from the front while two more held him from behind. He couldn't see that pair, but the two in front of him he recognized as Box D cowboys named Stanton and Fenner. Even though they rode for the same brand, Dan didn't consider either man a friend.

He knew they were cronies of Jube Connolly's, though, and he saw the anger on their faces. The men holding him were probably more of the same.

He threw himself backward as hard as he could, staggering the men behind him, but their grips on him didn't come loose. Dan raised a foot and drove his boot heel into Fenner's belly as soon as the man was close enough. Fenner gasped and folded up.

Stanton was in reach, too, but Dan didn't get a chance to kick him. Stanton slammed a fist into

Dan's jaw and rocked his head back and to the side. A heartbeat later, Stanton's other fist sank into Dan's belly with enough force to sicken him. Stanton swung and hit him in the face again.

"Lemme at him," Fenner rasped as he recovered a little from the kick Dan had landed in his midsection. He bored in and crashed a left and a right into Dan's face.

A lot of shouting was going on, and Dan thought he heard Laura pleading with her husband to stop the beating, but he couldn't be sure. The punches didn't stop, though. Again and again, Stanton and Fenner hit him. Pain washed through Dan's body. He felt blood dripping from his nose and mouth.

"By God, that's enough!" somebody bellowed. "That's enough, I say!"

The shout might not have done any good, but the boom of a shotgun did. Nobody could ignore that. The blows stopped, although the men holding Dan hung on to him.

That was probably a good thing, because he would have fallen flat on his face if they had let go of him.

Through slitted, swollen eyes, Dan saw Lew Martin stride up in front of him. The foreman held a shotgun. Wisps of powder smoke still curled from the right-hand barrel. The left barrel was still loaded and menacing.

"There's no need for you to interfere in this, Lew," Dempsey snapped. "It's a matter between the men."

"Men who ride for the same brand I do," Lew said. "Men who are fixin' to beat to death one of their own, a member of the same crew."

Jube Connolly had made it to his feet by now. Grimacing in pain because of his injured tongue, he rubbed his throat and said hoarsely, "Aw, Hartford ain't one of us, Lew. He never has been, and you know it. He's been lookin' down his nose at us ever since he rode in, and he's nothin' but a saddle tramp!"

"And he assaulted my wife and was about to strike me," Dempsey said. "I wouldn't have let the men kill him, but he had a beating coming to him."

Laura began, "Abel, that's not the way it—"

Dempsey turned toward her so sharply that she took an involuntary step back.

"I mean . . ."

"Everyone here saw what happened," Dempsey interrupted her again. He stalked over so that he was in front of Dan, shouldering Lew Martin aside as he did so. "You're fired, Hartford. I'll give Lew the wages you have coming, and he can pay you. I can't stomach looking at you anymore. I want you off this ranch tonight, and if you're caught on Box D range again, you'll be considered a trespasser and my men will be within their rights to shoot you." Dempsey raised his voice. "I think everyone here understands what I just told you. Do you?"

"Yeah, I . . . reckon I understand," Dan ground out. The words were slurred as he forced them through his bloody, swollen lips.

"Good." Dempsey jerked his head commandingly. "Get him out of my sight." Then he turned away, put a smile on his face, and raised his hands as he went on, "Sorry for the interruption, folks. Nothing important, just a no-account cowboy getting too big for his britches. Let's get back to the party, shall we?" He held out a hand to Laura. "A dance, my dear?"

The men who had hold of Dan were already hustling him away, but he was able to glance back over his shoulder. He saw Laura standing there with her husband. All the color was drained out of her face. She hesitated . . .

Then she reached out and took Dempsey's hand.

Dan groaned. What he had just seen hurt worse than any of the punches he'd endured tonight.

CHAPTER FIVE

The two riders jogging their horses along one of the trails that cut through the Tonto Basin were a study in contrasts.

The one in the black, high-crowned hat was tall and lean, with a sun-browned face like a hawk and a thick black mustache that drooped over his wide mouth. He wore a cowhide vest and a white shirt and had chaps strapped on over his denim trousers. The trouser legs were stuck down inside high-topped black boots. The man carried a heavy, ivory-handled Colt in a black holster on his right hip.

His companion was much shorter and stockier, facts that were evident even though both men were on horseback. This second man had a thatch of red hair under a thumbed-back brown Stetson, wore a buckskin shirt and whipcord trousers, and packed a Colt with plain walnut grips. His face was open and friendly, with a scattering of freckles across his nose and cheeks.

The two riders had a couple of things in common.

Each carried a Winchester in a saddle sheath, and their gazes were alert and intelligent as they looked around at the countryside they rode through.

"Well, we're back in Arizona Territory, Stovepipe," the redhead commented.

His gangling companion nodded slowly and drawled, "Yep, we appear to be."

"You reckon we'll run into as much trouble as we did the last time we were here?"

"You mean when we got tangled up with those fellas Bodine and Two Wolves?"* The man called Stovepipe shook his head. "I hope not. That whole mess was plumb fatiguin'."

"You don't fool me none. There's nothing you like better than sticking that big ol' nose of yours in some ruckus where it don't belong."

"Are you makin' disparagin' comments about my countenance, Wilbur?"

"No, I'm making disparaging comments about how you always poke around and stir things up until before you know it, folks are shootin' at us!"

Stovepipe reined in and sat up straighter in the saddle as he lifted his head to listen.

"You mean like that?" he asked.

Wilbur had tensed as well. He listened to the distant popping and banging for a moment and then said, "Not exactly. All that gunfire is a ways off. Somebody else besides us is gettin' shot at for a change."

"Yeah, I think you're right," said Stovepipe. He heeled his Appaloosa into a faster pace.

*See the novel *Blood Bond: Arizona Ambush*.

"Dadgum it!" Wilbur called. He hurried his dun after his partner's Palouse. "You're going the wrong way!"

Stovepipe pointed and said, "I'm goin' toward whoever's burnin' all that powder."

"That's what I mean!"

Wilbur's objections didn't stop him from pulling alongside his lanky companion. Both men rode like they had been born to the saddle, looking almost like centaurs as they galloped across the sage-dotted range.

The flats they were crossing ended about half a mile away in a rocky bluff that had pine trees jutting from its top. Beyond it, far in the distance, the higher escarpment of the Mogollon Rim was visible.

"The shots are comin' from the other side of that bluff," Stovepipe said, raising his voice over the drumming of hoofbeats so Wilbur could hear him.

"Do you know what's on the other side?"

"Don't have a clue," answered Stovepipe with a grin. "That's one more reason to go and have a look-see."

Wilbur muttered something Stovepipe couldn't make out, but it didn't really matter. The tall, lanky cowboy knew his old friend was just as curious about such things as he was. Wilbur just didn't like to admit it, that's all.

As they drew closer to the bluff, Stovepipe's keen eyes searched for a trail leading to the top. He spotted one and pointed it out to his redheaded companion. Their horses, both strong, spirited animals, took the steep trail with relative ease, and a few moments later, they rode out onto the tree-covered bluff.

The terrain was mostly flat up here, too, though some green hills rose a couple of miles away, which Stovepipe saw as the trees thinned out some and the landscape opened out into grassy pastures. Brown spots here and there marked areas where the vegetation was sparser, but that was to be expected in this semiarid climate. There was enough graze to make this good ranching country.

Stovepipe reined in, pointed again, and said, "Yonderways."

"Yeah, I see 'em," said Wilbur. "One man being chased by . . . how many would you say? Eight or ten riders?"

"At least that many," Stovepipe responded.

"And that don't sit well with you, does it?"

Stovepipe shook his head and said, "Nope."

"Even though we don't have a shadow of an idea what it's all about. For all we know, that hombre bein' chased may be the worst varmint in the whole territory."

"Might be," drawled Stovepipe, "but I still don't like ten-to-one odds."

With that, he jabbed his boot heels into the Appaloosa's flanks and sent the horse galloping forward again.

The seemingly desperate chase was taking place in front of them, moving from right to left about a quarter of a mile away. At that distance, even Stovepipe's eagle-eyed vision couldn't make out many details. He had a good pair of field glasses in his saddlebags that would have told him a lot, but he had a hunch that it wasn't a good time to stop and study the matter.

Over the years, Stovepipe had learned to play his hunches, too.

He didn't look back as he rode. He knew Wilbur would be pounding along just behind him. The two of them had been best friends and trail partners for a long time as they drifted from here to there across the frontier. If there was one thing in this world Stovepipe counted on, it was knowing that Wilbur would back his play to the very best of his ability.

Stovepipe looked to his left. About half a mile away, the ground broke up into a mess of little canyons and draws. The fugitive would stand a lot better chance of giving the slip to his pursuers if he could reach those breaks. As things stood, though, it appeared that the men would catch up to him before he could get there.

"We need to slow those fellas down!" Stovepipe called over his shoulder to Wilbur as he grasped his Winchester and drew the repeater out of its sheath.

Stovepipe looped the reins around the saddle horn and guided the Palouse with his knees as he raised the Winchester to his shoulder. He didn't expect to hit anybody at this range, from the back of a galloping horse, but on the other hand, he didn't *want* to hit any of the pursuers. Despite instinctively sticking up for the underdog, he didn't plan on gunning down anybody without a good reason. He just hoped to scatter the group of riders chasing after the lone man. That might give him and Wilbur a chance to find out what was going on here.

The rifle cracked as Stovepipe triggered three swift shots, working the Winchester's lever between each round. He aimed really high, knowing the bullets would drop some as they traveled. He wanted to make sure they went over the heads of the pursuers.

Wilbur's rifle began speaking as he swung out to Stovepipe's right. He fired three times as well.

Stovepipe hoped a few of the bullets came close enough for the riders to hear them whistling over their heads.

An instant later, one of the men threw his arms in the air and pitched out of the saddle. He landed in a limp heap.

Wilbur yelped a surprised oath.

"Stovepipe, did you see that?" he asked. "One of those fellas looked like he was hit!"

"You shot over their heads, didn't you?"

"I thought I did! Blast it, I didn't mean to hurt anybody, let alone kill one of 'em!"

"We don't know he's dead," Stovepipe pointed out.

"He sure landed like he was!"

Stovepipe couldn't argue with that. He had seen men die from being shot—more than he liked to think about, actually—and the way this man had fallen bore a distinct resemblance to that unfortunate outcome.

He and Wilbur had accomplished their goal, however. The rest of the pursuers reined in and stopped chasing the man they'd been after. A couple of them dashed their horses back to the place where the man had fallen, obviously intent on checking on him.

The others swung around and pounded toward Stovepipe and Wilbur. Smoke spurted from gun muzzles.

"Oh hell!" cried Wilbur. "Now they're after *us*!"

"They appear to be!" Stovepipe called as he stuck the Winchester back in its sheath and hauled the Appaloosa around in a hard turn to the left.

Wilbur followed, although he asked, "Where are we going?"

"Those breaks are closer than any cover back the

way we come from," said Stovepipe. "We'll try to get amongst 'em, like that other fella."

Indeed, the lone rider who had been the group's original quarry had vanished into the rugged terrain. Stovepipe could still see a cloud of dust hanging in the air, but the rider himself was no longer in sight.

That was what he and Wilbur needed to do right about now: disappear.

As he galloped toward the breaks, Stovepipe felt bad about the man who had been shot and even worse for his partner. It was pretty obvious from the way the man had toppled from the saddle that one of Wilbur's bullets had brought him down. Wilbur was going to be racked with guilt about that, at least until they found out who the pursuers were and why they had been after that other hombre.

If it turned out the men had been up to no good, that would ease Wilbur's conscience, at least somewhat.

Of course, at the moment Wilbur's conscience wasn't that much of a consideration. Survival was. Because of the angles involved, it looked like the other men might be able to cut Stovepipe and Wilbur off from the breaks.

But then their horses began to falter. Stovepipe's Appaloosa and Wilbur's dun were fresher. The other men's mounts must have had a long, hard run already.

"We're gonna make it!" Wilbur called exultantly.

"Don't jinx it!" said Stovepipe. "You know what a hoodoo you are, Wilbur."

"Me a hoodoo? You're the hoodoo, you long drink of water! Bad luck follows you around—"

Wilbur ducked as a bullet whined over his head. The pursuers might not be able to catch them before they reached the breaks, but those men could still shoot.

Less than a minute later, though, Stovepipe and Wilbur raced through the mouth of a narrow, shallow, twisting canyon. A bend not far inside the canyon cut them off from view of the men who were after them.

"Slow down a mite," Stovepipe told his friend as he drew back on the reins. "They ain't gonna be too eager to charge in here, knowin' we might stop and set up an ambush."

"Yeah, but they're mighty mad at us," Wilbur said as he slowed his mount. He shook his head ruefully. "It took even less time than usual before somebody got themselves a hankerin' to ventilate us—"

He stopped short as a gun boomed and a slug kicked up dirt and gravel right in front of them.

CHAPTER SIX

Stovepipe reached for his gun, but a man's voice called, "Don't do it, mister! You're covered!"

Stovepipe moved his hand away from the ivory-handled Colt. He gestured to Wilbur, a gentle motion that Stovepipe knew Wilbur would understand as a signal to take it easy.

He put the sentiment into words as he expressed it to the unseen shooter, drawling, "Take it easy there, amigo. We ain't lookin' for trouble."

"Then how come we find it all the dad-blasted time?" asked Wilbur under his breath.

"Just lucky, I guess," Stovepipe answered in the same fashion. He raised his voice as he went on, "If you're the fella who got chased into these breaks a few minutes ago, you should know that we're the ones who slowed down those jaspers doggin' your trail."

"Why would you do that?" demanded the man. "I've never seen you before."

"Let's just say I didn't care for the odds."

Between the shot and the conversation they had

exchanged, Stovepipe had been able to pin down the unseen man's location. He was in a narrow crease in the canyon wall about twenty feet ahead of them, a dark line that Stovepipe had taken merely for a shadow on the wall at first. Now he realized it was an opening barely wide enough for a man to slide into.

"Where's your horse?" Stovepipe went on. "Those fellas who were after you might be a little leery of chargin' in here blind, but it won't be long before they show up."

The man didn't answer for a moment, then he said, "You're sure you're not part of that posse?"

"Posse?" repeated Wilbur. "Uh-oh."

Before the stranger could answer, a deep voice boomed from outside the canyon.

"You boys might as well come outta there!" a man bellowed. "You've taken cover in a box canyon! No way out!"

The stranger stepped out of the crack in the wall. He clutched a revolver tightly in his hand. He was fairly young, probably in his midtwenties, Stovepipe estimated, but he had the look of a man who had knocked around some. His range clothes were covered with trail dust, and dark beard stubble covered his cheeks and jaw.

"If you're telling me the truth, come on," he said as he gestured with the gun for Stovepipe and Wilbur to follow him.

"In there?" asked Stovepipe. "There ain't room for all of us to hide."

"We're not hiding. We're getting away."

From outside the canyon, that same powerful voice shouted, "This is Sheriff Frank Olsen from Hat Creek!

I'm ordering you to give yourselves up in the name of the law!"

Despite what Stovepipe considered to be their generally peaceable nature, this wasn't the first time he and Wilbur had found themselves on the wrong side of the law. Usually those problems were caused by a misunderstanding, and now and then they ran into star packers who were crooked as a dog's hind leg.

Stovepipe didn't want to wait around and find out which case this was. With one of their number downed by a bullet, the other members of the posse likely wouldn't be in any mood to listen to explanations or apologies. Depending on how firm a hand Sheriff Frank Olsen had, they might decide a little lynching was in order.

The sheriff might even be the sort to lead that necktie party himself.

So Stovepipe nudged the Appaloosa ahead and said, "If you really and truly know a way outta here, amigo, now'd be a good time to share that little secret."

"Right here," the man said as he pointed to the crack in the canyon wall. "The sheriff just thinks this is a box canyon. The passage is pretty tight starting out, but it's wider than it looks. A horse can get through it."

"Most horses, maybe," said Stovepipe. "These are pretty big fellas."

"Well, you can wait around and talk to Olsen if you want."

Stovepipe dismounted in front of the cleft in the wall. Wilbur followed suit. Stovepipe said, "Lead the way, mister."

The young man went first, followed by Stovepipe leading the Appaloosa. The Palouse's flanks scraped the sides of the narrow crack, which made him reluctant to go through it, but the horse trusted Stovepipe and the lanky cowboy's gentle-voiced urging kept him moving.

Wilbur came next, leading his dun. He said, "I think this hoss of mine has that, what d'you call it, closetrophobia."

"That ain't quite right, I don't think," said Stovepipe, "but I know what you mean."

"I reckon I've got a touch of it, too. I don't like this, Stovepipe."

The young man said, "It's not this narrow for much longer."

He was true to his word. The passage widened after a few more yards. It was still narrow enough that they had to proceed single file, but at least the walls weren't closing in quite so oppressively.

Behind them, Sheriff Frank Olsen was still yelling, telling the fugitives they were trapped and calling on them to surrender.

"Where's your horse, amigo?" Stovepipe asked their newfound companion.

"Up ahead a little ways in a clearing where there's a spring and some grass."

"Sounds like a hideout."

The man glanced back over his shoulder and said, "I'm not an outlaw, if that's what you mean." He paused, then went on, "But it's true I've been staying there for a while because I didn't want anybody to find me. That's how I knew this crack was here. I've been exploring some."

"You mind sayin' why you're hidin' out?"

"I'm not sure that's any of your business."

"We helped you get away from those fellas," Stovepipe pointed out. "They might've grabbed you if we hadn't slowed 'em down."

He didn't say anything about the man Wilbur had apparently shot out of the saddle.

From the spot where Wilbur was bringing up the rear of this procession, the redhead said, "You might as well tell him what he wants to know, mister. Once Stovepipe gets curious and starts asking questions, he's mighty stubborn."

"Fine," the young man said. "This is Box D range, right at the edge of the spread but still Abel Dempsey's property. I'm not welcome here. I used to ride for Dempsey, but he fired me and told me to stay off his ranch."

"And yet you stay," said Stovepipe. "What's your name, son?"

"Dan Hartford."

"Pleased to meet you, Dan. Probably. Dependin' on how this turns out. They call me Stovepipe Stewart."

"On account of he's as tall and skinny as a stovepipe," Wilbur put in.

"Dan looks like he's smart enough to figure that out on his own. The caboose back there's Wilbur Coleman."

"Grub-line riders?" Dan asked.

"You could say that."

Dan shook his head and said, "I wouldn't recommend signing on with the Box D, even if Dempsey's hiring."

"Yeah, it looks like his punchers get treated kinda rough," said Stovepipe.

Dan looked back at him again and asked, "What makes you say that?"

"You got some bruises that are almost healed, but not quite. Looks like you got a pretty good whippin' a while back."

Dan made a disgusted noise.

"You mean I got ganged up on," he said.

"How many of 'em did it take?"

"Four. Two to hold on to me and two to do the punching. Plus the hombre who jumped me in the first place."

"With odds like that, nobody could blame you for gettin' licked. Were they all Box D hands, the fellas who done it?"

"Yeah. And Dempsey himself started it by slapping me a couple of times."

"Hard for a man to take bein' treated like that."

"I wasn't going to take it," said Dan. "I would have gone after him, no matter what the consequences—but then those other men jumped me, and I never got the chance."

Wilbur said, "If somebody I was working for did that, I'd draw my time and leave. And if he fired me before I could do that, I'd sure shake the dust of the place off my boots as fast as I could."

"Maybe," Stovepipe said. "But some hombres'd be more likely to want to settle the score. Ain't that right, Dan?"

The young cowboy didn't answer the question. Instead, he said, "This is the place I was telling you about, right up here."

Stovepipe looked past Dan and saw that the passage ended in a bowl-like depression with a small, spring-fed pool in the bottom of it. Grass grew around the pool, a little on the sparse side but enough for a horse or two to graze on it. There was even a little stunted cottonwood to provide some shade. Conditions here would be fairly primitive, but compared to some places in Arizona Territory, it was downright idyllic.

"I'll show you the best way out of here," Dan said as he stepped out of the passage into the bowl. Stovepipe and Wilbur followed him, both of them glad to get out of the narrow crack. "I reckon you fellas will want to drift—"

"Hoist 'em!" a voice ordered sharply. "Keep your hands away from that gun, Hartford, or you'll never live to hang for Abel Dempsey's murder!"

CHAPTER SEVEN

"Murder?" Stovepipe repeated softly.

Dan Hartford had gone pale. He looked at Stovepipe and said, "It's a lie. I didn't kill anybody."

Before he could say anything else, men with guns crowded around them, emerging from behind the rocks around the bowl where they had been hidden. Clearly, they had been lying in wait, hoping to capture Dan when he returned.

They probably hadn't figured on bagging two extra fugitives.

With this many guns pointed at them, Stovepipe knew that he and Wilbur couldn't afford to make a play. He hoped that Dan would keep his wits about him and realize the same thing. If any gunplay broke out, it was likely that all three of them would go down.

A tall, horse-faced man wearing a badge stepped up and plucked Dan's gun from its holster. He prodded Dan in the chest with the barrel of the revolver he held and said, "You thought you was gonna get away, didn't you, Hartford? You didn't figure on me knowin' these breaks better 'n anybody else in these parts. I used to ride for the Box D years ago before I took up deputyin'. I combed many a head of stock outta here, and I told Sheriff Olsen I'd bet a hat this was where you'd hole up. That's how come him split the posse like he done, on account o' my advice."

Wilbur said quietly to Stovepipe, "That fella seems almighty fond of his own voice."

The deputy caught that comment and turned to glare at the two old friends.

"And who are you?" he demanded. "Hand over them guns, but be mighty easy-like about it! After what you done, shootin' Alf Swenson like you did, I'd love an excuse to ventilate the both o' you!"

"You don't understand," Wilbur began. "That was a—"

Stovepipe nudged him with an elbow, and Wilbur fell silent. Stovepipe reached across his body, carefully drew the ivory-handled Colt from its holster, and handed it to one of the posse members.

"Be careful with that six-shooter," said Stovepipe. "I set a lot of store by it. It's gotten me out of some mighty bad fixes."

"Gunfighter, are you?" the man asked with a sneer.

"Not so's you'd notice, but I know which end of the barrel the bullet comes out of."

Wilbur's snort indicated that was an understatement. Equally carefully, he removed his own gun from its holster and passed it over to one of their captors.

The deputy moved away a few steps, pointed his gun in the air, and squeezed off three rounds in what was obviously a prearranged signal.

"That'll bring the sheriff and the rest of the boys on the run," he said, then gave Dan a self-satisfied smirk. "You'll be behind bars where you belong before the day's over, Hartford, and so will these compadres of yours."

"I don't know these men," Dan said. "I never saw them before, until just a little while ago. They only tried to help me because they saw I was outnumbered and thought I needed some help."

"Well, if that's true, that was their mistake," said the deputy. "They mixed in on the wrong side of the law, *and* they shot a member of this here posse, so now they got to pay the price, too."

Wilbur heaved a sigh. Stovepipe knew that what had happened was eating at his friend. He wished there was something he could say to make Wilbur feel better, but at the moment he sure couldn't think of what it might be.

The echoes of the three shots rolled across the breaks and died away. It wasn't long before they were replaced by the sound of hoofbeats. A trail led down into the bowl from one of the ridges that surrounded it, and several riders appeared at the top of that trail and started down, led by a barrel-chested man with a white, bristling mustache. The sun reflected off the badge he wore, and from the man's air of authority, Stovepipe pegged him as Sheriff Frank Olsen.

One of the riders following the lawman was hatless and had a bloodstained rag tied around his head as a makeshift bandage. The sight of him drew a startled oath from the deputy.

"Well, what do you know? Swenson ain't dead after all. I thought sure he would be, shot in the head like that and all." The deputy glanced at Stovepipe and Wilbur. "You musta just creased him. You might not hang after all . . . less'n we find some other charges outstandin' against you, of course."

Wilbur didn't exactly heave a sigh of relief, but Stovepipe could tell his old friend was pleased by this development. Wilbur had gunned down a star packer or two in his time, but they'd all really been owlhoots who had it coming.

"I see you got him, Warren," the white-mustached lawman said to the deputy. "Good job. And these are the two who were shootin' at us and wounded Alf, I take it."

"That's right, Sheriff," said the deputy. "Hartford met up with 'em, just like I figured he would. They must've had the whole thing planned."

Dan said, "I'm telling you, you've got it all wrong—"

"You'll have a chance to tell your side of it," the sheriff interrupted him. "Not that it'll do you much good. Witnesses heard you shoot Abel Dempsey and found you standing over his body with a smoking gun in your hand. If ever anybody was bound for the gallows, it's you, son."

"There's a thing you may have heard of, Sheriff," said Stovepipe. "It's called the presumption of innocence and says the law's got to prove somebody's guilty of a crime before he's punished for it."

Olsen glared at the tall, lanky range rider.

"I know damn well what the law's responsibilities are," he said. "Who are you? What's your connection to this murdering saddle tramp?"

"*Alleged* murderin' saddle tramp," drawled Stovepipe. "As for my name, it's Stewart. I sort of disremember what the legal front handle is, it's been so long since anybody called me by it. Generally folks just know me as Stovepipe, when they ain't callin' me *Hey, you.*"

"Like to spill a lot of words when you talk, don't you?" the deputy said.

"The same could be said of others in these parts, as I recall."

"Never mind that," said the sheriff. He fixed his cold-eyed glare on Wilbur. "What about you?"

"Name's Wilbur Coleman."

"Stewart and Coleman, eh? I don't recall seeing those names on any wanted posters, but I'll go through all the dodgers back at the office. Friends of Hartford, are you?"

"Dan has the right of it," said Stovepipe. "We just met less than half an hour ago. And we don't know a blamed thing about any murder, or anything else that's been goin' on in these parts."

"Don't believe 'em, Sheriff," the deputy said. "I'll bet they're part of that gang o' rustlers that's been raisin' hell all over the basin."

"Rustlers, eh?" Stovepipe said quietly. "Sounds plumb lawless around here. Maybe Wilbur and I never should've drifted in this direction."

Olsen grunted and said, "You got that right, cowboy." He turned toward the other members of the posse, jerked his head at the prisoners, and ordered, "Get them on their horses. I want to get back to Hat Creek and lock them up before anything else has a chance to happen."

Wilbur said, "We're just gonna go along with this, Stovepipe?"

"Don't see as we have any choice in the matter right now," Stovepipe replied with a meaningful nod at the heavily armed men surrounding them.

"We could—"

"Naw, we'll just go along without any trouble. I'm sure the sheriff'll get everything sorted out the way it should be."

"Damn right I will," Olsen said, "and you'll be sorry when I do."

Hat Creek was the only settlement of any size in the area. It served the supply needs of the Box D, the HS Bar, the Cholla, the Big Nine, the Double R, the Leaning T, and all the other spreads in the basin. It was built around a courthouse square. The courthouse was a square, sturdy, stone building with two floors. The sheriff's office took up part of the first floor, along with the other county offices.

The entire second floor was the jail. All the windows had iron bars set into them, and only one door, made of thick beams and reinforced with iron straps, led in and out of the cell block. Once a man was locked up there, getting out wouldn't be easy.

A crowd gathered quickly as soon as the posse and its prisoners came in sight of the town. People lined the boardwalks as if they had assembled to watch a parade. Stovepipe supposed it *was* a parade of sorts, with more than a dozen riders traveling slowly along the street. The three prisoners were in the middle, surrounded by men holding rifles at the ready.

If the bystanders were expecting a show, they were disappointed, because nothing unusual happened. The closest thing to entertainment was the way Deputy Warren Purdue managed to preen even though he was on horseback. He was mighty proud of himself for having masterminded the capture of the accused murderer Dan Hartford and two apparent accomplices.

Stovepipe wasn't surprised by the interest the townspeople showed. Anything that broke up the monotony of frontier life was always appreciated. Also, although Stovepipe had no way of knowing at this point how folks in the basin felt about Abel Dempsey, anybody who owned a big ranch like the Box D was important. Important people always got more attention in life—and in death. That might not always be fair, but it was the way of the world.

The group drew up in front of the courthouse. Sheriff Olsen dismounted first and ordered his deputy, "Take them upstairs and lock them in, Warren. Separate cells with some space between 'em. I don't want them working together on anything."

"No need to worry, Sheriff," Deputy Purdue said confidently. "That jail's escape-proof."

"There ain't no such thing," growled Olsen, which struck Stovepipe as the most sensible thing the lawman had said so far. "Just do what I told you."

"Sure, boss, sure," Purdue said. He swung down from the saddle, drew his revolver, and pointed it at the prisoners, whose hands were tied in front of them but whose legs were free because they had to be able to ride. "Get down from those horses and don't try anything funny."

"Funny's about the farthest thing from my mind right now," Wilbur said with a sour look on his normally affable face.

The prisoners were marched into the building at gunpoint and then up a broad staircase to the second floor, where a couple of men would stand guard at a desk right outside the cell block door. That door stood open at the moment. Evidently no other prisoners were locked up in the Hat Creek jail.

Purdue ushered Dan into a cell on the right side of the aisle, then put Stovepipe and Wilbur in separate cells on the left side. He left an empty cell between the two of them, as Sheriff Olsen had ordered. The cells had bars between them, so the prisoners would still be able to talk, but they couldn't make physical contact with each other.

"Reckon you'll be wantin' a lawyer," Purdue said to Dan.

"I don't know any lawyers around here."

"Well, the judge don't like it when somebody comes into court without a lawyer." Purdue scratched his long jaw and frowned in thought. "I'll send Simon McGilvray up to talk to you."

"I don't know— Wait a minute. McGilvray. Isn't he that old drunk who's always hanging around the Blue Oasis Saloon cadging drinks? He's a lawyer?"

"That's what the sign on his office says. Of course, he ain't usually there, because he's at—"

"The Blue Oasis Saloon," Dan finished bleakly.

Purdue grinned and said, "Yeah. That's your attorney, all nice and legal-like." He looked over at Stovepipe and Wilbur. "I reckon he can represent you fellas, too."

"I didn't notice any tracks coming into town," said Wilbur.

"Tracks?" repeated a puzzled Purdue.

"Yeah, this sure seems like a railroad job to me."

Purdue snorted and went out, slamming the cell

block door behind him. With a heavy *thunk!* the key turned in the lock.

Dan grasped the bars of his cell door, sighed, and shook his head as he looked across the aisle at Stovepipe and Wilbur.

"I'm mighty sorry you men got into this mess on my account," he told them. "I'll talk to that lawyer and make sure he understands that you didn't have anything to do with killing Abel Dempsey."

"You said you didn't, either," Stovepipe pointed out.

"I didn't. I know that things, well, look mighty bad for me . . . but that doesn't mean I'm guilty."

"No, it sure don't," agreed Stovepipe. "So why don't you tell us the whole story . . . and start at the beginnin'."

"Why do you want to know?"

Wilbur said, "Remember what I told you about how Stovepipe gets curious and starts asking questions? He'll keep at you until you tell him everything he wants to know, mark my words."

"Well, what harm can it do now?" Dan laughed bitterly. "We're already locked up, and they're probably fitting a noose for my neck right now. So if you want the story, here goes . . ."

CHAPTER EIGHT

"It started back in Saint Louis," Dan said. "I was a driver for a freight outfit. I'd been knocking around the river, up and down from Saint Louis to New Orleans, doing whatever work I could find, since I left my folks' farm back in Ohio and set out on my own."

"Fiddle-footed, eh?" said Stovepipe. "I know the feelin'."

"If it had been forty or fifty years ago, I would have headed for the mountains and become a fur trapper. There was an old fella who grew up on a farm not far from my folks' place, and that's what he did. He came back for a visit every now and then and told stories like you wouldn't believe about the adventures he had out there in the Rockies. But the fur trade's been over for a long time, so I decided I'd be a cowboy instead."

"You didn't start reading those yellowback novels and get a bunch of crazy ideas about what it's like out here, did you?" asked Wilbur. "The gents who write those yarns don't know anything about the real frontier. They just make it all up."

"I might have looked at one or two of them," Dan admitted grudgingly. "Anyway, I figured to go west, but I hadn't taken into account the fact that you need money to do that. So I worked at those odd jobs, like I told you, and saved my money to buy a horse and a gun and everything else I'd need to outfit myself."

Stovepipe tossed his hat on the bunk, ran his fingers through his tangled dark hair, then stuck his hands through the bars on his cell door and rested his forearms on one of the horizontal bars. As he leaned there casually, cool as could be under the circumstances, he said, "Reckon this is about the point in the story where a girl shows up."

"How'd you know that?" asked Dan with a frown.

"Because every fella's tale of woe has a gal in it somewhere."

"Stovepipe's what they call a misshogamist," Wilbur put in.

"Not hardly," objected Stovepipe. "I like gals just fine and think the world of 'em. But I know how bein' around 'em sometimes makes a fella's thinkin' take some mighty odd turns."

Dan said, "Well, as a matter of fact, I did meet a young woman in Saint Louis. Her name was Laura Tyson." The cowboy's voice took on a wistful note as he went on, "I'd never met anybody quite so beautiful, or so nice . . ."

"See?" Stovepipe said. "That's just what I was talkin' about."

"She felt the same way about me, too," Dan said. "Problem was, her father was well-to-do. Owned some warehouses and other property along the riverfront."

"And he didn't cotton to the idea of his daughter

gettin' mixed up with a young, would-be cowboy who didn't have two coins to rub together," Stovepipe said.

"You've got that right," said Dan, sounding bitter now. "He did everything he could to keep Laura away from me, including throwing her at a friend of his, somebody who had fought in the war with him. He was bound and determined to get the two of them hitched so that Laura would go to live on the fella's ranch, all the way out in Arizona Territory."

Stovepipe's casual attitude vanished as he straightened. He closed his hands around the bars.

"Wait a minute," he said. "Are you tellin' us this gal Laura was married to Abel Dempsey, the hombre you're accused of killin'?"

"I'm afraid so."

"You're right to be afraid," muttered Wilbur. "You're so far up the creek it'd take you a year to get back, even if you had a paddle, which it sounds like you don't."

"Go on with the story," Stovepipe said. "How'd Miss Tyson wind up gettin' hitched to Dempsey? Her pa forced her into it?"

"Pretty much," Dan replied with a nod. "He wrote to Dempsey and had him come to Saint Louis for a visit, then sent Laura back out here with him to the Box D. Tyson sent his old maid sister along as a chaperone, so there was nothing improper about it, but he and Dempsey both hoped Laura would like the place, so she'd be more likely to agree when Dempsey asked her to marry him. But it didn't work out that way."

"Gal's got a stubborn streak in her, eh?"

"She does," said Dan. "When Dempsey proposed

to her, she told him she'd have to think about it and went back to Saint Louis. She didn't intend to ever come back here." He sighed. "But Dempsey followed her, and he and Tyson finally pressured Laura into going along with the marriage idea."

"Wait a minute, wait a minute," Wilbur said. "If Dempsey knew that you and Laura were sweet on each other, why in blazes would he hire you to ride for him?"

"You're sort of gettin' ahead of the story, Wilbur," Stovepipe said. "But I got to admit, I was wonderin' the same thing myself, Dan."

Dan shook his head and said, "Dempsey didn't know who I was. He never laid eyes on me back there in Saint Louis, and Laura never told him my name. All he knew was that somebody Laura's father didn't approve of had been courting her."

"All right, I reckon that makes sense," said Stovepipe as he nodded slowly. "But it don't explain how you come to be ridin' for the Box D in the first place. And Miss Laura was bound to have recognized you."

"She did," Dan admitted. "As soon as we laid eyes on each other, we both knew." He sighed and went on ruefully, "The best thing to do would have been if I had gotten back on my horse and rode away. Instead, I told myself I could stay—you know, sort of keep an eye on things and look out for Laura's best interests— and that it would be all right. It didn't have to go beyond that."

"Reckon it must've, though, or you wouldn't be in the fix you're in now."

"That's right. Back in Saint Louis, after Laura told me she was getting married, I quit my job with the freight company and came west to follow that dream of being a cowboy. I figured I could still have that, even if I didn't have her. I rode for several spreads over in New Mexico and here in Arizona, but I always got restless after a while and had to go on the drift again. I heard the Box D was hiring—"

"Now, hold on," said Wilbur. "There you go again. You didn't know that Dempsey was the fella who married this Laura gal?"

Dan shook his head.

"She never told me his name, just that he was a rich rancher who was an old friend of her father's. I know it sounds far-fetched, but that's the way it happened, I swear."

Stovepipe said, "All right. We been jumpin' around in the story, but I reckon I've got the straight of it now, up to the time this trouble between you and Dempsey got started. Go on about that."

"Well, Laura and I had more and more trouble staying away from each other—"

"Who'da thunk it?" muttered Wilbur.

"And after a month or so, we couldn't stand it anymore," Dan went on as if he hadn't heard the redhead's comment. "Now, don't go getting that puritanical look on your face, Stovepipe. I admit, I kissed her one night when the two of us were alone in the barn, but that's all that happened. That's as far as I compromised her honor. And after that, I resolved all over again to keep my distance from her. I didn't really trust myself—or her, to be honest." He shook his head. "She wasn't happy being married to Dempsey. He treated her decent enough, I suppose, but . . . well . . . he was a lot older than her. Sometimes that works, I reckon, but they weren't a good match."

"You must not've been able to keep your distance."

"I did until that blasted birthday party," said Dan. "It was Laura's birthday, and Dempsey threw a big celebration for her. She insisted on dancing with me. That's what really set the match to the fuse. You see, even though Dempsey didn't know about what happened between her and me back in Saint Louis, he was really jealous of her. He'd caught her talking to me one day out on the range, and he didn't like it. When he saw us dancing, his temper slipped loose from its reins."

"That's when he slapped you and those other fellas jumped you," Stovepipe guessed.

"That's right, and when the fight was over—it wasn't much of a fight, I'm afraid, outnumbered like I was—he fired me and told me to stay off his range."

"But you couldn't, because you were worried about Laura."

Dan nodded and said, "I rode off, heading east, so the men Dempsey sent to run me off the place saw me going in that direction. But then I circled way back around to those breaks, and I've been camping there ever since, sneaking out every now and then to see Laura."

"So she knew you were still around?"

"That's right, and why the hell shouldn't she?" Dan challenged. "After what happened, I knew I couldn't leave her with a man like Abel Dempsey. I got word to her through a friend on Dempsey's crew—no need to mention any names—and she started meeting me on the range when we knew none of the Box D riders would be around. We were making plans for her to leave him. We figured we'd go to California and start over there."

Stovepipe nodded and said, "California's not a bad

place for that. But then somethin' else happened, didn't it?"

"Yesterday . . ." Dan had to stop for a moment before he forced himself to go on. "Yesterday Laura and I met at a place called Apache Bluff. That was one of our usual spots. We were talking when we heard a gunshot close by. I told her to light out for home while I went to see what had happened."

"That's when you found Dempsey's body," said Stovepipe.

"Yeah, it doesn't take a genius to figure that out, does it?" Dan said wryly. "He was dead. He'd been shot in the back at close range. Whoever did it was still close by, too, close enough to take a shot at me from some rocks. Without thinking, I grabbed my gun and fired back . . . and right about then, Lew Martin—he's the foreman of the Box D—rode up with several more of the hands. They saw Dempsey, saw that smoking gun in my hand . . . I guess I can't blame them for thinking what they thought. A couple of them opened fire on me, even though Lew told them to wait, and I did the only thing I could unless I wanted to stay there and shoot it out with them. I lit a shuck."

"Forget what I said about the creek and the paddle," Wilbur told him. "You're halfway up the gallows' steps."

Dan sat down on the bunk in his cell, put his head in his hands, and said miserably, "I know."

Stovepipe didn't want the young man sinking into self-pity. Not before he had told the rest of the story. Stovepipe asked sharply, "What happened today?"

"I snuck out of the breaks in the hope of seeing Laura. We had a rendezvous scheduled at one of our usual spots, and I hoped she would show up, even though I knew it was unlikely. Instead that posse was waiting for me—"

"She tipped 'em off," said Wilbur.

"I . . . I don't want to think so. Maybe they just happened to be there . . ."

Stovepipe let that go for the moment, although he agreed with Wilbur. Chances were, Laura Dempsey had told the law about the rendezvous.

"What about the rustlin'?" he asked. "How's that tied in with what happened to Dempsey?"

"Those two things don't have anything to do with each other," Dan said.

"Tell me anyway."

Dan scratched his head and then said, "A lot of the ranches in the basin have been losing stock over the past few months. Some of it happened before I got here, so I don't see how the law can blame me for that. Of course, they probably will anyway . . ." A frown creased his forehead. "You know, I said there wasn't any connection, but maybe I was wrong. Abel Dempsey isn't the first cattleman who's been killed in these parts."

"Now, maybe you're gettin' somewhere," said Stovepipe. "Go on."

A look of excitement appeared on Dan's face as he gripped the bars of his cell.

"One of the Tomlinson brothers, they own the Leaning T, was shot from ambush and killed a while back. And the body of Jack Hogan, the owner of the Big Nine spread, was found at the bottom of a ravine not long ago. Everybody thought his horse bucked him off and he happened to fall in the ravine, but somebody could've maybe roped him out of the saddle and then thrown him in there so he broke his neck."

"Or broke it some other way and tossed him in the ravine to make it look like the fall killed him," Stovepipe suggested.

"Sure, it could have happened that way," Dan agreed. "If the rustlers killed Dempsey, it could be because they're getting the ranchers out of the way so they can clean out the whole basin."

Wilbur said, "I don't think the sheriff will put much stock in that theory. If you tell him about it, it'll just sound like you're trying to shift the blame for Dempsey's murder to these mysterious rustlers."

"But they really could have killed him!"

"There's a little matter of provin' it," said Stovepipe. "And it ain't likely you'll get a chance to do that while you're locked up in here."

"We could poke around and see what we could find out," said Wilbur. "Stovepipe's biggest weakness is that curiosity of his. But . . ."

The redhead spread his hands and nodded gloomily at their surroundings.

"Yeah, we're all pretty much in the same boat," said Stovepipe, "and it's takin' on water. We'll have to figure some way of gettin' out before we sink."

A key rattled in the cell block door. Deputy Purdue opened it, and a slender figure shuffled unsteadily through the door. Purdue had a big grin on his horsey face as he said, "Your lawyer's here, boys."

Wilbur looked at the newcomer and muttered, "That water's gettin' deeper in the bottom of the boat."

CHAPTER NINE

Simon McGilvray looked like he was in his seventies, but he might have been younger than that. Whiskey aged a man, and judging by the tracery of broken veins across his nose and gaunt cheeks, he had imbibed plenty of it in his time.

The black suit he wore had once been a good one, but like its owner, the years had taken their toll on the suit. A string tie was draped around McGilvray's neck, but the grimy collar of his shirt was open and the tie hung loose. He had wispy white hair and watery, pale blue eyes, and his hands trembled. The skin on those hands was like thin parchment, with a network of blue veins showing through it.

He was not a figure to inspire confidence.

His voice sounded a little like the squeaking of a rusty gate as he said, "I'm told you men need legal repre—" He made it that far before his apparent resolve to sound sober and dignified lost its steam. "Repre . . . represen . . . representation!"

Getting the word out made him stagger a little. He

reached out with a shaky hand to grasp one of the bars of the empty cell between Stovepipe and Wilbur.

"Take it easy there, old-timer," Stovepipe advised him. He looked at Purdue, who still stood in the open door. "You reckon we could get a chair or a stool in here for Mr. McGilvray, Deputy?"

Purdue was still grinning, but his voice was surly as he said, "I'll see what I can do." He disappeared into the jail office and came back a moment later with a short, three-legged stool. He set it on the floor and gave it a shove with his foot.

Stovepipe leaned down and reached a long arm through the bars to snag the stool before it could slide past. He said, "Have a seat there, Mr. McGilvray."

"I . . . I'm obliged to you, young man," the lawyer said as he sank onto the stool. He swayed a little, as if he might topple off it, then seemed to steady himself. "That's better."

Stovepipe looked along the aisle to the open door where Purdue still stood.

"You can't be listenin' while prisoners talk to their lawyer, Deputy," he said.

"I reckon I can do anything I want to in this jail," blustered Purdue.

"Well, not exactly. The law's got rules to it."

Purdue sneered and said, "And a saddle tramp like you would know those rules?"

"You can't always tell what a fella knows just by lookin' at him. If you don't believe me, I reckon you can go find the sheriff and ask him about it."

McGilvray raised a finger and said, "The gentleman is . . . is correct. The accused has a right to con . . . to consult with counsel in private."

The deputy made a disgusted noise, turned away,

and slammed the door behind him. The key rattled in the lock again.

Dan said, "He could still be listening just on the other side."

"He could be," Stovepipe said. "Best be careful what you say. Right now, why don't you just tell Mr. McGilvray about what happened yesterday. *Just* what happened yesterday."

Dan's eyes narrowed as he frowned, then his expression cleared as he seemed to realize what Stovepipe was trying to tell him. Having met Stovepipe only a couple of hours earlier, Dan had no real reason to take his advice about anything, but the young cowboy seemed sharp enough to realize that the two drifting range riders were on his side.

"They say I shot Abel Dempsey," Dan began, "but it's not true. I was out riding yesterday near Apache Bluff when I heard a shot, and when I went to investigate it, I found Dempsey's body. He'd been dry-gulched. Whoever ambushed him was hidden in some rocks nearby and took a shot at me, too. I fired back at them, and then some of the Box D riders came galloping up from the other direction." Dan shrugged. "That's the whole story, Mr. McGilvray."

Wilbur frowned and said, "You didn't—"

Stovepipe caught his friend's eye and silenced him with a tiny shake of the head. Dan had his own reasons for not mentioning Laura Dempsey and the fact that the two of them had been together when Abel Dempsey was murdered.

McGilvray rubbed a hand over his face and said, "That's . . . that's a very weak story, young man. I doubt that a jury would . . . would believe it. I'm a bit in my cups, to be honest, and I'm not sure *I* believe it. And I'm your lawyer."

"I can't help that," Dan said stiffly. "That's what happened."

"Is there anyone who can corrob . . . corrobor . . . corroborate your testimony? Someone who saw you before the . . . before the shooting took place?"

"No. I was alone."

Dan looked across the aisle at Stovepipe and Wilbur as if asking them to keep quiet about what he had told them earlier. Wilbur looked like he wanted to say something, but he tightened his lips and remained silent.

"Well, that's unfor . . . unfortunate. Can't build a defense . . . solely around the word of the accused. Need something to back it up." McGilvray frowned in what appeared to be intense thought. "I remember hearing something . . . about a fight between you and Abel Dempsey."

"We had our differences," said Dan.

"You used to ride for him."

"He fired me."

"Then what were you doing . . . on his range? There's talk around town . . . that you're in with those rustlers."

"That's a lie. I don't have anything to do with any rustlers."

"But can you prove it?"

Stovepipe muttered, "It's a lot harder to prove you *ain't* somethin' than to prove you *are.*"

"I've told you everything there is to tell," Dan insisted. "What do you think, Mr. McGilvray? Can you help me?"

The elderly lawyer thought it over for a long moment and then finally nodded.

"Yes," he said. "Yes, I'm sure I can help you."

"You can?"

"Certainly. But I'll need a list of all your worldly possessions."

"What in the world for?" asked Dan.

"If I'm going to prepare your last will and testament, young man, I need to know what you're going to be leaving behind when they hang you."

Dan refused to talk to the drunken old attorney after that. McGilvray stood up, tottered over to the cell block door, and called for Deputy Purdue to let him out.

"That was a waste of time," Dan said bitterly once the lawyer was gone and the door was closed again.

"Why didn't you tell him about Mrs. Dempsey?" asked Wilbur. "She can prove you didn't shoot her husband. You were with her when he was killed."

"She's already gone through enough," Dan said. "I'm not going to ruin her reputation, to boot. If word got around that she was meeting some no-account cowboy her husband had fired . . . well, you know what people would think about her. You know what they'd say."

"So you'll let them stretch your neck just to protect her feelings? You must really love her!"

Stovepipe said, "I reckon that's what started this whole mess, Wilbur."

Dan sat down on his bunk again and said, "I

shouldn't have told the two of you. I'm not sure why I did."

"I got what folks say is a trustworthy face," said Stovepipe with a smile.

"I'm going to have to trust you, all right. Trust you not to say anything about Laura. I'll take my chances without bringing her into this."

"What about our chances?" asked Wilbur.

"The two of you didn't even ride into the basin until today. Nobody can blame you for Dempsey's killing, even indirectly."

"I dunno that I'd go so far as to say that. The deputy was already makin' noises about how we must be part of that gang o' rustlers. We can't prove we just got into these parts today."

"Sure we can," said Wilbur. "We stayed in a hotel in that settlement over west of here last night, and our horses spent the night in the livery stable there. Plenty of folks saw us."

"They don't know where we were before that," Stovepipe pointed out. "We could've been right here in the basin, wide-loopin' cows."

"Blast it! Whose side are you on, anyway?" Wilbur said in exasperation.

"Just playin' devil's advocate."

"Well, let ol' Beelzebub find his own damn advocate!"

"All you did was try to help me get away," said Dan. "They won't hang you for that."

"No, but they might put us in prison, and I don't have a hankerin' to wind up behind bars." Wilbur shuddered. "Just the thought of being locked up, of not being able to drift on over the next hill when the time came, gives me the fantods!"

"You're right," Dan said. "I can't ask you two to give up your freedom just to protect Laura. If she clears me of killing her husband, then chances are the law will go a lot easier on you."

"Well, it might not be that easy," Stovepipe said. "You got to remember, even if you tell the truth about what happened and so does Mrs. Dempsey, a jury might not believe her. They might think that if you and her have a romance goin' on, she'd lie for you." He paused. "After all, I reckon as of yesterday, she's the owner of one of the biggest, most successful spreads in the basin. A smart prosecutor might even argue that it was *her* idea for you to ambush her husband—"

Dan came up off the bunk and lunged at the bars, gripping them tightly as he glared at Stovepipe.

"Shut your lying mouth!" he exclaimed. "You can't say things like that about Laura! She wasn't happy being married to Dempsey, but she didn't . . . she would never . . ."

"That devil's advocate stuff again, eh, Stovepipe?" said Wilbur.

"That's right. Take it easy, Dan. For what it's worth, I believe the story you told us earlier. I think you're tellin' the truth about what happened, and I got my brain to percolatin' on ways to maybe prove it."

The anger went out of Dan, causing his shoulders to sag again.

"There's no way to prove it," he said, "not without ruining Laura's reputation, and maybe not even then—"

The cell block door opened. Sheriff Olsen strode in. Stovepipe knew as soon as he saw the triumphant look on the lawman's face that things had just gotten worse.

"I don't know what all the yelling is about in here," Olsen said, "but I don't suppose it matters. There's an old saying about how thieves fall out."

"None of us are thieves," Dan said tightly. "I know you don't want to believe that, but it's the truth."

"I got the truth right here," said Olsen as he reached into his shirt pocket and pulled out a folded piece of yellow paper. Stovepipe recognized it as a telegraph flimsy, and he grew even more worried.

The sheriff went on, "I got to wondering if maybe there was some connection between you and Dempsey before you ever came to the basin, Hartford. You know, bad blood between the two of you. I recalled hearing that Dempsey and his father-in-law were old friends from the war. His name was in the story printed in the Hat Creek *Gazette* when Dempsey brought his new bride home with him. So I sent Mr. Lawrence Tyson a wire in Saint Louis and asked him if he recognized *your* name."

"Well, that kicked a hole in the bucket," muttered Stovepipe.

Olsen didn't pay any attention to him. The sheriff was too busy grinning at a stunned Dan Hartford.

"I was mighty surprised to find out that you and Mrs. Dempsey were old friends," Olsen went on. "More than friends, from what her father said. Seems you had your sights set on marrying her, and then she up and married Abel Dempsey instead. That would give you a mighty good reason to come out here to Arizona and put a bullet in the man's back!"

CHAPTER TEN

Sheriff Olsen seemed to be waiting for Dan to respond. Dan was still holding the cell door. His hands tightened on the bars as he said, "You just leave Mrs. Dempsey out of this, Sheriff. She had nothing to do with anything."

"Are you denying that you and her were sweethearts?"

"Damn right I am! It's true, I was acquainted with her back in Missouri, but that's all there is to it. There's no need to drag her into this mess. She's already gone through enough, what with her husband being murdered."

"That's real considerate of you, seeing as how you're probably the one who put that bullet in Abel Dempsey's back." Olsen refolded the telegram and tucked it into his pocket. "I reckon I'll take the word of a successful businessman over that of a shiftless cowboy."

Dan let go of the bars and turned away with a sigh. He looked utterly defeated as he sat down on the bunk. His head drooped forward and his hands hung limply between his knees.

"I'll confess," he said. "Leave Laura out of it, and I'll say anything you want me to say, Sheriff."

Olsen let out an offended snort.

"All I want is the truth," he said. "That's all the law ever wants."

Stovepipe wasn't so sure about that. Olsen had already made up his mind what the truth was, and so had Deputy Purdue. Probably most of the other folks in Hat Creek had done the same. In their minds, Dan Hartford was just as guilty as if a jury had already proclaimed it so.

At this moment, Stovepipe knew there was a good chance he and Wilbur were the only ones who believed the boy . . . and he wasn't that sure about Wilbur.

"Hang on, Dan. I don't think you should be sayin' anything else until you've had a chance to talk to your lawyer again."

"That old sot?" Dan shook his head. "He's not going to do me any good."

"Still, you don't need to be confessin' to anything that ain't true."

Olsen glared at Stovepipe and said, "You stay out of this, mister. It doesn't concern you."

Stovepipe waved a hand at the cell around him.

"I reckon it does," he said. "What are we bein' charged with?"

"Right now, attempted murder of a duly deputized peace officer and aiding and abetting a fugitive."

"Blast it!" Wilbur burst out. "We didn't mean to

hurt anybody, and the fella who got shot isn't even dead!"

"That's why it's *attempted* murder," said Olsen. "If it turns out you fellas knew anything about Abel Dempsey's killing, you'll be an accessory to that, too. Once it's all said and done, I don't expect you'll see the outside of those prison walls at Yuma for at least twenty years, probably more."

"Yuma," Wilbur said in a hushed voice. Everybody in these parts knew what a hellhole the territorial prison was.

Quietly, Stovepipe asked, "When do we go before the judge to be arraigned?"

"First thing tomorrow morning," the sheriff said.

Wilbur looked at his old friend and said, "Stovepipe, we gotta—"

Stovepipe raised a hand to stop the redhead from going on.

"I reckon you're right, Wilbur," he said. "We've gotta play out this hand and see what happens."

"That's not what I was gonna say," growled Wilbur.

Stovepipe ignored him and told Olsen, "We'll need to see Lawyer McGilvray again, Sheriff. That's our right. And it would sure help if you'd pour a pot of black coffee down his gullet first to sober him up."

"Sobering up the old souse isn't my job," Olsen snapped. "I'll send word to him. Whether or not he comes—and what condition he's in—is up to him. I can't force him to represent you." He looked at Dan. "You can still just confess, like you said a few minutes ago. It would sure make things simpler."

Stovepipe looked hard at Dan. The young cowboy returned the stare for a second, then shook his head.

"I've said all I'm going to say, Sheriff."

"Your decision," Olsen said with a shrug. "I reckon you'll swing either way. A confession would save the county some time, trouble, and expense, but with the outcome the same . . ."

His voice trailed off grimly. He turned, walked out of the cell block, and slammed the door behind him.

Dan looked across the aisle at Stovepipe and said, "You heard him. They're going to hang me either way, so what difference does it make? I'll make a deal with the district attorney and the judge. I'll confess to killing Dempsey because of the trouble that happened at the birthday party, but other than that, nothing about Laura will be said in court. I'll testify that I never saw you fellas before today, and that you didn't know anything about Dempsey's murder. Maybe I can talk the judge into taking it easy on you in return for my cooperation."

"What it comes down to is that they don't need your cooperation," said Stovepipe. "They've got the whip hand, so they can do whatever they dang well please . . . or at least they think they can."

"What do you mean by that?"

"We're not gonna be charged officially until to-morrow mornin'. That's more than twelve hours from now." Stovepipe smiled. "A lot can happen in that amount of time."

Dan leaned forward and asked, "You have some sort of plan?"

"Nope."

Wilbur said, "He's just hoping for the best. He's what they call a cockeyed hoptomist."

"I've been called worse," said Stovepipe as his smile widened into a grin.

* * *

Simon McGilvray seemed to be a reasonable fac-simile of sober when he returned to the jail late that afternoon. He was plagued by a splitting headache, though, as he was quick to inform his clients.

"You already know you're going to be arraigned before Judge Snow in the morning," said McGilvray. "It's my duty as your attorney to ask you how you want to plead to the charges."

"Not guilty on all counts," Stovepipe answered without hesitation.

"Yeah, I'll plead not guilty, too," added Wilbur.

McGilvray looked at Dan and said, "What about you, young man?"

"Might as well be hanged for a wolf as a sheep," said Dan. "I didn't shoot Abel Dempsey or anybody else, so I'm not guilty. That's what I'm going to say."

"All right. Have you thought of anything else that might help your case? Anything at all? Perhaps a witness?"

"Nothing," Dan said stubbornly.

McGilvray sighed.

"You can't brazen out a charge this serious," he said. "You're just asking to be convicted."

"I'm just telling the truth."

"There's not much I can do to help you, but I'll be there at your side," said McGilvray. "Sometimes that's all a lawyer can do, assure that the defendant isn't alone. If you think of anything else—"

"I won't," Dan said.

"Very well. I'm going to see if I can eat something."

The attorney shuddered. "The very thought of it is revolting. What I need is—"

Stovepipe said, "What you need is to stay away from that tonsil varnish tonight, counselor."

McGilvray glared at him, then left the cell block.

A short time later, a heavyset young man with a deputy's badge pinned to his shirt came in carrying a tray with three plates and three coffee cups on it. His blond hair was thinning rapidly despite the fact that he probably wasn't twenty-five years old yet.

"Hello, Brock," Dan greeted the deputy.

"Howdy, Dan. Sorry to see you locked up in there."

Dan shrugged and said, "Maybe I was born to hang."

"I don't believe that," said Brock. He handed plates and cups to the prisoners through the slots in the cell doors. The food was simple—roast beef, beans, and a hunk of corn bread—but it looked and smelled good. The aroma of the coffee was appealing, too.

The three men sat down on their bunks to eat while the deputy lingered outside the cells.

"I'm supposed to collect the plates and cups when you're finished with 'em," he explained.

"You take care of the jail, son?" asked Stovepipe.

"That's right. And I'm the night deputy, too."

"Stovepipe, Wilbur, this is Brock Matthews." Dan performed the introductions. "Brock, meet Stovepipe Stewart and Wilbur Coleman. We know each other from when we were both cowboying over in New Mexico Territory."

"Yeah, but I decided to get into the law business." Brock grinned ruefully. "I never was much good at sittin' a saddle all day."

"You're better at riding a swivel chair, aren't you?"

Dan's friendly grin took any sting out of the words, so Brock laughed and replied, "Yes, sir, I sure am. Never had one buck me off yet."

Stovepipe said, "If you and Dan are old friends, you probably don't believe that he's guilty of the things he's accused of."

Brock's open, affable face closed up abruptly. He said, "I don't get into things like that. I just follow the sheriff's orders and try to uphold the law." He glanced at Dan. "Sorry."

"Don't worry about it, Brock. I understand. You've got a job to do, and I wouldn't expect anything less from you than to have you do it."

"I'm obliged to you for that." Brock gestured at the plates. "Now you fellas go ahead and finish your supper, so I can get that stuff back over to the café."

The prisoners polished off the food and coffee, then handed the plates, cups, and utensils through the bars to Deputy Matthews. Once he left, there was nothing for them to do except sit and watch through the barred windows as the last of the day's light faded from the sky over the basin.

The cell block was lit by an oil lamp mounted in a wall sconce just inside the door. The flame was turned low, so shadows gathered inside the cells as the evening wore on. Wilbur stretched out on his bunk and was soon snoring. Dan paced back and forth, his nerves obviously too tight to let himself relax.

Stovepipe sat with his long legs stretched out in front of him and crossed at the ankles. He was motionless and looked totally at ease, but that was deceptive, because the wheels of his brain were turning over as rapidly as if they'd been attached to a runaway wagon.

After a while, he said quietly, "Dan, who knew about—"

Before he could finish the question, a key rattled in the lock of the cell block door. It swung open. Deputy Matthews stood there with a worried look on his round face. He muttered, "I shouldn't be doin' this."

Then he stepped aside and a slender figure brushed past him. The young woman let out a dismayed gasp at the sight of Dan Hartford behind bars. She hurried toward him as Dan stopped short in his pacing, stared at her, and exclaimed, "Laura! What in blazes are you doing here?"

CHAPTER ELEVEN

Dan reached through the bars as Laura held her hands out toward him. The deputy started forward and said sharply, "Hey, don't do that! Dadgum it, I'll be in enough trouble already if Sheriff Olsen or Warren Purdue find out I let you in here to see the prisoner, ma'am. I can't be lettin' you get close enough to pass him a gun."

Laura's hands were within inches of Dan's, but she stopped and lowered her arms.

"You're right, of course, Deputy," she said. "I'm sorry. I really appreciate what you're doing. I don't want to cause more problems for you."

"Well, just, uh, get your visitin' done," said Brock. "I reckon it's safe enough for the next ten minutes or so, but that's all I can risk."

"All right." Laura stood there in the aisle, just out of Dan's reach, and looked longingly at him. "I'm so sorry, Dan."

Stovepipe had heard quite a bit about Laura Dempsey today, but this was the first time he'd laid eyes on her. He had to admit, it was a mighty pleasant experience. She was in her early twenties, about the same age as Dan Hartford, and her figure, in a white blouse and a long brown skirt, had the graceful curves of youth. Her hair was a darker shade of brown and was pulled into a ponytail that hung halfway down her back.

"You shouldn't have come here," Dan told her. "People are going to talk—"

"Do you think I care?" she broke in. "People can say whatever they want about me. I don't give a damn."

Dan's mouth tightened as he said, "Maybe not, but I do. I won't see you ruined, Laura. I just won't."

"But Dan, if I tell the sheriff—"

He lifted a hand and said, "Stop right there. Please, don't say another word." Dan turned his head to look at the deputy. "Brock, no offense, but get out of here. I thank you for what you're doing, but you don't need to be here."

Brock frowned and said, "I sort of reckon I do. If it ever comes out that I let Mrs. Dempsey in here, it'll go even worse for me if the sheriff finds out I left the two of you alone."

"They ain't alone, Deputy," Stovepipe pointed out. "Wilbur and me are here to keep an eye on 'em."

Roused from sleep by Laura's arrival, Wilbur had sat up on his bunk. He ran his fingers through his tousled red hair and yawned.

"I don't think that'd make Sheriff Olsen feel any better about things," said Brock. "No, I'm sorry, but I got to stay here, Dan."

"Then you have to promise, Laura, that you won't say anything about . . . well, you know."

"But it could save you," she whispered.

Dan shook his head and told her, "I don't care. It's not worth it to me."

"Saving your life isn't it? Building a future . . . for us . . . isn't worth it?"

"There's not any future for us," said Dan. Bleakness filled his voice. "Fate's seen to that."

Stovepipe couldn't see the young woman's face, but he could tell from the set of her shoulders and the way her back stiffened just how much Dan's grim words hurt her. She didn't want to accept his stance, and Stovepipe understood why. She knew Dan was innocent. If Stovepipe had harbored any doubts about that, they vanished now as he witnessed her reaction to his self-sacrifice. The two of them had been together when Abel Dempsey was shot, all right.

"I . . . I suppose you're right," she said. Stovepipe could tell that she had to force the words out. "I don't want to leave, though, without . . . without touching you one more time." She turned to Brock Matthews and held her hands out toward him. "Deputy, you can see I don't have anything. If you stand right there and watch, can't . . . can't I hold Dan's hands, just for a moment?"

Brock grimaced. He was obviously torn by the request, and ultimately, he couldn't deny it.

"All right," he said. "But just for a minute, and then you've got to leave, ma'am. We're runnin' out of time."

"I know," murmured Laura. She extended her hands to Dan, who reached out and took them, squeezing with a fierce desperation.

"I wish . . ." he began.

"I know," Laura said as his voice trailed off. "I do, too."

They stood there in silence then, hands clasped, and anything they were telling each other was said with their eyes and their touch.

Finally, as the deputy began to get more anxious, Laura said, "You're sure, Dan? You won't let me help you?"

"I'm sure." He managed to get a smile on his face. "Something else might still turn up to clear me."

She slipped her hands out of his and turned away. Brock blew out a breath in relief and said, "All right, ma'am, if you'll just come this way . . . You can go down the back stairs in the courthouse so nobody'll see you leavin'."

Laura stepped through the doorway first. Brock turned to take hold of the handle on the heavy door so he could pull it shut.

That put his back to Laura for a second, so he couldn't see—but Stovepipe, Wilbur, and Dan could—as she reached into a pocket on her skirt and pulled out a small revolver.

"Laura, no!" exclaimed Dan.

She put the gun's muzzle against the back of the deputy's head and said, "I'm sorry, Dan. You won't let me help you one way, so I'll just have to help you another way."

"This doesn't help me," Dan told her. "You're just digging a hole for yourself."

Laura smiled and said, "I think it's already dug." She pressed the gun harder against Brock's head. "Deputy, unlock that cell."

"Don't do it, Brock," Dan urged. "She doesn't mean it. She's just a little loco right now because she's upset about everything—"

Stovepipe could have told the youngster it wasn't a

good idea to say anything about a gal being loco where she could hear it, even though it might be true.

In this case, Laura exclaimed, "Loco! I'll show you how loco I am." She pulled back the gun as if she were about to hit the deputy in the head with it.

"Laura, no!" Dan said hastily. "Brock, do what she says. She means it."

"Wait a minute," said Brock. He licked his lips nervously as Laura once again pressed the gun muzzle to his head. "Ma'am . . . Miz Dempsey . . . I'll get in all sorts of trouble if I let Dan go, and I like this job better 'n any other I've ever had. So I reckon, well, you're just gonna have to shoot me, 'cause I ain't unlockin' that cell."

"I'm not joking, Deputy," she told him angrily.

"Neither am I, ma'am."

For a second, Stovepipe thought Laura was going to pull the trigger, which would have ruined her life, Dan's life, and probably a lot of other things.

But her nerve and resolve broke, even as her finger tightened on the trigger, and she let off on the pressure before the gun exploded. She stepped back, lowered her arm, and let the pistol slip from her fingers. It thudded to the floor.

Laura started to cry, great, racking sobs that shook her whole body as she buried her face in her hands.

Like most men, the deputy seemed to be thoroughly discombobulated by the sight of a woman crying so miserably. He said, "Aw, shoot, ma'am, don't take on so. I'm sure everything's gonna be all right . . ."

Laura just cried harder.

Brock looked around helplessly, then moved closer

to her and awkwardly and gingerly put his arms around her so he could pat her on the back and say, "There, there . . ."

Laura lowered her shoulder, rammed it into his chest, and shoved him backward as hard as she could. The way they were turned, that took him toward the cell where Wilbur was locked up.

Wilbur's air of sleepiness vanished instantly. He lunged forward, shot an arm through the bars, and looped it around Brock's neck from behind. He jerked the deputy against the bars hard enough that Brock's head banged against the iron with considerable force. Brock sagged, stunned or perhaps even knocked out.

Wilbur hung on to the deputy as Stovepipe snapped, "Grab his keys, ma'am!"

"No!" Dan cried as he gripped the bars of his cell. "Laura, don't make things worse than they already are. You can't bust me out of here—"

"We're all going," said Wilbur. "You heard the sheriff. You don't want to hang, Dan, and Stovepipe and I don't want to spend the next twenty years in Yuma."

"Wilbur's right," Stovepipe said calmly. "We got to git while the gittin's good. You know good and well that folks around here ain't gonna believe your story, Dan. This is the only chance you got." A sly grin appeared on the lanky cowboy's rugged face. "And who knows, if we're free to move around a little, we might even stumble over some way of provin' what really happened."

Dan still looked reluctant, but Laura said, "There's no point in arguing." She jerked a ring of keys from where they hung on Brock's belt and turned toward the door of Dan's cell. As she began trying the keys,

Wilbur let go of the deputy so that Brock slid down the bars to lie in a heap on the floor just outside the cell.

There were only a few keys on the ring, and the second one Laura tried turned in the lock. She jerked the door open.

"Do you want me to let these other men go?" she asked.

"The only reason they're here is because of me," he said grimly. "And I think they really do want to help."

"Dang right we do," said Stovepipe. "Let us outta here, ma'am, and we'll do everything we can to get to the bottom of this mess."

Dan nodded to her, and Laura hurried to unlock the other cells. While she was doing that, Dan bent over and pulled Brock Matthews's gun from its holster.

"The guns they took from us are probably locked up in the desk in the sheriff's office," he said. "I don't know if we can risk going down there. Like Brock said, there are some back stairs we can use."

Stovepipe and Wilbur stepped out of their cells. Stovepipe said, "Lead the way. You know where you're goin' and we don't."

"What about our horses?" asked Wilbur as they left the cell block.

"Probably already at the livery stable, unsaddled," said Stovepipe. "We might have to steal some mounts."

"They don't send horse thieves to Yuma," Wilbur said ominously. "They hang 'em on the spot, mostly."

"That's true." Stovepipe looked at Laura. The skirt she wore wasn't split for riding. "How did you get to town, ma'am?"

"I brought the buckboard from the ranch."

A high-crowned, wide-brimmed hat hung from a nail on the wall behind the desk right outside the cell block door. Stovepipe figured it belonged to Brock. He snagged it from the nail and handed it to Dan.

"Put that on and pull the brim down," he said. "You and Miz Dempsey head back to her buckboard and drive outta town nice and peaceful-like."

"You don't think anybody will recognize me?"

"Keep your head down, and you'll have a chance. Wilbur and me will see if we can sneak our horses outta the livery stable. I'd just as soon not get a reputation as a hoss thief if I can avoid it. Just tell me where to find the stable."

"A couple of blocks west of here on Front Street, the one right outside. It'll be on the left."

Stovepipe nodded and said, "We can find it."

"Where should we go?"

"Pick a spot, tell us how to get there, and we'll meet you as soon as we can."

"All right. The Needles are a couple of rock spires about five miles north of town. We'll wait there as long as we can. But if I spot a posse coming, we're lighting a shuck for California."

"Fair enough," said Stovepipe. He stuck out a hand. "Good luck."

Dan was about to grasp the lanky cowboy's hand when Brock Matthews reeled out of the cell block with his mouth open, ready to let loose a shout of alarm.

CHAPTER TWELVE

Stovepipe's reactions were lightning swift. His left hand shot out and clamped around Brock's throat, choking off any outcry. His right hand balled into a knobby-knuckled fist that crashed into the deputy's jaw a split second later. Once again Brock's eyes rolled up in their sockets as his knees unhinged.

Wilbur caught the stocky young man under the arms and lowered him to the floor behind the desk.

"He'll stay quiet for a spell," said Wilbur. "When Stovepipe wallops 'em, they stay walloped."

"Come on," Dan said. "Those stairs are back here."

He led the way along a narrow corridor and around a corner to a door that was barred with a thick wooden beam.

"How'd you know this was here?" asked Stovepipe. "Been locked up in this jail before?"

"No, but one time I rode in with Lew Martin, the Box D foreman, when he had to pay the fine for a couple of the hands who'd gotten into a drunken brawl. I saw the stairs then."

Stovepipe and Wilbur lifted the beam from its

brackets and set it aside. The door opened onto a wooden landing with a narrow flight of stairs attached to it that angled down the back side of the court-house. There were no lights back here, but enough of a glow came from the moon and stars for the four people to descend the steps without any trouble.

When they reached the bottom, Stovepipe got that quick handshake from Dan that the deputy had inter-rupted.

"Take care," Stovepipe said. "Saunter around the corner like you belong there, climb on the buck-board, and drive away nice and easy-like."

Dan nodded and then put on Brock's big hat.

"I'm obliged to you for all your help—" he began.

"Save it," said Stovepipe. "We'll see you at the Needles."

He and Wilbur waved farewell to Dan and Laura and slipped away into the shadows.

"You figure that young fella's tellin' the truth, don't you, Stovepipe?" Wilbur whispered as they trav-eled through the back alleys of Hat Creek, heading for the livery stable.

"I sure do," replied Stovepipe. "Did you see the way the gal reacted when he said he didn't want her testifyin' about what really happened because they don't have any future together? That plumb ripped her heart out. I can't see any woman feelin' that way if she had any doubts about a fella. She *knows* Dan's innocent because she was with him when Dempsey was shot, just like he said."

"Yeah, he sure was caught between a rock and a hard place. Either face the gallows or let the woman he loves be ruined. Especially when it might not even do any good for her to tell her story, like you pointed out to him." Wilbur paused in his speech, though not in his hurrying to keep up with his old friend's long-legged strides. "You know, there *is* one other thing we can do besides go on the run from the law."

"I ain't ready to do that yet," Stovepipe said stubbornly. "That'd just make things harder for us in a lot of ways. This way, nobody in these parts knows what to expect from us."

"I do," Wilbur said. "I expect we'll wind up neck-deep in trouble, as usual."

They followed Dan's directions and found the livery stable without any problems. They paused at the establishment's back door. Stovepipe tried the knob and found it locked.

"Blast it," muttered Wilbur. "That door looks flimsy enough we could bust it down—"

"But that'd make enough racket to wake up the night man, if he's sleepin' in the tack room like most of 'em do," Stovepipe finished the thought for him. He stepped back and tilted his head to look above them. "There's a door up there leadin' into the hayloft. If you'll gimme a boost, I think I can reach it."

"How come it's always me giving you a boost?"

"Because even though I'm a head taller 'n you, I weigh less," Stovepipe replied with a grin.

"That's just because you're so dang scrawny." Wilbur sighed, bent over slightly, and laced his fingers together to form a makeshift stirrup. "All right, cowboy. Up you go."

Stovepipe put his booted left foot in Wilbur's hands and pushed off with his right foot as Wilbur lifted. Stovepipe's left hand pressed lightly against the wall for balance as he reached up as far as he could with his right. He grasped the bottom of the hayloft door. It swung open freely. He was able to grab hold of the opening's bottom edge with both hands and pull himself up as Wilbur gave him an added boost.

Stovepipe levered himself up and over, rolling onto the planks that formed the loft. Straw dust filled the air and threatened to make him sneeze. He sat up, opened his mouth, caught his breath, and held a finger under his nose until the almost irresistible urge passed.

As he relaxed and started to breathe again, the overpowering need to sneeze struck again. He was unable to suppress it this time, but he managed to get his hand over his nose and mouth in time to muffle the sound.

Then Stovepipe waited, motionless and intent, to see if anyone inside the stable was going to raise the alarm.

Everything was quiet except for the faint sounds of horses moving around restlessly in the stalls below.

Satisfied that nobody had heard his sneeze, Stovepipe crawled on hands and knees between stacked bales of hay to the ladder. He swung around and climbed down. The place was almost pitch-dark, shut down for the night. Snoring came from somewhere toward the front of the cavernous barn. Just as Stovepipe had thought, the night hostler was asleep.

It would be better all around if he stayed that way for a while.

Stovepipe went to the back door, unfastened the simple latch, and opened it for Wilbur, who was waiting just outside.

"All clear?" asked the redhead.

"Got a fella sawin' logs somewhere."

"Yeah, I hear him."

"Lemme strike a match so we can find our horses."

Stovepipe fished a lucifer out of his pocket and snapped it to life with a flick of his thumbnail. The sulfur match put out a little stink along with its light, but that was unavoidable. Stovepipe held it above his head, squinted against the glare, and spotted his Appaloosa in one of the stalls. Not surprisingly, Wilbur's dun was in the adjacent stall.

"I see our saddles," Wilbur whispered. A note of excitement entered his voice as he went on, "Our rifles are still with 'em."

"We won't be completely unarmed, then," said Stovepipe. "Grab your saddle. We'll have to work in the dark."

That didn't prove to be a problem. These two had saddled their horses thousands of times before, sometimes in pitch darkness, or in pouring rain, or with bullets whipping around their heads. In a matter of minutes, they had the animals ready to ride.

Stovepipe led the Palouse out into the center aisle. Wilbur did the same with the dun. Wilbur whispered, "We'll have to go out the front. It'll be risky."

"Yeah, but they can't hang us for stealin' our own horses."

"No, but they'll add that jailbreak to the list of charges against us. That ought to be good for another five years in the territorial pen."

"They got to put us there first," said Stovepipe.

Slowly, carefully, and as quietly as possible, he and Wilbur led their mounts toward the entrance. But it was impossible for animals as big as horses to move around without making some sound, and as they neared the closed double doors, the snoring stopped abruptly.

Stovepipe had been listening for that. He handed his reins to Wilbur as he turned in the direction the snoring had been coming from until just now.

"Somebody out there?" a man's voice called. "Who's there? If you want your horse, I'll get it for you. That's my job."

A yellow glow sprang into existence as the man scratched a match and lit a lantern. Stovepipe's eyes narrowed. They were accustomed to the darkness, and the light half blinded him as the night hostler, holding the lantern, stepped out of the tack room.

Stovepipe caught a glimpse of a beard-stubbled, middle-aged face as he muttered, "Sorry about this, hombre." The next instant his rock-hard fist crashed into the hostler's jaw.

With his other hand, Stovepipe caught the lantern's bail as the man dropped it. That was the most nerve-racking part of the whole thing. If that lantern had busted, it could have easily caught the livery stable on fire, and all that wood and straw would have turned the place into an inferno in a few heartbeats.

"Get him?" Wilbur called softly.

"Yeah," said Stovepipe. He studied the sprawled hostler in the lantern light and saw that the man would be out for a minute or two, more than likely. That would be long enough. He blew out the lantern and told Wilbur, "Get one of those doors open."

He set the lantern aside and hurried to take the Appaloosa's reins back from Wilbur. With any luck, Dan Hartford and Laura Dempsey had already left the settlement behind them, Stovepipe thought as he and Wilbur led the horses outside.

Wilbur swung the door closed behind them. It was quiet around the livery stable. The other businesses in this block on both sides of the street appeared to be closed, although light and music and the occasional sound of a woman's laugh came from saloons up the street.

One of the cafés was still open, too. A squat, rock building with a slate roof, its sign proclaimed it to be the Red Top Café. As Stovepipe and Wilbur were about to swing up into their saddles, the door opened and a burly man stepped out onto the boardwalk, digging at something in his mouth with a toothpick. He must have spotted the two men and horses half a block away and recognized them, because he suddenly threw the toothpick aside and started forward.

"Hey!" the man called. "You two! Hold on there."

"Blast it, that's Sheriff Olsen!" exclaimed Wilbur.

"Yeah," said Stovepipe. "Let's rattle our hocks, Wilbur!"

They practically leaped into the saddles and then dug their heels into the animals' flanks. Sheriff Frank Olsen was running toward them now as they wheeled the mounts around.

"Stop, damn it!" Olsen bellowed as he yanked his revolver from its holster. The weapon roared and belched flame as he started thumbing off shots as fast as he could.

"There's that old familiar sound again!" Wilbur called over the racket as he and Stovepipe leaned forward in the saddles and the horses lunged into a gallop that carried them along Front Street.

CHAPTER THIRTEEN

The light in the street wasn't very good for shooting. One of Olsen's bullets came close enough that Stovepipe heard it whine past a few feet above his head, but that was the best the lawman did.

Olsen wasn't the only threat, however. More men poured into the street in response to the shots, and the sheriff yelled at them, "Stop those varmints! They're escaping prisoners!"

Several men yanked out guns and started blazing away. Stovepipe and Wilbur had to run a gauntlet of angry townspeople. They couldn't pull out their Winchesters and shoot their way through, either, because those folks were innocent of any wrongdoing, at least in this matter.

The Appaloosa and the dun were moving fast, though, and the hastily aimed bullets missed the two fugitives.

Some of the men firing those shots weren't so fortunate. As Stovepipe and Wilbur flashed past, the townies found themselves inadvertently shooting at each other. One man let out a yelp as a slug burned his arm, and another howled and collapsed with a bullet hole in his thigh. Rather than run right into the middle of that storm of lead, Sheriff Olsen stopped and roared, "Hold your fire! Hold your fire, damn it! They're getting away!"

It was true. The horses pounded around a corner into a side street and were gone.

"Get your horses!" Stovepipe heard Olsen yell. "I need a posse to go after those fellas!"

That was the last Stovepipe heard from the sheriff. The drumming hoofbeats drowned out anything else Olsen had to say.

Barely slowing their racing mounts, Stovepipe and Wilbur made another sharp turn, this time into an alley, and thundered along it. When it came to an end, they had reached the edge of the settlement and rode out onto the sage-and-saguaro-dotted flats. They were headed west.

"We'll keep goin' this way for a while!" Stovepipe called to Wilbur. "Then we'll swing north toward those Needles Dan told us about."

"We'd better try to cover our trail," warned Wilbur.

"That's what I figured."

Right now, though, they couldn't slow down and worry about anything except putting as much distance as possible between themselves and the inevitable pursuit from Hat Creek. The horses had plenty of stamina, but they'd already had one hard run today and Stovepipe knew it could be disastrous to push them too much. They had to walk that fine line between all-out flight and caution.

When he thought enough time had passed, he hauled back on the reins and slowed the Appaloosa. Wilbur followed suit with the dun.

"They won't be able to read sign very well until mornin'," Stovepipe said. "We'll do a few things to try to throw 'em off the scent."

The first of those things was to follow a rocky arroyo for almost a mile before climbing back out. When they came to a shallow creek, they rode out into it and followed it for another mile. Stovepipe, leading the way, started curving to the north, the direction they ultimately wanted to go.

As they rode, they listened for the sound of riders behind them. A couple of times, Stovepipe thought he heard distant hoofbeats, but the posse failed to close in on them.

"We had too good a lead by the time they started on our trail," commented Wilbur. "They don't know where we are."

"More than likely," Stovepipe agreed. "We can't afford to get careless, though. We'll keep movin'."

They rode all night, in fact, stopping now and then to let the horses rest. Stovepipe kept rough track of the time by watching the stars that wheeled through the ebony sky overhead. The air was so clear and dry those glittering diamonds looked close enough for a man to reach up and pluck one of them from its mounting.

The dry air also cooled off efficiently, so that by the time the eastern sky began to turn gray with the approach of dawn, it was downright chilly.

The breakneck flight from Hat Creek had taken Stovepipe and Wilbur far out of their way, so it was almost sunup by the time they spotted the two towering rock spires ahead of them.

"That's got to be the Needles," said Wilbur. "I

don't see anything else around here that looks like it'd have a name like that."

"Nope, I don't, either," Stovepipe agreed. "Wonder if Dan and Miss Laura are here already."

As they came closer, the horses moving at a walk now, Stovepipe spotted a buckboard in the gray light, parked in the twenty-foot gap between the spires. Two draft horses had been unhitched from the vehicle and picketed to graze on the sparse grass that grew around the base of the Needles.

"They must be here," commented Wilbur, "but I don't see 'em."

Stovepipe pointed to a shape underneath the buckboard.

"Looks like one of 'em wrapped up in a blanket," he said.

"Or both of 'em," Wilbur said with a grin.

Stovepipe cocked his head to the side and said, "I don't reckon that's very likely. A fella as worried about a gal's reputation as Dan was wouldn't be likely to try to take advantage of her."

"Yeah, you're probably right about that. Of course, if folks ever find out they spent the night out here together, just the two of them, it'll still be a scandal."

"Some people can make a scandal outta dang near anything," Stovepipe said.

A figure stepped out from behind the closest spire, pointed a revolver at them, and ordered, "Hold it right there! Stovepipe, is that you?"

"In the flesh, Dan," Stovepipe replied as he reined in. Beside him, Wilbur did likewise.

Hatless now, Dan Hartford lowered the gun as he walked toward them.

"You're both all right?" he asked.

"Yep."

"We were out of town, heading in this direction, when I thought I heard some shooting."

"That was us," said Wilbur. "Or rather, that was us being shot *at*. The sheriff spotted us just as we were about to ride out of town. Just pure bad luck . . . the sort that seems to follow us around all the time."

"I wouldn't say that," Stovepipe put in. "After all, we've been in some mighty tight spots, some bad scrapes, and come out of 'em all with our hides in one piece."

"For the most part," Wilbur added dryly.

"So I figure we've had our share of good luck, too."

"Maybe, but it's gonna run out one of these days. Maybe today, for all we know."

Dan holstered the gun and said, "Well, we're all here now. We need to figure out what we're going to do next."

From underneath the wagon, Laura Dempsey said, "We can still head for California, Dan."

She had sat up while the men were talking, no doubt awakened by their voices. Her hair was loose now and spilled in flowing, dark waves around her shoulders. She climbed out from under the buckboard, stood up, shook her head, and knuckled sleep from her eyes.

Dan turned toward her and said, "If we run off to California, we'll always be fugitives, Laura. We'll always be looking over our shoulders, expecting to see some lawman there ready to arrest us."

"We'd be together, though," she said. "We probably wouldn't have any trouble finding a preacher to marry us. That's what we've both wanted for a long time, isn't it? To be married?"

"That's what I wanted," said Dan.

"And you think I didn't?" she asked.

"You said yes to Abel Dempsey, so yeah, I reckon you wanted to be married, all right."

Stovepipe pointed with a thumb and said to Wilbur, "Let's wander over yonder to that other rock and unsaddle these horses. I'm sure they'd appreciate some rest, some grass, and a drink."

They had filled their canteens at one of the creeks they'd crossed, so once they had the horses unsaddled and picketed, Stovepipe poured water into his hat and let both horses drink from it. While he and Wilbur tended to those chores, Dan and Laura continued to talk in low, angry voices.

"Times like this, I'm glad I never got hitched," Stovepipe commented quietly to his friend.

Wilbur snorted and said, "No woman'd be fool enough to marry a long drink of water like you who's always getting mixed up in shooting scrapes."

"Oh, I dunno. I seem to recollect a few widows who might've set their caps for me if we hadn't shook the dust of those places off our boots. There were even a few who made eyes at you."

"Sitting in some house behind a white picket fence for the rest of my days . . ." Wilbur shuddered. "Nope. I think maybe that gives me the fantods worse 'n the thought of going to Yuma Prison."

Dan and Laura must have finished what they had to say to each other. Dan came over to Stovepipe and Wilbur and told them, "I'm not going to run. I'm going to find out who really killed Abel Dempsey and clear my name."

"You convinced the little lady to go along with that?" asked Stovepipe.

"It's my decision," Dan said. Then he added, "But Laura sees it my way . . . for now, anyway."

"We're gonna have to have a long talk, then. There are some things I need to know. But first . . . what do you think the odds are that a posse will come lookin' in this direction?"

"It's possible. What direction were you going when you got chased out of town?"

"West."

"It's more likely they'll start by searching in that direction, then. But Frank Olsen's not a fool, just as stubborn as a mule. He's liable to send search parties out in every direction, if he can round up enough men who are willing to volunteer."

"Somebody's gonna need to keep watch, then, while Wilbur and me get a little shut-eye. We were in the saddle all night."

"I can do that," Dan said, nodding. "In fact, I can climb up on top of one of these spires. From up there, if anybody starts in this direction I'll be able to see them while they're still several miles away."

"It'll get mighty hot up there by the middle of the day."

"I'll be all right."

"It's your decision. I don't suppose you and the lady have had any breakfast?"

Dan shook his head and said, "That sort of seemed like the least of our worries."

"Maybe so, but you've got to keep your strength up," said Stovepipe. "We've got some jerky in our saddlebags we can share with you. It ain't much, but it's better 'n nothin'."

"Sure wish we had some coffee, too," Wilbur said wistfully.

"Reckon we'll have to settle for bein' alive," Stovepipe said as the orange ball of the sun began to peek over the Mogollon Rim in the east.

CHAPTER FOURTEEN

After their meager breakfast of jerky washed down with canteen water, Stovepipe and Wilbur took their bedrolls off the horses and spread them in the gap between the spires. The eastern Needle would provide some shade from the rising sun. The air was still chilly, but it would heat up quickly as the morning progressed.

They slept for several hours before Dan called from the top of the western spire, "I see some riders south of here!"

Stovepipe roused from sleep and sat up, rubbing his rather craggy face.

"Are they headed in this direction?" he asked Dan.

"Sort of. Not straight at us, but drifting in this general direction."

"Bound to be a posse," muttered Wilbur from where he had sat up, too. "We'd best light a shuck."

"And go where?" asked Stovepipe.

"I dunno. I figured you had some ideas along those lines. There's always a lot more percolating in that head of yours than you let on, Stovepipe."

That brought a chuckle from the lanky cowboy. He stood up, stretched, and looked around for Laura Dempsey. He spotted her sitting on a rock slab near the other spire with a carbine across her knees.

"You brought that repeater with you in the buckboard, ma'am?" he asked her as he gestured at the carbine.

"I may not have been raised on the frontier, Mr. Stewart," she said, "but I've picked up some of its ways pretty quickly. Lew Martin told me never to ride out anywhere without taking a gun with me, because you never know when you might come across a rattlesnake or some other varmint."

"That's good advice," said Stovepipe. "If there's one thing these parts are full of, it's varmints . . . four-legged, no-legged—and them that go on two legs as well."

Dan was climbing down the spire where he had posted himself. The thick column of rock appeared smooth from a distance but in reality was rugged enough that there were plenty of handholds and footholds for a man to climb up and down. Dan dropped the last few feet and landed gracefully.

"Are we pulling out?" he asked.

"Yeah, I reckon," said Stovepipe. "I didn't intend to stay here all day. How far are we from Box D range?"

Dan pointed southwest and said, "It's seven or eight miles that way. But won't it be awful risky going there?"

"Seems to me like that's one of the last places the sheriff'd think to look for you."

"You may have a point there," Dan said with a

shrug. "Anyway, with posses scouring the whole basin, I suppose one place is just about as good as another." He glanced at the young woman who sat there holding the carbine. "And going there would get Laura back home."

"I'm not sure I'll ever consider the Box D truly my home," she said. "Not unless you're there with me, Dan."

"Y'all can talk about that later," said Stovepipe. "Right now, let's get ready to move."

He and Wilbur hitched the horses to the buckboard, then gathered up their gear. As they worked, Wilbur said, "Remember what I said when we got here about wishing we had some coffee?"

"Sure."

"Well, it goes double now. I need a pot of Arbuckle's, good and black, along with a plate full of bacon and some fried eggs and a big ol' stack of flapjacks and maybe some fried potatoes."

"You always was a bottomless pit when it comes to eatin'," said Stovepipe with a grin. "Right now you're just torturin' yourself, though. I reckon we'll get some decent grub sooner or later."

"If we don't starve to death first," muttered Wilbur.

In a few minutes, they were ready to go. Dan helped Laura climb onto the buckboard seat, then pulled himself up beside her and took hold of the reins. The big hat that belonged to Brock Matthews was in the back of the buckboard, and Dan left it there. Stovepipe and Wilbur fell in alongside the vehicle as Dan got it rolling toward the distant ranch.

As they rode, Stovepipe said to Dan, "I wouldn't

mind takin' a look at that Apache Bluff place you mentioned yesterday."

He didn't add anything about Apache Bluff being the spot where Dan and Laura had had their rendezvous the day that Abel Dempsey was killed. He didn't see any point in upsetting the young woman unnecessarily.

"I suppose I could take you there," Dan replied. "First, though, there's somewhere else I want to go." He turned to Laura. "I've been thinking about it, and we have to take you someplace you'll be safe. You can't just go back to the ranch. Sheriff Olsen might ride out just to make sure you're not there." He frowned. "Besides, I don't trust some of the men, like Jube Connolly. He might try to hurt me by tipping off the sheriff that you're there."

"I suppose that's possible," said Laura. "But I can't really think of anywhere else I can go."

"What about the line shack up in the high pastures?" asked Dan. "Hamp Jones and Charley Bartlett are staying up there for the summer. They're good men. They'd look after you."

"I'm not so sure I need looking after," Laura said. "I'm the one who got *you* out of jail, remember?"

"I'm not likely to forget," Dan said grimly. "You may have ruined your whole life in the process."

"It's my life to ruin if that's what I choose to do."

Dan didn't say anything to that. They rode on in silence for a few moments, then she continued, "There's something you may not have considered, Dan. Mr. Jones and Mr. Bartlett rode for A—for my husband, for a long time. They were loyal to him. How do you know they'll agree to help us and let me hide out there? They might try to take us prisoner and turn us over to the law."

"Maybe, but I've gotten along pretty good with them. I think they'd at least hear me out. It's a chance we'll have to take. You'll be safer there than anywhere else I can think of, while Stovepipe and Wilbur and I try to figure out what to do next."

Stovepipe said, "Not tryin' to stick my nose in where it don't belong, ma'am, but Dan's got a point. If we're gonna figure out who really killed your husband and come up with evidence to prove it, we're liable to need to move around in a hurry for a while. That'll be easier—"

"If you don't have to worry about keeping track of me," Laura finished for him. She sighed. "You're right, Mr. Stewart. I know that. After everything that's happened, I just don't like the idea of being separated from Dan. There's always a chance we . . . we might never see each other again."

"That's not going to happen," Dan promised as he looked over at her. "So much has happened to try to keep us apart, and yet here we are. I'm starting to think it's our destiny to be together."

"I thought you said we didn't have a future," she reminded him.

"I'm going to fight like a wildcat to make sure I was wrong about that," Dan said.

Dan knew this range better than any of the other three, even though he hadn't been in the area for very long, so Stovepipe let him pick their route as they headed toward the Box D. As much as possible, Dan tried to avoid trails where they might be spotted, but at the same time he had to stick to places the buckboard could negotiate. It would have been easier if they had all been on horseback.

Dan was canny, though, and stuck to areas where they were screened by trees or ridges, and he avoided anywhere they might be skylighted. Several times, Stovepipe's keen eyes spotted horsemen in the distance, and when that happened, Dan pulled the buckboard into cover and they waited until the distant riders were out of sight.

Eventually, he said, "We're back on Box D range now," and drove the buckboard along a trail that began to climb toward the higher pastures. It wasn't much of a trail, just a pair of faint ruts left from the times when a wagon had taken supplies up to the line shack. The buckboard jolted back and forth, throwing Laura's shoulder against Dan's.

Even under the circumstances, Dan didn't look like he minded all that much, thought Stovepipe. A faint smile curved the lanky cowboy's mouth under the drooping mustache. There was an old saying about how love conquered all, he recalled. That might not always be true . . . but love usually put up a good fight, that was for dang sure.

After a hard climb, the trail leveled out and crossed a meadow to where a blocky log cabin was nestled at the edge of a thick stand of pine. A creek tumbled over a rocky bed nearby, which was one reason the line shack had been located at this spot, Stovepipe surmised.

He hipped around in the saddle and looked back in the direction they had come from. The basin spread out to the north and east, and the dark line of the Mogollon Rim was clearly visible from here. This would be a good hideout, he mused, since it was isolated and commanded a good field of view.

The sun was high in the sky by now, almost directly overhead. Gray smoke curled from the cabin's stone chimney, and Dan commented, "One of the boys must be here. I sort of figured they'd be out on the range right now. But that's good, because it'll give us a chance to talk to whoever is here and make sure they understand what's going on."

As the group approached, the cabin door swung open on leather hinges and a man stepped out, balancing himself on a makeshift crutch tucked under his left arm. In his right hand he held an old cap-and-ball pistol with a muzzle so big it looked sort of like a cannon as he raised it toward them.

The gun was just a precaution, though, because the old-timer lowered it immediately as his eyes got big with recognition.

"Miz Dempsey!" he exclaimed. "And I'll be da— I mean, is that you, Dan Hartford?"

"It's me, Hamp," said Dan as he pulled back on the reins and brought the buckboard to a halt. "What happened to you? Are you all right?"

"Yeah, I'm fine. Danged ol' cow stepped on my foot yesterday." Hamp Jones grimaced. "All these years cowboyin', and this is the first time that's happened. But it was swole up enough this mornin' that it wouldn't fit in a stirrup, so Charley said he'd take care of the chores by himself today and let me rest it."

Laura said, "You probably need to have a doctor look at that, Mr. Jones."

"Naw, no offense, ma'am, but when it comes to all the aches and pains a fella can pick up workin' with cows, I reckon I know as much about 'em as any sawbones would. Besides, the foot's considerable better already. It'll be back to normal by tomorrow, I expect. In the meantime, again no offense . . . but what in blazes are you folks doin' up here?" Hamp looked at Stovepipe and Wilbur. "And who are these two rannihans?"

"This is Stovepipe Stewart and Wilbur Coleman," said Dan. "They helped me out when—" He stopped short and frowned. "Has anybody from headquarters been up here in the past few days, Hamp?"

"Nope. Ain't seen hide nor hair of anybody 'cept each other for nigh on to a week."

"That means you don't know what happened," said Laura. "Mr. Jones, I need help from you and Mr. Bartlett."

"Anything we can do, ma'am," said Hamp. "You know that. You're the boss's wife."

"Actually, she's the boss," said Stovepipe as he caught on to what the conversation meant. "Somebody murdered Mr. Dempsey and is liable to come after the lady next, but we mean to keep her safe and round up the polecat who done it."

CHAPTER FIFTEEN

Hamp stared at them goggle-eyed for a couple of seconds before bursting out, "Murdered! The boss? Good Lord! What happened?"

"We don't know yet," said Dan. "That's what we want to find out. Stovepipe and Wilbur are giving me a hand with that. But we need someplace safe for Mrs. Dempsey to stay so nothing will happen to her while we're investigating."

"You don't reckon anybody'd think to look for her up here?"

"That's what we're hoping."

Hamp nodded and said, "Sounds like a good idea to me." He looked at Laura. "Ma'am, the conditions are plumb primitive and I'm a mite embarrassed that you'll have to put up with a couple of old rapscallions like Charley and me, but we'd be honored to have you stay here for a spell. Got plenty of supplies on hand, and we can sleep in the shed around back with the horses so's you can have the cabin to yourself."

"I hate to put you out—" Laura began.

"Shoot, no, don't give it another thought. Light

down from that buckboard and come on in. I got a mess o' beans cookin'. Figured since I was stuck here today I might as well put the time to good use, and Charley said he'd ride in for lunch instead of takin' his grub with him. He ought to be showin' up pretty soon. You other fellas are welcome to grab a surroundin', too."

"Mister, you don't know how good that sounds to me," said Wilbur as he swung down from the dun's saddle.

"Yeah, ol' Wilbur here was about to have a fadin' spell from hunger," added Stovepipe with a grin.

Hamp hadn't mentioned it, but he also had a pan of corn bread cooking, and there was still coffee in the pot. The smells inside the line shack were heavenly at the moment, although as the abode of two rough-and-ready cowboys, the place didn't really resemble anything to be found on the other side of the pearly gates.

A few minutes after everyone had gone inside, making the cabin rather crowded, Stovepipe heard a rider approaching. The swift rataplan of hoofbeats told him that the newcomer was in a hurry. He stepped into the open doorway with his Winchester in his hands.

"Who is it?" asked Dan. He was standing beside the rough-hewn table where Laura had taken a seat in an old ladderback chair.

"Stocky fella with a gray mustache," Stovepipe reported.

"That'd be Charley," Hamp said from the pot-bellied stove, where he was stirring the pot of beans.

Dan went to the door and looked out past Stovepipe. He said, "That's Charley Bartlett, all right. He must have seen the buckboard and the strange horses and figured something was going on."

Dan stepped out where Charley could see him and waved to let the elderly puncher know that everything was all right. Charley slowed his horse and finished crossing the pasture at an easy trot.

"Dan, what're you doin' up here?" he asked as he reined in. "And who's this?"

"Charley, meet Stovepipe Stewart, a friend of mine," said Dan. Solemnly, he continued, "There's trouble down at headquarters. Mr. Dempsey was shot and killed a couple of days ago."

Charley let fly with a startled oath.

"What in blazes happened, Dan?" he asked. "Who done it?"

"We don't know." Dan lowered his voice and added in a flinty tone, "But we're damned sure going to find out."

Charley dismounted and came inside, where Dan introduced him to Wilbur and then told him the story they had made up on the fly earlier with Hamp. Charley was in firm agreement that Laura should stay at the line shack and added his pledge to protect her from anyone who tried to harm her.

"It really means a lot to me that you two feel like that," she told the old cowboys.

"Shucks, ma'am," Charley said. "Hamp and me ride for the brand, and now that Mr. Dempsey's gone, God rest his soul, *you're* the Box D."

Laura lowered her eyes, clearly embarrassed, and Dan looked away, too, Stovepipe noted. Even though nothing really improper had happened between them, this show of loyalty to Laura's late husband by

Hamp and Charley must have made them a little uncomfortable.

Judging by everything Stovepipe had heard about Abel Dempsey, the man really hadn't been evil, but the way he and Laura's father had conspired to push her into marrying him showed that he possessed a large degree of arrogance and had a ruthless streak when it came to getting what he wanted. To Hamp and Charley and the rest of the crew of the Box D, though, Dempsey had just been the boss. According to their code, when you took wages from a man, you gave him your loyalty, no matter what.

And no matter what Abel Dempsey's faults might have been, he hadn't deserved a bullet in the back. That was reason enough for Stovepipe to want to discover the killer's identity, but in addition to that, his finely honed instincts told him that Dempsey's murder was tied in with something bigger, something that threatened the whole basin . . .

"Grub's ready," announced Hamp, breaking into Stovepipe's reverie. "It might be a little crowded, but everybody gather round the table."

The food was simple but good. Hamp had cooked a couple of pieces of salt pork with the beans, giving them an excellent flavor, especially when combined with the corn bread and washed down with strong, black coffee.

After Wilbur had polished off two plates, Stovepipe grinned and told Hamp and Charley, "It's a good thing this pard of mine ain't stayin', boys. He'd plumb eat you outta house and home."

"You're a fine one to talk," said Wilbur. "I've seen

you put away practically a whole side of beef at one sitting."

"Red meat's good for a man. Keeps the juices flowin'."

Hamp said, "I don't want to disturb anybody's digestion, but I'd sure like to hear what happened to the boss."

Stovepipe and Wilbur looked to Dan, since he was the natural one to answer that question. He said, "Mr. Dempsey was bushwhacked a couple of days ago over by Apache Bluff. I happened to be close by and heard the shot, but by the time I got there and found him, he was gone."

Charley frowned and said, "I don't mean to talk outta turn here, Dan, but seems to me the last I heard, you'd been run off the Box D. Didn't the boss fire you and tell you to never come back?"

"That's true," Dan admitted. "But he had cooled off and sent word to me that he was willing for me to hire on again. In fact, that's where I was headed when I heard the shot."

That lie would be easily disproved if Hamp and Charley were to talk to anyone from the rest of the Box D crew or from Hat Creek, but as long as they stayed up in these high pastures and nobody else came around, they would accept what Dan had told them. Stovepipe's hope was that the respite would last long enough for him and Wilbur to discover the truth about what was going on in the Tonto Basin.

"Well, I'm glad to have you back," said Hamp. "I always took you for the decent sort. Not to speak ill o' the dead, and I'm beggin' your pardon, ma'am, but I thought the boss sort of flew off the handle when he fired you."

"Things happen," Dan said with a shrug. "I don't hold any grudges."

"It's good of you to try to find out who bush-whacked him," said Charley.

Again Dan looked away. He needed to find Demp-sey's killer to clear his own name, not out of any sense of wanting justice for the murdered man. But Hamp and Charley didn't need to know that.

With the meal finished, Stovepipe, Wilbur, Dan, and Charley went outside, leaving Hamp and Laura in the line shack to clean up. Stovepipe and Wilbur unhitched the team and watered the horses.

"I need to borrow a mount from the string you and Hamp brought up here," Dan said to Charley. "Hate to leave you short, but I might need a better horse than those draft animals."

"Sure, that's all right. We'll still have a few extra cayuses."

"You expectin' any visitors in the next few days?" asked Stovepipe.

Charley shook his head and said, "Nope. Willie brought a wagonload of supplies up from the home ranch four or five days ago. He won't be back for a week, more 'n likely. I reckon some of the boys could ride up here, but there ain't no way of knowin' that."

"If you see anybody coming, lie low," Dan said. "And whatever you do, don't let them know Mrs. Dempsey is here."

Charley frowned.

"Even if it's somebody like Lew? He'd never double-cross the boss."

"Maybe not, but until we find out who shot Mr. Dempsey, we can't take any chances."

Charley's frown deepened as he looked over at Stovepipe and Wilbur.

"You know, nobody ever told me who you fellas are or how you fit into this."

"We're just a couple of driftin' waddies who met Dan and got a hankerin' to play detective when we heard what was goin' on in these parts," said Stovepipe.

"Yeah? And how do we know you didn't have anything to do with the boss gettin' shot?"

"They didn't," Dan said. "It's not possible. They were nowhere around when that happened. They didn't ride into the basin until yesterday."

"Yeah, well, maybe I ain't that trustin'," said Charley. "They seem like good hombres, but you better keep an eye on 'em anyway."

Stovepipe grinned and said, "We'll all keep an eye on each other. How's that?" He grew more serious as he went on, "What can you tell me about the rustlin' that's been goin' on around here, Charley?"

"I don't know much except that it's got to be a slick gang behind it. Practically every spread in the basin has lost some stock here and there. Never a big bunch at a time, you understand, but it sure adds up. I got a hunch the wide-loopers are just feelin' us out, tryin' to decide just how much they can steal and still get away with it. One of these days, there's liable to be a big strike, and they'll clean out the whole basin."

"That would ruin everybody in these parts," said Dan.

"Well, I don't reckon a bunch of damn rustlers would care about that, do you?"

"No," said Stovepipe. "They sure wouldn't. With Dempsey dead, along with those other two ranchers, that'll make things easier for them."

Charley stared at him and said, "You figure whoever shot the boss is tied in with them rustlers?"

"That's what we intend to find out," Stovepipe said.

CHAPTER SIXTEEN

Dan picked out one of the horses from Hamp and Charley's string and put an old saddle he found in the shed on the animal. It was time for him, Stovepipe, and Wilbur to leave.

Stovepipe could tell that Dan didn't want to be parted from Laura. The young cowboy would have liked to take her in his arms and bid her a proper farewell.

But to have done so would have shocked and scandalized Hamp and Charley, and for the time being, they needed the two old-timers on their side. Dan was smart enough to know that, so he just nodded and told Laura, "So long, Mrs. Dempsey. We'll be back as soon as we can, hopefully with good news."

"And good luck to you, Mr. Hartford," Laura said. She held out her hand. Dan hesitated for just a second, then grasped it and shook it as he would have a man's hand.

It was a poor substitute for a kiss, thought Stovepipe as he concealed a smile, but better than nothing, he supposed.

Dan didn't look back as they rode away, although

Stovepipe figured he wanted to. Quietly, Stovepipe said, "You done the right thing back there. Havin' those two old pelicans around to look after Miz Dempsey gives us a fightin' chance."

"That's all I'm asking for," Dan said with a grim cast to his face.

Now that they were heading lower in the basin, onto the main part of the Box D range, the likelihood of running into some of Dempsey's punchers was greater. All three men remained as alert as possible and stuck to the trees when they could. They didn't want to be spotted.

Because of the need for stealth, they couldn't move very fast. It took more than an hour to reach the crest of a bluff where the landscape fell away into a rugged stretch similar to the one farther west where Dan had been hiding out in recent days.

They rode out of a stand of trees to the edge of the rocky promontory. Dan reined in, nodded to the rough terrain in front of them, and said, "When the Apaches were still giving trouble around here, back in the early days when the basin was still being settled, that was where they holed up between raids. That's how this bluff got its name. At least, that's what I've heard the old-timers say, like Hamp and Charley and Willie Hill, who's the cook for the Box D now. That was a long time before I was ever in these parts, but the name stuck. I suppose when you've had to fight the Apaches, you never forget what you went through."

"I reckon not," said Stovepipe. "Chances are the 'Paches ain't forgot about those days, neither. They were smart enough to know they were fightin' a losin' battle in these parts and beat what they call a strategic retreat down to the area around the border."

"The Apaches may have headed south," said Wilbur, "but there are still plenty of rustlers and owlhoots around here, I'll bet. There's always somebody lookin' to make trouble." He nodded toward the badlands. "Could be that gang's hiding out in there right now."

That comment made all three men sit in solemn silence for a moment. Then Stovepipe said, "Tell us again about what happened the day Dempsey was bushwhacked, Dan."

"Laura and I were sitting here on our horses, right where we are now," said Dan. "We were talking."

"What about?"

Dan frowned and said, "I don't see what that has to do with Dempsey being killed."

"I don't know that it does. I just like to round up all the information I can. You can't never tell when somethin' will turn out to be important."

"We were talking about running away together," Dan said bluntly. "I told you before, we considered starting over in California. We were trying to figure out when we could go, and how we could manage it so that Dempsey wouldn't try to hunt us down."

"You figured he might come after the two of you," said Stovepipe.

"And from what I've heard of Dempsey, he might come gunning for you," added Wilbur. "Or at least pay somebody to do that."

Dan looked back and forth between them and said, "What are you trying to do, give me even more of a motive for murdering Dempsey?"

"Just linin' up the facts," said Stovepipe. "I don't reckon Sheriff Olsen needs any help figurin' out your motive."

"Whether or not I had a good reason to shoot the old buzzard, I didn't do it," Dan said. "While Laura and I were talking, we heard a shot from that direction." He pointed north along the bluff. The trees came closer to the edge in that direction, blocking the view. Dan went on, "I knew there might be trouble, so I told Laura to get out of here. Then I rode up yonder to have a look."

"Let's do the same," said Stovepipe with a nod.

They walked their horses slowly along the bluff toward the pines. Stovepipe kept a close eye on the ground as they proceeded. He wasn't looking for anything in particular, just looking. That was a habit he had gotten into over the years, and it had served him well many times in the past.

They entered the trees, which grew close enough together to form a screen, although the trunks were far enough apart that it was no problem for a rider to weave through the growth. The stand wasn't very thick, and when the three men reached the far side, Stovepipe reined in and turned his horse so that he could look back to where they had come from.

"If a fella wanted to spy on somebody on the bluff, he could sit here and do that," he commented. "You can see well enough through the trees to make out what's goin' on, but if you were quiet about it, the folks you were watchin' might not ever notice you."

"You're saying that Dempsey was sitting here spying on Laura and me," Dan said with a frown.

Stovepipe's bony shoulders went up and down in a shrug.

"I don't reckon we'll ever know for sure, since the fella's crossed the divide, but it makes sense."

"I told you, we weren't doing anything except talking."

"And I ain't disputin' that. Howsomever, a lot of gents would take exception to their wives talkin' to some other fella out in the middle of nowhere, especially one they'd done fired and thrown off their ranch."

Dan sighed and nodded. He said, "We were foolish, and we were wrong in some ways. But so was Dempsey. He had no right to force a young, vibrant woman like Laura to marry him. He knew she wouldn't be able to stand up to the pressure from both him and her father."

"I ain't makin' excuses for the man, just tryin' to figure out who dry-gulched him." Stovepipe gestured toward the ground. "This is where you found him?"

"Yeah. He was laying right there, facedown, with a good-sized bloodstain already on the back of his shirt. I knew as soon as I saw him that he'd been shot."

"Was his horse still here?"

"Yeah, about fifty yards that way." Dan pointed along the line of trees. "It must have spooked when Dempsey was shot out of the saddle."

"Or Dempsey had dismounted and was holding the reins when he was shot," said Wilbur. "Either one works to explain what you found."

"I suppose, but I don't see how that matters."

Stovepipe said, "You never know what matters until you figure out exactly what happened." He nodded toward a cluster of boulders approximately seventy-five yards away. "The killer was hidin' in those rocks, you said?"

"That's right. I got off my horse to make sure Dempsey wasn't alive and needed help. I saw right away that he was dead, though, and as I straightened up, there was another shot. The bullet came close enough for me to hear it go over my head."

Stovepipe turned his head slowly, looking back and forth between the rocks and the place where Dan had found Abel Dempsey's body. After a moment, he said, "What did you do?"

"After that potshot, you mean? I grabbed my gun and fired back. It was just a reflex. Any man would do the same, don't you think?"

"I reckon most would," Stovepipe agreed. "How long was it after you triggered that shot that some of the Box D hands rode up?"

"I don't know. Thirty seconds, maybe."

"You stood out here in the open for that long after somebody'd tried to ventilate you?"

Dan shook his head and said, "Well, no. I ducked back into the trees and took cover. But then I heard hoofbeats from the other side of the rocks and decided the bushwhacker was lighting a shuck. I had just stepped out of the trees and was standing beside Dempsey's body when Lew Martin, the Box D foreman, and some of the other hands came galloping up from the other direction."

Wilbur said, "You couldn't have had more bad luck if you'd tried, son."

Dan sighed and nodded.

"I know," he said. "I mean, what were Lew and those other fellas supposed to think? They found me standing over Dempsey's body with a gun in my hand."

"What did they do?" asked Stovepipe.

"They threw down on me, of course. Lew yelled for the others to hold their fire, but they were too worked up to listen to him. I knew they'd fill me full of holes if I stayed there and tried to shoot it out with them, so I jumped in my saddle and took off."

"Where?"

"Back through the trees and along the bluff until I got to a spot where I could get down into that rougher country. They chased me for a long time, but I stayed ahead of them and finally gave them the slip."

"Then you headed for the breaks west of here, where you'd been hidin' out."

"That's right," said Dan. "I've told you the whole story—*again*—and no offense, Stovepipe, but I don't see what good it does to go over the ugly mess so many times."

"Because sometimes it takes more than one tellin' for all the details to come out. For example, you said somethin' yesterday while we were locked up in the Hat Creek jail that you didn't mention this time, and I got a hunch that it's important."

"I did?" Dan said with a puzzled frown. "I can't think of what it might be."

"You told us that when you found Dempsey, he'd been shot in the back *at close range*. Are you certain about that part, Dan?"

Dan's frown deepened, as if he were casting his mind back to the grim scene that had played out here a couple of days earlier. After a moment, he said, "There were powder burns on the back of his shirt. I'm sure of it. They were hard to see because the blood had spread enough to sort of hide them, but I remember noticing them and thinking that . . . Wait a minute . . ."

"Yeah," said Stovepipe. "Those powder burns prove that he wasn't bushwhacked from those rocks.

The killer had to be closer than that. Right behind him, in fact. You think anybody could sneak up on Dempsey like that?"

Dan shook his head and said, "Not a chance. I'll give the man credit. He'd been here in the basin for a long time, and he fought Indians and outlaws to establish his ranch. He wouldn't be caught like that. But what does that mean?"

"It means he knew whoever shot him," said Stovepipe. "Knew him—and trusted him."

"So whoever it was . . . knew that Laura and I were over there on the other side of the trees."

"Yep. He gunned down Dempsey and then hid in the rocks, figurin' that you'd come to see what the shootin' was about. He must've spotted Martin and the other hombres headin' this way, so he fired a shot over your head, knowin' you'd be likely to shoot back at him. That'd put you practically on top of Dempsey's body with a smokin' gun in your hand for the others to find."

"Damn it," Dan grated. "What you're saying is that it wasn't just bad luck I found myself in so much trouble."

"That's right. The killer may have made up the plan on the spur o' the moment when he spotted Martin and the others comin', but it worked just like the varmint wanted. He gunned down Abel Dempsey and framed you for the killin'." Trenches appeared in Stovepipe's weathered cheeks as he added, "That's a pretty good day's work for a murderer."

CHAPTER SEVENTEEN

Stovepipe walked the Appaloosa toward the boulders, with Wilbur and Dan coming along behind him. Again Stovepipe studied the ground. He saw a number of hoofprints, but there was nothing really distinctive about any of them and he knew quite a few riders had milled around here since Dempsey was shot.

He was more interested in any tracks he might find among the boulders, but the ground was too rocky there. He spotted a few places where the stone had been nicked by a horseshoe, but they didn't tell him anything.

"The shot the hombre took at you from over here," he said to Dan. "Could you tell if it came from a rifle or a handgun?"

"A handgun, I'd say. That's what it sounded like, and I remember thinking the range was pretty far for a handgun. I knew that when I shot back with my Colt, too, but I did it anyway. Like I said, it was just instinct to return the fire."

"Yeah. The varmint didn't want to hit you, anyway. It would've ruined his plan if he'd killed you, because then you wouldn't have been around to take the blame for murderin' Dempsey."

Stovepipe swung down from the saddle and studied the ground more closely, then turned his attention to the boulders themselves. He wasn't sure what he was going to find, if anything, but he hadn't been searching for more than a minute when he spotted something caught on a rough spot on one of the big slabs of rock. He reached out to pull it loose and rubbed it lightly between his fingers.

"What've you got there, Stovepipe?" asked Wilbur.

"It's a thread of some sort—" Stovepipe began.

He stopped short as he felt the wind-rip of a bullet passing within inches of his ear. It slammed into the boulder and whined off, leaving behind a splash of lead. At the same time, the whipcrack of a rifle tore through the air.

Stovepipe twisted around and reached for his gun before he remembered that his holster was empty.

"Take cover!" he called to Wilbur and Dan as more shots slammed out. The two men leaped from their saddles. Dan wheeled around and drew the revolver he had taken from Deputy Matthews back in Hat Creek. He triggered two rounds toward the trees. From the sound of the shots directed at them, the rifleman was hidden in there.

That distraction gave Wilbur time to haul both his and Stovepipe's Winchesters from their saddle boots. Carrying the two rifles, he lunged toward the rocks. Dan was right behind him. Bullets sizzled through the air around them.

"Stovepipe!" Wilbur said as he tossed one of the rifles toward his friend. Stovepipe caught the weapon and had it spitting flame and lead in an instant as he dropped to one knee behind a small boulder. Slugs ricocheted wildly as more than one man opened fire from the pines.

Dan and Wilbur flung themselves behind the rocks, too, and had to catch their breath for a second before they could join the battle. Meanwhile Stovepipe kept up a steady fire toward the pines. His bullets rattled low-hanging branches and chewed big chunks of bark from the tree trunks.

Wilbur rose up into a crouch, brought his rifle to his shoulder, and started firing as well. He called to Stovepipe, "Can you see any of the varmints?"

"No, but they're in there!" Stovepipe replied.

Dan took a couple of fresh cartridges from the loops on his shell belt and thumbed them into the Colt's cylinder, replacing the rounds he had fired.

"I can't do much good at this range," he said. "How much ammunition do you fellas have?"

"Maybe a dozen spare rounds in my pockets," replied Stovepipe.

"Yeah, same here," Wilbur added. "We've got plenty of cartridges in our saddlebags, but they're not going to do us much good where we are now."

That was true. The Appaloosa and Wilbur's dun weren't easily spooked, but enough gun-thunder had roared to make them trot off along the bluff. They had come to a stop about thirty yards away, far enough that crossing the open ground between them and the rocks would likely prove fatal for anyone who attempted it.

"They've got us pinned down," Dan said. "All they have to do is wait for us to run out of ammunition and then rush us."

Stovepipe looked behind him. The edge of the bluff was only ten feet away. It was a drop of twenty-five or thirty feet, depending on where along the rugged bluff a fella was.

"Dan, is the face of that bluff rough enough that an hombre could climb down it?" he asked.

"Probably," Dan replied, "but if we did that, we'd have to leave our horses behind. We wouldn't have a chance afoot. Whoever's after us would be able to run us down without much trouble."

"I ain't plannin' to leave the horses behind. But like you said, we can't just squat here, empty our guns, and wait for those varmints to kill us. Toss me that six-shooter o' yours."

Dan frowned and said, "I don't much cotton to the idea of being unarmed."

"You won't be," Stovepipe assured him. "I'll slide my rifle over to you, tie up the extra shells I got in a bandanna, and throw them to you as well. You and Wilbur will be able to keep those fellas in the trees busy for a spell. Just be sure and pick your shots, so you're not wastin' too much lead."

"And what are you gonna be doing?" asked Wilbur.

"Thought I'd take me a little scenic excursion," replied Stovepipe with a grin. "I'm gonna climb along the face o' that bluff until I can get up in the trees and circle around behind the bushwhackers."

"You'll fall off and bust your fool noggin open!"

"Not if I'm careful, I won't." Stovepipe put his Winchester on the ground and shoved it over to Dan, who was kneeling behind a boulder about fifteen feet away. The rifle slid close enough for Dan to reach out, snag the barrel, and pull it the rest of the way. Stovepipe followed it a moment later with the little bundle of extra bullets he had tied up in a neckerchief.

Dan loaded the sixth chamber in his revolver, which customarily was kept empty, and threw it to Stovepipe, who caught it with both hands.

"You've got a full wheel," Dan told the lanky cowboy. "You want my extra shells?"

Stovepipe shook his head and said, "If six rounds won't do the job, it ain't likely any more would."

He pouched the iron in his empty holster and went down on his belly. As he crawled backward toward the edge, Wilbur laughed and said, "You're doodlebuggin', Stovepipe."

With his legs already hanging over the brink, Stovepipe didn't reply to that gibe. Instead he eased over the edge and searched for handholds.

As Dan had said, the face of Apache Bluff wasn't sheer. There were fissures, rocky knobs, the occasional hardy little bush. Stovepipe considered trying to climb all the way to the ground, but it was so rough down there he thought he might make better time working his way along just below the rim.

Above him, shots rang out from Wilbur and Dan. They were taking their time now, trying to make the ammunition last. More shots blasted from the trees. Stovepipe tried to estimate how many gunmen might be hidden in the pines. He knew there were at least two and might be as many as four. Those weren't very good odds, so he would have to make every bullet count.

Assuming he ever got in position to use the borrowed revolver, he reminded himself. He had to reach the trees first, and it was slow going.

A couple of times during the arduous journey along the bluff, he almost fell. His feet slipped, and he found himself hanging from his hands. There was a lot of strength in his wiry body, though, so he was able to cling to the precarious grip until he got his toes wedged in another crack. Slowly but surely, he came closer to the trees. When he tipped his head back, he could see the tops of the pines sticking up above the rim.

Finally, he was below them, and it was only a short climb to the top. Stovepipe pulled himself up and over and sprawled belly-down among fallen pine needles. Shots still boomed, close by now. He came up on hands and knees and drew the Colt, then rose lithely to his feet and pressed himself against one of the tree trunks.

With all the stealth of one of the stalking Apaches who had given the bluff its name, Stovepipe slipped through the growth toward the bushwhackers. He heard a horse whicker and stamp somewhere not far away. A moment later, an empty rifle clicked, and a man cursed.

"We never should have given them a chance to fort up in those rocks," he said in a harsh voice.

"Well, it's not like we were trying to," another man said impatiently. "If we'd been able to kill Hartford and those other two gents, whoever they are, we could wrap up this whole thing."

Stovepipe stayed where he was, barely breathing, as he eavesdropped on the would-be killers. It was possible they would hand him all the information he needed to figure this out, right on a silver platter.

Or maybe not, because just as that thought went through his head, another man yelled, "Hey!" and a gun blasted. Splinters of pine bark stung Stovepipe's cheek as a bullet slammed into the tree trunk only inches from his head.

CHAPTER EIGHTEEN

Stovepipe pivoted and saw a man charging toward him. The gun in the man's fist blasted again. Stovepipe felt the bullet tug at his vest as he dropped to one knee and drew the revolver he had borrowed from Dan Hartford. That gun got around a lot, from Brock Matthews to Dan and now to him, thought Stovepipe as the weapon roared and bucked against his palm when he triggered it.

The slug smashed into the attacker's right shoulder, likely shattering it. The hombre howled in pain as the bullet's impact knocked him halfway around. His gun went flying. He dropped to his knees and then fell the rest of the way to the ground, where he lay writhing.

Underbrush crashed as the other bushwhackers trampled through it. One of them shouted, "Lonnie!" Stovepipe figured that was the man he'd just shot.

He stood up and darted over to another tree just as two men with rifles came in sight. They spotted him at the same time and opened fire. Stovepipe crouched, thrust the gun barrel past the rough-barked trunk, and squeezed off another shot. One of the bushwhackers yelped but didn't seem to be hurt badly, considering how spry he was as he jumped for cover.

Stovepipe caught a glimpse of a trailing foot and risked another shot. The man who belonged to that foot screamed as the bullet tore through his boot and smashed his ankle to bits. He toppled out from behind the pine where he had taken cover. Stovepipe could have killed him easily then, but the lanky cowboy held his fire. The man was in too much agony to be much of a threat.

That appeared to leave just one of the bush-whackers, and the man didn't seem eager to risk exposing himself to Stovepipe's deadly accurate fire. He called, "Lonnie! Pete! Can you get to the horses? Let's get the hell outta here!"

Stovepipe pressed himself to the tree trunk and grinned. He had only three rounds left and didn't hanker to continue this battle, either. On the other hand, if he was able to capture at least one of these varmints, it could bust the whole thing wide open. Cheap gun-wolves tended to spill their guts, especially when they were facing the threat of a hangrope.

That wasn't going to be the case here, however. The unwounded member of the trio opened fire again, and he must have known which tree Stovepipe was hidden behind. He concentrated his fire there, slamming bullet after bullet into the trunk until there was a veritable shower of splinters filling the air. Stovepipe didn't dare budge from his concealment.

When the shooting stopped and he risked a look again, he saw that both of the men he had shot were no longer where they had fallen. They had managed to crawl or hop to where their horses were hidden.

A moment later, a sudden rataplan of hoofbeats confirmed that theory. The bushwhackers were making their escape, and there wasn't a blessed thing Stovepipe could do to stop them.

He was still alive and with a whole skin, though, and he hoped Wilbur and Dan were in the same shape. From the sound of the shots that were still ringing out from the rocks, that was the case.

"Hey, fellas, hold your fire!" shouted Stovepipe. "I think the bushwhackin' polecats are gone!"

"Stovepipe, are you all right?" called Wilbur.

"Yeah. Stay where you are and let me do a little scoutin'."

For the next few minutes he stalked through the trees, the gun in his hand ready for instant use if he needed it.

That wasn't necessary. The would-be killers were gone. And he and his friends needed to rattle their hocks, too, thought Stovepipe, because it was possible there were Box D cowboys within earshot, and they would be coming to see what all the gunfire was about.

Stovepipe trotted out of the trees and headed for the boulders. Wilbur and Dan emerged from the rocks at the same time, and the three of them met in the middle of the open area where Dan had found Abel Dempsey's body a couple of days earlier.

"Let's round up those hosses and get outta here," Stovepipe said as he traded the Colt for the Winchester Dan held.

As he reloaded the revolver, Dan said, "Sorry I shot up all those cartridges you gave me, Stovepipe."

"That's all right. There're more in my saddlebags, and you kept those dry-gulchers busy while I was climbin' along that bluff like a dang monkey."

"Did you get a look at those fellas?" asked Wilbur as they walked toward the horses.

"I caught a glimpse of a couple of 'em, but it didn't do me any good. Never seen either of them before, leastways not that I recall. And I got a good memory for faces. They looked like run-o'-the-mill hard cases to me, though. I heard a couple of names. Lonnie and Pete. Those mean anything to you, Dan?"

The young cowboy shook his head.

"No. I've known a few fellas named Pete, but none around here. And I don't think I've ever met a Lonnie. Why would they want to kill us? You think maybe they were members of a search party from Hat Creek? Some of Sheriff Olsen's temporary deputies?"

"Could be, I suppose," said Stovepipe. "But it's more likely they're tied in with whoever's responsible for Abel Dempsey's murder."

"How do you figure that?"

They had reached the horses, and Stovepipe didn't answer until he and his two companions had caught the animals and swung up into their saddles again.

Then Stovepipe said, "My hunch is that those three varmints were keepin' an eye on the place where Dempsey was killed on the chance that you'd come back here and look for evidence to clear your name . . . which is exactly what happened, of course. That was pretty smart of 'em. If they killed you, after you'd been arrested for Dempsey's murder and then broke jail, that'd tie everything up with a pretty little bow. Everybody around here would just accept that you killed Dempsey, and that'd be that."

"Which means the real killer would get away with it," added Wilbur. "Yeah, that makes sense, Stovepipe. And it means that whoever shot Dempsey wasn't acting by himself. He's tied in with a bigger bunch."

Dan frowned in thought and said, "You're talking about those rustlers."

"Dempsey's the third cattleman in these parts who's died under mysterious circumstances," Stovepipe said. "They're tryin' to throw the basin into enough chaos that when they start their big roundup, there won't be anybody able to stop them."

"That would take a big, well-organized gang."

Stovepipe nodded and said, "I reckon that's what we're dealin' with."

"How in the world can we stop them, just the three of us?"

"Well, it'll be a tall order, all right," drawled Stovepipe. "But we'll start by seein' if we can trail those fellas who just tried to kill us. We got to be quick about it, though. We ain't got much time."

They rode through the trees and searched for the tracks left behind by the fleeing bushwhackers. Stovepipe had heard the hoofbeats and knew where to look, and it didn't take long to locate the trail.

The sign led away from the bluff and then curved back toward it, well away from the spot where Dempsey had been killed and Stovepipe and his companions had traded shots with their mysterious enemies. After a while, Wilbur said, "They're heading for those badlands."

"You said a while ago that they might be holed up

in there," Stovepipe pointed out. "Looks like you were right, Wilbur."

Dan said, "You mean they've been right here on Box D range all along?"

"Did Dempsey run any stock in those badlands?"

Dan shook his head and said, "No, it's not good enough grazing land for that. It's pretty much worthless, in fact."

"Unless you're an outlaw lookin' for a place to hide."

"Yeah," Dan agreed grimly.

The bluff began to shallow out into an easier slope. Dan led the way down an arroyo that cut through it and took them into the region of razorback ridges and dry washes.

"This stretch is a couple of miles wide," Dan told Stovepipe and Wilbur. "Then there's some better range again before you come to those breaks where my camp was."

Wilbur said, "So this ugly bit of country was plopped down in the middle of the Box D for no good reason."

Stovepipe chuckled and said, "I reckon *el Señor Dios* had His reasons, all right, but you'd have to ask Him about that, Wilbur. Some things are beyond our understandin'."

"Yeah . . . like how we've managed to live so long when you're all the time getting us mixed up in one shooting scrape after another."

"Well, you don't have much of a chance to get bored, do you?"

Wilbur laughed and shook his head.

"No, you can say that for it, that's true," he agreed.

They were still following the trail left by the bush-whackers, but in this rugged terrain it was getting more difficult to do so. Finally the ground became so rocky that it wouldn't take any prints at all, and even Stovepipe had to admit defeat, though it galled him.

"Let's see if we can get back to the line shack without runnin' into any more trouble," he said. "Reckon we've done all we can for today. We'll put our heads together and figure out our next move."

"We've got to find that rustlers' hideout," said Dan. "That's the only way we're going to get to the bottom of this."

Stovepipe nodded and said, "I expect you're right."

He was pondering some other things, though, but as usual he kept them to himself. It wasn't his custom to start spouting theories until he had worked out as many of the details as possible.

Their route took them far to the north as they circled toward the high pastures on the other side of the Box D. Dan didn't want to cut across the heart of the spread, and Stovepipe agreed that was a good idea. They wanted to avoid not only any of Abel Dempsey's punchers who might be riding the range, but also posses from Hat Creek who could be out searching for the escaped prisoners.

They were just crossing the shallow stream that flowed on eastward to the settlement named after it when a group of riders followed the bank around a bend to their left. The grass was thick along the bank, so the horses hadn't raised any dust, and the grass had muffled the hoofbeats as well. Stovepipe, Wilbur, and Dan were taken by surprise and couldn't get out of sight in time.

"Uh-oh," muttered Wilbur.

"Uh-oh is right," said Stovepipe, and hard on the heels of his words came the popping of gunshots as the horsemen surged toward them, firing as they charged.

CHAPTER NINETEEN

Instantly, Stovepipe, Wilbur, and Dan jabbed their boot heels in their horses' flanks and sent the animals leaping forward. Water flew high, filling the air with sparkling droplets, as the horses splashed through the creek and lunged up onto the bank.

Stovepipe glanced at the group of riders and recognized the burly figure of Sheriff Frank Olsen in the lead. Wilbur's earlier comment about their luck ending appeared to be coming true. Nothing but pure happenstance had led them to cross this creek just as the sheriff and the posse came along.

"Don't shoot back at 'em!" Stovepipe called to his companions as they raced toward some distant trees. "We'll wind up in even more trouble if we do!"

Wilbur ducked and winced as a slug whined over his head.

"Yeah, we wouldn't want to get in trouble!" he exclaimed.

The horses had done quite a bit of hard traveling during the day, and now the three men were calling on them for a valiant effort. The mounts responded, stretching out and covering the ground swiftly.

The members of the posse were riding hard, too, though. They seemed to have stopped shooting and were concentrating on chasing down their quarry instead. At least, Stovepipe couldn't hear any guns going off over the rolling thunder of the horses' hooves.

They had to slow down as they reached the trees. Wilbur glanced back and yelped, "They're gaining on us!"

"Hang on!" Dan called. "I've got an idea!"

"Lead the way, son!" urged Stovepipe.

They pounded through the pines, then Dan angled sharply to the right. The trail he followed led across a broad, open area.

"Oh hell!" Wilbur moaned. "We might as well be targets in a shooting gallery!"

The ground suddenly dipped down in a grassy trough that wasn't visible more than a few yards away. That dropped them below the level of the surrounding landscape. The three men leaned far forward in their saddles to make themselves even less visible.

Stovepipe let out a laugh.

"When Sheriff Olsen and those old boys come outta those trees, it'll look like we dropped off the face of the earth!" he said. "You musta known about this little gully, Dan."

"I remembered it from chasing cows through here when I worked for Dempsey," Dan replied. "And I've used it since he kicked me off the place, too."

"You reckon Olsen knows about it?" asked Wilbur.

"No telling. He might."

"We better hustle along as much as we can, then," said Stovepipe.

The trough ran straight for about a quarter of a mile before rising and coming to an end in some thick brush. The three riders forced their way into the growth and then dismounted. Stovepipe parted some branches a little and peered back toward the creek.

"I don't see 'em," he said quietly, "but I hear some horses . . . Hold on. There they are. They're clean on the other side of this pasture, looking around. Appears they've lost the trail."

"They'll probably work their way in this direction eventually, though," Dan said. "We can't just wait here."

"Naw, that'd be too risky. This chaparral's mighty thick, but I reckon we can lead the hosses through it. We just need to be careful not to make too much racket while we're doin' it."

Once again, stealth had become more important than speed as the three men worked their way through the brush, leading the horses. Dan went first to break a trail of sorts, which made it a little easier on Stovepipe and Wilbur, but all three men wound up with skin scratched and clothes snagged. The horses' hides took a beating from thorns and branches, too, but they didn't balk at going through.

At last they came to the end of the growth and emerged into some rolling hills dotted with rocks. The green heights where the upper pastures were located were visible now. Stovepipe and the others mounted up and rode in that direction, still alert for any sign of the men searching for them.

They didn't relax until they came in sight of the

line shack, and even then Stovepipe was still cautious and said, "Hold on, fellas. Let's take a look before we go ridin' up there."

He reached into his saddlebags and brought out a pair of field glasses. It was late afternoon, and the westering sun splashed golden light all over the cabin and the pine-covered slopes behind it. Stovepipe studied the line shack and the surrounding area through the lenses and didn't see anyone or anything moving except birds flitting around in the nearby trees. The presence of those birds told him there hadn't been any recent disturbances around here.

"All right, let's go," he said as he lowered the glasses.

Despite the apparent peacefulness of the scene, Stovepipe and Wilbur both pulled their rifles from the saddle sheaths and rode with the Winchesters held in front of them. As they approached the cabin, Dan said, "I sort of thought Laura might come out to wave at us."

"Thought we might see Hamp, too," mused Stovepipe. "Charley could be out on the range again, but Hamp wasn't in any shape to ride with that swole-up foot."

Dan glanced over at the lanky cowboy and asked, "Do you think something's wrong?"

"Don't know. But I don't know of any way but one to find out, either. Just in case, though . . . Wilbur, why don't you swing out and come in from the side while Dan and me ride straight on?"

"You'll be sitting ducks if you do that," Wilbur protested.

"Yeah, but that's why we'll be countin' on you to pull our fat outta the fire if there's a ruckus."

"All right," Wilbur said with obvious reluctance. He turned his horse and trotted off to the right.

Dan said, "If somebody's watching from in there and saw Wilbur do that, he'll know that we're suspicious."

"Reckon he probably figured that anyway from the fact that we're holdin' guns," Stovepipe pointed out. "Can't do nothin' now except play out the hand."

"I'll bet you like to bluff when you play cards, don't you?"

Stovepipe chuckled and said, "I've been known to."

They were close enough now to see that the door of the line shack was standing part of the way open. Dan frowned and said, "I don't like the looks of that. It almost seems like nobody's here."

"It's startin' to appear you're right, amigo." Stovepipe lifted his voice and called, "Hamp! Charley! You boys in there?"

No response came from inside the cabin. Dan leaned forward anxiously in his saddle.

"Laura!" he said. "Laura, are you all right?"

Once again, silence was the only answer.

"Something's happened, damn it!" Dan exclaimed. Without waiting to see what Stovepipe thought of the idea, he kicked his horse into a gallop.

Stovepipe hurried along behind him, holding the Winchester ready. He glanced to the right and saw that Wilbur was about fifty yards away, closing in on the line shack from that direction.

Dan reached the area of hard-packed dirt in front of the cabin and swung down from his saddle almost before his horse had stopped moving. He called Laura's name again as he charged into the squatty log building with his gun up and ready.

By the time Stovepipe dismounted, Dan appeared in the open doorway with a distraught look on his face.

"They're gone!" said the young cowboy. "The chairs are turned over, and the pot Hamp cooked the beans in is lying on the floor. It looks like there was a fight in there!"

"Take it easy," Stovepipe advised. "Let me take a look."

He moved past Dan and cast his eyes around the shack's interior. The signs of a disturbance were there, just as Dan had said.

Stovepipe spotted something Dan obviously hadn't, or else the young man would have been even more upset. There were several dark spots on the puncheon floor near the table, and when Stovepipe dropped to one knee and touched a spot with a fingertip, he found it to be sticky. Some of the substance clung to his skin, and when he rubbed it with his thumb, he was sure of what he had found.

Somebody had lost some blood here. Not a lot, but enough to confirm that things had gone wrong.

Of course, there was no way of telling who that blood belonged to . . .

Stovepipe came to his feet and found Dan staring at him from the doorway. He pointed and said in a voice that shook a little with emotion, "What is that, Stovepipe? What did you find?"

Stovepipe didn't figure there was any point in lying. He said, "There are a few drops of blood over here, Dan."

"Blood!"

"Hold on. It don't look like anybody was hurt bad."

Dan came over and stared down at the dark spots

on the floor. He said, "Somebody was wounded, though. There's no doubt about that."

"No, I reckon not," Stovepipe agreed.

Dan looked up at him.

"We've got to find Laura. She could be hurt. And I know good and well she didn't leave here of her own free will!"

From the doorway, Wilbur said, "I'll go along with that, Stovepipe. I had a look around back in the shed. Three horses are gone, and it looks like more than that were milling around here for a while."

"How many more?" asked Stovepipe.

"I'd say three, but that's just a guess. I'm pretty sure six rode out, though."

"Can you tell which way they were goin'?"

Wilbur leaned his head toward the north.

"Headed higher on the slopes, I'd say."

"Then that's where we're going, too," Dan snapped. He stalked out of the line shack, still tightly clutching the Colt in his hand.

Stovepipe and Wilbur followed him outside, where Stovepipe said, "Wait just a minute, Dan. We need to think about this."

"You think about it. I'm going after Laura. You know good and well somebody *took* her from here, Stovepipe, and it wasn't anybody who has her best interests at heart."

"You don't know that—" began Wilbur.

"Actually, I reckon Dan's right," said Stovepipe. "There's really only two possibilities: some of the sheriff's men came along and found Miss Laura here, in which case they would have hung around, figurin' that we'd show up sooner or later so they could arrest us."

"And what's the other possibility?" Dan asked tensely.

"That bunch who wants us dead grabbed her and those two old-timers," said Stovepipe, "and now they'll use 'em as bait to lure us into a trap."

CHAPTER TWENTY

Dan was almost beside himself with worry, but Stovepipe calmed him down.

"They want us to follow them," he assured the young man. "They won't be goin' to any trouble to hide their trail."

"Then let's get started," Dan said. "I don't want Laura to be in the hands of those killers one minute longer than she has to be."

"Hold on," said Wilbur. "We can't just waltz right into whatever trap they've got set for us. We'll just wind up dead, and that won't do Mrs. Dempsey a bit of good."

Stovepipe nodded and said, "Wilbur's right. You and I will follow that trail, Dan, while he shadows us."

"We're gonna split up?" asked Wilbur with a frown. "I'm not sure I like that idea. Anyway, won't they be suspicious when they see there's just two of you?"

"Maybe a little, but you got to remember, they don't know what happened while we were out roamin' around today. For all they'll know, you might've got shot or nabbed by a posse, Wilbur. They'll have to go ahead and spring the trap on Dan and me—and then you'll spring our trap on them, once they've given themselves away."

Wilbur rubbed his chin as his frown deepened, but after a moment he nodded.

"Reckon it might work," he said. "And I've got to admit, I don't have a better idea."

"We'd better get movin'," said Stovepipe. "The sun'll be down in a while, and we don't want to run out of light."

They had found some biscuits wrapped up in a cloth inside the line shack. Each man took one of the biscuits to nibble on as they set out. Stovepipe and Dan left first. Wilbur would wait a few minutes and then follow them, staying far enough behind that he wouldn't be noticed but close enough that he could pitch in and take the enemy by surprise when trouble erupted.

And it really was a matter of *when*, not *if*, thought Stovepipe as he and Dan headed higher in the hills. Logically, he knew an ambush would be waiting for them, and what he felt in his gut confirmed that.

The dark, brooding brow of the Mogollon Rim hung over them as they climbed. Stovepipe had no idea how far they would have to go before they sprung the trap. All they could do was keep their eyes open.

"If they've hurt Laura, I'll kill every one of them," vowed Dan as they rode.

"They won't do anything to her," Stovepipe assured him. "You know even rustlers and killers won't mistreat a decent woman."

"But she's seen their faces now. They can't afford

to leave her alive. The same goes for Hamp and Charley."

Stovepipe knew he was right. Whoever had carried off Laura and the two old punchers, in the end they wouldn't want to leave anybody alive to tell what had really happened. More than likely, they wanted to kill everybody and make it look like Dan was responsible for the murders, losing his own life in the process. That would write a bloody finish to the whole affair and leave the impression the killers wanted to leave, that Dan Hartford was a mad dog and a murderer.

That would leave them a free hand to carry on with their long-term plan of looting the Tonto Basin.

"Are there any more line shacks up here?" Stovepipe asked. "Any good places they can hide out?"

"No line shacks that I know of," Dan replied. He thought for a moment. "But there's a box canyon where some of the Box D crew have camped before. Sometimes they hold cattle there when they're combing these hills for stock to drive back down to the lower range in the fall. I haven't been there myself, but I remember hearing the place mentioned in the bunkhouse."

"Could be that's where they've holed up, then," mused Stovepipe. "Reckon you could find it?"

Dan shook his head and said, "I never heard it described in anything but the most general terms. If we keep going in this direction, though, we ought to come across it."

Stovepipe nodded to the tracks they were following.

"That seems to be what those fellas have in mind."

Dan frowned and said, "These trees are thick enough that they shouldn't be able to see us. Why don't you drop back, Stovepipe, and join up with

Wilbur? I'll go on alone while the two of you circle around a little. Maybe you can find the canyon, and if the bunch we're after is there, you could get behind them and take them by surprise while they're concentrating on me."

Stovepipe's forehead creased in thought as he scraped a thumbnail along his lean, beard-stubbled jaw.

"You really would be paintin' a target on yourself if you did that," he said.

"I don't mind the risk if it means we're able to rescue Laura." Dan's voice caught a little. "I don't even mind that much if they kill me, as long as she's safe. I reckon I can count on you and Wilbur to keep poking around until you find out who really killed Dempsey."

"Yeah, that's the truth," said Stovepipe. "Once I've got my teeth set in somethin', I don't like to let go, as Wilbur'd be only too glad to tell you if he was here." He came to a decision and nodded. "All right, we'll give it a try like you said. Keep your eyes open, though. There's still no tellin' what we might run into up here."

Dan returned the nod and kept riding as Stovepipe reined in. After a moment the young cowboy disappeared in the thick growth of pines that covered these slopes. Stovepipe turned the Appaloosa and rode slowly downhill.

A few minutes later he came in sight of Wilbur, who looked surprised to see him. The redheaded cowboy reined in and asked, "What in blazes, Stovepipe? I thought you were going with Dan."

"He had another idea, and I think it's a pretty good one," Stovepipe explained. "He remembered there's a box canyon up here that'd be a good place for that bunch to set their trap for us, so you and me are gonna swing around and try to find it first while he keeps goin' the way he was. The hope is that while those varmints are watchin' him and waitin' for him to ride into their trap, we can spring one on them."

Wilbur considered the idea and shrugged.

"Might work," he said. "Sounds like it's worth a try, anyway."

"That's what I thought. Come on."

Since they didn't know exactly where they were going, they turned and rode west for a short distance before turning northeast again. That put them on a parallel course to the one Dan was following.

The sun, as it always did, continued to drop toward the western horizon. That was worrisome, thought Stovepipe. If night fell before they located the men who had captured Laura, Hamp, and Charley, finding them was going to be that much harder.

Then Stovepipe sat up straighter in his saddle and lifted an arm to point at a long ridge above them.

"See that openin'?" he said to Wilbur. "I've got a hunch that's the box canyon Dan was talkin' about. I don't see anything else up here that looks like it could be the place."

"Can we get there from here? In time?"

"We got to," Stovepipe said solemnly. He heeled the Palouse into a faster pace. The horse was worn out, and Stovepipe was getting that way himself, but they had to keep going for a while longer, anyway.

Instead of heading straight for the canyon Stovepipe had spotted, they approached it at an angle so they'd be less likely to be seen. As they came closer, he was more sure than ever that it was the right place. Of course, there was no guarantee that was where the kidnappers had stashed their captives, but the search had to start somewhere and that seemed like as good a place as any.

"We'll have to leave our horses and climb that ridge on foot," Stovepipe said. "That way we can get above the canyon and look down into it."

"Then what?" asked Wilbur.

"If they're there, you can stay up above on the high ground while I try to climb down and get the drop on the varmints. We'll have 'em whipsawed, especially if Dan shows up in time to give us a hand."

They reined in at the foot of a rugged slope about eighty feet high. Stovepipe eyed it in the reddish light from the sun that was now hanging just above the horizon. The slope was too steep for the horses, but he and Wilbur wouldn't have any trouble climbing it. The mouth of the canyon was about half a mile to their right.

They dismounted and ground-hitched the horses. The Appaloosa and the dun wouldn't wander off. For one thing, the animals were too tired to do anything other than crop at the sparse grass. The two drifters pulled their Winchesters from the saddle boots, filled their pockets with spare cartridges, and started up the ridge.

The climb had both men a little breathless by the time they reached the top. By then the sun had started to slide behind the horizon. Stovepipe paused to catch his breath and then pointed again.

"Down there," he said to Wilbur. "It's Dan."

A rider had come into sight and was proceeding slowly toward the canyon. Stovepipe and Wilbur had no trouble recognizing Dan, since the young cowboy wasn't wearing a hat. As Dan continued toward the canyon, Stovepipe and Wilbur trotted in that direction, too. Stovepipe's nerves were taut as he listened for gunshots. It was possible the men they were after might ambush Dan before he and Wilbur could get in position.

As they approached the notch in the ridge that the canyon formed, Stovepipe saw that it was only a couple of hundred yards deep. That was plenty big enough for a range camp or a temporary holding pen for stock, though.

Or for killers to hole up in.

"What if they're not there?" Wilbur asked quietly.

"Then we'll look somewhere else," answered Stovepipe. "I reckon there's a good chance they are, though. Dan's still followin' those tracks they left, and he's headed straight for the place, looks like."

They slowed as they neared the rimrock above the canyon, then eased forward until they could peer down into it. Several big slabs of rock stood at the entrance, where they had fallen from the canyon walls in ages past, and almost immediately, Stovepipe spotted the men kneeling behind those rocks and holding rifles.

"Dan's hunch was right," he whispered to Wilbur. "There they are."

"And there's Mrs. Dempsey and those two old pelicans," Wilbur whispered in return as he pointed to several figures sitting on a log about fifty yards inside the canyon. Stovepipe recognized Laura, Hamp, and Charley, and a man stood near them, pointing a gun at them. The six horses that had brought the group here were tied to small trees deeper in the canyon.

The guard held the revolver in his left hand. Bloody rags tied into a makeshift bandage swathed his right shoulder. Stovepipe frowned and said, "I think that's one of the fellas I shot when they jumped us back over yonder at Apache Bluff. Reckon the others must be the two who were with him."

"I'll bet we can drop all of them from up here, Stovepipe."

"I expect we could, too, but we ain't gonna. For one thing, that'd be cold-blooded murder."

"No, it wouldn't," protested Wilbur. "They already tried to kill us once today, which makes it self-defense, and they're about to bushwhack Dan, to boot."

"For another," Stovepipe went on, "I want to grab at least one of 'em so I can ask him a few questions. I got some ideas, Wilbur, but I need more answers."

"You've always got ideas . . . but I reckon I see your point. You still plan to climb down there?"

"Yep."

"Better get at it, then. The light's going, and they're liable to open fire on Dan as soon as he gets close enough."

Stovepipe knew his old friend was right. The canyon walls were steep, and he couldn't hurry too much in his descent or he risked slipping. A fall from up here would be disastrous.

So there was no time to waste, thought Stovepipe as he swung over the edge, found some footholds, and started lowering himself into the box canyon where death waited.

CHAPTER TWENTY-ONE

Dan was as tightly wound inside as a spring, and he felt like he might explode at any second as he approached the canyon. The thought that Laura might be in there, the helpless captive of men who wanted to kill her, gnawed at his mind like a hungry rat. He had to fight down the impulse to kick his mount into a run and gallop toward the canyon as fast as he could.

He had no way of knowing if Stovepipe and Wilbur were in position yet, though, so he had to drag out his approach as long as possible and give them plenty of time. He studied the ground as he rode, as if he were having trouble following the trail.

Stovepipe and Wilbur were strange birds, he mused. He had known them for only a day and a half, and yet for some reason he trusted them completely. Dan hoped that faith wasn't misplaced.

At the same time, he couldn't help but wonder about them. As far as he could see, they had no real stake in his problems. It was like they had befriended him on impulse when they'd seen him being pursued by Sheriff Olsen and that posse, and once they had thrown in with him they were willing to do anything, even risk their lives, to help him.

Puzzling though it might be, he sure couldn't complain about that. Without Stovepipe and Wilbur, by now he would either be in jail, awaiting trial and an all-but-certain date with the hangman—or else already dead, leaving Laura defenseless against whatever came next.

And there would be another move, he was sure of that. The men behind this trouble wouldn't be satisfied until they had everything they had set their greedy sights on.

The mouth of the canyon was only about a hundred yards away now. Without being too obvious about it, Dan's eyes searched for any sign of an ambush. The light of the setting sun might reflect off a gun barrel or a belt buckle. He might spot a hat rising above a rock as a hidden bushwhacker drew a bead on him. Anything that would tell him what he was facing . . .

The sudden roar of a gunshot made him jump. He braced himself for the shock of a bullet striking him.

But none came, nor did he hear a slug come anywhere near him. Rifles began to crack, but the reports came from inside the canyon.

Hell had broken loose in there, and Dan jabbed his boot heels into his horse's flanks to send the animal lunging forward in a gallop. Desperate worry flooded through him.

Laura might be in the middle of all that furious gunplay!

Laura Dempsey had been trying not to be frightened, but it wasn't easy. Ever since the three men had shown up at the line shack, she had felt like she was only a hair away from dying.

They were keeping her alive only to use her as bait to lure Dan into their trap, and she knew that. She could only pray for Dan's sake that he wouldn't allow himself to fall into it . . . but she knew with despairing certainty that he would.

The three men were named Lonnie, Pete, and Carver. She had picked that up from listening to them talking to one another. The fact that they showed their faces and used their names so freely could only mean that they didn't intend to leave anyone alive when they were finished here. Laura was smart enough to know that.

Hamp must have seen the fear and worry on her face as she sat on a log next to him. He leaned toward her and said quietly, "Don't worry, Miss Laura. It's gonna be all right."

"I don't see how you can say that," she told him.

"Because I trust Dan, and those two fellas he had with him struck me as bein' pretty resourceful hombres, too. They'll figure out some way to get us outta this mess, and then those three varmints will wish they'd just lit a shuck outta these parts."

Charley sat on the other side of Hamp. The burly puncher leaned forward and nodded to Laura.

"Listen to this old codger, ma'am. He may not look

like it, but he's pretty smart . . . a heap smarter 'n me, anyway. He ain't the one who let those polecats get the drop on him."

The three gunmen had ridden up to the line shack with Charley as their prisoner. They had jumped him while he was out checking on the stock in the high meadows. With Charley's life at stake, Laura and Hamp had had to cooperate with the men, although Charley had urged them to hole up in the shack and blast away at the would-be kidnappers.

Things hadn't played out that way, and the three of them had been captives ever since. Now the day was waning, and Laura knew this couldn't go on much longer.

She wasn't sure what it was that made her glance toward the back of the canyon, but when she did, her breath hissed between her teeth and she looked again to make sure her eyes weren't playing tricks on her.

They weren't. A man was climbing down the canyon wall. Laura wasn't sure, but she thought he was the lanky cowboy who called himself Stovepipe.

Lonnie stood near the three captives, gun in hand. He was turned so that his left side was toward Stovepipe, but if he happened to glance in that direction, as Laura had, he might spot the man. Laura knew she couldn't let that happen.

She stood up.

"Hey," snapped Lonnie. "I told you to stay on that log."

"It's not comfortable," Laura said as she took a couple of steps toward the canyon mouth. Lonnie's eyes followed her as he half turned away from Stovepipe.

"I don't care if you're comfortable or not, lady. Sit down."

"I'm just trying to ease my muscles. They're getting stiff. I'll sit down in a minute."

"Damn it, you ain't in charge here. You do what I tell you—"

A whistle from one of the men behind the boulders at the canyon's entrance made Lonnie look in that direction. A grin creased his rugged face.

"Your beau's on his way, just like we figured he would be. He'll be in easy range in a minute, I'll bet, and then this'll all be over. I just hope those two waddies who've caused us so much trouble are with him, so we can kill them, too. Do you know who they are?"

"They're strangers," said Laura, which was true as far as it went. She knew their names, but not why they had thrown in their lot with her and Dan.

She was just grateful they had.

"My shoulder's never gonna be the same," Lonnie groused. "I hope they gut-shoot that tall drink of water and he takes a long time dyin'. He's got it comin' to him."

The men weren't going to shoot Stovepipe unless they turned around, thought Laura, because he was behind them now. She stole a glance in that direction and saw that Stovepipe wasn't climbing down the canyon wall anymore.

She hoped that meant he had reached the ground safely.

Lonnie started to turn that way again. Laura moved

to place herself between him and the back of the canyon, blocking his view.

"Listen, whatever you're planning, you don't have to go through with it," she said, stalling for time the only way she knew how. "I'll gladly cooperate with you. I'll help you." She forced a smile onto her face. "I'll do anything you want."

"Lady," Lonnie said with a leer, "you're gonna do that anyway, just as soon as we've finished killing everybody that needs it."

That threat was more than Laura could stand. The combination of terror and anger that welled up inside her made her snap. She lunged at Lonnie, grabbing for the gun he held. She knew he was right-handed and was using his left only because he was wounded in the right shoulder. She was counting on that awkwardness to slow down his reactions . . .

The gun exploded, and the blinding flash from its muzzle filled her face.

Stovepipe dropped the last couple of feet, landed with agile grace, and cat-footed toward the spot where Laura, Hamp, and Charley were being held prisoner. He hugged the canyon wall as he did so, hoping that would make him harder to spot if their guard happened to look toward him.

Laura was on her feet, though, keeping the hombre occupied. Stovepipe wondered if she had spotted him and was distracting the guard deliberately. She seemed like a pretty smart gal, so he wouldn't put that past her.

Suddenly, however, something went wrong. Laura lunged toward the man. The flame that spouted from his gun was bright in the gathering shadows inside the canyon. Stovepipe bit back a curse as Laura flew backward, evidently hit by the shot. Yelling, the two old punchers bolted up from the log where they'd been sitting. The gunman swung his revolver toward them.

Stovepipe didn't have any choice. He snapped the Winchester to his shoulder and fired.

The bullet punched into the guard's body before he could pull the trigger again. As he fell, the two men who'd been lurking at the canyon mouth waiting to dry-gulch Dan Hartford swung around and opened fire. Hamp and Charley hit the dirt as slugs sizzled past them.

Stovepipe hoped they would have the good sense to stay down and would keep Laura down, too, assuming she was still alive. The possibility that she wasn't was like a bad taste in the back of Stovepipe's throat. He worked the rifle's lever rapidly and sprayed several shots toward the other two kidnappers. Their bullets kicked up dirt and rocks around him, and one of the slugs seemed to whisper in his ear as it went past.

Wilbur opened fire from the rimrock. From that vantage point, he was able to rain down bullets on the men at the canyon mouth. Stovepipe wanted to take one of them prisoner, but in a desperate fight like this, there was no time for anything fancy. It was a battle for survival now, and one of the men was flung back off his feet as slugs from both Stovepipe and Wilbur smashed into him.

That still left one man, though, so Stovepipe hadn't given up all hope of taking him alive. But at that instant, Dan came boiling into the canyon on horseback, and as the kidnapper instinctively jerked his rifle toward the newest arrival, Dan's pistol boomed. The third gunman spun off his feet and collapsed, facedown.

As the echoes of the shots bounced back and forth from the canyon walls, Stovepipe lowered his Winchester and ran toward Laura, Hamp, and Charley. Dan galloped in from the other direction. The two old-timers were sitting up now, but Laura was still down.

Dan reached her first, leaping from the saddle while the horse was still moving. He landed running and cried, "Laura!" He reached down, caught hold of her, pulled her upright, and hugged her to him.

Stovepipe felt sick when he saw the way her head lolled loosely on her neck as Dan continued calling her name and she didn't respond.

CHAPTER TWENTY-TWO

Then, abruptly, Laura moaned. She lifted one hand shakily and clutched at the front of Dan's shirt. He exclaimed, "Laura! Thank God!" and held her even tighter to him.

She was alive, but Stovepipe couldn't tell if she was hurt or how badly. He said, "Dan, help her sit down on that log there while I go check on those varmints."

Charley Bartlett bent over and picked up the revolver the man with the busted shoulder had dropped when Stovepipe shot him. The old cowboy said, "Let Hamp and me do that, mister, while you help Dan tend to Miz Dempsey."

"All right," Stovepipe said with a nod. He handed his Winchester to Hamp. "Better take this, just in case any of the varmints still have any fight left in 'em."

The two old-timers set off on the grim errand, first making sure that the man who had been guarding them was dead. Satisfied that he was, they started toward the mouth of the canyon.

Stovepipe took Laura's left arm while Dan supported her on the other side. Carefully, they lowered her onto the log. She shook her head groggily and asked, "Wha . . . what happened? Am I shot?"

"I don't think so," Dan told her. He brushed her hair back from her face. "I don't see any blood."

"What?" She started to look alarmed. "I . . . I can't hear you, Dan! What's happened to me?"

Stovepipe looked over her clothes and didn't see any bloodstains. He said, "That gun went off practically right in her face, Dan. Bullet probably didn't miss her by more 'n an inch or two. The shock of it stunned her, and she's deaf from the sound of the shot right now, that's all."

Dan knelt in front of her, put his hands on her shoulders, and said loudly and distinctly, "You're all right, Laura. You're just having trouble hearing right now. It'll get better."

She frowned, shook her head, and said, "I can't understand you." She looked alarmed. "I . . . I can't even hear myself."

Dan pointed at his ear, then at hers. Understanding dawned on her face, and then her eyes widened with fear.

"I'm deaf?" she said.

"It'll go away," Dan told her. Whether she was able to read his lips or her hearing was already starting to come back, Stovepipe didn't know, but she nodded as if she had heard at least a little of what he said.

Hamp and Charley came back and reported that the other two kidnappers were dead as well. So much for questioning them, thought Stovepipe. But he would trade that opportunity for saving the lives of Laura, Hamp, and Charley any day.

Stovepipe looked up on the rim and didn't see Wilbur. He figured his old friend had climbed down to fetch their mounts. Sure enough, Wilbur appeared in the canyon mouth a few minutes later, riding the dun and leading Stovepipe's Appaloosa.

"Everybody all right?" asked the redheaded cowboy as he trotted up.

"Reckon they will be," Stovepipe told him. "Miss Laura's havin' a mite of trouble hearin' just now because a gun went off right beside her head."

"We've all had that problem at one time or another, I suppose," said Wilbur. He asked Hamp and Charley, "You boys aren't hurt?"

"No, just mad as can be," Charley replied. "Who in blazes were those fellas?"

Hamp added, "I know they wanted to ambush the three of you and were just usin' us as bait, but how come they hankered to see you all dead?"

Stovepipe exchanged a glance with Dan and Wilbur. Maybe the time had come to tell the truth to the old punchers after all, instead of keeping them in the dark. After a moment's thought and a nod from Wilbur, Stovepipe said, "You tell 'em about it, Dan. I reckon you know more of the story than anybody else."

"Story?" repeated Charley. "What story?"

"You boys may find this hard to believe, but I swear it's the truth," Dan said. "Here's what's been happening for the past few days."

He spent the next ten minutes explaining everything to Hamp and Charley, including his history with Laura. At first the two old-timers looked angry, which was understandable enough because of the natural loyalty they felt toward Abel Dempsey. But they were very fond of Laura, too, Stovepipe sensed, which tempered their reaction.

They were angry again when they heard about Dempsey's murder. Hamp said, "We're supposed to believe that you didn't have nothin' to do with that, Dan?"

"He didn't," said Laura, taking them all by surprise because they hadn't realized she was able to hear that well yet. She went on, "Dan was with me when Abel was shot. I swear he was. We were sitting on our horses on Apache Bluff, talking. He couldn't have had anything to do with Abel's murder, no matter what everyone else thinks."

"Sheriff Olsen and a posse caught me and threw me in jail," said Dan, "along with Stovepipe and Wilbur because they tried to help me get away."

Charley frowned at the two drifters and asked, "How do you boys figure in this?"

"We're just natural-born hoodoos, I suppose," said Wilbur. "Always stumbling into one mess of trouble after another."

"Yeah," agreed Stovepipe. "That seems to be our lot in life. And once we're up to our necks in it, we don't have no choice but to try to straighten ever'thing out. Otherwise we'd've been strung up or shot a long time ago. Ain't that right, Wilbur?"

"Unfortunately, it is."

Dan told Hamp and Charley how they had gone to the site of Abel Dempsey's murder to investigate, and run into the three gunmen who later had kidnapped Laura and the two of them.

"I don't suppose you recognized any of them," he said.

"Never laid eyes on any of the varmints before," said Charley as Hamp shook his head, "but you could tell by lookin' at 'em that they were the scum o' the earth."

"Owlhoots, pure and simple," added Hamp.

"That's what we figure," said Stovepipe. "My thinkin' is that there's a gang of rustlers behind all the devilment in these parts, includin' Abel Dempsey's murder. They've laid the blame for that at Dan's feet and got away with it, as far as everybody in the basin is concerned except for the six of us here."

"You're assumin' we believe you," Charley pointed out.

Laura stood up from the log. She was still a little shaky on her feet as she faced the two old-timers, but her back stiffened and she said, "I'm asking you to believe us. We needed your help before, and we still do."

"You want to go back to the line shack and keep hidin' out there?" asked Hamp.

"No," Laura replied as she shook her head. "I've been thinking about that, and I believe it would be best if we got off the Box D entirely."

Stovepipe had considered that himself and decided it might not be a bad idea. Sheriff Olsen wasn't likely to give up searching the spread, and clearly the rustlers knew they were here, too.

He wasn't sure where it would be safe for them to go, however. It sounded like Laura had some thoughts on the matter, so he said, "What do you mean, ma'am?"

"My friend Jessica Stafford will help us. I'm sure she will."

A dubious frown creased Dan's forehead. He said, "I don't know about that. Henry Stafford and Abel

Dempsey were old friends. I'm sure he thinks I'm guilty, just like everybody else in the Tonto Basin."

"If Jessica asks him to let us stay with them, he'll go along with it," Laura insisted. "If we sit down with him and tell him the truth, he'll believe us."

Stovepipe wasn't so sure of that, but he didn't know Henry and Jessica Stafford, had not even heard of them until this moment, in fact. Clearly Laura considered Jessica a good friend, though, and if she was right, it was unlikely anyone would suspect that they were hiding on the Stafford ranch.

If Stafford was like everybody else in the basin, his herd had been hit by rustlers, too, so that would give him another reason to help Stovepipe and Wilbur get to the bottom of this. Stovepipe was convinced that when they uncovered the truth about the gang, they would also find proof of who was behind Dempsey's murder.

As usual, those thoughts flashed through his brain, leading him to make up his mind swiftly. He said, "Sounds to me like an idea worth tryin', Dan. Where is this Stafford spread?"

"The HS Bar is up at the northern end of the basin," Dan replied. "Stafford's range partially borders the Box D."

"So we can get there without havin' to ride back toward Hat Creek."

"Yeah, we can." Dan looked up at the sky, which had turned a deep, deep blue now that the sun was gone. The stars would be popping out within minutes. "Night's falling. We can get to Stafford's place by midnight, I'd say. Before morning, for sure."

Laura laid a hand on his forearm and said, "I'd like

that, Dan. To soak in a hot bath and be able to sleep for a while in a real bed . . ."

"All right," Dan said with a nod. "We'll go. And if Stafford refuses to believe the truth, we won't be in much worse shape than we already are. We know the Box D isn't safe for any of us."

"What about Charley and me?" asked Hamp. "I don't know if I'd feel right about leavin' them cows we was told to look after."

"You don't have to leave them," said Stovepipe. "You two fellas can stay here and go on about your regular business—just keep your eyes open. Since the three varmints we just tangled with are all dead, the bunch we're after don't know that you've thrown in with us. If you come across anything you think we ought to know, you can send word to Miz Dempsey at the Stafford ranch. Just be careful about it."

"I don't recall sayin' we were gonna throw in with you," said Hamp. "What do you think, Charley?"

"Well . . ." Charley rubbed his chin as he frowned in thought. "Ever'thing Dan and these other fellas told us sort of had the ring of truth about it, don't you think?"

Hamp shrugged his scrawny shoulders and said, "Yeah, I reckon so."

"And with the boss dead, Miz Dempsey's callin' the shots now. That's just plumb simple." Charley nodded. "I say we help as much as we can, Hamp."

"Good enough for me," Hamp agreed. He stuck out a hand to Dan and added, "Shake on it, boy, and if you're lyin' about any of this, heaven help you."

"I'm not lying," Dan said as he clasped Hamp's hand and then shook with Charley as well. "And I'm mighty glad you're going to give me a chance to prove I'm innocent."

"If you ain't, I figure it'll catch up to you sooner or later."

Wilbur waved a hand at the horses tied nearby and asked, "What about the horses those three varmints were riding? If Hamp and Charley take them back to the line shack, some of the gang might come around, see them, and recognize them."

"We'll take off their saddles and throw 'em in the back of the canyon here," Stovepipe decided. "Then we can turn the horses loose and let 'em wander. There's plenty of graze for 'em." He frowned. "Or maybe we ought to just turn 'em loose and then follow 'em. Could be they'd lead us right back to the hideout."

"That's a good idea," said Dan with some excitement in his voice.

"Not you," Stovepipe said. "You need to make sure Miss Laura gets safely to where she's goin', and then both of you lie low there while Wilbur and me see if we can round up that bunch of no-good cattle thieves."

Dan frowned, clearly torn between wanting to make sure Laura was safe and feeling an obligation to help Stovepipe and Wilbur backtrack the rustlers.

"Why should the two of you have to risk your lives like that, just to help us?" he asked.

"Just consider it sort of our job," Stovepipe told him.

CHAPTER TWENTY-THREE

Laura said that her hearing was back to normal, except for a slight ringing in her ears, by the time she and Dan rode out of the canyon a short while later. Dan was glad to hear that, although of course he would have still loved her if her ears had been affected permanently. It was good that she would be able to hear him when he told her how he felt about her—if they ever got a chance to talk about such things again, instead of rustlers and murder and the desperate situation in which they found themselves.

Dan wasn't familiar with the Stafford ranch, since he had only set foot on HS Bar range one time, to retrieve some cattle that had strayed over the border between the two spreads. Because of Laura's friendship with Jessica Stafford, though, the two women had been back and forth between each other's homes many times, and even in the dark Laura was able to find the trail that ran between the two ranch headquarters.

"We'd better keep our eyes open," Dan said as they rode along at an easy pace. "I don't expect to run into anybody after dark like this, but you never know. If we hear anybody coming we'll need to get off the trail and lie low until they've gone past."

"I understand," said Laura. "Who would be out in the middle of the night like this, though?"

"*We* are," Dan pointed out with a smile.

Laura laughed and said, "Yes, that's true."

It was good to hear her laugh, he thought. After everything she had been through in the past few days, no one could blame her if she never laughed again. She had the sort of resilient streak, though, that people needed to live on the frontier. The two of them could make a fine life together, he knew, if they ever got the chance.

He was still musing on that a few minutes later, when his senses and instincts alerted him and he hauled back on his reins. Laura came to a stop beside him and asked tautly, "What is it?"

"I thought I heard hoofbeats up ahead somewhere," said Dan. "Wait . . . There they are again!"

There were horses coming toward them, all right. A good number of them, from the sound of it. Dan looked around in the starlight, spotted a clump of brush about twenty yards off the trail, and turned toward it.

"Come on," he told Laura. He wasn't sure if the brush was thick enough and tall enough to conceal them, but it was the only cover nearby.

The horses pushed through the branches, then Dan and Laura dismounted and stood holding the reins. Dan put a hand over his horse's nose to keep the animal quiet and whispered to Laura that she should do the same. Then they waited tensely.

A large group of riders, at least a dozen in all, came

in sight, trotting along the trail between the Box D and the HS Bar. Dan wondered if the men were a posse from Hat Creek, then another even more chilling possibility occurred to him.

These hombres could be part of the outlaw gang that had murdered Abel Dempsey and at least two other men, along with wreaking havoc in the basin. They could be the ones responsible for the threat of the gallows that loomed over Dan's head. A part of him wanted to ride out there, confront them, and demand the truth—but of course that wouldn't accomplish anything except to get him killed and put Laura in even more danger.

So he stayed where he was and waited as the mysterious riders swept past. In the poor light, it was almost impossible to make out any details about them. Dan certainly didn't see anybody he recognized.

Between the shadows and the brush, he and Laura must not have been visible from the trail. The riders thundered past without slowing. Dan heaved a sigh of relief when they were gone.

"Who in the world was that?" asked Laura.

"You didn't recognize any of them?"

She shook her head and said, "No. I couldn't make them out. They were just dark shapes."

"Yeah, me, too," said Dan. "But if you stop and think about it, there are only two real possibilities. Either that was a posse from Hat Creek—or some of the rustlers who are raising hell around here."

She took a sharp breath and said, "You mean . . . the men who killed Abel and framed you?"

"Yeah. It was a little hard not to stop them and demand some answers. But of course, that wouldn't have done us any good. For the time being, I reckon we're going to have to rely on Stovepipe and Wilbur for that."

"They're turning out to be good friends, for men you haven't known very long."

"That's the truth," agreed Dan. "I get the feeling that Stovepipe is a lot smarter than you might think from the way he talks and acts. If I was an outlaw, I'm not sure I'd want to tangle with either one of them."

With the group of riders safely gone, Dan and Laura swung up into their saddles again and continued on toward the HS Bar. It wasn't long before Dan estimated that they were on Stafford range.

They didn't encounter anyone else, but even so, it was after midnight according to the stars before they came in sight of the ranch headquarters. The main house was surrounded by large, carefully tended trees, and there were a lot of outbuildings scattered around it as well. Dan saw a large barn with a sprawling array of corrals attached to it, a long, low bunkhouse, a building with a stovepipe sticking up from its roof that probably meant it was the cook shack, and other structures that were undoubtedly a smokehouse, a blacksmith shop, and cabins for the foreman and any married ranch hands. Everything Dan could see told him that the HS Bar was quite a successful spread.

He reined in when they were still a couple of hundred yards from the house and motioned for Laura to do likewise. When they were both stopped, he said quietly, "We don't want to ride up and raise enough of a ruckus to rouse the whole place. The fewer people who know we're here, the better. I know you trust Mrs. Stafford and figure she can convince her husband to help us, but we can't count on everybody else on the place keeping quiet about us."

"You're right," Laura said. "What should we do?"

Dan thought about it for a moment, then said, "We'll leave the horses here and go the rest of the way on foot. Once we've talked to the Staffords and know that they won't turn us over to the law, I can slip back out here and fetch the horses."

They dismounted and tied the reins to a scrubby bush, then walked toward the ranch house, circling a little to avoid most of the other buildings. Dan had his right hand resting on the butt of the gun in his holster. Laura was to his left, and without thinking he reached out with that hand and clasped her right hand. It was an instinctive gesture, but when he did it, it felt right, natural.

"Jessica would never betray us," said Laura in a voice a little above a whisper. "I'm certain of that."

"I believe you," Dan said. Deep down, though, he still remained to be convinced, and he knew the tension inside him wouldn't go away until they had talked to Henry Stafford.

The buildings were all dark except for a faint glow from the partially open door of the one Dan had pegged as the cook shack. Even though the hour was very early in the morning, it was possible the ranch cook was already in there getting started on the biscuits for the crew's breakfast. They gave that building a wide berth.

As they approached the house, a dog began to bark. It was a deep-throated sound, and as the animal stood up on the front porch, Dan saw that it was a large dog with a massive torso. Laura's hand tightened on his.

"You've been here quite a few times," he said. "That dog might know you, might recognize your scent."

"Yes, he might," Laura said. "I know his name, too."

"That'll help. Call to him."

Softly, Laura said, "Dash! Dash, it's me. You know me, sweetheart. Remember how I rubbed your ears the last time I was here and we were all sitting on the porch?"

The dog wouldn't understand the words, of course, thought Dan, but Laura's voice might be enough to strike a chord of familiarity in him. He was counting on that, along with the animal's sense of smell, to tell the dog that they were friends.

It seemed to work. The dog stopped barking and sat down, although it remained alert. Dan felt the eyes watching him as he and Laura came to the bottom of the steps leading up to the porch.

The front door opened and a man stepped out. He said, "Dash, what the devil were you raisin' a ruckus about, you big ol'—"

The man stopped short as he spotted the two figures standing at the bottom of the steps. Dan saw him lift something, then recognized the double barrels of a shotgun. He started to push Laura behind him, just in case.

She stepped past him, though, and said, "Henry, it's Laura Dempsey."

"Laura!" exclaimed Henry Stafford. "What in blazes are you doin' here in the middle of the night? Who's that with you?"

"It's Dan Hartford," Laura said.

"Hartford!" Stafford had started to lower the

shotgun, but now it came up again in a hurry. "Don't move, you bushwhacking son of a—"

"Henry, no! It's all right." Laura moved up onto the first step and raised her hand. "Please listen to me. Dan didn't kill Abel. He's innocent."

"Innocent, hell!" snorted Stafford. "Sheriff Olsen rode out here to tell us what happened and warn us to be on the lookout for Hartford. There's a rope waitin' for you, you no-good—"

From behind the rancher, a woman's voice interrupted him, saying, "Henry, what is it? Who's out there? What—" The questions stopped abruptly as Jessica Stafford, wrapped in a silk dressing gown, came out onto the porch. Instead she exclaimed, "Laura! My God!"

Laura went the rest of the way up the steps. Stafford didn't try to stop her as she and his wife embraced. He continued to scowl at Dan, though, and hold the shotgun pointed in the young cowboy's general direction.

"I want to know what's goin' on here," Stafford declared in a rumbling voice.

Laura turned to him and said, "We need your help, Henry, yours and Jessica's."

"You know if there's anything we can do for you, dear, we will," said Jessica.

"I ain't so sure about that," said Stafford, "if it includes helpin' Dan Hartford."

Laura ignored that and said to Jessica, "I know you've been told that Dan murdered Abel, but it's not true."

"I know you want to believe that . . ." Jessica began.

"I know it for a fact," said Laura. "I know it because . . . Dan was with me when Abel was shot."

Stafford said, "Hmmph." Like a lot of rugged frontiersman, he was fine with battling against outlaws or savages or wild animals or the elements, but any hint of scandal or impropriety made him uncomfortable.

"Please," Laura went on, "if you'd just hear us out . . . We need a place to stay while some . . . some friends of ours are trying to uncover the truth of what really happened."

"What friends?" Jessica asked, but before Laura could answer, she went on, "Never mind about that now. Both of you come in. Of course we'll listen to what you have to say. Won't we, Henry?"

For a couple of long seconds, Stafford didn't answer. Then he said, "I reckon since you and Jess are such good friends, we can listen. But I got to warn you . . . I'm gonna take a heap of convincin' before I'll believe that this young varmint didn't bushwhack my friend Abel Dempsey!"

CHAPTER TWENTY-FOUR

Stovepipe and Wilbur waited in the box canyon while Hamp Evans and Charley Bartlett headed back to the line shack. Hamp and Charley understood that they needed to carry on as they normally would have, except for the fact that they would be even more alert for any signs of trouble.

While the two drifters waited for morning, they carried out the unpleasant task of dragging the dead men to the far end of the canyon. Neither Stovepipe nor Wilbur felt like digging graves, especially in such hard, rocky ground, for hombres who had tried to kill them not once but twice, but they laid the corpses against the canyon wall and piled rocks on them to protect the bodies from scavengers.

For one thing, Stovepipe didn't want buzzards circling overhead and drawing attention to the canyon. It might be better, at least for the time being, if the disappearance of the three gunmen remained a mystery.

"As soon as it gets light enough to see to follow those three hosses, we'll turn 'em loose," Stovepipe declared. "By then, they'll probably be gettin' anxious to head home."

"Are we gonna just leave the saddles on 'em?" Wilbur wanted to know.

Stovepipe considered that question for a moment and then nodded.

"Might as well," he said. "The rest of that bunch is gonna be plumb puzzled either way when they show up at the hideout without their riders."

"Assuming that they go back to the hideout."

"Turn a horse loose and nine times outta ten, he heads for whatever place he thinks of as home."

"With our luck, this is probably that tenth time. Those nags will probably lead us straight to a posse that wants to string us up."

Stovepipe grinned and said, "No need to be pessimistic, Wilbur. Maybe *I'm* right and they'll lead us to a bunch of rustlers who'd rather fill us full o' lead."

"Yeah," Wilbur responded dryly, "I sure wouldn't want to be a pestimist."

Since they had been on the move, riding and shooting and fighting, for what seemed like forever and it appeared that that trend might continue for a while, these few hours gave them their best chance to get some rest. Stovepipe flipped a silver dollar to see who would get some shut-eye first. Wilbur called tails and the dollar came up heads.

"Give me a couple of hours," Stovepipe said as he sat down with his back against a rock and stretched his long legs out in front of him, crossing them at the ankles. He tipped his black hat down over his eyes, although he didn't really need the shade at night like this, and was soon snoring softly.

It seemed like he had just dozed off when Wilbur

kicked his foot to wake him. Stovepipe stood up, yawned mightily, rolled his shoulders, swung his arms in circles, and arched his back to get the kinks out of it. A glance at the stars told him it would start getting light in a couple of hours.

"Everything quiet?" he asked Wilbur.

"Yeah," replied the redhead. "Now, hush up your usual jabbering. I'm sleepy."

"Go ahead and turn in, then. Shoot, you make it sound like I don't never do nothin' except flap my jaws."

Wilbur grunted, then sprawled on his belly, rested his head on his folded arms, and closed his eyes.

"I'll just walk over yonder to the canyon mouth and keep an eye out," Stovepipe told him.

"Go ahead," growled Wilbur without raising his head. "Go on before I take my hat and start swatting you with it, you dang blabbermouth."

Stovepipe chuckled and ambled over to the opening that looked out on the vast sweep of the Tonto Basin. Shadows cloaked the basin right now, but Stovepipe knew he would see movement if anyone headed in their direction.

In truth, two hours of sleep hadn't been anywhere near enough to refresh him. His eyes felt gritty and his muscles were still weary. But the rest had been better than nothing and all he was likely to get for a while. What he really would have liked was a fire and a pot of hot coffee, but that wasn't going to happen. A fire would announce their presence to anybody who was looking for them.

He hunkered on his heels as he stood guard, and as usual any time he had a spare moment, the wheels of his brain began to revolve, clicking faster and faster.

He couldn't remember when he had discovered that he liked to solve mysteries and was good at it. He had been poking into things that assorted schemers regarded as none of his business for a long time now, from the Mississippi to the Pacific and the Rio Grande to the Milk River. As Wilbur liked to complain, getting into trouble seemed to be as natural as breathing for the two of them, but Stovepipe knew that in truth, his old friend wouldn't have it any other way.

At the moment, Stovepipe considered the ruction that had the basin in an uproar. Ranchers dying under mysterious circumstances, a young cowboy framed for a killing he hadn't committed, rustlers looting the area's herds at an ever-increasing pace . . . all those things were tied together—Stovepipe was sure of that. And if he could find the thread that held them together and pulled on it, likely the whole thing would come unraveled . . .

Thread.

Stovepipe smiled in the darkness.

The eastern sky had started to turn a faint shade of gray when Stovepipe kicked the sole of Wilbur's right boot, just as Wilbur had done to wake him earlier, and said in cheerful tones, "Rise and shine, sleepyhead."

Wilbur groaned, lifted his head, and peered around.

"Dang it, Stovepipe, I just closed my eyes ten seconds ago," he complained.

"More like seventy-two hunnerd seconds ago, if I

did the cipherin' right in my head," said Stovepipe. "You been asleep for two whole hours."

"That's not possible." Wilbur pushed himself up to a sitting position, scrubbed both hands over his face, and raked fingers through his red hair. He looked up at the sky and sighed. "Reckon it *is* getting on toward morning, isn't it?"

"Yep. Come on. Let's haze those horses outta here and see where they go."

Before doing that, they saddled the Appaloosa and the dun, then let them drink water that Stovepipe poured from a canteen into his hat. After resting most of the night, the horses were a little frisky this morning and ready to go. Stovepipe and Wilbur were ready to go, too, but *bedraggled* described them a lot better than *frisky* did.

Breakfast was a strip of jerky and no coffee. They were still gnawing on the tough strips of meat when they swung up into their saddles and started pushing the gunmen's mounts toward the canyon mouth. Stovepipe took off his hat, leaned over to slap it against the rump of one of the animals, and called, "Hyahhh!"

The horses took off at a fast trot.

Stovepipe and Wilbur followed. The sky was light enough now that the stars were getting harder and harder to see. It was as if, one by one, they all went out overhead. A small strip of rosy sky appeared along the eastern horizon.

The horses had grazed in the canyon, so they weren't particularly hungry. Still, they stopped from time to time to crop at the grass. Stovepipe and Wilbur let the animals proceed at their own pace, knowing the horses would be more likely to head back to what they considered home that way.

This strained the patience of both men as they followed at a good distance, close enough to keep the horses in sight but unlikely to be spotted themselves if anybody came along and found the animals. That was possible, because they were on Box D range and some of the ranch's punchers were liable to be out and about. In fact, it was likely that they were, so Stovepipe and Wilbur had to keep their eyes open for that potential danger and stay out of sight as much as they could, too.

The sun still wasn't up when the outlaws' horses reached Apache Bluff. Stovepipe and Wilbur hadn't seen anyone else, which Stovepipe thought was a stroke of luck and Wilbur regarded as a sign that the odds against them were rising.

"When things go along too smooth-like, you know life's just getting ready to smack you a good one right in the mush," the redhead commented.

"I swear, Wilbur, if a good-looking gal came up to you and offered you a whole pile o' money and told you she came along with the deal, you'd find somethin' to complain about," said Stovepipe.

"Beautiful women are always trouble," Wilbur said. "You ever know a man who was married to a beautiful woman who wasn't worried all the time that some smooth-talking fella was gonna come along and steal her away from him? Same thing with money. We've run into plenty of rich hombres in our time, Stovepipe, and I don't recall a single one of them who was truly happy. No, sir. When a man's *got* something, he has to spend all his time worrying that he's going to *lose* it."

"Well, then, you and me ought to be downright giddy, old son, 'cause other than our hosses and saddles and guns, we ain't got a blasted thing."

"And that's just the way I like it," said Wilbur.

By now the horses they were following had found a way down the bluff and entered the area of rugged terrain just below. Stovepipe and Wilbur were still on their trail, and the two drifters had to increase their pace a little in order to keep their quarry in sight. The horses were trotting along a dry wash that twisted and turned among the ridges. There wasn't a straight stretch more than a hundred yards long. If there were any other washes branching off from this one, Stovepipe and Wilbur might not be able to tell which way they had gone.

Because of that, they probably weren't watching their surroundings quite as closely as they normally would have been. Otherwise they wouldn't have been so surprised when a man suddenly dived off the top of a rock they were riding past, crashed into Stovepipe, and drove him out of the saddle.

CHAPTER TWENTY-FIVE

Stovepipe's hat flew off as he fell. He hit the ground hard with his attacker on top of him, but his wiry body was tough as whang leather so he didn't think the crash did any real damage.

That situation might not last, because the man who had tackled him clamped both hands around Stovepipe's throat and proceeded to bang the lanky cowboy's head against the ground.

Stovepipe's brain seemed to be jolting around inside his skull with each impact. Blindly, he shot a punch upward and felt his bony fist collide with something hard. The man on top of him grunted in pain and slewed to the side, knocked that way by Stovepipe's blow smashing into his jaw. Stovepipe heaved his body from the ground and threw the man the rest of the way off.

Stovepipe was short of breath from being choked, but he forced his muscles to work and rolled after the man who had jumped him. He planted his right fist in the man's midsection, then bounced a left off the hombre's chin with enough force to make the man crack the back of his head against the ground. He proved less resilient than Stovepipe had. His eyes rolled up in their sockets and he passed out.

Stovepipe looked up and saw Wilbur sitting on the dun a few yards away. The redhead held his Winchester ready, but he hadn't been able to use it because if he had fired, he would have risked hitting Stovepipe.

Wilbur's back was turned toward the rock from which Stovepipe's attacker had leaped. Another man appeared there now with a revolver in his hand. As the gun barrel rose toward Wilbur's back, Stovepipe yelled to his friend, "Behind you!"

Wilbur twisted in the saddle and drove his heels into the dun's flanks, making the horse leap aside. Flame geysered from the muzzle of the gunman's Colt, but Wilbur's swift reaction caused the shot to miss. The Winchester in his hands cracked as he fired instinctively without aiming.

The man standing on top of the rock doubled over as the bullet punched into his guts. He dropped his gun and clutched at his belly, then toppled forward to land in a sprawled heap in front of the boulder.

Wilbur covered the man, although it appeared he was no longer a threat, while Stovepipe scrambled to his feet and pulled his Winchester from the sheath strapped to the Appaloosa's saddle. Only when Stovepipe was armed did he pick up his hat and clap it back on his head.

"You think these two are more of that gang of wide-loopers?" asked Wilbur.

Stovepipe looked at the coarse, beard-stubbled features of the two men and said, "I don't see how they could be anything else. They sure don't look like the townsmen from Hat Creek who volunteered for one of Sheriff Olsen's posses."

"That one's not dead, is he?" Wilbur asked as he nodded toward the man who had tackled Stovepipe.

"Nope, just knocked silly for a few minutes. I reckon he'll be comin' around soon. Better check on the other one while I got the chance."

Stovepipe stepped over to the man Wilbur had shot, hooked a boot toe under his shoulder, and rolled him onto his back. The man's shirt was soaked with blood, and his eyes were already starting to turn glassy.

"This hombre's done for," announced Stovepipe.

Wilbur grunted. Stovepipe knew that his partner didn't like taking lives, even those of outlaws, but sometimes the varmints just didn't give a fella any choice.

Stovepipe went back over to the man he had knocked out, rested the Winchester's muzzle against his shoulder, and prodded him.

"Wake up, mister," he said. "You got some talkin' to do."

The man's eyelids fluttered for a few seconds before opening and staying open. Blearily, he peered up at Stovepipe for a moment, not seeming to know where he was or what was going on.

Then understanding settled in and the man's face twisted in a hate-filled scowl that only became darker as Stovepipe backed off a few steps and said, "All right, fella, get on your feet."

The man sat up, shook his head groggily, and then said, "Go to hell, mister."

"You'd better listen to him, friend," Wilbur advised. "You put a dent in Stovepipe's hat when you knocked him off his horse, and he sets a heap of store by that hat."

"I got a dent in my hat?" exclaimed Stovepipe. "Cover the polecat, Wilbur."

He took the high-crowned black Stetson off, gently brushed some dust from it, and then carefully poked it back into acceptable shape. His rugged face was grim as he put the hat back on his head.

"Now I got even less patience than I did," he told the prisoner. "I know you're one of those rustlers who've been raisin' so much hell around here. You might as well admit it."

"I'm not gonna admit anything," the man said stubbornly.

"Then how come you tackled me the way you did? How come your pard tried to gun my pard?"

The prisoner glared at Stovepipe in stony silence.

"Are you the one who bushwhacked Abel Dempsey," asked Stovepipe, "or was it somebody else from your bunch?"

This time he saw a flicker of *something* in the man's watery eyes. It wasn't denial so much as it was confusion, thought Stovepipe. He wouldn't have bet money on it, but he had a hunch this fella didn't actually *know* who had killed Dempsey.

And that was puzzling, since Stovepipe was convinced the gang was responsible for that killing.

"Not to rush you, Stovepipe," said Wilbur, "but if there are any more of those varmints close by, they must've heard those shots. They're probably on their way here now to find out what happened. They'll really be curious if these two fellas don't report in."

"Yeah, you're right about that." Stovepipe gestured

with the Winchester. "I told you to get on your feet, hombre. Do it now or—"

"Or what?" the man interrupted with a sneer. "You're gonna shoot me? Blow my head off? The hell you are. You're not a cold-blooded killer. I can tell that by lookin' at you."

"Appearances can be deceivin'," said Stovepipe coldly. He stepped closer to the prisoner. The man's eyes widened as he probably realized that he might've overplayed his hand.

But instead of pulling the rifle's trigger, Stovepipe swung the weapon instead so that the stock slammed against the man's head, knocking him out again. He slumped to the side and didn't move.

"Dang, Stovepipe, you might've busted his skull," said Wilbur.

"Naw, I know how to wallop an hombre so I knock him cold without doin' any permanent damage to him . . . I hope."

"What are we gonna do with him?"

Stovepipe thought for a second, then said, "I don't particularly want to haul him around with us. I'll tie him up and gag him and leave him stashed behind that rock with the other fella."

"The dead one, you mean?"

"Yeah." Stovepipe smiled. "He won't be much company for this one, but I figure the fella would rather be bored than dead. Then we'll finish havin' our look around and come back for him if we can."

"If we don't run into the rest of the bunch and get ventilated."

"Yep," said Stovepipe as he leaned his rifle against the rock and set about the task of tying and gagging the man he'd knocked out. Wilbur dismounted and dragged the corpse behind the rock, out of sight.

"It appears that I've taken up a new line of work," said Wilbur. "Hauling bodies."

"Somebody's got to do it," said Stovepipe, "because there's never gonna be any shortage of dead people in this world."

"Yeah . . . especially around us, seems like."

A few minutes later they were mounted again and riding along the wash in the same direction as the horses they'd been following. Those horses were out of sight now. Stovepipe listened intently. If the rest of the gang had been bearing down on him and Wilbur, out for blood, he thought he would have heard their horses by now. Instead the countryside was quiet. There weren't even any sounds of birds or small animals, because those had hushed due to the gunplay a short time earlier and hadn't started back up again.

"You know, I'm startin' to wonder if there's anybody else in these parts," mused Stovepipe after a few minutes. "Maybe the gang cleared out and left those two behind to stand guard in case anybody showed up lookin' for 'em."

"Like the three hombres we shot it out with at Apache Bluff and then in that box canyon," suggested Wilbur. "They were watching the place where Abel Dempsey was bushwhacked."

"Yeah. Could be the gang moves around so they'll be harder to find, or maybe they pulled up stakes because they got spooked when their plan to frame Dan for Dempsey's murder didn't go exactly the way they expected."

"I'd say it worked out pretty well. Everybody in the

basin thinks Dan is guilty except for you and me and a few other people."

Stovepipe grinned and said, "Maybe they're scared of us."

"Not likely. As far as they're concerned, we're just a couple of shiftless saddle tramps who got caught in the middle of this ruckus. They don't know how hard we work at being unimpressive."

Stovepipe let that pass as they rode on. A few more minutes went by, and then they came to a broad, shallow depression that was thick with grass and had a small pool on one side of it. The three horses they had been following earlier were grazing contentedly on the grass near the pool. No other signs of life were visible at the moment, but when Stovepipe gazed at the ground and saw a multitude of hoofprints, as well as the way the grass was pushed down in places, he knew what he was looking at.

"Somebody's been holdin' stock here," he said to Wilbur.

"Yeah, there's the remains of a campfire over yonder." The redhead pointed. "This was the gang's hideout, Stovepipe. Has to be. But they're gone now."

"Yeah, they pulled up stakes, like I said, and it ain't likely they'll be comin' back. They'll shift the operation somewhere else in the basin. That's good news for the Box D but bad news for whichever spread they set up shop on next."

The two men sat on their horses and stared disconsolately at the empty hideout. After a moment, Wilbur asked, "What do we do now?"

"Reckon we're sort of at a dead end. About the only thing we can do is try to trail that bunch to wherever they're headed next."

"What about that fella we left back up the wash?"

"He can work his way loose after a while. He'd just slow us down, and I don't reckon he knew much. That's the impression I got, anyway. When I said somethin' about the rustlers killin' Abel Dempsey, he looked downright puzzled."

"Is our thinking on the whole business wrong, Stovepipe?"

"Nope, I don't believe it is." Stovepipe shook his head slowly. "There's just somethin' we ain't come across yet, and when we do, the whole thing'll make sense."

"I suppose you're right. You haven't been wrong yet."

Stovepipe grinned and said, "There's a first time for most things. I hope this ain't one of 'em."

CHAPTER TWENTY-SIX

At the HS Bar the previous night, Jessica Stafford ushered Dan and Laura into the parlor. Henry Stafford followed them with the shotgun tucked under his left arm and a suspicious frown still on his rugged face.

"Sit down," Jessica told the two visitors as she gestured toward a divan. "You both look exhausted. Can I get you something? There might still be some coffee in the pot on the stove." She smiled ruefully and added, "Although I'm sure it's just about turned into mud by now."

"You can be hospitable later, Jess," said Stafford. "Right now I want to hear the story these two promised us."

"It's not that pretty a story, I'm afraid," said Laura.

Stafford grunted and said, "Life ain't pretty most of the time, and folks who thinks it is, or ought to be, are just foolin' themselves."

"Most of this mess is my fault," Dan said. "*Not* what happened to Abel Dempsey, but the rest of it, so I should be the one to tell it."

Laura laid a hand on his and told him, "Don't blame yourself, Dan. I certainly don't. I had just as much to do with everything that happened as you did."

"Just get on with it," growled Stafford.

Dan started talking. He told Stafford and Jessica about how he and Laura had known each other back in Saint Louis, how her father had come between them and pressured Laura into marrying Abel Dempsey, and how they had encountered each other again unexpectedly out here in Arizona Territory.

Stafford let out a skeptical snort at that and said, "You really want us to believe you didn't know Laura was here, Hartford? That you didn't come to these parts plannin' to steal her away from her husband?"

"It's the truth," Dan insisted. "I know it's quite a coincidence, but that's not any more unbelievable than a lot of other things that have happened in life."

"I was completely surprised when Dan showed up at the Box D," added Laura. "Please believe us, Henry. We really didn't plan to see each other again and . . . and rekindle all those old feelings . . ."

Stafford made a curt gesture and said, "You can leave out that part. Just get on with the rest of it."

"No, you need to hear this, Henry," Laura insisted. "I was never unfaithful to my husband. It's true that Dan and I had feelings for each other. We still do. But I wasn't going to cheat on Abel, regardless of the circumstances that led to our marriage in the first place. In fact, that's what I was going to tell Dan . . . that day on Apache Bluff . . ."

"You were?" said Dan.

Laura swallowed hard and nodded.

"That's right. I know we had talked about . . .

running away to California. I was going to tell you that's where you ought to go . . . but without me." She shook her head. "But before I could say anything about that, we heard that shot . . . the shot that killed Abel . . . and everything was different after that. In that one moment, everything changed."

"Yeah," grunted Stafford. "You were a widow, so you were free to play around with this no-account cowboy—"

"Henry, please," said Jessica. "From everything Laura and Dan have told us, you're making things sound a lot more scandalous than they really were."

Stafford grumbled something, then snapped at Dan, "Get on with the story."

Dan told them about finding Dempsey's body, the shot directed at him from the rocks, and then returning that fire only to be discovered a moment later by Lew Martin and some of the other Box D hands.

"I knew how it would look to them," he said. "They weren't going to give me a chance to explain. All I could do was get out of there before they filled me full of lead. Even as fast as I moved, it was a mighty close thing."

"Might've been better if they had ventilated you."

"Henry, how can you say that?" Jessica admonished her husband. "Haven't you heard a word Dan's said? He didn't shoot Abel, so why should he be gunned down for it?"

"You believe that yarn he spun?"

"I believe Laura," Jessica insisted. "If she says Dan was with her when Abel was shot, then it's the truth."

"Thank you, Jessica," said Laura. "Most of the time, it seems like nobody in this basin even wants to listen to me, let alone believe what I'm telling them. If it weren't for you, and Mr. Stewart and Mr. Coleman—"

"Who?" Stafford interrupted.

"The two fellas who helped me get away from Sheriff Olsen's posse the other day," Dan explained. He sighed. "Of course, that didn't last very long, and then we all wound up in jail anyway."

"Yeah, I heard about that," said Stafford. "You're talkin' about those saddle tramps who broke outta jail with you. Who in blazes are they, and how'd they get mixed up in this?"

"Just a couple of drifters, from what I can tell," replied Dan with a shrug. "But they believe in me, and they've been good friends so far."

"Where are they now?" asked Jessica.

"I don't really know. Off somewhere trying to get to the bottom of this mess, I suppose." Dan laughed humorlessly. "Although if they had any sense, they'd light a shuck out of this whole part of the country and never come back."

"Maybe that's what you ought to do," Stafford said.

Dan shook his head and said, "I don't want the law on my trail the rest of my life. The only way to prevent that is to find out who really killed Abel Dempsey."

"What can we do to help?" asked Jessica.

"What we really need is a place to stay for a while," said Laura. "That will give Stovepipe and Wilbur a chance to look into things more."

"That's those two saddle tramps?" Stafford said.

When Laura nodded, Jessica said, "You're putting an awful lot of faith in them, it seems to me."

Dan said, "There's something about them that makes you have confidence in them, almost like you can tell they've done this sort of thing before."

"Well, of course you're welcome to stay here." Jessica looked at her husband. "Isn't that right, Henry?"

Stafford looked like he wanted to disagree with his wife, and vehemently, at that. But after a long moment, he overcame his reluctance and said, "All right . . . for now. I ain't sayin' I believe you, Hartford, and even if you're tellin' the truth about what happened to Abel, I still don't like you. But I reckon you can hide out here for a spell."

Dan's face flushed with anger. He didn't like the way Stafford had phrased that about him and Laura hiding out here on the HS Bar, but he supposed there was some truth to it. They actually were fugitives from the law, after all.

"Thank you, Henry," Laura said. "And thank you, Jessica. This means so much to us."

"Yeah," said Dan with a curt nod to the rancher. "We're much obliged to you."

"Did anyone see you when you came up to the house?" asked Jessica.

"I don't think so," Dan replied. "We walked in on foot and stayed away from the other buildings as much as we could."

"Where are your horses?" asked Stafford.

"We left them tied up a couple of hundred yards from here." Dan told the older man where to find the mounts.

"I'll go out and get 'em," said Stafford. "Can't bring them back here to the barn or one of the corrals, though. My hands would spot 'em and know right away they're strange horses. Reckon the boys'd want to know where they came from. There's an old rock pen up in the hills where I can put 'em for now, though."

"That's smart thinking, Henry," Jessica told him.

Stafford grunted and said, "I ain't sure we're doin' the right thing, Jess, but if we're gonna do this, we might as well try to do it right."

"That's exactly what I thought," she replied with an affectionate smile.

"There's one more thing . . ." said Dan.

"What do you want now?" Stafford asked impatiently.

"I'm just curious about something. While Laura and I were on our way here, we had to get off the trail for a little while and let a group of riders go past. Looked like at least a dozen of them, and they were moving along at a good clip. I was just wondering who they were."

Stafford's forehead creased in a frown. He said, "These hombres you saw were comin' from this ranch?"

"That's what it looked like. They were headed south, toward the Box D, or maybe Hat Creek."

Stafford shook his head.

"They weren't any of my crew," he insisted. "None of the boys went to town tonight. Reckon they're all accounted for. If you don't believe me, we can go out to the bunkhouse and roust 'em from their bunks."

"I believe you," Dan said. "The sheriff wasn't out here with a posse last evening?"

"I ain't seen Frank Olsen in a couple of days."

Jessica, who'd been sitting in an armchair while they talked, leaned forward until she was perched on the edge of the chair cushion. She asked anxiously, "Who could those men have been, Henry?"

Stafford rubbed his jaw, which at this hour was dotted with silvery beard stubble.

"I don't reckon I know . . . unless they were up to no good."

"Like that gang of rustlers who've been bleeding off stock throughout the whole basin," said Dan. "Stovepipe figures they're behind Abel Dempsey's murder, as well as the deaths of Fred Tomlinson and Jack Hogan."

Stafford's frown deepened. He said, "Tomlinson was bushwhacked, all right, but Hogan fell in a ravine and busted his neck."

"We don't know that for sure," Dan said. "The killers could have made it look like that."

"Yeah, I reckon . . . You mean to say this fella Stewart thinks the rustlers are goin' through the basin, killin' off all the cattlemen?"

"It seems possible."

"Why would they do that? They're out to steal cows, not slaughter a bunch of folks."

"Yes, but if they throw the basin into enough of an uproar, they can strike in force, round up every cow that's out there, and drive them out of here, say, down across the border into Mexico. It would be a cleanup the likes of which has never been seen around here."

"Yeah, maybe. If Stewart's right, and all the ranchers in these parts have got targets on their backs . . ."

Jessica stood up and hurried over to her husband to clutch his arm. Eyes wide with fear, she said, "My God, Henry, you could be next. You can't . . . You have to stay right here in the house where you'll be safe."

Stafford blew out his breath disgustedly and said,

"I ain't never hid from trouble, and I don't plan to start now. Besides, somebody's got to deal with the horses these two rode here."

"Henry, no," Jessica said, shaking her head.

Stafford put the shotgun back in the rack where it had come from and took down a Winchester instead. He checked the repeater to make sure it was loaded, then said, "I won't be gone long."

He plucked his hat from a hat tree near the door and stalked out, leaving his wife staring after him as she stood there gnawing her bottom lip worriedly.

Laura said, "Jessica, I'm sorry for the trouble we've caused—"

"You didn't cause it, Laura," said Jessica. "I'm just married to the stubbornest man on the face of the earth, that's all!"

CHAPTER TWENTY-SEVEN

It appeared that only a small herd of cattle had been kept at the rustlers' hideout Stovepipe and Wilbur had located, but the stock had left enough of a trail for the two men to follow. It was difficult to move even a small herd without leaving a considerable amount of sign.

They tracked the cattle toward the northwest as the sun rose in the east, over their right shoulders. After a while, Wilbur commented, "It looks like they're headed for those breaks where Dan was holed up when we first met him."

"North of there, I'd say," mused Stovepipe. "Of course, we don't know how far those breaks extend in that direction. They may run along the whole edge of the basin on this side, all the way up onto Henry Stafford's range."

"That'd make sense if they were going after some of Stafford's beeves next."

"Or goin' after Stafford himself," Stovepipe said grimly.

Wilbur frowned, shook his head, and said, "I don't follow you, Stovepipe."

"Think about it. The two ranchers who were killed before Dempsey were one of the Tomlinson brothers from the Leanin' T, who was bushwhacked first, then Jack Hogan from the Big Nine."

"Yeah, but we don't know for sure that Hogan's death wasn't an accident."

"I'd bet my hat it was murder just like the other two, and you know how much store I set by this hat, Wilbur."

"Well, that's true," Wilbur agreed. "I still don't see what you're getting at."

"The Leanin' T and the Big Nine are southwest and west of Hat Creek, down on the other end of the basin. If you work your way up this side, you come to the Box D next, and then the HS Bar. We know that from the maps we looked at before we ever headed in this direction."

"Yeah, come to think of it, I guess you're right. That could mean . . . Yeah, I see what you're saying, Stovepipe. The gang's knocking off the ranchers one after the other, just following the way the spreads are laid out in the basin. They've got themselves a nice little system going. And if you *are* right, they'll be targeting Henry Stafford next, just like you said."

"What I'm wonderin' now," said Stovepipe, "is if we ought to be followin' this herd, or if we should head for Stafford's place to warn him."

Wilbur frowned and said, "We're on the run from the law, remember? If we show up at Stafford's ranch, he's liable to point a gun at us and try to hold us for the sheriff. He and Dempsey were old friends, after all, and as far as Stafford knows, we've been helping the man who dry-gulched Dempsey."

Stovepipe shook his head.

"You're forgettin' that Dan and Miss Laura were headin' for the HS Bar the last time we saw 'em. Chances are, they've made it there by now, explained the whole thing to Stafford and his wife, and they've agreed to help 'em."

"What if Stafford didn't believe their story and turned *Dan* over to the law?"

"Then we'd be ridin' into trouble, sure enough. That's why I figure we'd best be careful when we get there, maybe do a little scoutin' first before we let anybody know we're around."

"Be careful, eh?" said Wilbur. "Well, that might be a nice change for us." He waved a hand toward the tracks they had been following. "So we're not going to trail that herd anymore?"

"We can always find that herd later on," Stovepipe said confidently. "Right now I just want to make sure Henry Stafford don't wind up dead like so many other folks around here."

Laura had said that she wanted a hot bath and the chance to sleep in a real bed. The bed sounded good to Dan, too, although he was willing to pass on the bath for the time being.

Once he had stretched out in one of the spare bedrooms in the Stafford ranch house, though, he'd found that he had trouble dozing off. Too much upsetting had happened in recent days, and his thoughts were whirling so fast in his brain that he wasn't able to relax and go to sleep.

But no matter how much he pondered, he wasn't able to come up with any answers to the dilemma that faced him, other than waiting for Stovepipe and

Wilbur to sort everything out. Relying on someone else to solve his problems rubbed Dan the wrong way, but right now he didn't see any other option.

At one point he heard a horse and figured that was Henry Stafford coming back from hiding his and Laura's horses up in the hills.

Exhaustion finally claimed him, but his sleep was restless and not very refreshing. When he woke up, the gray light coming through a tiny gap in the curtains at the window told him it was dawn and he had slept for only a few hours. He hoped that Laura was getting more rest than that.

Dan had taken off only his shirt, boots, and gun belt when he lay down. Now he pulled them on and went downstairs, drawn by the smell of coffee brewing.

He found Jessica Stafford in the kitchen, pouring herself a cup from the pot that was heating on the stove. She turned toward Dan, forced a smile, and asked, "Would you like some, Dan? I promise it's fresh this time."

She was already dressed, wearing a dark green silk blouse and a brown riding skirt. Her honey-colored hair was loose and tumbling around her shoulders. She would have been stunningly beautiful, even at this hour of the morning, if not for the haunted look in her eyes and the taut lines of her face.

"What's wrong?" asked Dan. All he had to do was look at Jessica to know that something wasn't right.

Her hand started to shake. She turned and set the coffee cup on the table so she wouldn't drop it. Then she said, "It's Henry. He . . . he hasn't come back."

"Good Lord," Dan said. "You mean from wherever he was going to take our horses last night?"

"That's right. That rock corral up in the hills he mentioned."

"Do you know where it is?"

"I've seen it before," said Jessica. "Henry pointed it out to me once when we were out riding."

"Reckon you could find it again?"

She nodded and said, "I believe I could. In fact, I was thinking about going up there. That's why I'm dressed the way I am."

"You're not going alone. I'll come with you."

"You can't. You shouldn't leave the house. That was the whole purpose of you and Laura coming here, remember? To hide out?"

"Maybe so," Dan said, his face and voice grim. "But if anything's happened to Mr. Stafford, it's because he was trying to help us. I can't forget about that. If he needs help . . ."

Dan didn't finish the sentence. Jessica looked intently at him for a moment, then said, "The crew will be at breakfast right now. I'll go out to the barn, saddle a couple of horses, and bring them around back of the house. I think we can ride out without anyone noticing us, if we're careful and don't waste any time."

"I have to let Laura know what's going on."

Jessica nodded and said, "Of course. And get a couple of rifles for us, too."

She started out of the kitchen. Dan stopped her by saying, "Mrs. Stafford . . . I'm sure sorry we've brought all our trouble down on you like this."

She managed a faint smile as she shook her head.

"You didn't bring all the trouble down on the basin, Dan," she said. "Whoever's behind the rustling . . . they're responsible for everything that's happened. I believe that now, and sooner or later . . . they're going to pay for what they've done."

Dan was waiting on the back porch a few minutes later when Jessica rode around the corner of the house on a big, cream-colored gelding. She led a chestnut horse with white stockings and a blazed face for Dan.

"Did anybody see you?" he asked as he swung up into the saddle.

"I don't think so. Did you talk to Laura?"

"Yes. She's upset and worried about Mr. Stafford, too. But she understands that she needs to stay out of sight while we're gone."

"You may not be able to come back, Dan. You may have to stay in the hills and lie low until after dark."

"Yeah, I already thought about that. But I'm not going to worry about it at this point. I just want to find out what happened to Mr. Stafford and make sure he's safe."

"That's the way I feel, too. Come on."

Jessica turned her mount and heeled it into a trot. Dan fell in alongside her.

The sun was still well below the horizon, although the eastern sky was rosy enough that it provided plenty of light for them to see where they were going. The sky quickly grew brighter, although the two riders were well out of sight of the ranch house before the orange orb poked its way into sight.

The HS Bar was a vast spread, like the Box D, and according to Jessica, the old rock corral where her husband had been taking the horses was miles away from the ranch headquarters.

"This was all a Spanish land grant at one time," she explained. "The rock corral dates back to that time period. There are also the remains of an old rock house up there, but most of it has fallen in. Henry talked about wanting to rebuild it sometime—it would be a place where he and I could go during the summer, he said, so it would be cooler—but of course he's never gotten around to it."

"Sounds nice," said Dan. It wasn't the sort of romantic notion he would have expected from Henry Stafford, but of course he didn't really know the man at all.

The sun rose higher by the time they approached a range of low hills covered with pine and juniper. Jessica pointed and said, "We go through that gap there and on the other side is a trail that leads higher."

Dan had been listening for shots. If Stafford had been thrown off his horse and broken his leg or encountered some other sort of mishap like that, he probably would have fired signal shots in the air to alert searchers to his location. He had to know that his wife would be worried about him by now and would send men to look for him, if she didn't come herself—as, of course, she actually had.

But Dan hadn't heard a thing, and that silence didn't bode very well, he thought. He didn't say anything about that to Jessica, however.

She was smart enough to figure out things for herself, and he knew from her increasingly worried expression that she probably had.

The trail they were following led higher into the hills. Stafford was right: the air was cooler up here than down on the flats, although the bright sunshine was still warm.

"The corral is up there, just on the other side of that hill," said Jessica, pointing. She stiffened in the saddle and went on, "Wait a minute. Is that—"

She broke off with a gasp, because she had seen the same thing Dan had.

Buzzards were circling over that hill.

"No," Jessica said, her voice catching in her throat. "No . . ."

"Stay here," Dan told her.

"No, I have to—"

"Stay here!" he said again, sharper this time. He jabbed his boot heels into the chestnut's flanks and sent the horse lunging forward at a run.

More death, he thought as he rode hard toward the hill. More death that might not have struck if he hadn't ever come to this basin, or if he'd had the sense to ride on as soon as he recognized Laura.

Then he remembered what Jessica had said about the rustlers being responsible for everything that had happened. Maybe that was true, but Dan couldn't help but feel that his presence in the basin had contributed to it as well.

He shoved those bleak thoughts out of his brain and concentrated on his riding instead. He topped the hill, started down the slope, and spotted the stone corral ahead of him. Two horses were in the enclosure, and Dan recognized them immediately as the ones he and Laura had been riding the night before.

Another saddled horse stood outside the corral. That had to be Henry Stafford's mount . . .

Then a bitter curse erupted from Dan's mouth as he saw the motionless figure of a man lying sprawled facedown on the ground nearby. He started toward the man, knowing in his gut that he was going to find Henry Stafford dead.

That was when a gun blasted somewhere nearby and a bullet whistled past Dan's ear, barely missing him.

CHAPTER TWENTY-EIGHT

Stovepipe and Wilbur were familiar with the general layout of the spreads in the Tonto Basin, but they didn't know where the headquarters of each ranch was located. So all they could do was head in the approximate direction of the Stafford ranch house.

"This is good range, Stovepipe," Wilbur commented as they rode. "Maybe not as prime as some we've seen, but with hard work a fella could wind up with a mighty nice outfit here in this basin."

"And those old-time cattlemen like Dempsey and Stafford knew how to work hard," said Stovepipe. "That's how they were able to carve places for themselves outta the frontier, surrounded by enemies who wanted to kill 'em."

"These days people don't appreciate that," Wilbur groused. "They just want to come in and take away from the folks who worked so hard to make this a decent place to live."

"Reckon you're always gonna have greedy varmints like that," said Stovepipe. He grinned. "But as long as there are outlaws, we'll never be outta work, will we?"

"I suppose you could look at it like that," Wilbur replied with a shrug.

They continued riding until a few minutes later when Stovepipe raised a hand and said, "Hold on. You see those riders way over yonder, Wilbur?"

"Where?" asked the redhead.

Stovepipe pointed across a broad expanse of flats and said, "They're about a mile away, headin' for those hills."

"You've got eyes that'd put an eagle to shame, Stovepipe. I think I see something moving over there, but I never would have spotted it if you hadn't pointed it out."

Stovepipe reached in his saddlebags and brought out his field glasses. He lifted the lenses to his eyes, studied the distant riders through them for a moment, and said, "Jehoshaphat! That's Dan, ridin' with some woman I don't know."

"It's not Miss Laura?"

"Nope. This gal's just as good-lookin', but she's got lighter-colored hair."

"Mrs. Stafford, maybe? Miss Laura's friend?"

"Could be," said Stovepipe as he lowered the field glasses. "Likely, in fact, considerin' that we've got to be on HS Bar range by now."

"Well, what are we gonna do?"

"What do you reckon we're gonna do?" Stovepipe asked with a chuckle. "We're gonna follow 'em."

"Yeah, that's what I figured you'd say."

The two men heeled their horses into motion again.

The riders they were following had a long lead on them, but the Appaloosa and the dun were still fresh and strong enough to run free and easy across the flats toward the hills. Their hooves raised some dust, which worried Stovepipe a mite because somebody might spot it, but it was still early enough in the morning that he considered that unlikely.

He was more concerned about the fact that Dan was out riding the range when he was supposed to be lying low and hiding out at the Stafford ranch along with Laura. It must have taken something important to get him out in the open like this.

Or something pretty bad . . .

They had cut down the distance between themselves and their quarry enough that Wilbur could make out the other riders with the naked eye. He said, "That's a bright green shirt the lady has on. Or is that Dan?"

"No, that's Miz Stafford," said Stovepipe. "Reckon she likes bright colors."

"Sometimes that's not too smart out here on the frontier. Makes you too easy to spot."

"Yeah, but nobody's gonna mistake you for a wild animal and shoot you, either," Stovepipe pointed out.

"I dunno. I've seen birds that were a bright green like that. Remember when we were down in Central America on the trail of that owlhoot who called himself the Macaw?"

"Ain't likely to forget it," said Stovepipe. "As I recollect, we almost got ourselves killed."

Wilbur snorted disgustedly and replied, "You could say that about almost every place we've ever gone."

Dan and Mrs. Stafford—assuming that's who the woman was—had reached the hills by now. They were about half a mile ahead of Stovepipe and Wilbur, maybe a little less. As they rode over a hilltop and went out of sight, the two cowboys pushed their mounts a little harder.

Stovepipe suddenly exclaimed, "Dadgum it!"

"What's wrong?"

"Look yonder," said Stovepipe, pointing again. His finger indicated some black shapes wheeling above the hills, stark against the blue sky of morning.

"Oh, I hate to see that," Wilbur said.

"Yeah, me, too. Them *zopilotes* are never good news."

"Could be just a dead cow."

"Maybe," said Stovepipe. "I ain't gonna pin my hopes on that, though. Come on."

From what he could tell, the two riders they were following were heading toward the spot the buzzards were circling, too. Stovepipe couldn't see them anymore, but he knew they couldn't be very far ahead.

With no warning, a shot slammed through the morning air. From the sound of it, Stovepipe didn't think it was directed at him and Wilbur, but he couldn't be sure of that. Even if someone was shooting at them, they had to keep going and find out what was happening up ahead.

Stovepipe pulled his Winchester from the saddle boot. Wilbur did likewise. They reached the base of the nearest hill and sent the horses pounding up the slope.

Dan jerked the borrowed horse to the side as he felt the wind-rip of the slug next to his ear. He yanked his revolver from its holster and looked around for the source of the shot, but he didn't see anything and he didn't want to return the fire blindly.

Fear for Jessica Stafford welled up inside him. Laura might not ever forgive him if her friend was hurt, or worse, killed. Dan was about to charge back over the hill toward the spot where he had left Jessica when another shot cracked from the hidden rifleman and the chestnut staggered. The horse was hit, and Dan could tell it was about to go down.

He kicked his feet free of the stirrups and flung himself out of the saddle before the chestnut could collapse and pin him underneath it. He landed hard on the ground and rolled over, and as he did another bullet kicked up dirt right beside him. Out in the open like this, he was an easy target.

The old stone corral was the nearest cover. The gate, made out of peeled pine poles, was closed, but Dan knew he could climb it. He leaped to his feet and sprinted toward it, another shot whistling past him as he did so. He jammed the Colt back in the holster so he would have both hands free.

He jumped onto the gate, grabbed the top pole, and vaulted over as a slug chewed splinters from the pine less than a foot from him. Dropping to the ground on the other side, he rolled behind the protection of the old stone wall.

He was penned in here with the two horses he and Laura had ridden the night before, but at least now he had that thick wall between him and the man who was trying to kill him.

Unfortunately, Jessica Stafford was still out there somewhere, in deadly danger herself. Dan grimaced as he tried to figure out his next move.

Then he heard hoofbeats drumming in the distance

as they steadily drew closer, and he wondered what else was about to go wrong now.

The shots fell silent as Stovepipe and Wilbur galloped toward the top of the hill. Stovepipe spotted a flash of green on the ground under some trees near the crest and pointed it out to Wilbur.

"Looks like that gal's hurt!" he called to his friend. "Check on her while I see what's on the other side of the hill!"

"Be careful!" Wilbur responded as he veered the dun toward the sprawled shape under the trees.

Stovepipe held the reins in his left hand and the Winchester in his right as he leaned forward in his saddle and sent the Palouse charging to the top of the hill. As he reached the crest, he saw an old stone corral part of the way down the far slope. A couple of horses were in the corral, and another saddle mount was moving around skittishly nearby.

A fourth horse, a chestnut that Stovepipe didn't recognize, was down on the ground, evidently badly wounded, judging by the way it was thrashing around feebly.

A man stood up behind the stone wall and pointed a revolver at him. Stovepipe almost jerked the rifle to his shoulder and blasted the hombre, but he recognized the man at the same time the fella realized who he was.

"Stovepipe!" Dan called.

"You all right?" Stovepipe asked him.

"Yeah, but there's a bushwhacker around somewhere!"

"Yeah, we heard the shootin'." Stovepipe pulled the Appaloosa around in a tight, 360-degree turn as he searched for the source of those shots.

No one else was in sight. It was possible the bushwhacker had taken off as soon as he spotted the two riders galloping up the hill toward him. Most varmints who would dry-gulch a man were back shooters who didn't like having the odds against them, Stovepipe knew.

He rode back and forth, keeping his eyes open, but after a few minutes had to admit that the gunman was gone. He turned the Appaloosa back toward the corral, where Dan waited.

"Looks like the polecat got away," Stovepipe reported as he reined in.

"What about Mrs. Stafford?" Dan asked anxiously.

"She might've been hit. Wilbur's checkin' on her."

Dan climbed quickly over the gate and caught the reins of the other saddled horse. He swung up and rode hard toward the hilltop. Stovepipe was right with him.

They topped the hill and saw Wilbur kneeling beside the woman, who was sitting up now and slowly shaking her head as if she were groggy. Stovepipe and Dan rode up to them and dismounted quickly. Dan knelt on the woman's other side and asked, "Mrs. Stafford, are you all right?"

"Yes, I . . . I think so," the woman said. She lifted a hand to her forehead, where a scratch was bleeding a little. That appeared to be her only injury. She went on, "When I heard that first shot I rode up to the top of the hill, Dan, even though you told me not to, and spotted a man under the trees with a rifle. He must have heard me, because he turned around and snapped a shot at me. It missed, but it spooked my horse and he threw me. That . . . that's all I really know until a minute or two ago when I came to and found this gentleman taking care of me."

She smiled at Wilbur, who immediately blushed.

Stovepipe said, "Looks like you must've hit your head when your horse throwed you, ma'am. Best be careful for a day or two. Gettin' knocked out's a tricky business. Sometimes you can't be sure how bad you're really hurt."

"That's good advice, Mr. . . . ?"

"Stewart, ma'am. They call me Stovepipe. That redheaded runt hoverin' over you is my pard Wilbur Coleman."

"Dan's told me a lot about both of you. I'm Jessica Stafford. My husband owns this ranch."

Stovepipe pinched the brim of his hat and said, "It's a plumb pleasure to meet you, ma'am. Just wish it was under better circumstances, that's all."

"You don't know how bad it really is, Stovepipe," Dan said. "Mrs. Stafford, I sure hate to tell you this, but—"

"It's Henry, isn't it?" she broke in. A look of bleak acceptance settled over her face. "Those buzzards we saw . . . it was his body attracting them, wasn't it?"

"I'm afraid so. He's down there by that old corral."

Jessica looked at Wilbur and said, "Please help me up."

"Of course, ma'am," he said.

While Wilbur was doing that, Stovepipe said, "Miz Stafford, it might be better if you was to wait here—"

"No," she interrupted sharply. "I want to see him. I *have* to see him."

With a solemn look wreathing his craggy face,

Stovepipe nodded. He wasn't going to tell a bereaved woman what she could or couldn't do. Everybody handled tragic losses in a different way.

With Wilbur beside her, his arm linked with hers in case she stumbled on the rough ground, Jessica headed down the hill to look at the body of her dead husband.

CHAPTER TWENTY-NINE

Henry Stafford had been shot once in the back. The bullet had gone through his body and exploded out of his chest, making a fist-sized hole in the process. He was lying on his stomach, but his head was turned far enough to the side so that his face was visible. His expression was one more of surprise than pain. He'd had just about enough time to realize that something bad had happened before he died, mused Stovepipe.

Jessica made a choking sound and turned toward Wilbur, who awkwardly put his arms around her, patted her tentatively on the back, and looked like he wished he could be anywhere else right now, even facing a horde of bloodthirsty Apaches. He grimaced as he looked over Jessica's shoulder to Stovepipe for help.

"Come on, Miz Stafford," the lanky cowboy said. "There ain't nothin' you can do here. We'll load up your husband's body and take it back to the ranch for you."

Jessica lifted her head from Wilbur's shoulder,

sniffled a little, and said, "You can't. You two and Dan are hiding out from the law, remember?"

"That doesn't matter," said Dan. "What's important is getting you home, where you'll be safe."

"Is any place in this basin safe anymore?" she asked.

None of the three men could answer that question.

"The three of you should stay here," Jessica went on. "I can get back to the ranch with Henry's body by myself."

"No, that's not going to happen," said Dan. "With rustlers and bushwhackers roaming around and killing people at will, it's not safe for you to ride back there by yourself. We're coming with you, and that's all there is to it."

Jessica looked like she wanted to argue some more, but instead she said, "All right. It'll be the middle of the day by the time we get there. Maybe most of the crew will be out on the range. There's a slim chance you'll be able to get out of sight in the house before anyone notices you."

"Don't worry about that, ma'am," Wilbur told her. "You've, uh, got more important things to concern yourself with right now."

"Yes. My husband is dead." For a second Jessica looked like she might crumple into tears again, but then she squared her shoulders and held her head up higher. "And if there's one thing I learned from being married to Henry, it's how to be a frontier woman. I'm not going to break down again, gentlemen—and I'm not going to rest until whoever murdered my husband is brought to justice."

Jessica walked back up into the trees while the men loaded Stafford's body on the horse that had brought him out here. Since the chestnut Dan had been riding was dead, he would travel back to the HS Bar headquarters on Stafford's horse with the rancher's corpse. When the men headed up to the hilltop, they found that Jessica was already mounted and ready to go.

"You folks head on," Stovepipe told the others. "I'll catch up."

"What are you going to do?" asked Dan.

"I want to take a look at the area where that bushwhacker was lurkin'."

The others continued south while Stovepipe turned back. He rode in and out of the trees along the hilltop for several minutes, studying the ground, the trunks, and everything else he could see. Then he wheeled his Appaloosa around and trotted after his companions, who were moving at a slower pace.

As he trotted up alongside them, Dan asked, "Did you find anything?"

"Nothin' helpful," replied Stovepipe. He noticed that Jessica was frowning and picking at one of the sleeves of her blouse. "Are you all right, ma'am, or as all right as you can be under the circumstances, anyway?"

"Yes, I'm just . . . This blouse is ruined! It got all snagged up when I fell off my horse. And . . . and Henry always loved it . . ."

Tears welled from her eyes again and rolled down her smooth, tanned cheeks. The men rode in silence, allowing her to work through her grief. Stovepipe turned his head and stared into the distance as he tugged briefly at his right earlobe, then ran his thumbnail along the line of his jaw.

As Jessica had said, it was close to midday by the

time they came in sight of the ranch headquarters. She reined in next to a brushy knoll, and the men followed suit.

"Surely it would be safe for me to go the rest of the way on my own," she said. "You can turn back now and hide out in the hills. Dan, you and I trade horses and I'll take Henry's body the rest of the way."

"I don't know," Dan began dubiously. "I'd like to make sure Laura's all right."

"She's bound to be. She's smart enough to have stayed out of sight in the house—"

Before Jessica could go on, hoofbeats suddenly sounded as a large group of riders surged around the knoll toward them. Jessica gasped in surprise, and Stovepipe, Wilbur, and Dan reached for their guns, only to stop as they realized that the newcomers were bristling with weapons, all pointed at the four of them.

Sheriff Frank Olsen, in the forefront of the group, bellowed, "Hold it, you varmints! I knew I'd catch up to you sooner or later. Nobody busts outta my jail and gets away with it!" He leveled the Colt in his fist at the three men and went on, "Get away from 'em, Miz Stafford. You're safe now."

"Sheriff, what are you—" Jessica began.

By now the posse had surrounded the four riders. Olsen frowned darkly as he exclaimed, "Good Lord! Is that—begging your pardon, ma'am—is that your husband draped over that horse?"

"Yes," said Jessica. "Henry was murdered last night, up in the hills where that old Spanish stone corral is. But these men had nothing to do with it."

"I don't know about that, but they're already in trouble for busting out of jail and Hartford still has a murder charge hanging over his head from Abel Dempsey's killing. Now, ma'am, please . . ."

Jessica looked helplessly at Stovepipe, Wilbur, and Dan. Stovepipe told her quietly, "It's all right, ma'am. You just need to go on inside your house and take care of ever'thing in there."

She looked at him for a moment, then nodded, seeming to understand that he was talking about Laura Dempsey. Just because he and Wilbur and Dan had been captured, there was no need for Laura to be locked up, too. Stovepipe knew Dan wouldn't mention that she was here at the HS Bar.

Jessica sighed and said, "All right. But don't worry, gentlemen. I'm sure the truth will come out sooner or later."

"I reckon you can count on that," Stovepipe told her.

The ring of possemen parted to let Jessica through. Olsen snapped, "Hartford, get down off that horse. Warren, you take Mr. Stafford's body and go on to the house with Mrs. Stafford."

"Sure, Sheriff," the deputy said as he moved his horse forward to take the reins from Dan, who dismounted and stood there.

"Ride double with Coleman," said Olsen as he gestured with his gun toward Wilbur.

"Careful, Sheriff," Wilbur said. "You don't want that hogleg going off by accident."

"If it goes off, it won't be an accident," Olsen said gruffly. "Now, hand over your guns, all of you."

Dan surrendered the revolver he had taken from Brock Matthews during the jailbreak, along with the rifle he had brought from the HS Bar ranch house early that morning. Stovepipe and Wilbur handed their Winchesters to members of the posse. Then, with Dan riding behind Wilbur, they all headed toward the house.

"Oh Lord, no," breathed Dan as they came in sight of the porch. Laura stood there with a couple of the temporary deputies flanking her.

"That's right," said Olsen. "We searched the house, too, and found her. Did you think we wouldn't?"

"I was hoping you'd have the sense to know that Laura is blameless in this whole mess," Dan said.

"I'm not so sure about that. I've had some time to think while we've been scouring the range for you fellas, and it's pretty obvious to me now that Mrs. Dempsey was in on the whole thing with you all along. Shoot, for all I know, she's the one who came up with the plan to murder her husband."

Dan stared at him in horror and said, "You can't mean that, Sheriff!"

"That would explain why she risked her neck breaking you out of jail," Olsen went on stubbornly. "She couldn't afford to leave you there and take a chance that you'd talk. I don't know if we can prove that killing Dempsey was her idea, but I reckon she's guilty of enough we *can* prove that she'll spend a good number of years behind bars."

Stovepipe could tell by the look in Dan's eyes that the young cowboy was about to lose control. If that happened, there was no telling what he might do. He might try to tackle one of the possemen and grab a gun, and if he did, they would probably all wind up getting shot. Stovepipe knew he couldn't get to the bottom of this mess with half a dozen holes blown through him.

"Dan," he said with an unmistakable intensity in his voice, "you got to take it easy here. Losin' your head ain't gonna do anybody any good."

"Take it easy?" Dan repeated. "Stovepipe, this badge-toting idiot is about to lock us up again!"

Olsen growled and moved his horse closer to the one carrying Wilbur and Dan.

"You'd best watch what you say, mister," warned the sheriff. "I'm about out of patience with you, and a good pistol-whipping won't keep you from standing trial for your crimes."

Wilbur turned his head to look at the man riding behind him and said, "Stovepipe's right, Dan. We've still got a few tricks up our sleeves."

"Well, you'd better not try 'em," snapped Olsen.

They had reached the house by now. Laura looked miserable as she said, "I'm sorry, Dan. There was no way I could keep them from finding me."

"It's not your fault," he told her. "None of it is."

Olsen moved his horse closer to the porch and told Laura, "You'll need to mount up now, ma'am. We're all on our way back to Hat Creek."

"So you can lock us up when we get there?" she challenged him.

"So I can do my job," Olsen said. "And yes, ma'am, that includes slamming a cell door behind each and every one of you!"

CHAPTER THIRTY

It was a gloomy quartet of prisoners who rode slowly toward Hat Creek with the members of the posse surrounding them. Dan and Laura both looked upset and worried. Stovepipe figured each of them was more concerned with the other, rather than with their own plight. Wilbur rode along stoically. Sheriff Frank Olsen and Deputy Warren Purdue led the group. Both of them seemed well pleased with themselves.

Being in captivity didn't stop Stovepipe's brain from working. His thoughts were racing as he considered all the things he had seen and heard since he and Wilbur had arrived in the Tonto Basin. There was a lot of information to sift through, but a vague picture was beginning to form in Stovepipe's mind. All the details weren't clear yet, though, and he still had to come up with evidence to support the nebulous theory.

After thinking for a few minutes longer, he nudged his horse ahead of the others. Several of the posse members immediately swung their guns toward him, and Deputy Purdue looked back over his shoulder and snarled, "Hey, there! You get back where you're supposed to be, mister."

"I need to talk to the sheriff," said Stovepipe.

"Save the talkin' for your trial—"

"I just want to ask a question," Stovepipe insisted.

Purdue was about to berate him some more, but Sheriff Olsen half turned in the saddle and lifted a hand to silence the deputy. Olsen frowned at Stovepipe and said, "What is it you want, Stewart?"

"All right to come up alongside of you?"

"Yeah, I suppose." Olsen drew his revolver and rested the barrel across the saddle in front of him. "Just don't try any tricks."

"No tricks," Stovepipe assured Olsen as he pulled the Appaloosa up alongside the lawman. Quietly, he continued, "How come you happened to be at the HS Bar to nab us like that, Sheriff?"

"What do you mean, 'happened to be'? I've been searching all over the basin ever since you varmints broke out of jail."

"I don't doubt it, but I've got a hunch somebody tipped you off to look for us today at Henry Stafford's ranch."

The creases on Olsen's forehead deepened as he said, "What makes you think that?"

"I'm right, ain't I?" asked Stovepipe, not answering the sheriff's question.

Olsen hesitated, then asked, "What if you are?"

"We can volley questions back and forth all day, Sheriff, without accomplishin' a durned thing."

"All right, blast it," snapped Olsen. "Yeah, a fella showed up in town this morning and came to the office to say he thought he'd spotted you out here. He was sure enough about it that I figured it was worth checking out."

"The hombre was a stranger, wasn't he?"

"How'd you know that?"

"Just a guess," said Stovepipe. "Some fella just driftin' through these parts, eh?"

Olsen glared at him and said, "You sound like you're trying to get at something, Stewart. Whatever it is, spit it out."

"Nope, just curious, is all," said Stovepipe with a shake of his head.

Olsen's skeptical snort made it clear that he didn't believe the lanky cowboy, but he didn't press the issue. Stovepipe dropped back again to ride next to Wilbur.

"I heard what you were saying to the sheriff," Wilbur said, quietly enough that only Stovepipe could hear him. "I agree with what he said. You've got something on your mind." He shrugged. "But then, when *don't* you have something on your mind?"

"Just a glimmerin' of an idea, Wilbur," said Stovepipe. "And it's so dang far-fetched I don't want to say anything about it. If I did, chances are you think I was a pure-dee idiot."

"You're about as far from a pure-dee idiot as anybody I've ever met." Wilbur shrugged. "But I also know it's no use trying to get you to talk when you're not ready, so I won't push you." He paused. "Are we *really* going to let Olsen lock us up again?"

"We'll see," Stovepipe said.

* * *

The arrival of the posse and its prisoners caused quite a bit of excitement in Hat Creek, just as had occurred a couple of days earlier in similar circumstances. If anything, the uproar in the settlement was even more dramatic this time, because Laura Dempsey, the widow of one of the basin's biggest ranchers, was among the prisoners being taken to jail.

As they approached the stone building, Dan said, "Sheriff, you can't lock Mrs. Dempsey in the same cell block as the rest of us. That just wouldn't be right, and you know it."

"Don't worry," said Olsen. "There's a special holding cell downstairs, attached to the sheriff's office. That's where the lady will stay."

"But that's still a jail cell," Dan said. "Can't you, I don't know, put her in a hotel room and have a deputy stand guard outside it?"

Laura said, "Dan, I don't need any special treatment."

"Well, ma'am, you'll be getting it whether you need it or want it or not," said Olsen. "Nobody's ever gonna be able to say that a woman was mistreated in my jail. But I'm not putting you up in a hotel room, either, not until a judge and jury have had their say about whether you had anything to do with your husband's murder."

"Blast it—" Dan began angrily.

"No, Dan, it's all right," Laura told him. "The sheriff's wrong, and sooner or later he's going to realize that. Until then I want to handle this with as much dignity as possible."

"You see that," Dan snapped at Olsen. "That's a lady for you."

"I never denied that," said the sheriff. "Problem is, a woman can be a lady and still be a murderer, too."

They reached the building housing the sheriff's office and jail and reined in. Olsen told the prisoners to stay on their horses until all the members of the posse had dismounted. Once they had done that, the men trained their guns on Stovepipe, Wilbur, Dan, and Laura. Olsen motioned for them to get down.

While they were doing that, a man wearing sleeve garters and a green eyeshade came along the boardwalk and stepped up to Olsen. Stovepipe saw the man hand a piece of paper to the sheriff. Olsen took the paper, which Stovepipe realized was a telegraph flimsy, and unfolded it.

The sheriff's bushy white eyebrows seemed to climb up his forehead as he read the message and his eyes widened in surprise.

Then the eyebrows dropped precipitously as the lawman scowled. He crumpled the telegram and shoved it in his pocket before giving the man who had delivered it a curt nod. If the fella expected a tip, he was clearly destined to be disappointed, because Olsen turned away in dismissal.

"See to it that Hartford's locked up in one of the cells upstairs, Warren," he told Deputy Purdue. "Stewart, Coleman, you're coming with me."

Purdue looked surprised. He said, "Sheriff, hadn't we better get these two behind bars, too?"

Dan said, "They shouldn't even be locked up. They haven't done anything wrong. Sheriff, no matter what you think of me, Stovepipe and Wilbur are innocent."

"Shut up." Olsen jerked a thumb toward the stairs. Purdue sighed, took hold of Dan's arm, and steered him roughly up the staircase toward the cell block.

The sheriff went on to Laura, "Ma'am, you're coming with me, too."

"All right," she said with a cool and reserved nod.

One of the possemen asked, "You want some of us to come with you to keep an eye on those prisoners, Sheriff?"

"No," Olsen said heavily. "I don't think they're going to give me any trouble."

Stovepipe and Wilbur exchanged a glance, then Stovepipe said, "No, sir, Sheriff, we sure won't."

He was telling the truth. He had an idea what might have been in the telegram the lawman had received, but he wanted to be sure of that before he said anything else.

Olsen kept his gun out and pointed in their general direction as they went inside. The building's thick stone walls meant that it was cooler in the shadowy hallway, and after riding in the sun for more than an hour, Stovepipe was grateful for that. Their footsteps echoed in the corridor.

The sheriff said, "Through that door up there on the left, Stewart."

The upper half of the door was pebbled glass. Painted on it in gilt letters were Olsen's name and the words COUNTY SHERIFF. The county seal was below the legend. Stovepipe opened the door and then stepped back to let Laura go first into an office with a couple of desks in it, at the moment unoccupied. One wall had a gun rack and a couple of cabinets on it; the other was decorated with photographs of Arizona's territorial governors, as well as the current president of the United States.

In the center of the back wall was a plain wooden door, again with Olsen's name on it, obviously leading to his private office. There was also a door in the right-hand wall, and when the sheriff opened it, it led into a small foyer with a barred cell on the left.

"This won't be the most comfortable place in the world for you, Mrs. Dempsey," Olsen said to Laura, "but at least you'll have some privacy. And I'll do what I can to make it better for you. I think we can get a better mattress and more blankets for the bunk, for starters."

"I appreciate that, Sheriff," she said. "I'm saddened, though, that you believe I could have had anything to do with my husband's death."

Olsen cleared his throat and said gruffly, "It's not my job to decide such things, ma'am. I just gather all the evidence I can and turn it over to the court to figure out."

Laura went into the cell and sat down on the bunk. She had said she wanted to be dignified about this, and she was managing that quite well, thought Stovepipe.

Olsen closed the cell door and said, "Somebody'll be around. If you need anything, just holler."

Laura nodded without saying anything.

Olsen stepped back out of the foyer in front of the holding cell and closed the door into the office. He went to one of the cabinets, took a key from his pocket, and unlocked it. Reaching inside, he took out two Colt's revolvers: one with an ivory handle, the other with plain walnut grips.

Stovepipe instantly recognized his gun, as well as Wilbur's.

Olsen set both guns on one of the desks, glared at the two drifters, and said, "You might as well take 'em back. I'm turning both of you loose."

"Now, why would you do that, Sheriff?" asked Stovepipe, although he was pretty sure he already knew the answer, and judging by the look on Wilbur's face, so did the redhead.

Olsen leaned forward, rested his hands on the desk, and said, "What else am I gonna do with a couple of dad-blasted range detectives?"

CHAPTER THIRTY-ONE

"Reckon the telegram that fella handed you outside musta spilled the beans," drawled Stovepipe.

"Yeah. It was from Cuthbert Farmington, president of the Arizona Territorial Cattle Raisers' Association, letting me know that a couple of undercover investigators named Stewart and Coleman, working for the association, are going to be in the Tonto Basin soon. He said you've been sent here at the request of some of the local ranchers to look into the rustling that's been going on and asks me to extend you every professional courtesy and as much assistance as I can."

Stovepipe smiled and said, "Yeah, ol' Cuthbert never uses one word when ten will do."

Sheriff Olsen straightened and then slammed an open hand down on the desk.

"Damn it, Stewart, when were you gonna tell me that we're on the same side of the law?"

"Seemed like we might have more of a chance of diggin' out the truth of what's goin' on around here if we kept quiet about that," Stovepipe said with a shrug. "Gen'rally speakin', when Wilbur and me ride into a case, we don't announce who we are until we've at least had a chance to get the lay of the land. This time, so much hellfire kept poppin' it seemed like there never was a good moment to bring it up."

Olsen's eyes suddenly narrowed suspiciously.

"I suppose you two can prove you're really the fellas that telegram was talking about?"

Stovepipe reached for his belt and said, "Sure."

From a little pocket cunningly concealed on the inside of the belt, he withdrew a folded square of paper. Wilbur took a similar piece of paper from a hiding place inside his right boot. They unfolded the documents and placed them on the sheriff's desk.

"Those are our bona fides," said Stovepipe. "You can see they give our names and descriptions and state that we're employees of the Cattlemen's Protective Association, the overall organization that the Arizona bunch belongs to."

Olsen studied the papers for a moment, then nodded even though he still appeared somewhat reluctant to accept the truth. It was pretty clear that Stovepipe and Wilbur weren't lying about their identities, though.

"How come you got here a couple of days before that telegram did?" asked the sheriff as he returned the identification papers.

"We made better time on the trail than Mr. Farmington expected us to," said Wilbur.

"And that's a good thing because it gave us a chance to poke around some," said Stovepipe. "Before we got here, we didn't know anything about the killin's. We just thought we were gonna be investigatin' some rustlin'. So it's even more of a hornet's nest here in the basin than we expected."

"Why'd you throw in with Hartford?"

"Well, that was just a matter of seein' a fella who was outnumbered and tryin' to give him a hand just on gen'ral principles. We've been tellin' you the truth about that part of it all along, Sheriff."

"Then you don't really know if Hartford is innocent or guilty," snapped Olsen. "For all you know, he really did bushwhack Abel Dempsey because he's in love with Mrs. Dempsey, or he could be part of the gang that's operating in these parts . . . or both. No reason it couldn't all be true."

"Except for the fact that we believe Dan."

Olsen shook his head and said, "You may believe him, but you don't have any proof he's innocent."

"Wellll . . ." drawled Stovepipe, "that ain't strictly true. We've come up with a few things. Some physical evidence, and some educated guesses—"

"Then tell me, by God!" exclaimed the lawman.

Stovepipe shook his head.

"There's a bunch more I ain't got figured out yet, and until I do, it'd probably be best to keep all those thoughts just a-meanderin' around inside my head."

"Blast it, I'm telling you as an officer of the law to explain what you're talking about!"

Wilbur said, "You're wasting your time, Sheriff. Until Stovepipe's ready to talk, you couldn't blast anything out of him with dynamite. Trust me, I know that from bitter experience."

Olsen continued to glare across the desk at them for several seconds before he put his hands on the guns and shoved them forward.

"Go on, take those hoglegs and get out of here."

"Not just yet," said Stovepipe.

The sheriff looked flabbergasted. He said, "Let me

get this straight . . . Now you don't *want* me to turn you loose? You'd rather be locked up with Hartford?"

"I didn't say that. But there's still a crowd outside, and it'll look mighty odd to them if Wilbur and me just walk outta here wearin' guns again, free as birds. There's a chance some of the bunch we're after might be in town, and if they see that, they're gonna be suspicious that there's more to the two of us than what they figured. For now, I'd rather have 'em keep on believin' that we're just a couple o' saddle tramps."

"How are you going to accomplish that?" Olsen wanted to know.

Stovepipe frowned in thought for a moment, then said, "Have the judge and the county attorney brought over here, that is, if you trust both of 'em."

"Judge Snow and Bert Wainwright are two of the finest men I know!"

"Been around these parts for a while, have they?"

"Going back twenty years, almost," said Olsen.

Stovepipe nodded and said, "Chances are they don't have any connection with the rustlers, then."

"If you knew them, you'd know how ridiculous it is to even consider that."

"I'll take your word for it, Sheriff. We'll swear 'em to secrecy, and then you can tell folks that the county attorney reduced the charges against us to misdemeanors and the judge fined us. It ain't the strongest story in the world, but it'll at least smooth over some suspicions, I reckon. That way we can get out and move around again."

Stovepipe could tell that the sheriff was mentally chewing over the idea. Finally Olsen said, "That might work. Some folks are liable to still be leery of you two, though."

"Can't be helped. We do the best we can with what we've got." Stovepipe smiled. "For now . . . just to make it look better . . . it might be a good idea for you to lock us up."

Wilbur groaned and said, "We're going behind bars again? You know how much I hate that, Stovepipe!"

"It'll only be for a little while," Stovepipe assured his old friend.

He hoped that prediction proved to be accurate.

Sheriff Olsen called a couple of his deputies, including Warren Purdue, and had Stovepipe and Wilbur taken upstairs to the cell block.

"No offense, Sheriff," said Purdue, "but I wondered how come these two weren't clapped behind bars right off."

"Because I wanted to question them, that's why," snapped Olsen. "Now get busy doing what I told you."

Dan Hartford looked downcast when the deputies brought in Stovepipe and Wilbur. He stood at the door of his cell, gripping the bars, and said, "Blast it, I was hoping that Olsen had come to his senses and realized that the two of you don't really have anything to do with this mess."

"Actually, maybe he's comin' around," said Stovepipe as he stepped into one of the empty cells. "He said somethin' about talkin' to the judge and the county attorney about the charges against us."

Wilbur added, "Maybe he's going to see about getting them reduced. He seemed to believe us this time when we told him we didn't have any connection with you until we rode into the basin a couple of days ago."

Deputy Purdue looked on, wide-eyed, as Stovepipe and Wilbur laid the groundwork for their impending release. After a second, he exclaimed, "You two are loco! Everybody knows you hellions are neck-deep in all the trouble that's been goin' on around here."

"Just 'cause we're neck-deep in it don't mean we caused any of it," Stovepipe pointed out.

Purdue's contemptuous snort showed how much he believed that idea—not at all.

The deputies went out, leaving Stovepipe, Wilbur, and Dan alone in the cell block. For a moment, Stovepipe considered telling Dan who he and Wilbur really were, since the sheriff knew now, but then he decided against it. As long as Dan was unaware that they were range detectives, he couldn't reveal that secret accidentally.

"I hope you're right about the law giving you a break," Dan said. "It's really not fair for you to be locked up, even though you did try to help me."

"And we busted outta jail," Stovepipe reminded him. "Most star packers tend not to look kindly on that, no matter what the facts o' the case are."

"Still, I'd like to see the two of you get out of here. For one thing . . ." Dan paused, then went on, "For one thing, I'm thinking maybe you'd keep on poking around in the basin. I think this whole thing has gotten your curiosity aroused, Stovepipe."

Wilbur said, "Ha! You've got this tall drink of water pretty well figured out, Dan, even if you've only known him for a few days. He's part bloodhound, part bulldog."

"Are you sayin' I've got fleas, Wilbur?" asked Stovepipe with a smile.

"Well, that, too, maybe."

Dan said, "So, if you get out of here, you'll keep on trying to find out the truth?"

"I reckon you can count on that, Dan," said Stovepipe.

Half an hour dragged by, then the cell block door opened and Deputy Purdue came in again, a scowl creasing his long, horsey face. He thrust a key into the lock on the door of Stovepipe's cell.

"Danged if I know why," he said, "but the sheriff's got Judge Snow and Bert Wainwright, the county attorney, down there in his office and he wants to see you two saddle tramps. I don't like it. No, sir, I don't like it one bit."

"It's all right, Deputy," Stovepipe told him. "I suspicion it's like the old hymn says, we'll understand it all by and by."

Judging by Purdue's unhappy expression, that assurance didn't do anything to make him feel better about the situation. He unlocked Wilbur's cell, too, however, and motioned with his drawn gun for both prisoners to leave the cell block and head downstairs.

A stocky, white-haired man in a brown tweed suit and a lean hombre with thinning gray hair, dressed in a sober black suit that made him look like a preacher, were waiting in Sheriff Olsen's office when Purdue ushered in Stovepipe and Wilbur. Olsen nodded to the deputy and said, "That'll be all, Warren."

Purdue said, "Don't you reckon I'd better stay and keep an eye on these two troublemakers?"

"That won't be necessary."

Purdue didn't like it, but he went out and closed the door behind him. Stovepipe did his best not to grin at the deputy's frustration. He figured Purdue would soon be a lot more discombobulated.

Olsen nodded at the white-haired man and said, "This is Judge Thaddeus Snow."

Stovepipe said, "Pleased to meet you, Your Honor."

"And County Attorney Bert Wainwright," added Olsen, indicating the sober fellow who looked as much like a sky pilot as a lawyer.

Judge Snow said, "Sheriff Olsen has explained the situation to us, gentlemen, and asked for our cooperation in the matter. As representatives of the law, Mr. Wainwright and I are always happy to cooperate with such an esteemed organization as the Arizona Territorial Cattle Raisers' Association."

By which the judge meant that since he and Wainwright were elected officials, and the ATCRA could wield a lot of influence in political campaigns, they didn't want to get on the wrong side of that bunch, mused Stovepipe. But he certainly wasn't averse to taking advantage of such influence if it helped him and Wilbur uncover the truth behind the hell-raising in the Tonto Basin.

"Therefore," continued the judge, "after much consultation between the sheriff, Mr. Wainwright, and myself, we have decided to drop the charges of attempted murder against the two of you and reduce the other charges to two counts of creating a public disturbance. I find you guilty on both counts and as empowered by the laws of the Territory of Arizona, I fine you ten dollars apiece for these misdemeanors."

Stovepipe took a double eagle from his pocket and placed it on the sheriff's desk.

"There you go," he said. "I reckon Wilbur and I are free to go now?"

Olsen shoved their guns across the desk and growled, "I tried to get you to leave an hour ago, but you wanted to do it this way."

Stovepipe picked up the ivory-handled Colt, checked the cylinder, and then holstered the gun. Wilbur did likewise with his plainer revolver. It felt good to have a gun on his hip again, thought Stovepipe. He'd been packing iron for so long that being without it almost made him walk slantwise.

Stovepipe touched a finger to the brim of his black hat and said, "Much obliged to you, fellas. Wilbur and I will be around. Just keep it under your hats who we really are."

"Go on, get out of here," said Olsen. The sheriff was cooperating with them, but Stovepipe could tell he wasn't that happy about having outside investigators poking around in his county. Most lawmen felt the same way.

The two of them walked out of the building. Stovepipe paused and took a deep breath.

"Nothin' like breathin' free air and feelin' free sunlight shinin' on your face," he said.

"What are we gonna do now, Stovepipe?" asked Wilbur.

"Now we see if anybody has any interest in hirin' a couple of driftin' cowboys," said Stovepipe.

CHAPTER THIRTY-TWO

Before they could get started on that, Stovepipe noticed a wagon down the street as it pulled up and came to a stop in front of one of the buildings. A man who looked like a typical cowpuncher was at the reins, but sitting beside him was a woman dressed all in black, including the veil that covered her face.

Despite the mourning outfit, something about the woman caught the eye. Perhaps it was the slight flash of golden hair under the black hat and veil, or the way the sober dress didn't quite conceal the appealing lines of her body.

Stovepipe set off toward the wagon with his usual long-legged stride. Wilbur hurried to catch up and then keep up.

"Stovepipe, what are you doing?" asked the redhead.

"Payin' my respects to the widow," Stovepipe said. "That's Miz Stafford yonder."

"Yeah, I can see that. I'm not sure she wants anything to do with us, though."

"Well, it don't cost nothin' to be polite, and it don't hurt nothin', neither, my mama always said."

As the two men approached the wagon, they doffed their hats and held the Stetsons in front of their chests. The driver had already climbed down from the vehicle, but Jessica Stafford was still perched on the seat.

"Ma'am," said Stovepipe as he and Wilbur came to a stop beside the wagon, "Wilbur and me would like to extend our deepest condolences."

Up close like this, Jessica's face was visible through the veil. Stovepipe could see the surprise on her features as she said, "Thank you, Mr. Stewart, and you, too, Mr. Coleman." She paused. "To be honest, I didn't expect to see the two of you like this. I was under the impression Sheriff Olsen was going to lock you up."

"Oh, he did, ma'am," Stovepipe told her. "But the county attorney decided to reduce the charges against us, and the judge done fined us already. We paid up, and we're free men."

Jessica smiled faintly under the veil.

"Actually, I'm glad to hear that, Mr. Stewart. The two of you strike me as honest men who were unfortunate enough to find yourselves in a bad situation. And you certainly helped me as much as you could under the . . . the tragic circumstances."

She glanced over her shoulder into the back of the wagon, where a blanket-shrouded form lay. Stovepipe knew that was the body of her husband, Henry.

"If there's anything else we can do for you . . ." he said.

"I'm afraid everything that needs to be done right

now is the province of the undertaker." She hesitated. "Although . . ."

"Yes'm?" asked Stovepipe.

"What do the two of you intend to do now? Will you be moving on out of the basin?"

"Well, it's true Wilbur and me are a mite fiddle-footed . . . but we thought we might stay around these parts for a spell yet, even though they ain't been very hospitable so far."

"Perhaps we can change that. I feel like I owe you something for the help you gave me—"

"Oh no, ma'am, not really."

"Yes," Jessica insisted. "I'd like for you to come work for me. The HS Bar can always use another couple of good hands, especially at a time like this when things are in such an uproar. You *have* worked with cattle before, haven't you?"

Wilbur said, "Ma'am, Stovepipe here was one of the top hands in the whole blamed state of Texas when he was younger. And I've looked at the south end of more northbound cows than I could ever re-member, let alone count!"

"It's settled, then," said Jessica as she smiled again under the veil. "The two of you are now riding for the HS Bar."

"You don't want to check with your foreman before you go to hirin' anybody?" asked Stovepipe.

A note of steel entered Jessica's voice as she said, "It's my ranch now, Mr. Stewart, and I'll hire whoever I want to."

"Yes, ma'am."

The man who had driven the wagon into town had gone into the building, which according to the sign on the awning above the boardwalk was the Hat Creek undertaking parlor. He came back out now, accompanied by a lean, middle-aged, fair-haired man in a gray suit.

"Mrs. Stafford, my deepest sympathy on your loss," he said.

"Thank you, Mr. Brewer," Jessica said.

"If you'd care to come inside with me, out of the heat, we can make all the necessary arrangements. Wilkins can drive the wagon around to the back, where my boys are waiting, and they'll take care of everything else."

"You're too kind," murmured Jessica. As she started to get down from the wagon, Stovepipe quickly clapped the hat back on his head and held out a hand to help her.

Once she was on the boardwalk, she turned to look at Stovepipe and Wilbur again and told them, "I'll see you gentlemen out at the ranch."

"Yes'm, we'll be there," Stovepipe assured her.

"The foreman's name is Bob Ridgewell. When you get there, tell him that I hired you. There won't be any problem."

"Yes, ma'am."

The undertaker stood aside from the door and ushered her into the building. The HS Bar puncher climbed onto the wagon, took the reins, and drove around the building, leaving Stovepipe and Wilbur standing there in the street next to the boardwalk.

"Riding jobs," said Wilbur. "You got us riding jobs. Was that what you intended when we walked over here?"

"Not exactly, but I reckon the idea might've been in the back of my mind," admitted Stovepipe. "Think about it, Wilbur. The rustlers pulled out o' that hideout on the Box D and seemed to be headed toward the Stafford spread. Chances are, whatever hell breaks loose next is gonna be on the HS Bar."

"And we'll be right in the middle of it," Wilbur said.

"Well," said Stovepipe with a grin, "that seems to be the way it's workin' out."

Their horses had been put in the livery stable when they reached Hat Creek as prisoners, so that was where they headed now to reclaim the Appaloosa and the dun. They drew a lot of suspicious looks. The big crowd that had been on hand earlier had dispersed, but there were still quite a few people on the street and it appeared that most of them were surprised to see the two drifters out of jail and walking around free.

The old-timer who ran the livery stable certainly was. He was holding a pitchfork when Stovepipe and Wilbur walked in, so he clutched it tighter and leveled the tines at the two of them.

"Did you fellas bust outta jail again?" he asked.

"No, the judge fined us and let us go," said Stovepipe.

"Fined you? For throwin' in with a killer and breakin' jail?"

Wilbur said, "Dan's no killer, and as for the jailbreak, there were what you call mitigrating circumstances."

The liveryman frowned and said, "I never heard of no such blasted thing."

"Well, if Wilbur says it, you can be sure it's right,"

Stovepipe told him. "Anyway, we're free men again, and we've come to get our hosses."

"Gonna rattle your hocks and shake off the dust of this part of the country, eh?"

"Actually, we're stayin' around for a while. Got ridin' jobs out at the Stafford spread."

"What? You mean Bob Ridgewell hired you? I didn't know he was even in town."

"Nope. Miz Stafford did the hirin'. Seems like she's gonna take the reins and run the ranch."

The old-timer's frown deepened as he said, "A woman runnin' a ranch? I don't know how the crew's gonna take to that. But I reckon it ain't none o' my business." He pointed. "Your nags are in those stalls over yonder. You can saddle 'em your ownselves. The county pays me a mere pittance for stablin' prisoners' horses, and it ain't enough for me to have to saddle the blamed things, to boot!"

Chuckling to themselves at the irascible oldster's complaints, Stovepipe and Wilbur went to saddle the Appaloosa and the dun. A few minutes later they rode out of Hat Creek, still on the receiving end of quite a few curious, even suspicious and hostile, stares.

"Appears that folks around here don't like us—or trust us," commented Wilbur as they left the settlement behind.

"I don't figure on losin' much sleep over that. The time'll come when they understand what's goin' on."

"Assuming *we* ever figure that out."

"Oh, we will," Stovepipe said with easy assurance.

Wilbur looked over at his old friend. After a moment, he said, "You've got the whole thing figured out already, don't you?"

"Nope, not hardly. Like I told you before, there's

just a far-fetched idea rattlin' around up there in my noggin, and it's liable to die for lack of company if I don't come up with somethin' else pretty soon."

"Yeah, sure," said Wilbur, his tone making it clear he didn't really accept Stovepipe's explanation.

It was late afternoon by the time the two men reached the headquarters of the HS Bar. They had seen punchers tending to the stock grazing on HS Bar range, but no one had challenged them. That changed now as a short but wide-shouldered man with curly brown hair emerged from the bunkhouse and strode toward them. Stovepipe and Wilbur reined in.

The man kept his hand close to the butt of the revolver on his hip as he said, "I recognize you two. You were with Dan Hartford earlier today. When you left here, you were under arrest."

"Well, now we ain't," said Stovepipe. "The judge believed us when we told him we didn't have anything to do with Hartford and didn't even know him until a couple of days ago. He fined us for disturbin' the peace and makin' public nuisances of ourselves, since none of the trouble was deliberate-like, and then let us go."

"So what are you doing here?" the man wanted to know.

"We talked to Miz Stafford in town, and she hired us."

"Hired you!" exclaimed the man. "What the hell!"

Stovepipe said, "Reckon you must be Bob Ridgewell, the foreman around here."

"That's right. And I do the hiring and firing, along with Mr.—"

Ridgewell stopped short and frowned. Stovepipe

said, "Along with Mr. Stafford, I reckon you were fixin' to say. I understand how you feel, Bob. Truth to tell, I was a mite worried that Miz Stafford might be steppin' on your toes a little by offerin' us ridin' jobs. But we can use the work, and if you'll allow me a little braggin', we're pretty good hands."

"Top hands," added Wilbur.

"But if you want to go against Miz Stafford's decision and tell us to ride on," continued Stovepipe, "we'll sure do it. We ain't keen on stayin' anywhere we ain't wanted. Ain't that right, Wilbur?"

Before the redhead could answer, Ridgewell shook his head and said, "No, no, that's all right. With the boss gone, I reckon Mrs. Stafford is calling the shots around here now. I can put up with that, as long as she doesn't get too high-handed about it."

"So we can stay on for a spell?"

Ridgewell pointed and said, "Put your horses in the corral over there. There are several empty bunks in the bunkhouse. Claim whichever ones you want. Supper's not far off. Get yourselves a meal and a good night's sleep and then get up in the morning ready to work."

"Oh, we will be," Stovepipe said. "Come mornin', we'll be ready to do our jobs, you can count on that."

CHAPTER THIRTY-THREE

Even if Stovepipe and Wilbur had been mere strangers, the crew of the HS Bar would have wanted to take their measure. As it was, their connection, however tenuous, to Dan Hartford and their presence that morning soon after Henry Stafford's body had been found, combined to make the other hands in the bunkhouse downright suspicious.

The men kept that feeling in check until after the evening meal, when everyone had returned to the crew's quarters. After unsaddling their horses and putting them in one of the corrals, as Bob Ridgewell had told them to, Stovepipe and Wilbur had carried their war bags and rifles into the bunkhouse and placed them on a couple of empty bunks in the far rear corner. Those bunks were the farthest from the stove and the windows, so that corner would be chilly in the winter and hot and stuffy in the summer.

Stovepipe didn't figure he and Wilbur would be around here long enough for either of those things to become a problem.

They were sitting on their bunks, Wilbur reading a dime novel he had taken from his bag and Stovepipe cleaning and oiling the ivory-handled Colt, when one of the punchers approached them. The man was heavy shouldered but had a born horseman's lean hips. Dark beard stubble dotted his jaw, which he thrust out belligerently as he said, "Bob tells us you hombres have signed on to ride for the HS Bar."

"That's right," Stovepipe said mildly. "My name's Stewart. My pard is Coleman."

"We know who you are," the man snapped. "You left here under arrest this mornin'."

"Well, we're not under arrest now," said Wilbur without looking up from the book with its flimsy yellow cover and dense, tiny print.

"That's right," said Stovepipe. "We've done paid our debt to society."

"That doesn't explain what you were doing with Dan Hartford, or how come the three of you showed up so convenient-like not long after the boss was killed."

"Are you saying you think we had anything to do with that?" asked Wilbur. "If you are, you'd better go ahead and spit it out plain."

"I wasn't talkin' to you, you little redheaded gink," said the man. He gestured toward Stovepipe. "I was talkin' to this scarecrow."

That finally prompted Wilbur to set the book aside and start to stand up from his bunk, but Stovepipe lifted a hand slightly and Wilbur subsided.

"Reckon I do have a mite of a resemblance to a scarecrow," Stovepipe said. "That don't mean I enjoy bein' reminded of it."

"I don't give a hang what you enjoy, jailbird. This is an honest crew, and we don't like havin' no-account saddle tramps forced on us."

"Well, I reckon you can take that up with the boss," said Stovepipe coolly.

"No, I can't. He's dead. And if he was still alive, he never would've hired the likes of you two!"

Stovepipe had continued working on his revolver while he talked. He didn't need to pay a great deal of attention to the task. He had carried it out so many times over the years that his fingers did the necessary work almost without any mental urging.

Finished now, he picked up the cartridges he had removed from the gun earlier and laid them on the bunk. As he thumbed them into the cylinder, he said quietly, "Looks like this might turn out to be a plumb unfriendly place, Wilbur."

"Yeah, I'm getting that idea," Wilbur responded in a hard, angry voice.

The burly cowboy who had confronted them looked a little less sure of himself now, and that feeling seemed to grow as Stovepipe snapped the gun's cylinder closed. The man relaxed slightly, however, as Stovepipe slid the Colt into the holster attached to the coiled shell belt he had also placed on the bunk.

Stovepipe stood up. With a friendly smile on his rugged face, he said, "Wilbur and me, we ain't lookin' for any trouble. Now, I'll admit, sometimes it seems like *trouble* looks for *us*, because it sure enough finds us pretty often. But all we want is to do the jobs we signed on for."

The cowboy must have thought that Stovepipe's mild tone meant he had succeeded in buffaloing the two newcomers. He sneered and said, "Well, trouble's sure found you this time, mister, because we don't want you here."

With that, he reached down to the bunk and shoved Stovepipe's war bag off onto the floor. The bag was open, and Stovepipe's spare clean shirt fell out.

Stovepipe looked down at the shirt and with a solemn expression on his face, he shook his head.

"I sure wish you hadn't done that," he said.

"Yeah?" said the troublemaker. "Why not?"

"Well, there's been enough mud and who knows what else tracked in here over the years that I reckon I wouldn't feel right about wearin' that shirt until I'd washed it. I never was much of one for doin' laundry."

The cowboy let out a harsh laugh and said, "Is that it? I figured you were gonna take a swing at me."

"Over a shirt?" Stovepipe shook his head. "No, I reckon I'm a lot more peaceable man than that. I don't care much for fightin'."

"A peaceable man, eh? Then you won't mind if I do this."

The cowboy poked Stovepipe in the chest hard enough to make the lanky drifter move back a step.

"I don't much cotton to bein' laid hands on, though," said Stovepipe.

"What are you gonna do about it? You already said you weren't gonna fight."

"When did I say that?" asked Stovepipe with a puzzled frown creasing his forehead. "I said I didn't *like* to fight. I never said I wouldn't do it."

That was all the warning the troublesome cowboy got, and it was just enough to cause a look of surprise to appear on his face before Stovepipe uncorked a thunderbolt of a punch that landed squarely on his jaw, lifted him off his feet, and spilled him across one of the other bunks, scattering the hand of solitaire that the occupant of said bunk was dealing there.

"Hey!" that individual exclaimed as he leaped to his feet and charged toward Stovepipe.

Wilbur surged off his bunk and got in the second man's way. He planted himself and hooked a right into the man's midsection with all the considerable power of his stocky body behind it. Wilbur's fist sunk almost wrist-deep in the man's belly. The hombre's eyes opened wide as his breath whooshed out of his mouth and he doubled over.

Wilbur brought up a left uppercut that clicked the man's teeth together and made his eyes go glassy. He toppled over backward.

Before the second man even hit the floor, several more members of the HS Bar crew had leaped to their feet and charged toward Stovepipe and Wilbur. The two old friends stood back to back and met the attack. Their rock-hard fists lashed out with blinding speed and landed with the sharp crack of bone against bone as they targeted their opponents' jaws and chins.

Some of the cowboys reeled back from those potent blows, but others ignored the punishment they received and pressed the attack. Stovepipe weaved aside from a punch, but it still landed on his shoulder with enough force to knock him back a step and disrupt his defense. Another man took advantage of that opportunity to bore in and slug Stovepipe a couple of times in the belly.

Wilbur had his hands full, too. The men crowded around him, raining punches on him. He hunched his shoulders and pulled his head in, sort of like a turtle, and tried to make the blows glance off as he moved back and forth. His fists snapped out and peppered the men around him with short but powerful punches.

Stovepipe, short of breath from the punches to his midsection, was being crowded backward. He knew he would trip over one of the bunks if he kept going in that direction, so he let one of the attackers get close to him, suddenly grabbed the front of the man's shirt, and heaved as he pivoted. The perfectly timed wrestling throw sent the man flying over Stovepipe's outthrust hip. The man yelled in alarm, but only for a second before he crashed down on one of the bunks, which broke under his weight and spilled him to the floor amidst the debris that was left. Tangled in the blanket, the man couldn't get back up.

That put one man out of the fight, at least for a few moments. Another cowboy lunged at Stovepipe and tried to grab him from behind. Stovepipe bent forward, reached back, grabbed the man, and executed another throw. This man landed on the first one. Their heads banged together with an audible *clunk!* and knocked them even sillier.

As Stovepipe wheeled around, he saw that he still faced two opponents. They were closing in on him, arms cocked to throw punches. Stovepipe glanced past them to the spot where Wilbur was fighting with three men and apparently getting the worst of it. The redhead was still landing some blows, but the cowboys around him battered him back and forth like a punching bag.

The cowboys facing Stovepipe charged at him. He ducked and went between them, sweeping his long arms up and out. His fists caught them on the ears and knocked them off their feet.

Stovepipe had a clear path to the men tangling with Wilbur. He never liked to hit a man from behind, but in this case he was going to make an exception. He clubbed his fists together and swung them against the back of the closest man's neck. The hombre went down, and the limp way he fell told Stovepipe he was out cold.

At that instant, Wilbur got a punch past another man's upraised arms and landed it on the fella's nose. Cartilage popped and blood spurted. The man reeled back, howling in pain.

Just like that, the odds were two to one in Stovepipe and Wilbur's favor. The lone remaining HS Bar puncher tried to back off, but the two range detectives had their dander up by now. Wilbur hooked a left to the man's jaw that knocked him halfway around, setting him up perfectly for the right cross Stovepipe threw. That punch landed with a sound like an ax biting into a block of wood, and the man's knees unhinged as his eyes rolled up in their sockets. He hit the floor, too.

Three men, all of them older cowboys who had probably participated in their own share of fracases when they were younger, had sat this one out, remaining on their bunks and grinning as they enjoyed the show. A little breathless now, Stovepipe looked at these three men and said, "You boys ain't takin' cards in this game?"

"Shoot, no," replied one of the punchers. "Miz

Stafford is the boss now, and if she wants to hire you fellers, that's her business."

The bunkhouse door opened, and Bob Ridgewell stepped in, stopping abruptly to stare in surprise at the bodies littering the floor in the far corner.

"What in blue blazes happened here?" the foreman exploded.

"I reckon you've got a pretty good idea, Bob," said Stovepipe. "Those fellas decided they wanted to see what sorta stuff Wilbur and me are made of."

Ridgewell grunted and said, "It looks like they found out. You didn't kill any of them, did you?"

"Appears they're all still breathin'."

"Break any bones so they can't work?"

"I don't think so."

"Well, then, I guess it's all over. This doesn't make me trust the two of you any more than I did, though."

"What were we supposed to do?" demanded Wilbur. "Just sit there and let them whale the tar out of us?"

"I suppose you're right," Ridgewell admitted with a shrug. "A man's got to defend himself." He looked over at the three older cowboys. "Is that the way it happened?"

"Stewart told you the truth, Bob," one of them said. "Bradley's the one who started the ruckus."

"Fine." Ridgewell started to turn away, then paused and added to Stovepipe and Wilbur, "Just don't make a habit of brawling."

"Don't worry, Bob," Stovepipe assured him. "We're plumb peace lovin'."

The foreman just gave him a dubious look and went out.

Wilbur said, "You do realize that was your bunk that got busted to pieces, don't you, Stovepipe?"

Stovepipe looked and sounded disgusted as he exclaimed, "Well, I'll be danged if you ain't right, Wilbur!"

CHAPTER THIRTY-FOUR

Stovepipe and Wilbur were both sore and bruised the next morning, but the battering the other men in the fight had taken meant that they were moving around even more stiffly. Some of them glared at Stovepipe and Wilbur and muttered under their breath, but none of them tried to stir up any trouble.

The three older hands seemed to have accepted the newcomers. At breakfast in the mess hall that morning, as dawn lightened the sky outside, they sat down at the same end of the long table where Stovepipe and Wilbur had been sitting alone.

"You fellas ain't worried you'll catch the leprosy from us?" asked Stovepipe.

"I reckon not," said one of the cowboys. He had gray hair and a mustache, and the hand he extended across the table bore the scars and calluses of many years working with horses and cattle. "Name's Gene Hawkins. These other fellas are Bill Cunningham and Jonas Powell."

"Pleased to meet you," said Stovepipe. He and Wilbur shook and howdied with all three men, then they all devoted their attention to the plates of food and cups of coffee. On a ranch, it was a long haul between breakfast and lunch, with plenty of hard work in between, so a fella had to stoke the fires when he had the chance.

Bob Ridgewell came in while the men were still eating. Evidently he didn't take his meals with the crew, because all he claimed from the cook was a cup of coffee. He stood at the head of the table sipping from the cup for a few moments before he started doling out the day's assignments.

Ridgewell worked his way down the table, finally getting to Stovepipe, Wilbur, and their newfound friends. The foreman said, "I want all five of you to ride over to the rim and comb those canyons along the base of it. You know how cows like to wander up in there and get themselves caught in the brush."

Hawkins said, "It ain't been that long since we been through there, Bob. I doubt if many head have strayed up yonder in that time."

"I'm the one who makes those decisions," snapped Ridgewell. "That's the job I've given you."

"And we'll do it," said Hawkins. "Just makin' sure."

"I don't give any orders unless I'm sure about them."

Ridgewell gulped down some more of the coffee, set down the cup, and stalked out.

"That hombre's sure got a burr under his saddle," said Stovepipe.

"And we're the ones who put it there," added Wilbur.

"Don't worry about it," the mournful-faced Bill Cunningham told them. "Bob's just got his nose a mite out of joint because he's been the foreman here for a long time and worked pretty close with Mr. Stafford. Havin' Missus Stafford in charge is a big change for him. But he's a fair man. Give him a good day's work, day in and day out, and he'll come around."

"That's what we intend to do," Stovepipe said, nodding.

When breakfast was finished, they went out to the barn and the corrals with the others to saddle their horses. The sun still wasn't up yet, but the eastern sky was a spectacular mix of blue and rose and gold above the dark line of the Mogollon Rim. That was where Stovepipe, Wilbur, and the three older punchers would be headed shortly.

As they rode out, Stovepipe said, "I'm guessin' this chore Bob gave us ain't one of the most coveted jobs around here."

The three men chuckled. Hawkins said, "You're right about that. That's rough country over there around the rim. Lots of canyons and draws, and every one of 'em is full of prickly pear, briar vines, and sticker bushes. Throw in the rattlers and scorpions, and everywhere you look there's liable to be something that wants to bite you, sting you, or stick you."

Wilbur said, "As long as the rattlesnakes and scorpions don't start shooting at us, I reckon we can deal with the rest of it."

Jonas Powell, who evidently didn't talk much, said, "Some of those scorpions are damn near big enough to handle a gun." That brought chuckles from the other men.

The sun peeked above the rim a few minutes later and sent golden light washing across the landscape, making even the rugged terrain beautiful. Stovepipe and Wilbur had been just about everywhere west of the Mississippi, because they were always moving around in their job. Stovepipe was the sort of hombre who found something to like about the places everywhere they went. Every part of the country had its own special beauty, he had reflected more than once. Sometimes that beauty was on the stark side, but he still appreciated it.

Like many Western ranches, the HS Bar sprawled out over a lot of square miles of acreage. It took half the morning just to get close to the Mogollon Rim. As they rode, the men saw quite a few head of stock grazing peacefully. Those cattle weren't their concern. They were after the animals that had wandered into the rough country along the rim's base and for one reason or another couldn't make their way back.

As they approached the rugged escarpment and entered a broad pasture, Gene Hawkins waved an arm to indicate the long, irregular sweep of the rim and said, "We'll have to split up to cover the ground. Any cows you find, drive 'em out here to this pasture. Jonas, you stay here to keep them from wandering right back to where we found them."

Powell nodded and said, "All right, Gene."

"Stewart, you and Coleman head north. One of you can go about a mile and then start working your way back in this direction. The other needs to ride on for another mile and do the same, until you get back to where the first fella started. Bill and I will do the same thing to the south. There'll be a lot of riding back and forth, but it can't be helped. Hope you boys don't mind me giving the orders."

"From the sound of it, you've been handlin' this

chore for a while," said Stovepipe. "Only makes sense that you'd be the straw boss."

"I'm glad you feel that way." Hawkins lifted a hand in farewell. "See you fellas later."

He and Cunningham headed south while Stovepipe and Wilbur turned north. Powell continued on toward the rim to look for a good place to hold the gather.

After they had ridden for a while, Wilbur commented, "Those three seem like pretty friendly hombres. Not like the bunch we tangled with last night."

"Aw, those other fellas'll come around, once they see we ain't as bad as they think we are," said Stovepipe.

"What do you think the chances are some of them are mixed up with that gang of rustlers?"

"Well, you can't ever rule out the possibility of a bad bunch havin' an inside man. But from all the talk I've heard, we're the first new hands on the HS Bar in a while, so I don't think it's very likely any of 'em have thrown in with the gang. Now, if there were a bunch of new men workin' on the ranch, that might be a different story."

"Are we really going to work those draws and canyons for strays?"

"Sure. Got to do our jobs, or the fellas really won't accept us. But there's nothin' stoppin' us from keepin' our eyes open for other things, is there?"

"Like what?" asked Wilbur.

"Our theory is that the gang has moved on to the HS Bar and is hidin' out someplace either on the spread or close by. From what I've seen of the ranch so far, most of it is open range. Good graze for the cattle, but not many places where a gang of outlaws could hide. Except . . ."

Stovepipe inclined his head toward the rim.

"And we're bound for that rough country anyway," said Wilbur. "I get your point. We need to watch for tracks of a big group of riders, or any other sign that bunch has been around here."

"That's my thinkin'," agreed Stovepipe. "Be mighty careful, though. If they're really up here, there's a chance we might stumble right into 'em. If that happened while we're split up, that wouldn't be good."

"Yeah, because two guns against thirty or forty is much better odds than one gun against that many," said Wilbur.

"Twice as good, if I'm doin' the cipherin' right," Stovepipe said cheerfully.

A short time later, they estimated that they had ridden a mile. Wilbur said that he would start his gather here and drift back toward Powell's position. Stovepipe waved to his friend and rode on.

The sun was high enough overhead by now that a mantle of heat lay over the landscape. In the draws and canyons it was even worse, Stovepipe discovered when he had covered another mile and begun his task.

The brush was as bad as Gene Hawkins had warned them, too. Stovepipe dismounted and took a pair of chaps from his saddlebags. He'd had them ever since his brush-popping days in the South Texas chaparral, learning the cowboy trade from a bunch of leathery brown vaqueros. Buckaroos, some folks had started calling them, adapting the Spanish word into something that was pure Texan.

The chaps helped, but Stovepipe still got stuck and

scraped and scratched quite a bit by the inhospitable vegetation. Sweat soaked his shirt as he pushed cattle out of those canyons and back onto open range. It was hot, dusty, miserable work, but having been raised a cowboy, a certain part of him still exulted in it.

Being a detective was better, though, even if it meant he got shot at on a fairly regular basis.

He didn't immediately drive the stock he found back down to the pasture where Jonas Powell was waiting. Instead he continued gathering them until he had a dozen or more. Even so, he made a couple of trips there as the day wore on. He didn't see Wilbur but knew his friend was around.

Lunch was biscuits and jerky brought from the ranch headquarters, washed down by water from his canteen. He had just finished the last of the food when the sound of a distant shot floated through the air.

Stovepipe tensed in the saddle. The shot had come from somewhere south of him, but he couldn't tell if it had originated in the area where Wilbur was searching or somewhere beyond that. He listened intently to see if there were going to be any more shots but heard only silence once the echoes had died away.

Worry gnawed at Stovepipe's gut. He had a small jag of five cattle that he had combed out of a draw, so he headed them south. He wanted to find out if his old friend was all right before he did anything else.

CHAPTER THIRTY-FIVE

Stovepipe spent a nervous ten minutes driving the cattle south before he caught a glimpse of a familiar figure on horseback several hundred yards away. The rider was pushing some cows along a course that would intercept his. Figuring that Wilbur had spotted him, too, Stovepipe took off his hat and waved it over his head. Wilbur returned the signal, and both men hurried on.

When they came together a few minutes later, Wilbur greeted Stovepipe by saying, "I reckon you heard that shot a little while ago, too."

"I sure did. Was a mite worried that it could've been aimed at you."

Wilbur shook his head and said, "No, it came from farther down along the rim, I think. I wasn't sure it was anything to worry about, but I didn't figure it would hurt to check it out."

"Same here," said Stovepipe. "One of the other fellas could've killed a rattler, I reckon, since there was only one shot and there are plenty of the scaly varmints around."

"That's the most likely explanation," Wilbur said with a nod.

Neither man looked like he really believed that, however. They pooled the cattle they had been driving and continued toward the big pasture.

A short time later, as they were drawing closer to their destination, Stovepipe suddenly reined in and pointed.

"Look there, Wilbur," he said. "Over by those trees. Ain't that a saddled hoss with no rider?"

"It dang sure is," snapped Wilbur. "It looks like the horse Jonas Powell was riding, too!"

Wilbur was right. Powell's mount was a black with a star on its face and one white stocking. From this distance, it appeared that description fit the animal they were looking at. They left the cattle they had been driving and heeled their horses into motion, galloping hard toward the riderless horse.

A few moments later, Stovepipe was certain the horse belonged to Jonas Powell, or more likely to the HS Bar ranch, since many cowboys didn't have personal mounts, using horses from the ranch's remuda instead. The star-faced black was grazing peacefully, but he shied a little as Stovepipe and Wilbur raced up to it.

Stovepipe swung down from the saddle, dropped his own reins, and caught those dangling from the black. He held tightly to them and ran his other hand over an irregular patch of something dark brown on the saddle.

"Sticky," he reported. "That's blood, Wilbur."

The redhead loosed an oath.

"Not much doubt about who that shot was aimed at now, is there?" he asked.

Stovepipe mounted up quickly, and he and Wilbur rode on, leading Jonas Powell's horse.

It wasn't long before they spotted a dark shape lying on the ground up ahead, underneath the spreading branches of a pine tree. Although the large splash of blood on Powell's saddle made it unlikely, Stovepipe knew there was a chance the cowboy was still alive. He and Wilbur didn't waste any time reaching the fallen man's side.

Stovepipe dismounted and dropped to a knee beside Powell, who was lying facedown. Gripping the man's shoulders, Stovepipe carefully rolled him onto his back. Powell's wide, sightlessly staring eyes immediately told Stovepipe that he was dead. The breast of Powell's bib-front shirt was dark with dried blood in a large, ragged circle. Some of the blood had soaked into the ground where he had been lying, too.

"Any powder burns around the wound?" asked Wilbur. His instincts and training were taking over.

"Don't look like it," replied Stovepipe. "That sounded like a rifle we heard earlier, so I'm bettin' he was shot from a distance."

Wilbur tipped his head back to gaze at the rimrock looming above them. He said, "From up there, more than likely. Powell never stood a chance."

"Drilled through the heart like that, he prob'ly never knew what hit him," Stovepipe said. "I sort of hope so, anyway."

He put his hands on his knees and straightened, some of his joints popping a little as he did so. He looked out across the pasture to the west, where close to fifty head of cattle were grazing, undisturbed by the nearby presence of the dead man.

"Whoever shot him, they didn't try to run off those cows," mused Stovepipe.

"Maybe they just hadn't gotten around to it yet. They probably saw some of us coming and going and knew we were around and would come to see about that shot." Wilbur rubbed his chin and frowned in thought. "But if it was the rustlers, why gun down Powell and not try to steal the cattle—"

Stovepipe leaped toward his friend, grabbed Wilbur's shirt, and hauled him out of the saddle. Wilbur let out a startled squawk as he toppled to the ground. The sharp crack of a rifle served as a counterpoint to that exclamation, and it was followed instantly by the high-pitched whine of a slug traveling through the space where Wilbur had been a split second earlier.

There were several trees nearby. Stovepipe jerked Wilbur to his feet and they scrambled for cover behind the trees. As they leaned against the rough-barked trunks, panting for breath, Stovepipe said grimly, "Bait."

"What?"

"You asked how come they shot Powell. Bait to lure the rest of us in. I had just figured that out when I spotted sunlight winkin' on a rifle barrel up yonder on the rim. Had time enough to grab you, but just barely."

Wilbur swallowed hard and said, "I reckon you saved my life, Stovepipe."

"More 'n likely," agreed the lanky cowboy. "But

you've saved my mangy ol' hide plenty o' times, too. I ain't keepin' count."

"Neither am I, but I don't forget, either." Wilbur drew his Colt and risked a peek past the trunk of the tree where he had taken shelter. "The range is too far for a handgun, blast it, but I feel like burning some powder anyway."

"Save your ammunition," Stovepipe advised him. "We're liable to need it later."

Wilbur cast a glance toward their horses. The Appaloosa and the dun were standing out in the open. Winchesters stuck up from the saddle boots.

"Sure would like to get my hands on my rifle."

"Yeah, so would I, but those varmints ain't taken any potshots at the horses yet, so let's don't give 'em any reason to by tryin' to call 'em over."

Wilbur nodded, knowing that Stovepipe was right.

Again, only one shot had been fired. Whoever was up there was patient. He had Stovepipe and Wilbur pinned down and could afford to wait.

After a few moments, Wilbur said, "Hawkins and Cunningham are bound to have heard both of those shots."

"Yeah, and I reckon there's a good chance they're on their way here to see what it's all about."

"That bushwhacker will cut them down."

"He will if he gets a chance. We can't let 'em just ride up out in the open the way we did."

"You think the fella missed the shot at me on purpose?" asked Wilbur. "More bait?"

Stovepipe shook his head and said, "Nope, he was aimin' to part your hair with that slug, all right. It's just good luck that he didn't."

"And your reflexes," Wilbur pointed out.

Stovepipe chuckled and said, "Well, it was good luck that the two of us partnered up all them years ago, ain't it?"

"Not for all the owlhoots we've put behind bars or in the ground."

"Bad luck for owlhoots," said Stovepipe. "I'll take that description any day."

The sound of hoofbeats drumming toward them made both men look up. Gene Hawkins and Bill Cunningham must have met up on the trail the way Stovepipe and Wilbur had, because both of the older punchers were galloping toward them, side by side.

Stovepipe pulled his Colt and fired three shots into the air, the universal signal for trouble. Normally, though, that would just prompt Hawkins and Cunningham to hurry toward them. To prevent that, now that he had their attention, Stovepipe pouched his iron, yanked the black hat off his head, and jumped out into the open. He waved the hat back and forth over his head and then motioned vigorously with it, trying to shoo the two riders away.

The rifle cracked from the rimrock. Stovepipe felt a slug pluck at his vest. He whirled around and dived for the shelter of the trees. He had done what he could. It was up to Hawkins and Cunningham to understand the danger they were in.

"They're turning around and heading back the other way!" Wilbur exclaimed. "Are you ventilated, Stovepipe?"

"Nope, I'm still all in one piece." Stovepipe picked up the tail of his vest and fingered the bullet hole in it. "Gonna have to do a little mendin', though, when I get a chance."

"That may not be too soon," said Wilbur, and now he sounded worried again. "Looks like more trouble's on the way!"

Stovepipe looked up and saw at least a dozen riders thundering across the pasture toward them, bristling with guns.

CHAPTER THIRTY-SIX

Stovepipe hesitated for a couple of heartbeats, hoping the newcomers might be Bob Ridgewell and some of the other members of the HS Bar crew, drawn to the rim by the gunfire.

That hope was dashed as the guns pointed at them by the riders began spouting flame and lead.

"Come on, Wilbur!" Stovepipe called as he darted out from the shelter of the trees. "We gotta risk makin' a run for it!"

He heard a slug whine past his head as he dashed toward the Appaloosa. The black-and-white horse, who had been a steady mount for Stovepipe during all sorts of trouble, didn't shy away but stood waiting for the lanky cowboy. Stovepipe grabbed the saddle horn and swung up onto the Palouse.

A few yards away, Wilbur practically vaulted into the dun's saddle. Both men had their horses moving before their feet even found the stirrups.

They leaned forward to make themselves smaller targets as bullets continued to whistle around them.

Caught between two fires this way, the odds against them escaping the trap were high. Neither man intended to give up, though. They would keep fighting to their last breath.

"Hope Hawkins and Cunningham had the sense to hightail it outta these parts," Stovepipe called over to Wilbur.

"Maybe they'll fetch some help!"

"We could use it, that's for dang sure!"

Stovepipe couldn't be certain, but he thought the shots from the rimrock had stopped. The bushwhacker probably didn't have a good angle on him and Wilbur anymore.

The men on horseback were still a threat, though, no doubt about that. As Stovepipe and Wilbur fled northward along the rim, the riders angled toward the escarpment. Their path would intersect that of the two range detectives.

"They're gonna cut us off, Stovepipe," said Wilbur. "We'll have to go up one of these canyons!"

"Most of them don't go anywhere," Stovepipe pointed out as another bullet whistled over his head. "Only a few of 'em lead to the top of the rim."

"You got a better idea?" Wilbur asked over the drumming of their horses' hooves.

"Nope," Stovepipe admitted. "Come on!"

He swung the Appaloosa toward the mouth of the nearest canyon. This was one that Wilbur had combed for strays, not him, so he didn't have any idea what they would find up there. Wilbur didn't object, though, so Stovepipe figured the redhead thought it was as good a choice as any.

The whole thing was a gamble, anyway, no matter what they did.

The canyon mouth was clogged with stickery brush, but there were gaps in it. The two riders plunged into one of those gaps, first Wilbur and then Stovepipe. The gap turned into a twisting trail that weaved back and forth among the bushes and the clumps of cactus. Briar vines whipped and caught and raked at the men, tearing shirts and the skin underneath. Wilbur yelped a few times but kept riding. Stovepipe followed him in grim silence.

At least the brush provided some concealment, as did the stunted trees that sprouted here and there. The growth wouldn't stop very many bullets, but it disrupted the aim of the men trying to kill Stovepipe and Wilbur. Slugs rattled and clipped through the branches, but Stovepipe didn't think they were coming as close as they had been.

After a few minutes, the gunfire died away. Stovepipe heard loud, angry voices behind them. He decided that the pursuers had stopped at the canyon mouth. They sounded like they were arguing about what to do next.

Wilbur looked back and said, "Some of them are going to follow us in here."

"More than likely," agreed Stovepipe.

"Maybe we should stop and set up a little ambush of our own. Give them a warm welcome."

"Not just yet," Stovepipe decided. "Let's keep movin' for a while. We might find a way out of here."

They followed the canyon for what seemed like at least a mile before Stovepipe called a halt. They had little threads of blood on their faces and hands from numerous scratches. As they sat there listening intently, both men heard the distant sounds of riders forcing their way through the thicket of brush.

"They're coming after us, all right," said Wilbur.

"It's worse than that." Stovepipe pointed to his left, then his right. "I think I hear horses over yonder in both directions. They've split up. They're combin' the canyon for us, just like we did when we were chousin' out those steers earlier."

"I reckon we'd better start looking for a good place to fort up, then."

In Wilbur's voice was a tone of dour acceptance that they probably wouldn't make it out of here alive. But they would go down fighting, taking as many of their enemies with them as they could.

That resolve was cold comfort. No matter how much punishment they inflicted on the outlaws before they crossed the divide, dying here would mean they had failed at their job. That had never happened before, and the potential that it might now was a bitter pill to swallow.

"Let's push on a ways," suggested Stovepipe. "I ain't ready to give up yet."

"Neither am I." Wilbur heeled the dun into motion.

A short time later, the end of the canyon came into sight. It narrowed down and terminated in a steep cliff riven with cracks. A mountain goat could climb that cliff. A man might be able to, if he had strong muscles and icy nerves. A horse couldn't, in a million years. Stovepipe and Wilbur weren't likely to abandon their mounts to the outlaws. Besides, if they tried to make that climb, men with rifles would be able to pick them off without much trouble before they reached the top.

Trees grew thickly at the base of the cliff. Stovepipe pointed to them and said, "Take the horses over there, Wilbur. Those trees should be pretty good cover."

"What are you gonna be doing?" Wilbur wanted to know.

Stovepipe pointed to some slabs of rock that lay in a haphazard arrangement next to the narrow trail through the brush and said, "I thought I'd find me a hidey-hole and wait for the varmints to go past. That way I'll be behind 'em. Might be able to whittle down the odds a little."

"Not enough to do much good, more than likely."

"There you go, bein' a pestimist again."

"But any time you whittle on something, you've got to start somewhere, I suppose," Wilbur went on as if Stovepipe hadn't said anything. "Give me your reins."

Stovepipe dismounted and handed the Appaloosa's reins to Wilbur. Then he began climbing into the jumble of rocks while Wilbur rode on toward the cliff, leading the Palouse.

Stovepipe kept a close eye out for rattlesnakes as he clambered among the rocks. The scaly critters loved to den up in places like this, and just about the last thing he needed right now was to have a sidewinder sink its fangs in him.

He worked his way through the rocks until he was no longer in sight of the trail, then looked around for a likely spot to wait for the pursuit to catch up to them. He crawled up the slanting face of one of the stone slabs, took his hat off, and chanced a look.

He could see the trail from where he was. In fact, it

passed about ten feet below him. None of the outlaws were in sight yet, but he heard the clopping of hoof-beats against the rocky ground as they approached.

Stovepipe slid back down where they couldn't see him and waited. He knew he would be able to tell by listening when they had passed him. Chances were, the pursuers were riding single file on the narrow trail, just as he and Wilbur had been forced to. Stove-pipe thought maybe he could jump the last man in line and then get the drop on the others before they knew what was happening.

Of course, this was just one group. There were others searching the canyon. But as Stovepipe had once heard a lawman acquaintance of his say, it was usually best to eat an apple one bite at a time.

The hoofbeats got louder, then abruptly stopped. Stovepipe frowned. From the sound of it, the riders were just on the other side of the rock where he was waiting. Had they spotted him somehow, or otherwise figured out he was up here?

Apparently, that wasn't the case. They had stopped just to rest their horses and palaver a mite. One of the men said, "Damn, it's hot in here."

"I don't reckon there's an inch of exposed skin that don't have a scratch on it," added another. "How long are we gonna chase those drifters, Benning?"

"Until we catch them and kill them," responded a third man. "You know what Rawson said. He doesn't like the way they keep showing up every time some-thing happens. He thinks they want to horn in on our game, and he wants 'em dead. If you want to go against what Rawson says . . ."

"I never said that," one of the other men replied

hastily. His uneasy tone didn't leave much doubt that he was afraid of the man called Rawson.

Stovepipe frowned as he listened. From the sound of what they were saying, this hombre Rawson was the gang's head man. The name was vaguely familiar to Stovepipe. Given his line of work, it was likely he had seen it on a wanted poster sometime in the past. Beyond that, though, he couldn't place it.

"All right, let's get moving," continued Benning. "This canyon runs out pretty soon. They can't have gone much farther."

"Unless they doubled back somehow," one of the other men said.

"They're probably up there waitin' to ambush us," another outlaw put in.

"Damn it!" grated Benning. "Are the whole lot of you turning yellow? Go on. I'll tell Rawson how you gave up the chase."

That got the men moving again. Stovepipe heard the horses start along the trail.

He crawled higher until he could see them. Three men, riding single file as he had figured, and the third and last man in line was just passing beneath the looming edge of the stone slab.

Stovepipe didn't pause to ponder the situation. This might well be the best chance he would get, so he seized it.

He stood up and launched himself from the top of the rock in a dive that sent him plummeting toward the third outlaw.

CHAPTER THIRTY-SEVEN

Stovepipe crashed into the man and knocked him sideways in the saddle. The outlaw managed to stay mounted instead of falling off. Stovepipe perched on the back of the suddenly panicky mount, just behind the saddle. He wrapped his left arm around the man's neck and pulled the ivory-handled Colt with his right hand.

He had thought to wallop the outlaw on the head with the gun, but before he could do that, the hombre's trigger-happy companions whirled their horses and opened fire. Stovepipe felt the third outlaw's body jerk under the impacts as bullets thudded into it.

Stovepipe thrust his revolver under the man's arm and triggered a shot at the second man in line. The bullet drove deep in his chest. The man threw up his arms and pitched off his horse to the side, landing in a clump of cactus. From his lack of reaction to being speared with hundreds of sharp needles, Stovepipe had a hunch the outlaw was already dead.

That left the man who had been in the lead, and

he was cussing up a storm as he emptied his gun at Stovepipe. Having a prisoner to question—and to use as a hostage—struck Stovepipe as a good idea, so he drew a quick bead on the fella's shoulder as he pulled the trigger again.

Unfortunately, the horse he was on jittered to the side just then, as did the leader's mount, and as a result Stovepipe's bullet struck the man in the throat. The man rocked back in the saddle as blood sprayed from severed arteries in a grisly fountain. He made a ghastly gurgling noise, then collapsed forward over his horse's neck. He stayed in the saddle, but the distinctive coppery smell of fresh blood flooding from his wound completely unnerved the horse. Pitching and bucking, it lunged off into the brush and screamed in pain as briars and thorns raked its hide.

Stovepipe let go of the man he'd been holding, who fell limply to the trail. He had been shot to pieces by his overeager compadres.

The whole ruckus had taken less than half a minute, but it had filled the canyon with resounding echoes from all the gun-thunder. Stovepipe knew the other outlaws searching for him and Wilbur had heard the shots and would be heading in this direction as quickly as they could through the thick brush.

At least there were three fewer varmints trying to kill them now, he thought bleakly.

Stovepipe left the horses and bodies where they were and raced along the trail to rejoin Wilbur.

The redhead, holding his rifle, came out from the trees to greet his old friend. He said, "Dadgum it, Stovepipe, I heard all that shooting and figured you'd been ventilated for sure."

"Sorry to disappoint you," Stovepipe said dryly.

"But we got three less polecats who're tryin' to kill us now."

Wilbur let out a low, admiring whistle and said, "That's pretty handy gun-work."

"Some of it was pure luck. In fact, it seems like me wantin' to take one of those fellas prisoner is just pure-dee jinxed. They keep windin' up dead no matter what I do."

"We can worry about that later. Come on back in the trees. I want to show you what I've found."

That sounded intriguing, to say the least. Stovepipe followed Wilbur into the trees at the base of the rim where the Appaloosa and the dun were tied.

A crack in the cliff that wasn't visible from farther out in the canyon formed a steeply sloping passage that led toward the top of the rim. Stovepipe eyed it and said, "You reckon it goes all the way up?"

"I don't know, but it's wide enough for our horses and there's only one way to find out."

Stovepipe knew his old friend was right. They went back to get the horses, then started up the fissure. Like the passage in the badlands through which Dan Hartford had led them several days earlier, this one was barely big enough for the horses to fit through. So much violent activity had been crammed into the time since then that it seemed like weeks ago they had made that trek with Dan, instead of mere days, Stovepipe reflected.

That made him think about Dan sitting there in the jail at Hat Creek, waiting for his trial and an almost inevitable date with the hangman. Unless Stovepipe and Wilbur could come up with some proof of who really killed Abel Dempsey, the young man probably was doomed.

"You know if this crack peters out, we'll have to try to back these hosses outta here," Stovepipe commented.

"Yeah, and if we do we'll probably find the rest of that gang of killers waiting for us, just ready to fill us full of lead."

"That's one good reason to keep goin' as long as we can, I reckon."

The cleft had several bends in it. From above, it would form a zigzag pattern as it penetrated into the rim, Stovepipe knew. That came in handy, because the jutting rock shielded them from any shots coming from below.

After a while, he heard voices. They were far off and distorted, so he couldn't make out any of the words. He heard the angry tone, though, and figured the voices belonged to more of the rustlers who had found the hidden escape route.

"You think they'll come up after us?" asked Wilbur.

"They'd be fools to. In a tight space like this, one fella could just about stand off an army." Stovepipe thought about it, then went on, "They're more likely to try to find some other way up so they can go around and be waitin' for us at the top."

"We'd better hurry, then. If they manage to do that, we'd sure enough be caught like rats in a trap."

They couldn't go much faster than they were already going, however. Stovepipe listened carefully as they neared the top but didn't hear anything. Of course, that didn't mean much, he mused. If any of the owlhoots were waiting up there, they'd be quiet about it, watching in silence as they trained their guns on the place where the passage opened onto the rim.

Finally, that came into view. Stovepipe passed the Appaloosa's reins back to Wilbur and told the redhead, "You wait here while I do some scoutin'."

"Don't go and get yourself killed."

"I'll sure try not to."

Stovepipe drew his gun as he cat-footed the final twenty feet. Crouching, he stepped out onto the rim and swept his keen-eyed gaze all around, seeing nothing except rocks, yucca plants, mesquite trees, and a few scrubby pines. The landscape was flat and open, without any good places to hide as far as he could see.

"Come on up," he called to Wilbur. "The coast is clear, as those seafarin' boys say."

Wilbur emerged from the cleft leading the horses. He looked around and said, "Huh. I thought we were a lot farther away from the rim."

It had seemed like they followed the passage for several hundred yards, but now as they looked back toward the southwest, they saw that they were only about a hundred yards from the edge of the Mogollon Rim. The way the crack in the cliff had twisted and bent back on itself had caused them to travel that farther distance.

"Come on," said Stovepipe. "Let's go have a look."

"From the top of the rim, you mean?"

"That's right."

"We might get spotted up here," warned Wilbur.

"Well, if we do, we've got the high ground now. I'd like to see anybody try to knock us off of it."

They mounted up and rode quickly to the edge. They could see down into the canyon where they had taken refuge from the gang. Nothing appeared to be moving down there.

"You reckon they lit a shuck?" asked Wilbur.

"Might have." Stovepipe took his spyglass from his saddlebags and extended the instrument. He swept it back and forth as he gazed through the lenses. After a moment he stopped as something out in the basin caught his interest.

Wilbur must have noticed Stovepipe's reaction. He asked, "What is it?"

"Dust cloud headed this way," Stovepipe replied. "Lemme see if I can focus in on the fellas causin' it . . ."

He focused the spyglass on the riders but couldn't make out any details about them. Patiently, he waited until they came closer, then reported, "Looks like Bob Ridgewell and some of the crew from the HS Bar. I see Gene Hawkins and Bill Cunningham, too. Reckon when they heard all the shootin' and then saw those hombres chargin' us, they turned around and rattled their hocks back to the ranch headquarters to fetch help."

Wilbur snorted and said, "They took their own sweet time about getting here."

"Well, to be fair, it's a pretty far ride. I figure they must have run into Ridgewell and the others on the way, 'cause they ain't had time to get to headquarters and back."

"Yeah, I suppose. What about those rustlers?"

"No sign of 'em. They must've pulled out. They could have spotted that bunch comin' and figured our lives weren't worth fightin' them." Stovepipe lowered the telescope, closed it, and stowed it away. "Wilbur, does the name Rawson mean anything to you?"

"Rawson," Wilbur repeated. "Rawson. Sounds familiar for some reason, but danged if I know why."

"Yeah, I felt the same way. I overheard those fellas I tangled with talkin' before I jumped 'em, and from the way they were jawin' with each other, this fella Rawson is the ramrod of the bunch. They made him sound like a bad hombre, too. I figure we've seen dodgers on him, sometime in the past."

"More than likely. Did they say anything else interesting?"

Stovepipe chuckled and said, "Just that Rawson wants the two of us dead. We were on the right track when we were tryin' to figure out why they dry-gulched poor Jonas Powell. They weren't after the cattle we've been combin' outta the rough country. They just aimed to dry-gulch us."

"Us?"

"You and me," said Stovepipe, nodding gravely. "Killin' us was more important to them than anything else right now. And you know what that tells me, Wilbur?"

"What?"

"We're gettin' too close to the truth for somebody's comfort." Stovepipe lifted his reins. "Let's see if we can find a way down off this rim, so we can go meet Ridgewell and the rest of that bunch."

CHAPTER THIRTY-EIGHT

They rode along the rim for half a mile before they found a wide coulee leading down into the basin. Once they were on the flats again, Stovepipe and Wilbur headed back toward the spot where they had seen the ranch crew approaching. It didn't take long to find the group of riders from the HS Bar. Hawkins and Cunningham spurred out to meet them, accompanied by Bob Ridgewell.

"Wasn't sure we'd ever see you boys again, unless it was at your buryin'," said the ever-mournful Cunningham as they all drew rein.

"It came pretty close to that," said Stovepipe. "They had us in a real bind for a while. Thanks to Wilbur, we got out of it."

Ridgewell said, "Gene and Bill tell me that Jonas Powell was shot. Is he dead?"

"I'm afraid so. Somebody drilled him from the top of the rim while he was watchin' over the cows the rest of us had combed out of the canyons."

"Is that right?" The foreman glared suspiciously at them. "You have any proof of that? Hawkins and

Cunningham said they saw you kneeling over his body. For all any of us know, one of you killed Powell!"

"Blast it, that's not true," said Wilbur. "We weren't anywhere close by when we heard that shot. We were up north along the rim, looking for strays just like we were supposed to be doing. We got back to the pasture where Powell was shot just a couple of minutes before Hawkins and Cunningham did."

"And whoever bushwhacked Powell took some potshots at us, too," added Stovepipe. "They durned near ventilated Wilbur, and I got a bullet hole in my vest to prove what I'm sayin'."

He lifted his vest and stuck a finger through the hole to demonstrate.

"That doesn't prove anything," said Ridgewell with a shake of his head. "You could have gotten that hole in your vest any time."

Gene Hawkins said slowly, "I'm not sure about that, Bob. I don't remember seein' it there before."

"And it looked to me like they was tryin' to help Jonas," put in Cunningham. "They was just too late to do anything for him."

Wilbur nodded and said, "That's the way it happened, all right."

Ridgewell didn't seem convinced, and neither did the other members of the crew, some of whom still bore bruises from the brawl in the bunkhouse the night before. Several of them glared at Stovepipe and Wilbur as if they were ready to string the two of them up from the nearest tree.

The word of Hawkins and Cunningham must have carried some weight with the foreman, however, because he grudgingly said to Stovepipe and

Wilbur, "All right, I'll listen to your story. Start from the beginning."

Stovepipe did so, explaining everything that had gone on since he'd heard the shot that killed Jonas Powell. Wilbur added a detail from time to time.

When they were finished, Ridgewell said, "If you're telling the truth, Stewart, the bodies of the men you killed ought to still be in that canyon."

"Maybe," said Stovepipe. "Maybe not. Their pards could've taken the carcasses with them."

"Let's go take a look anyway. What happened to the rest of that bunch you claim was trying to kill you?"

"Seems like they lit a shuck, prob'ly when they spotted you boys comin'. They didn't want to stay and fight a pitched battle."

Ridgewell let out a skeptical grunt and turned his horse.

"Show me that canyon," he said.

It didn't take long for Stovepipe and Wilbur to locate the canyon through which they had fled from the gang. Ridgewell told most of the men to wait outside and keep their eyes open in case of further trouble, then he, Hawkins, and Cunningham followed the two range detectives along the twisting trail through the brush.

Ridgewell let out an oath as a briar scratched him, then said, "I hate this stuff. Why the cattle are stupid enough to wander up in here, I'll never understand."

"Cows ain't the smartest critters *el Señor Dios* put on this earth, that's sure true," said Stovepipe, "but I reckon there are some dumber ones."

"Yeah, like grub line–riding cowpokes," Wilbur agreed dourly.

They came to the rocks where Stovepipe had

jumped the third outlaw. The man's body was gone, as was the hombre who had fallen in the cactus after Stovepipe shot him. There was no sign of their horses, either.

That was about what Stovepipe had expected. The rustlers had taken their dead with them. Except . . .

Since Stovepipe had reined in, the others had followed suit. Bob Ridgewell said, "I reckon this must be where you claim to have shot it out with those owlhoots." The way he phrased that comment made it clear he wasn't convinced Stovepipe and Wilbur had been telling the truth.

"Hold on a minute," said Stovepipe as he lifted a hand. "There was a third man. His horse spooked and went buckin' off into the brush. I thought I heard somethin' . . . Yeah, over yonder!"

He pointed. The other men sat up straighter in their saddles as they listened. Something was moving around in the brush, all right. Stovepipe hoped it was the other horse, drawn by the sound of human voices.

Ridgewell frowned at the thorny brush and said, "I reckon we'd better check it out."

"Or wait for the hoss to come to us," suggested Stovepipe. He whistled, thinking that might attract the animal even more. A lot of horses were trained to come to a whistle.

The noises in the brush got louder, and a few moments later, a big chestnut pushed through the growth and stepped onto the trail. Blood from hundreds of scratches covered its sleek hide. The dead rider still slumped forward in the saddle, arms dangling loosely on either side of the horse. The man's clothes were ripped to shreds by the brush.

Stovepipe was a little surprised the body hadn't

caught on something sturdy enough to drag it out of the saddle. He was glad that hadn't happened, though. The corpse was bloody evidence of what he and Wilbur had told Ridgewell.

"That fella's sure enough dead," said Hawkins. "Just like you claimed, Stovepipe."

Still wearing a frown, Ridgewell nudged his horse closer to the scratched-up mount. He reached out, grasped the dead man's hair, and lifted his head.

"I don't recognize the hombre," he said. "How about the rest of you?"

"Never seen him before," said Cunningham.

"Me, neither, Bob," said Hawkins.

Stovepipe said, "And the only time I ever saw him was when he was shootin' at me a little while ago. The fellas who packed the other two bodies away from here couldn't find this hombre. They might not have even realized he was missin' until they were long gone from here."

Ridgewell let the man's head down and said, "This doesn't prove you didn't shoot Powell, but it makes me more inclined to believe your story. This fella didn't have any reason to be on HS Bar range. Doesn't mean he was up to no good, but he sure looks the type."

"You can see his holster's empty," Stovepipe pointed out. "If we look around, we might find the gun he dropped when my slug hit him in the throat."

"That's a bloody way to go," said Ridgewell with a grimace.

The gun didn't turn up, but that didn't mean anything. It was lying somewhere in the thick brush, and it might stay there until it rusted away. After a few minutes, the men rode back out of the canyon. Hawkins led the horse carrying the body.

Bradley, the puncher who had started the ruckus with Stovepipe the night before, pointed and said to Ridgewell, "There's a mess of hoofprints over there, Bob, like a good-sized group of riders left out of here in a hurry. Could've been the bunch Stewart and Coleman were talkin' about."

Stovepipe was a little surprised that Bradley would say anything to help their cause, but just because the cowboy had acted proddy, that didn't mean he was less than fair. And any puncher worth his salt got his dander up in a hurry when it came to rustlers.

Ridgewell inspected the tracks, then said, "Can't tell much from them, but I suppose we could try following them for a while. Meeker, you take the body back to the ranch. The rest of you, come with me."

Hawkins handed the reins of the dead man's horse to one of the other cowboys, who didn't look happy about being sent back to headquarters. He didn't raise any objections, though, instead riding off leading the scratched-up horse.

"And take care of that mount," Ridgewell called after him. Meeker waved a hand in acknowledgment of the order.

The rest of the group, led by Ridgewell, Stovepipe, and Wilbur, followed the trail of the rustlers. Stovepipe was convinced they were the ones who had left the tracks, even if Ridgewell wasn't.

The trail followed the base of the rim until it reached a large, rocky slope where slides had taken place in the past. The incline angled upward between sheer walls. Clearly, the riders had gone up that slope because their tracks ended here.

"We'll go up to the rim and pick up their trail there," Ridgewell said. The horses had to pick their way along carefully to avoid slipping. Small rocks clattered down the slope behind them.

When they reached the top, the men reined in and studied the ground. Only a moment passed before the HS Bar foreman ripped out a curse.

"They split up," he said. "They rode out one at a time in all different directions."

"That appears to be the size of it," said Stovepipe as he rested his hands on his saddle horn. "Reckon they must have a rendezvous somewhere else, maybe up here, maybe back down in the basin." He turned his head to sweep his gaze over the vast area around them. "Not much tellin' where, though."

"I'll be damned if I'm going to let them get away with killing one of my men," declared Ridgewell.

"Does that mean you believe us now about what happened?"

"My gut says you're telling the truth," the foreman replied. "I've learned over the years to play my hunches."

"I'm glad to hear it. Because we want to round up the varmints responsible for all this trouble just as much as you do. Ain't that right, Wilbur?"

"It sure is," said the redhead. "We'll do it, too."

"How do you know that?" asked Ridgewell.

"Because I know Stovepipe," Wilbur said.

CHAPTER THIRTY-NINE

Henry Stafford was laid to rest in the little cemetery on a hill about half a mile from the ranch headquarters. The place was shaded by trees and surrounded by a black, wrought-iron fence. Stafford's first wife was buried there, along with the couple's two children, neither of whom had survived infancy. After that, there had been no more children. Several of the ranch's longtime employees had been interred on the hill as well.

Every member of the HS Bar crew attended Stafford's funeral, which was conducted by the Methodist minister from Hat Creek. Many of the settlement's citizens had made the trip out to the ranch for the service, including Sheriff Frank Olsen and Deputy Warren Purdue.

Stovepipe and Wilbur stood with the other cowboys, hats in hands, as the buggy carrying Jessica Stafford approached. Bob Ridgewell, dressed in a dusty black suit, was at the reins. A string tie was knotted tightly at Ridgewell's throat and appeared to be a source of discomfort for the foreman, although he ignored it as best he could.

Jessica was dressed in black as well, of course. The veil that hung from her hat was thicker today, so little of her face was visible as Ridgewell helped her down from the buggy and linked his arm with hers as they walked to the graveside.

The preacher was long-winded, as sky pilots tended to be, and the day was oppressively warm, especially with so many of those in attendance dressed in dark clothing. Stovepipe was glad when it was over. He had never liked funerals. They were inevitable, of course, and he and Wilbur knew that fact better than some because they had seen so much death in the course of their careers.

But Stovepipe was annoyed because funerals reminded him there were some mysteries he just couldn't solve, including what lay in store on the other side of the divide.

When the service was over at last, a lot of the folks from town lined up to shake hands with Mrs. Stafford and pay their respects. Stovepipe waited under a tree off to one side until Sheriff Olsen had shaken Jessica's hand. He caught the lawman's eye as Olsen put on his hat and started toward the horses that were tied to the buggies and wagons parked outside the cemetery.

Olsen changed his course and stalked toward Stovepipe. When the star packer was close enough to hear, Stovepipe told him, "Say somethin' that makes it sound like comin' over here was your idea, Sheriff."

Olsen frowned in surprise but played along. He raised his voice slightly and said, "By God, you and Coleman had better be keeping your noses clean out here, Stewart. I'm still not sure I did the right thing letting you two go, no matter what the judge said."

Keeping his voice low, Stovepipe nodded and said, "That's mighty fine. Won't nobody suspect anything about us talkin' if they think you're just checkin' up on me and Wilbur."

"What do you want, Stewart?" growled Olsen. The unfriendliness was at least partially genuine, rather than an act. The sheriff probably hadn't forgotten how Stovepipe and Wilbur had concealed their true identities from him. He had to feel at least a little like he'd been played for a fool.

"I'm gonna shake hands with you in a minute," said Stovepipe. "When I do, there'll be a note in my hand you need to take. It's a telegraph message, and I'd be mighty obliged if you'd send it for me."

"What kind of message?"

"You'll see that when you send it. It's all right for you to read it. Mostly it's to find out more about a fella whose name cropped up: Rawson."

Olsen's bushy white brows drew down.

"Rawson," he repeated. "Sounds familiar, but I don't place it."

"Wilbur and me feel the same way. Reckon he's bound to be a desperado of sorts, but I'd like to know more about him. From what I can tell, he's the ringleader of that bunch of rustlers and owlhoots."

Olsen was interested in spite of his hostility toward Stovepipe and Wilbur. He said, "Anything else?"

"How are Dan and Laura doin'?"

"They're in jail," Olsen snapped. "How do you think they're doing?"

"Pretty miserable, I expect. When's the trial?"

"Hartford goes on trial next week. Judge Snow

hasn't set a trial date yet for Mrs. Dempsey. I think he's waiting to see how things turn out with Hartford."

"Is that fella McGilvray still representin' Dan?"

"He's representing both of them."

Stovepipe shook his head and asked, "Is he sober, at least?"

"I think so. I haven't seen him in the Blue Oasis in several days." Olsen shrugged. "Of course, he could be nipping from a flask and I wouldn't know."

Stovepipe tugged on his earlobe and said, "Seems to me like the best thing to do would be to clear Dan's name before the trial ever starts, just to make sure there's no chance of him bein' convicted."

"How are you going to do that?"

"Round up the real rapscallions, of course. Maybe that wire you're gonna send for me will help with that."

Olsen grunted and said, "Does this tie in with that mysterious theory you've got? Or did you just make that up?"

"Oh, it's real enough," Stovepipe assured him.

"But you don't care to share it yet."

"Not just yet," Stovepipe said. He stuck out his hand. "Thanks for believin' in us, Sheriff, and givin' us a chance."

Olsen snorted again, but he gripped Stovepipe's hand. They transferred the small, folded piece of paper. Olsen stuck it in his pocket, then turned away.

When Olsen was gone, Wilbur wandered over and said, "What were you and the sheriff jawing about, Stovepipe?"

"I gave him a telegraph message to send for me, to

that deputy U.S. marshal amigo o' mine. I figure he can tell us more about that fella Rawson."

"We're pretty sure he's the boss rustler. What else do we need to know?"

"I've felt from the first that there's more to all this trouble than just wide-loopin' some cows," said Stovepipe. "I've got a hunch it all adds up to a heap more. And you know how my hunches usually play out."

"Yeah," responded Wilbur. "With hot lead buzzing all around our heads."

Jonas Powell was buried in the ranch cemetery as well, late in the afternoon of the day that Henry Stafford was laid to rest. The other members of the crew were on hand for this service, too, but everyone from Hat Creek had gone home, including the minister. Bob Ridgewell read from the Bible instead, and he was about to conduct a prayer when he was interrupted by the sound of hoofbeats.

The men all turned around to see Jessica Stafford approaching on horseback. She no longer wore mourning dress, hat, and veil, but the riding skirt she had on was black, and her shirt was made of dark blue silk. Her golden hair was pulled back and tied with a black ribbon, so she still had a somber appearance.

She reined in at the fence, dismounted, and looped her horse's reins around one of the sections of wrought iron.

"Bob, you should have told me you and the men were laying poor Jonas to rest," she said.

"Well, ma'am," Ridgewell began, "since he was just a member of the crew—"

"He rode for the HS Bar," Jessica broke in. "As far as I'm concerned, that's as close to being family as you can get without being blood."

"It's mighty kind of you to say that, ma'am."

"It's the way I feel," said Jessica. She walked through the open gate and took her place among the men standing around Powell's grave. "Go ahead."

"We were just about to say a prayer . . ."

Ridgewell lowered his head, as did all the others. The prayer was short, simple, and heartfelt, asking the Lord to have mercy on the soul of Jonas Powell, a good, hardworking cowboy, and when Ridgewell was done, Jessica murmured, "Amen," along with everyone else there.

With the service over, the men began to drift away, except for Gene Hawkins and Bill Cunningham, who had requested the job of filling in the grave since Powell had been their riding partner most of the time. Stovepipe and Wilbur had just stepped out of the cemetery when Jessica came up to them and said, "Mr. Stewart, I'd like to talk with you for a moment, if I may."

"Why, sure, ma'am," said Stovepipe as he held his black Stetson in front of him. "What can I do for you?"

"I saw you talking to Sheriff Olsen this morning, after . . ." Her voice caught a little. "After Henry's funeral. What did he want?"

"Oh, he was just checkin' up on Wilbur and me," Stovepipe replied easily. "Makin' sure we weren't up to any mischief."

"Did he say anything about Dan and . . . Laura?"

Stovepipe's voice was gentle as he said, "Well, they're still locked up. Dan's trial is set for next week. They don't know yet when Miz Dempsey's trial will be."

"It's selfish of me, I know, but I wish Laura could have been here today. She's my best friend out here, and I could have used her strength."

Wilbur said, "It appeared to me that you were plenty strong, ma'am. I didn't know your husband at all, but I'll bet he would have been proud of you."

Jessica smiled faintly as she said, "Yes, I believe he would have." She squared her shoulders and went on, "How's the search going for the rustlers?"

"Beg your pardon, ma'am?" said Stovepipe.

"Rustlers have invaded this ranch and killed one of our own. I may have been in the West for only a few years, but I think I know cowboys well enough to be aware that you and the rest of the crew have been looking for those criminals while you're doing your other work."

"We're keepin' our eyes open, that's for sure, but huntin' down owlhoots, that's the sheriff's job, ma'am." Stovepipe rubbed his chin and added, "But I got to admit, none of us cotton to the idea of those varmints still bein' on the loose."

"So if you come across any clues . . ."

"We'll make certain sure those sidewinders get what they've got comin'," said Stovepipe. "Ever' blasted one of 'em."

CHAPTER FORTY

Unfortunately, several days went by with no further progress in the case. In the brush-choked canyon where they had found the body of the dead outlaw, Wilbur had come close to spilling the fact that he and Stovepipe had an agenda of their own for wanting to bring the gang of rustlers and killers to justice, other than being employed by the HS Bar. Bob Ridgewell didn't seem to have noticed that near slip, however, so they were able to continue their pose as drifting cowpokes.

In order to do that, they had to ride the range every day, carrying out whatever tasks Ridgewell assigned to them. They did that with all the skill as top hands they had developed in their younger years.

But at the same time, they continued their search whenever they could, looking for any clues that might lead them to the gang's hideout.

So far, that search had proven unsuccessful.

Although Ridgewell no longer seemed suspicious of them, he usually had them working with some of the other hands since they were new to the ranch.

This made it more difficult for Stovepipe and Wilbur to wander off on their own and conduct any sort of investigation.

Today, however, when the foreman assigned the day's tasks after breakfast, he had told Stovepipe and Wilbur, "There's a water hole way up north, where the rim curves around and blocks the basin. That's as far as you can go and still be on the HS Bar, but the water hole is still on our range and somebody needs to check it out. Sometimes it tries to dry up this time of year."

"What do we do if it has?" asked Wilbur.

Ridgewell grunted and said, "Take a couple of shovels with you. You may have to dig it out some. It'll fill up. It always has in the past."

Stovepipe could tell from the expression on Wilbur's face that his old friend wasn't too happy to hear that. Wilbur never had cared much for digging. Post holes were the worst, though. Enlarging a water hole wasn't too bad compared to that.

While Wilbur grumbled, they fetched shovels from the tool shed next to the blacksmith shop and tied them onto their saddles, along with bags containing enough supplies to last them until the next day. It would take quite a while to ride to the water hole, and if they needed to dig it out more, they wouldn't have time to do that and still get back to the ranch headquarters before nightfall. In that case, they would camp until the next day, finish the work then if necessary, and return to ranch headquarters after that.

The prospect of spending a night on the range meant nothing to the two men. Sometimes Stovepipe thought they had spent more nights sleeping under the stars than they had under a roof. They set out, following the directions Ridgewell had given them for finding the water hole.

They had chewed over everything they had discovered about the rustlers, the murders, and the other events in the basin until there was nothing left to say, but they didn't mind riding along in companionable silence, either. They had done that plenty of times over the years as their work carried them from place to place.

Lunch was the usual jerky and biscuits, eaten in the saddle and washed down with water from their canteens. They were following the rim, and it was a couple of hours after they had eaten when they saw the looming escarpment twisting more to the west, marking the basin's northern boundary.

"We must be getting close to that water hole," said Wilbur. "It can't be much farther. We're running out of basin."

"I reckon," agreed Stovepipe. He pointed. "Look at those three pines growin' on top of that little bluff. That was one o' the landmarks Bob mentioned, wasn't it?"

"Yep. And over yonder the other way is a clump of rocks that looks like a sleeping buffalo."

"It sure enough does," said Stovepipe with a grin. "We're almost there."

A short time later, they came in sight of the water hole, which lay about half a mile south of the rim. Wilbur let out an oath as he looked at the sandy bottom of the depression.

"I thought Ridgewell said the water hole sometimes started to go dry at this time of year," the redhead complained. "That blamed thing is dry as a bone!"

"Yeah, but you can tell there's been water in it in the past," said Stovepipe. "There's still a little dried-up moss on the rocks down there that would've been layin' on the bottom."

"What do you think happened?"

"Dunno, but the cows grazin' up this way are gonna get mighty thirsty if we don't do somethin' about this."

"We'll have to dig clear to China to come up with any water," grumbled Wilbur.

"Maybe not. Let's get to work and see what we can do."

They dismounted, picketed their horses where there was a little stretch of hardy grass, and took the shovels off their saddles. They slid down into what had been the water hole, walked out to the center, and began digging. It wasn't long before the shirts of both men were soaked with sweat.

As he dug, Stovepipe looked around. Something was nagging at his brain, but he couldn't figure out what it was.

He and Wilbur had a hole about a foot deep and a yard in diameter, working on opposite sides of it, when the sand started getting a little damp on the north side of the hole, where Stovepipe was digging.

"Hold on a minute," he said.

"Gladly," replied Wilbur. He was red in the face from heat and exertion.

"You got any moisture in your dirt over there?"

"Let me check." Wilbur got down on his knees and reached into the hole. He picked up some of the sandy dirt and let it run through his fingers. "Not a bit. It's as dry as it was on top."

Stovepipe turned his head, narrowed his eyes, and squinted toward the rim. He studied the vegetation, then said, "Come around here and dig on this side with me."

"What in blazes is going on in that head of yours, Stovepipe?"

"I ain't sure yet. Maybe nothin'." Stovepipe grinned. "Or maybe I'm just sunstruck."

Wilbur blew out his breath and said, "I wouldn't doubt it. As tall as you are, your head's practically on the sun's front porch to start with."

He moved around to the north side of the hole and he and Stovepipe worked for a few minutes extending the excavation in that direction. After throwing aside one shovelful of dirt, Stovepipe paused and said, "Lookee there."

A tiny, almost invisible trickle of water was seeping out of the side of the hole they had dug.

Wilbur hunkered on his heels and frowned.

"Usually a water hole fills in from the bottom, not the side," he said.

"It does if it's spring fed," said Stovepipe. "I got a hunch this one ain't."

"What are you talking about?"

"Come on."

They climbed out of the water hole and Stovepipe pointed toward the rim.

"See anything?" he asked. "Look at the plants growin' between here and the rim. Notice any difference in some of 'em?"

For a long moment, Wilbur stared at the landscape in evident confusion, then he seemed surprised.

"There's a line of growth that's thicker and looks

healthier," he said. "That's what you're talking about, isn't it?"

"Yep. And it runs from the rim right here to this water hole."

"What does that mean?"

"It means there's an underground stream flowin' through here—or there was. It fed that water hole, then probably plunged deeper below the surface, which would explain why one side of the hole is dryer than the other. But somethin' happened. The stream's peterin' out. That's why the water hole looks like the dang Sahara desert. We'd likely get more water if we dug deeper, but I got a hunch it wouldn't be enough to fill the pool that used to be there."

"And what does all that mean, exactly?" asked Wilbur.

Stovepipe gazed toward the rim and said, "I don't know."

"Oh, I recognize that look! Something's intrigued you, and you'll move heaven and earth to figure out the answer."

"I don't know if I'd go that far, but I'll admit I'm a mite puzzled. From what Bob said, the ranch has been usin' this water hole for a good while. That means it's been a dependable supply of water. Somethin's happened to change that, and I'd like to know what it is." Stovepipe nodded toward the rim. "The answer's got to be in that direction."

"Well, then, let's mosey that way and take a look, cowboy."

"Just my thinkin'," Stovepipe agreed.

They carried the shovels back to their horses and paused long enough to wipe their sweat-covered faces with bandannas and take long drinks from their canteens. Then they mounted up and rode toward the Mogollon Rim, following the line of greener vegetation that Stovepipe theorized marked the course of an underground stream.

That led them to a beetle-browed bluff with a precarious look to it, as if the bulging rock face was poised up there, ready to fall at the slightest disturbance. In reality, it might have been like that for hundreds of years, thought Stovepipe, but the formation certainly had a threatening appearance to it.

"Dang it, Stovepipe," said Wilbur, "you know what that bluff looks a little like?"

"Yeah," said Stovepipe. "A big ol' skull."

Wilbur rolled his eyes and asked, "Would it have hurt you to let me say it?"

"Sorry, Wilbur. I thought it was a genuine question."

"Well, never mind that. If there really is an underground river, it comes out from under that bluff, don't you think?"

"I reckon it used to," said Stovepipe. "Now, I ain't so sure."

"What could have happened to interrupt its flow?"

"Let's take a closer look and see if we can find out."

As they approached the bluff, Stovepipe saw a line of thick brush along its base. He noticed something else as well: hoofprints. Bob Ridgewell had indicated that none of the HS Bar hands had been up to this isolated part of the ranch for a while, so that was puzzling.

Wilbur saw the same thing and said with excitement

creeping into his voice, "We're onto something here, Stovepipe."

"Seems like it." Stovepipe reached for his Winchester and drew the repeater from its saddle scabbard. He levered a round into the chamber. "Best be ready for trouble."

Wilbur followed suit. The tracks led toward the wall of brush. As they came closer, Stovepipe said, "Some of those bushes are dying, Wilbur."

"What does that mean?"

"That they've been pulled up and put here to hide somethin' behind 'em."

In fact, the bushes concealed a rather large opening, thought Stovepipe, and within minutes he and Wilbur had confirmed that as their horses pushed through the brush. The looming face of the bluff overhung a cavelike area that turned into the mouth of a tunnel not visible to casual observers.

Stovepipe reined in and motioned for Wilbur to do likewise. He threw his right leg over the saddle and slid to the ground, rifle in hand. He told Wilbur, "Stay here. I'm gonna have me a look-see."

"The hell you say. I'm coming with you."

Stovepipe shook his head.

"Nope. You need to be out here in case I don't come back. If that happens, you ride for Hat Creek and bring back Sheriff Olsen and a posse. My life may depend on it."

"Blast it, Stovepipe, I don't like it. I think we ought to stick together—"

"Not this time," Stovepipe declared. "I'll be all right." He flashed a grin. "I've never got myself in a scrape you couldn't pull me out of, have I?"

"No, I suppose not," Wilbur said gruffly. "All right. But you be careful in there. How long do I wait for you to come back?"

Stovepipe glanced at the sky. A couple of hours of daylight remained.

"If I ain't back by nightfall, you light a shuck for town. You can find this place again, can't you?"

"Of course I can. And if I have to go for help, I'll be back by dawn." Wilbur hesitated. "That's a long time, though. An awful lot could happen before then."

"Yep. I might have the whole gang corralled by then."

Wilbur snorted and said, "Just make sure they don't corral *you*."

With a grin and a wave, Stovepipe moved under the sinisterly looming rocks and headed for the tunnel.

CHAPTER FORTY-ONE

The area underneath the rock face wasn't really a cave, because it was open at both ends, but it might as well have been. With all the countless tons of earth and stone above his head, Stovepipe certainly *felt* like he was underground before he had gone very far.

With the time of day being what it was, light from the westering sun penetrated the area and allowed Stovepipe to see that the hooves of many horses and cattle had disturbed the dust. That was enough to tell him that his hunch was right, but he wanted to see what was up ahead with his own eyes.

He entered the tunnel, which was about forty feet wide. The ceiling was high enough for a man on horseback, as long as he wasn't too tall. Stovepipe thought he might have to bend over some in the saddle for his head to clear, but Wilbur wouldn't have any trouble with it. When he told his old friend and partner what he'd found in here, he might refrain from pointing that out, since from time to time Wilbur had been known to be a mite sensitive about his lack of height.

The gloom around him thickened as he penetrated deeper into the bluff. There was still enough light for him to see where he was going, but eventually that faded away. If men traveled regularly through this passage, they probably carried torches with them. That would explain the dark smudges he had noted on the roof of the tunnel when he could still see it. The marks came from the smoke of the torches the gang used.

Stovepipe had no doubt whatsoever that he and Wilbur had found the hideout the rustlers were using. Depending on what lay at the end of this tunnel, it might be the best one yet, a headquarters that would serve them for the rest of the time they were operating in the Tonto Basin.

And Stovepipe had a feeling that that time might soon be drawing to a close. If his theory was right, the hidden goal behind the plot had been achieved already. More than likely there would be a few more moves in the game, just for appearances' sake, but not many.

With the darkness thick around him, Stovepipe pressed forward. He had to move slowly now, since he couldn't see where he was going. He thought it unlikely that there were any pits or crevasses up ahead, since from all indications riders used this passage frequently, but he couldn't be sure about that. He probed carefully with each step before he committed his weight to it.

With no warning, he bumped into something and jerked back. A quick exploration with an outstretched hand told him he had run into an irregular stone wall. Either the tunnel had come to an end—

which was difficult for him to believe, considering the circumstances—or else it had turned. A bend was the more reasonable explanation. He carried the Winchester in his right hand while he rested the left lightly against the wall and kept going.

After several more steps, he saw a point of light in front of him. It was small, and if it marked the other end of the tunnel, as it seemed to Stovepipe that it must, it was still a considerable distance away. He moved toward it, eager to see what was out there.

The light steadily grew bigger as he approached. He could see the walls of the tunnel now, as well as the dust on the floor, which still showed the marks of numerous hooves. Impatience tried to prod Stovepipe into a trot, but he maintained his slow, cautious pace. It was possible, even likely, that the gang had a guard posted at the entrance to the tunnel.

When he was this close to the answers he needed, he didn't want to ruin everything by blundering into trouble.

He stopped about ten feet short of the opening. From here he could see that the tunnel led to a broad, steep-walled canyon that had been carved into the rim in ages past. Enough grass grew out there for cattle to graze on it. If there was water in the canyon, it would make a perfect hideout for a gang of rustlers. He had a hunch the underground stream that usually fed the water hole originated in this hidden spot, only it flowed on the surface here. The outlaws might have dammed it up to form a small lake. That would explain why the water hole had gone dry the way it had.

That was pure speculation at this point, though, so

Stovepipe edged forward to try to confirm it without exposing himself to the gaze of any sentries outside.

He stiffened as he heard the clatter of hoofbeats coming from behind him. Riders were in the tunnel. Wilbur wouldn't have brought the horses into the passage, so it had to be someone else coming toward him. The only ones who knew about this tunnel other than the two of them were the outlaws.

Stovepipe pressed himself against the rough stone wall and looked back toward the bend. He thought he saw light flickering beyond it. That meant one of the riders was carrying a torch. They couldn't fail to see him as they moved on through the tunnel.

That meant he had to risk going out into the canyon, sentries or no sentries.

Once his mind was made up on a course of action, he acted quickly, as always. He hurried to the tunnel mouth and paused briefly to look out. A flash of late-afternoon sunlight reflecting on water to his left confirmed his guess about the outlaws forming a lake by damming up the stream that ran through the canyon.

More important, Stovepipe spotted a thick clump of brush not far from the entrance. He dashed to it and pushed through the branches, ignoring the thorns that scratched at him. Turning back toward the tunnel, he dropped down to one knee and then waited, silent and motionless.

Nobody shot at him, and no cries of alarm sounded. Was it possible the rustlers felt so confident in the security of their hideout that they hadn't posted a guard on the tunnel? Stovepipe supposed it was. The place was well hidden, after all.

The question now was whether Wilbur had spotted

the outlaws coming in time to duck out of sight. Stovepipe hoped that had been the case. But he was definitely worried as he waited for the riders to appear.

Two men on horseback emerged from the tunnel. Stovepipe could see them through a small gap in the branches. He didn't recognize either of the riders.

The next face he saw was familiar, though, and the sight made his heart sink for a second before his natural determination and optimism asserted themselves. Wilbur rode behind the first two men, hatless, his face scratched and bruised from a struggle. He looked angry, but he didn't appear to be badly hurt, so Stovepipe was thankful for that, anyway.

Two more members of the gang, men with hard, angular faces, followed Wilbur, their guns drawn. Stovepipe had no doubt they would shoot the redhead down if Wilbur made a break for it. Evidently they preferred to keep him a prisoner, though, instead of killing him out of hand. They probably wanted to question him.

Stovepipe didn't see any sign of his Appaloosa. Wilbur might have sent the Palouse running off before he was captured. It was possible the outlaws didn't know anyone else had discovered their hideout.

That might give him at least a little chance to salvage this situation, thought Stovepipe.

Nobody else rode out of the tunnel. The odds were pretty bad anyway—four to one—but Stovepipe knew they would get even worse if he allowed the four men to take Wilbur to their headquarters. He had to act now if he was going to. At least he had the element of surprise on his side.

He eased forward, trying not to make too many crackling sounds in the brush.

The two men with guns in their hands were the most immediate threat. Stovepipe waited until they had ridden past his position, then stepped out of the bushes. He probably could have shot both men off their horses before they knew what was going on, but gunning a man from behind was cold-blooded murder as far as Stovepipe was concerned.

Besides, he didn't want the racket of any gunshots to alert the rest of the gang that something was going on.

Instead he leaped up, grabbed the shirt of the unsuspecting outlaw on the left, and hauled him out of the saddle. At the same time, he swung the Winchester at the other man bringing up the rear and cracked the rifle's barrel across the side of his head.

The man Stovepipe had unhorsed let out a startled yell. The one he'd walloped was out cold and didn't make a sound as he toppled off his horse. Stovepipe pivoted and kicked the first man in the head, stretching him out unconscious on the ground.

If he and Wilbur could get away without the rustlers knowing their hideout had been discovered, thought Stovepipe, they could lead Sheriff Olsen and a posse back here, bottle up the gang, and put an end to all the trouble in the Tonto Basin.

Yeah, that was all he wanted.

That wry thought flashed through his mind as he lifted the rifle. At the same time, Wilbur spurred his dun forward. The sturdy mount crashed shoulder to shoulder with one of the horses in front. Both horses and riders went down in a welter of flailing arms and legs.

Stovepipe leveled the Winchester at the remaining mounted outlaw just as the man touched the butt of the gun on his hip. The rustler's draw froze right there. Stovepipe had the drop on him, and he knew it.

But then a grin spread across his beard-stubbled face. He said, "You can't afford a shot, can you, mister? If that rifle goes off, you'll have the rest of us coming down on you like a ton of bricks."

"Not before we can get out of here," said Stovepipe grimly, "and you'll be just as dead either way."

That was true, and the outlaw knew it. He grimaced, but he didn't pull his gun.

A few yards away, Wilbur was on top of the other rustler, his fist rising and falling to land with solid thuds. The scrappy redhead could brawl like an hombre twice his size. The man he was battling with went limp. Wilbur pushed himself to his feet.

"Sorry, Stovepipe," he began. "They snuck up on me before I knew they were there—"

That was as far as he got before the fourth and final outlaw dived out of the saddle at him without warning. Stovepipe swung the Winchester in that direction, but he couldn't shoot because now Wilbur was in the line of fire.

The two men rolled over on the ground. The outlaw was behind Wilbur with an arm looped around his neck in a brutal chokehold. At the same time, Wilbur served as a human shield while the outlaw finally got his gun out. He shoved the barrel under Wilbur's arm and triggered the weapon in Stovepipe's direction.

Stovepipe tried to throw himself out of the way, but something struck his head with the fury and force of a sledgehammer. He felt himself dropping the rifle and spinning off his feet. As he crumpled to the ground, he heard cursing and the sound of a struggle, then a man roared, "Gun him down! Don't let him get away!"

Gun-thunder slammed through the red chaos in Stovepipe's head, and that was the last thing he knew.

CHAPTER FORTY-TWO

The first thing Stovepipe was aware of when he came to was pain. It filled his entire body, which at this point consisted only of his head since he couldn't feel anything else. He felt the impulse to groan, but he stifled it.

Somewhere far in the back of his head, stirring despite the pounding agony, was a small voice warning him not to reveal that he was awake.

He had a few bad moments when he thought he was paralyzed, but then feeling began seeping back into his arms and legs and torso. He could tell he was lying on some rough surface, maybe the puncheon floor of a cabin. He remained absolutely motionless except for his shallow breathing.

The throbbing in his head subsided a little, but it was still painful every time his heart beat and sent blood racing through his brain. He knew now that he had survived being shot. The bullet must have just grazed his head, knocking him out.

Then he remembered that the last thing he'd heard had been the outlaws shooting at Wilbur, and he went cold inside. There was a good chance his old friend was dead. And as the gang's prisoner, Stovepipe knew he probably didn't have much time left, either.

He tensed his muscles just enough to determine that his arms and legs were tied. Head wounds tended to bleed a lot, so he was probably a gory mess and they had believed he was dead at first. Discovering that he was still alive, his captors had tied him up and brought him here, wherever here was. Stovepipe figured they wanted to find out if anybody else knew about their hideout. They would question him when he came to, and they wouldn't be gentle about it.

That was one more good reason to let them think he was unconscious for as long as he could.

A strange noise gradually intruded on his consciousness. It stopped and started, and at first he thought it was just inside his own head, a result of being knocked out, maybe. Then he realized the sounds actually formed a tune.

Somebody was humming the song "Buffalo Gals."

Stovepipe heard the rasp of a match being struck, then a moment later smelled tobacco smoke from a quirly. Paper rustled. Somebody was standing guard over his supposedly unconscious body, mused Stovepipe, but the fella was distracted. He was humming, smoking, and reading a newspaper, from the sound of it.

Tied hand and foot as he was, Stovepipe couldn't take advantage of that distraction. But maybe it could come in handy later on, he told himself. If his guard's attention strayed at just the right moment . . .

A door opened. Heavy footsteps clomped on the floor. Stovepipe heard a chair scrape back quickly.

The guard must have stood up. The newspaper rattled as it was put aside.

"He's still not awake?" asked a harsh, impatient voice.

"The varmint ain't budged," came the answer. "Been nary a peep outta him."

"Jack's tired of waiting. Get that bucket of water and douse him with it. That'll bring him around."

Stovepipe knew he was about to get wet. He told himself to react properly, so they wouldn't know he'd been conscious before.

"I ain't sure why we kept him alive," said the first man. "Anybody stumbles on the hideout, they die. Ain't that the rule?"

"Jack wants to make sure those two didn't tell anybody else about this place," the second man replied, confirming Stovepipe's hunch.

"I ain't sure but what we ought to abandon it anyway, since that other fella got away."

Stovepipe's heart leaped at those words, but he was careful not to show it.

Anyway, the other man said, "He didn't get away. As much as he was bleeding, he had to be hit pretty bad. Even if those men the boss sent after him don't find him, he's laying out there somewhere in the basin, dead."

Stovepipe knew they were talking about Wilbur. He wasn't going to believe that his partner was dead as long as there was a single shred of hope for him to cling to. From what the outlaws had said, he guessed that Wilbur was wounded but had made it back through the tunnel. If that was true, Wilbur would go for help.

All Stovepipe had to do was hang on until it got there.

That determined thought had just gone through his mind when a bucketful of water slapped him in the face, drenching his head. He didn't have to do much acting as he sputtered and thrashed on the floor. Some of the water had gone up his nose and threatened to choke him.

"Set him up before he drowns," the second man snapped.

Strong hands gripped Stovepipe's left arm and shoulder and hauled him upright. He shook his head and blew water out of his nose. It had gotten in his eyes, too, and he blinked to clear his vision.

He was inside a crude cabin, he saw as he glanced around. Two men were with him, the one who had lifted him into a sitting position and another who stood in front of him, thumbs hooked in a gun belt sagging under a prominent gut. This hombre had a jowly face like a bulldog. He scowled as he drew his revolver and pointed it at Stovepipe.

"Cut his feet loose," the man ordered. "He needs to be able to walk."

The man who had been standing guard was loose limbed and gangly. He drew a bowie knife from a sheath on his belt and bent over to cut the ropes around Stovepipe's ankles. With his hands tied behind his back, Stovepipe couldn't make a try for the knife. He kept his face expressionless, but inside he seethed with frustration because he couldn't make a play.

When Stovepipe's feet were loose, the man sheathed the Bowie, went behind him, and grasped him under the arms. He lifted Stovepipe to his feet, which were numb and didn't want to support him at first. He would have fallen if not for the outlaw's grip on him.

"Better get your sea legs, old son," the man told him.

"We're a long way from the sea," said Stovepipe.

That brought a chuckle from Bulldog-face. He gestured with the gun he held and said, "Come on."

Unsteadily, Stovepipe shuffled toward the door. His stride strengthened as feeling flowed back into his legs and feet. Having his arms pulled behind his back and his wrists lashed together made his movements awkward.

Bulldog-face backed through the doorway so he could keep the prisoner covered. As Stovepipe stepped out onto a porch built on the front of the cabin, he looked around and saw sunlight slanting into the canyon from the east. It was early morning, not long after dawn. He had been unconscious all night.

Several other similar structures slapped together out of gray, weathered planks stood nearby. Smoke rose from their stone chimneys. Stovepipe said, "You fellas didn't build these shacks. They've been here awhile."

"That's right," the man agreed. "The way I hear it, there was some sort of religious colony out here at one time. They all went loco. Killed each other, ate each other—hell, I don't know. But nobody comes around here anymore, so it makes a good place for fellas like us."

"Rustlers, you mean."

"The boss didn't send me over here to jaw with you. Keep moving."

"Where am I goin'?" asked Stovepipe.

"That biggest cabin right in front of you."

As Stovepipe walked, his gaze roved over his surroundings, committing details to memory because there was no telling what he might need to know once he got out of here. He *was* going to get out of here, because he wouldn't allow himself to consider any other alternative, just like he devoutly believed that Wilbur was still alive somehow.

The cabins were clustered at one end of the cliff-enclosed canyon, with the pond formed by the dammed-up stream at the other end. In between, scattered jags of cattle grazed. Stovepipe had no doubt all the animals were stolen.

The two outlaws followed him, and other members of the gang were sitting on the porches of the cabins, drinking or playing cards or cleaning their guns. They watched the little procession with interest, adding to the impossibility of Stovepipe making any sort of a break right now.

As they approached the largest cabin, a man stepped out onto the porch and waited for them. He was medium sized, with a handsome, arrogant face and thinning fair hair under a thumbed-back brown Stetson. He wore a holstered Colt with the butt cocked forward on his right hip. Several rings glittered on his fingers. He was a bit of a dandy, but that didn't mean he was any less dangerous.

When Stovepipe reached the foot of the steps, Bulldog-face growled, "That's far enough." Stovepipe stopped.

The man on the porch grinned down at him and asked, "Do you know who I am?"

"I'm guessin' your name's Jack Rawson," drawled Stovepipe.

"That's right. So now you've got me at a disadvantage, because I don't know who you are. All I know is that you're pretending to be a drifting cowpoke named Stewart." Rawson drew his revolver, pointed it at Stovepipe's face, and eared back the hammer. "So tell me who you really are, mister, and what you're doing here, or I'll blow your brains right out the back of your head."

CHAPTER FORTY-THREE

Stovepipe didn't care for staring down the barrel of the gun, but he kept his face expressionless and his voice calm as he said, "What makes you think I ain't just a cowhand?"

"Because ever since you and that pard of yours showed up in the basin, you've been around every time trouble broke out," snapped Rawson. "That can't be a coincidence."

"Shoot, mister, didn't you ever hear of plain ol' bad luck? It seems to follow us around. Take yesterday. Bob Ridgewell, the foreman of the HS Bar, sent me and Wilbur up here to check on that water hole. When we seen it was dry, we took the shovels we brung with us and started diggin' it out. You can go take a look and see for yourself that I'm tellin' the truth."

"Then what brought you through that tunnel?"

"Well, I figured there was an underground stream that'd been feedin' the water hole, and somethin' must've happened to dry it up. You see, I took a few courses years back when I was a young fella thinkin' about becomin' a minin' engineer, so I know a little about things like that. I wanted to see what had happened to affect the water hole, so I started pokin' around. When I spotted that tunnel, naturally I was curious."

"You know what they say about cats and curiosity," Rawson said with an ugly grin.

"Yeah, I reckon, but I ain't no feline. Whatever you're doin' in here, mister, it ain't no business o' mine. Let me go and I'll ride away and forget ever'thing I saw in here."

Stovepipe knew the chances of the boss rustler agreeing to that ranged from slim to none, but he wasn't really trying to convince Rawson to let him go. He was just playing for time, giving Wilbur more of a chance to get back here with the sheriff and a bunch of gun-toting deputies.

Rawson let out a harsh laugh and said, "Let you go? That's not going to happen, Stewart. But if you cooperate and tell me what I want to know, I'll see to it that you die quick. Give me trouble and before you cross the divide, you'll be screaming like you'd been grabbed by a bunch of Apaches."

Stovepipe didn't doubt it. But he was going to hang on to the hope that it would never come to that.

"What happened to my pard?" he asked. "Is he all right? I might be more inclined to talk if I knew he ain't been hurt."

He didn't let on that he already knew that wasn't the case, from the conversation between Bulldog-face and the other man he had overheard earlier.

"Your partner's dead," Rawson said flatly. Stovepipe saw his finger tighten on the trigger. "And you will be, too, in another minute if you don't start talking."

Getting a bullet through the head wouldn't accomplish anything. Stovepipe remembered something else he had overheard and made his voice rougher than his usual soft drawl as he said, "All right, damn it. If you want the truth, here it is. It didn't take long for Wilbur and me to figure out what your game is here, and we wanted in on it."

"Our game, eh? What do you think that is?"

"You're after a big cleanup. You're going to sweep through the whole basin, steal all the cows you haven't already stole, and drive 'em down to Mexico. I reckon you'll sell 'em there for enough dinero to spend the rest of your lives south of the border, sippin' tequila and playin' with them little brown gals."

That was, in fact, the theory Stovepipe had come up with originally, before a few other discoveries had put him on a different path. The rustling was still an important part of what was going on in the Tonto Basin, but it wasn't the endgame as he had supposed it to be at first.

Rawson was still sneering at him, but the outlaw's gun was a little lower now. He said, "What makes you think you've got a right to horn in on that?"

"We can help you," said Stovepipe. "Or I reckon I can now, since you claim Wilbur's dead."

"Why would you want to help us if we killed your partner?"

Stovepipe shrugged and said, "It's true Wilbur and I rode together for a good spell, but hell, money's money, ain't it? And I wouldn't mind takin' life easy down in Mexico, neither."

"And how could you be of any help to us?"

"Well, think about it," said Stovepipe. "I ride for the HS Bar now. Don't you reckon it'd be easier to wipe the spread clean if you've got somebody on the inside workin' on your behalf?"

For the first time, Stovepipe saw a glitter of genuine interest in Rawson's faded blue eyes. Rawson said, "That doesn't explain how you got mixed up with Dan Hartford."

"Now that really was just pure bad luck, like I told you. We saw a fella bein' chased and figured we ought to give him a hand. Never did like to see an hombre with the odds stacked against him. But once we took cards in that hand, our luck ran out and we wound up on the sheriff's bad side. It took a while for us to convince him that we weren't really workin' with Hartford."

That story was basically true, which made it even easier for Stovepipe to sound believable as he told it. He went on, "By the time we'd done that, we had figured out what was goin' on around here and decided we ought to try to cut ourselves a piece o' the pie. That's how come we went to work for the HS Bar. It seemed pretty obvious that's where you fellas'd be movin' on next."

"You've killed some of my men," said Rawson. "You think we're just going to forgive you for that?"

Stovepipe shrugged again and said, "Well, you killed Wilbur, and like I told you, money is money. Comes right down to it, we all do what we got to do to get along, I reckon."

Rawson frowned and regarded Stovepipe intently as he lowered the gun the rest of the way. After a moment he pouched the iron and ordered, "Granville, you and Deuce take Stewart back to the cabin where you had him before. Keep an eye on him while I think about this."

"You're not gonna kill him?" The startled question came from Granville, or Bulldog-face, as Stovepipe had been thinking of him.

"Not just yet. Now, do what I told you."

"Sure, Jack," Granville said with a sigh. He motioned to Stovepipe with the gun he still held. "Get moving, you."

Stovepipe didn't show how pleased he was with this development as he turned and started trudging back toward the other cabin. He had been playing for time, and he had bought some. That might keep him alive until Wilbur showed up with help.

And if Wilbur *didn't* show up—although Stovepipe didn't like to think about that possibility and had to force himself to do so—wedging his way into the gang might well be the only way he could survive and still have a chance to bust up the scheme.

When they reached the cabin where Stovepipe had regained consciousness, the gangling, loose-limbed Deuce asked, "Are we supposed to tie his legs again?"

"Jack didn't say for us to," replied Granville. "He just said to keep an eye on him." To Stovepipe, the bulldog-faced man added, "Sit down at the table there, and don't try anything funny. Jack might not like it if we shot you, but if you were trying to get away, I reckon he'd understand."

Stovepipe lowered himself onto a stool next to the rough-hewn table in the middle of the cabin's single room. The place had four bunks in it, two on each of the side walls, a fireplace, and some crude shelves where supplies were kept. A coffeepot sat at the edge of the hearth, where a fire had burned down to glowing embers.

Stovepipe nodded toward the pot and said, "If there's still any coffee in there, I'd plumb admire to have a cup."

"How could you drink it with your hands tied behind your back?" asked Deuce.

"Well, I reckon you could untie me long enough for that . . ."

"Nix," said Granville. "We're taking a big enough chance leaving your legs untied. I'll be damned if I'm gonna have Jack walk in and find you sitting at the table loose and drinking coffee like it's some sort of blasted party."

Stovepipe figured that even a cup of coffee in these squalid surroundings would hardly qualify as a party, but he didn't say anything else. He was just glad he wasn't bound hand and foot anymore. He could move around a little now if he had to.

Deuce sat down at the far end of the table and picked up the folded newspaper he had tossed aside earlier. When the rustler opened the paper, which came from San Francisco, Stovepipe was able to make out the date, almost six months earlier. People out here on the frontier didn't care about such things. They were always glad to get any news, even if it was months out of date.

Granville took a tin cup from one of the shelves, went to the fireplace, used a piece of leather to protect his hand, and picked up the coffeepot. He poured some of the thick, black brew into the cup. It appeared to be about the color and consistency of tar, but Stovepipe felt a pang of longing for some of it, anyway.

Granville took a sip, then a grimace twisted his jowly features.

"Blast it, how old is this stuff?" he asked.

Deuce frowned and said, "I think it was brewed day before yesterday."

Granville tossed what was in his cup onto the embers, where it sizzled and smoked.

"Well, it's not fit to drink. Brew some more."

"I would, but I'm outta Arbuckle's," said Deuce. "Kettlebelly might have some he'd let you borrow."

"Which cabin is his?"

"Two over, toward the lake."

"I'll go see about it. You stay here and watch Stewart."

"Sure," Deuce agreed without hesitation. He seemed to be the easygoing sort. That didn't fool Stovepipe into thinking the outlaw was any less dangerous because of that.

Granville took the coffeepot, went out onto the doorstep, and poured out the rest of the contents. Then he set the pot on the hearth again and left the cabin. Rawson might not have liked that if he knew about it, but Stovepipe figured Granville planned on being back before his absence was discovered.

Stovepipe knew he might not get a better chance than this. He couldn't get to his feet and rush the length of the table without Deuce having time to draw a gun. He had to get closer . . .

"What's the story on the front page o' that paper say?" asked Stovepipe.

"What story?" Deuce asked as he lowered the paper, rattling it as he had before.

"Somethin' about some political scandal back in Washington, I think."

"Oh hell, there's always some scandal in Washington. Those politicians are such crooks they put fellas like us to shame."

Stovepipe got to his feet, grinning, and said, "Yeah, why waste your time stealin' a few cows when you can get elected to office and steal hundreds o' thousands of dollars?"

He moved around the end of the table toward Deuce, leaning forward and pretending to read the newspaper as he did so. He went on, "From what I hear, all them senators and congressmen have got lady friends what they ain't married to stashed away, too. I reckon you've got to steal plenty of money to afford that."

Deuce laughed and said, "Yeah, I—" Then he stopped short as he realized that Stovepipe had come halfway along the table toward him. He let go of the newspaper with his right hand and started to move that hand toward the butt of his gun as he said, "You'd better get back down where you—"

At that moment, a volley of gunfire erupted somewhere outside, shattering the peacefulness of the morning without any warning.

CHAPTER FORTY-FOUR

Stovepipe didn't hesitate. He reacted instantly, lowering his head and diving at Deuce, who threw the newspaper aside and started to bolt up out of his chair as he clawed at the gun on his hip.

Stovepipe rammed into the rustler before Deuce's iron could clear leather. The impact drove Deuce backward. He lost his footing and fell, and the back of his head banged into the floorboards so hard that his head bounced up several inches. He went limp all over.

The gunfire continued outside, punctuated by shouted curses. Stovepipe twisted around as he sprawled half on and half off Deuce's senseless form. He was all too aware that he might not have much time. He had no way of knowing how long Deuce would remain unconscious, although the outlaw certainly seemed to be out cold at the moment.

Stovepipe turned his back toward Deuce and fumbled around behind him until his fingers brushed the bone handle of the bowie knife. He pulled the knife from its sheath and turned it so he could rest the blade against the rawhide thongs around his wrists. Carefully, so he wouldn't slice any veins or arteries open, he started sawing on the bonds.

The rawhide was stubbornly tough, but evidently Deuce kept his knife honed to a razor-edge. It began parting the thongs. Stovepipe nicked himself a couple of times, but although the cuts stung, they weren't deep enough to worry about—he hoped. As he felt the warm trickle of blood, he began to wonder.

Then, abruptly, he was loose. He pulled his arms around in front of him, his muscles twinging painfully as he did so. They worked, however, and he was glad to see that he wasn't bleeding to death. The cuts were minor, as he had hoped.

Deuce's partially drawn revolver had fallen out of its holster and lay on the floor. Stovepipe scooped it up and then scrambled to his feet. He looked around and spotted something he hadn't noticed before, his ivory-handled Colt lying on one of the shelves, partially hidden by bags of flour and sugar. He quickly reclaimed it and tucked Deuce's gun behind his belt, along with the bowie knife.

Being well armed again made him feel better, as did the sounds of battle coming from outside the cabin. Only one explanation made any sense: the hideout was under attack by a posse from Hat Creek, possibly augmented by cowboys from the HS Bar, the Box D, or some of the other spreads in the basin.

One logical and very welcome conclusion followed from that. Wilbur was alive and had brought the men here to bust up the gang of rustlers and outlaws.

Stovepipe went to the door and eased it open. He saw puffs of gun smoke coming from the top of the cliffs around the canyon. Sharpshooters were up

there, picking off any of the owlhoots foolish enough
to expose themselves to the deadly fire. More shots
blasted down there inside the canyon, so Stovepipe
knew some of the attackers had come through the
tunnel as well.

No bullets seemed to be directed at the cabin
where he was, so he stepped outside. At that moment
he heard a man yell, "Stewart!" followed by a torrent
of obscenities. Turning toward the sound of the
voice, Stovepipe saw Granville rushing toward him.
The man's bulldog-like face was flushed with rage,
and flame spouted from the muzzle of the gun gripped
in his fist.

The slug sizzled through the air next to Stovepipe's ear. The ivory-handled Colt roared and bucked
in the range detective's paw, and Granville stopped
short like he had run into a stone wall as Stovepipe's
bullet drove into his chest. Granville's eyes opened
wide in shock and pain as he came up on his toes and
balanced there for a second with blood welling from
the wound, before he pitched forward on his face
and didn't move again.

"You damn—" another voice rasped behind Stovepipe. He whirled around to see Deuce lunging at him
with the stool that Stovepipe had been sitting on earlier upraised to strike with as a weapon. Deuce looked
a little groggy from being knocked out, but he was
still a threat.

Stovepipe ducked, making Deuce miss with the
stool. As Deuce stumbled against him, Stovepipe
brought a knee up sharply into the rustler's groin.
Deuce yelled and then doubled over, gagging. Stovepipe shut him up with a rap on the head from the
Colt. As Deuce collapsed, Stovepipe hoped his skull

wasn't getting too mushy from the repeated blows. The fellow hadn't seemed like a bad sort, for a rustler and killer. On the other hand, maybe he wouldn't waste any worry on the varmint, Stovepipe decided.

He turned back to survey the scene of battle in the canyon. He saw men running back and forth, stopping to trade shots with other men on horseback. Stovepipe spotted both of Sheriff Frank Olsen's deputies he knew by name, Warren Purdue and Brock Matthews. They were among the mounted men, so Stovepipe assumed the posse members were on horseback, with the outlaws who had been taken by surprise in their supposedly impregnable hideout on foot.

He looked for Wilbur but didn't see the redhead. That was a mite worrisome, but he figured Wilbur had to be alive, otherwise the sheriff and his men wouldn't have known where the hideout was located so they could raid it.

Unless Wilbur, mortally wounded, had lived long enough to reach Hat Creek with the news, then died—

No. Stovepipe wasn't going to let himself think that. Instead he ran toward the larger cabin where Jack Rawson had interrogated him earlier.

He wanted to get his hands on Rawson and take the boss rustler alive. He needed Rawson to expose the last bit of villainy in this scheme and wrap everything up so that Dan Hartford would be cleared of that murder charge.

A bullet kicked up dust at Stovepipe's feet. He realized that one of the men on the rim was shooting at him, probably having mistaken him for a member of the gang because he was on foot. He waved an arm and yelled, "Hold your fire, you blasted idiot! I ain't one o' them!"

That wasn't going to do any good, he knew. The air was too full of gun-thunder for anyone on top of the cliffs to hear him.

Then hoofbeats pounded behind Stovepipe and he whirled around, instinctively thinking he was under attack again. This time, however, he saw a burly, white-mustached figure on horseback bearing down on him. Sheriff Frank Olsen thrust a hand toward him and shouted, "Come on, Stewart!"

Stovepipe shoved his Colt in its holster, then reached up to grab Olsen's wrist. The sheriff clasped his wrist at the same time, and Stovepipe was able to swing up onto the horse behind the lawman. Olsen turned his head and asked, "Where can I find the boss of this bunch?"

Stovepipe pointed to Rawson's cabin and said, "Over there!"

Olsen called to his deputies, "Warren! Brock! Follow me!" and charged toward the cabin. Purdue and Matthews fell in with them, flanking the sheriff's horse.

Muzzle flame bloomed from inside the windows and beyond the open door as the men in the cabin opened fire on the star packers. Olsen and his men returned the shots, which made Stovepipe grimace. He didn't want Rawson to catch a slug, at least fatally, but he couldn't expect the lawmen not to fight back.

"Ride up next to the porch, Sheriff!" Stovepipe told Olsen. "I'm goin' in there!"

"Don't be a damned fool!" replied Olsen.

"I want the boss alive!" Stovepipe told him. Olsen grunted and sent his horse lunging forward, turning the animal at the last moment so that Stovepipe was able to throw himself off the horse's back and land running on the porch.

Stovepipe dived through the open door as a gun went off practically in his face. The explosion hammered his eardrums, and he felt the sting of burning powder on his face. But the bullet missed him, and as he somersaulted and came up on his feet, he lashed out with the gun in his hand and crashed it against the head of the man who had shot at him.

At the same time, he grabbed the second revolver from behind his belt and fired left-handed at a man on the other side of the cabin as soon as he realized the varmint wasn't Jack Rawson. The bullet thudded into the outlaw's chest and knocked him back into the fireplace behind him, scattering ashes and sparks.

Stovepipe dropped to a knee as a bullet from the other direction burned his cheek. A big, bearded man in a steeple-crowned sombrero was drawing a bead on him for another shot when Stovepipe punched two rounds into the man's ample belly. The man grunted, dropped his gun, doubled over, and collapsed.

That made two outlaws dead and the man Stovepipe hoped was Jack Rawson out cold. Stovepipe hooked a boot toe under the man's shoulder and rolled him onto his back.

An ugly face he had never seen before stared up at him.

Stovepipe bit back a curse. These three men were the only ones in the cabin, and none of them was the leader of the gang.

The shooting had stopped right outside, although it continued elsewhere in the canyon. Olsen, Purdue, and Matthews were holding their fire because Stovepipe was in here. He called, "Don't shoot," and stepped out onto the porch.

"What in blazes happened in there?" Olsen demanded.

"I cleaned house a mite," said Stovepipe. "I didn't come up with the varmint I wanted, though. Jack Rawson, the fella I had you send that telegram about, is the leader of this bunch, and this is his cabin, but he ain't in here. Must be somewhere else in the canyon."

"Then he's probably dead," said Olsen. The shooting had started to die away. "Sounds like the posse's mopping up now."

"Where's Wilbur?" asked Stovepipe, trying but not succeeding in keeping the worry out of his voice.

"Back in Hat Creek," the sheriff replied. "He'll be all right. He's got a bullet hole in his arm and the doc said he didn't need to ride all the way up here, but he was able to tell us just where to look and how to get in here." Olsen glanced around. "Looks like those skunks found themselves a pretty good hideout. They should've guarded the entrance to it better, though."

A wave of relief had gone through Stovepipe at the news that Wilbur was all right. He said, "I knew if anybody could hang on and get the word back to you, it was Wilbur."

"Yeah, he's a tough little galoot. He was worried sick that he'd gone off and left you, but he said it looked like you'd been shot in the head and were done for. He was determined to make this bunch pay for killing you." Olsen chuckled. "He'll be happy to see that you're still alive."

"I was mighty happy to hear that he'd made it, too." Stovepipe holstered his gun. The shooting was over now. "Reckon we'd better look for Rawson."

"That reminds me," said Olsen. He reached under his vest to his shirt pocket and brought out a piece of paper. "You got an answer to your telegram."

He leaned down from the saddle to hand the telegraph flimsy to Stovepipe, who took it and unfolded it. A feeling of satisfaction went through the lanky cowboy as he read the words printed on the paper. The information in the telegram confirmed all the hunches he'd had.

"Thanks, Sheriff," he said as he put the paper in his own pocket. "Let's find Rawson, and then maybe we can finish cleanin' up this mess."

A search of the basin produced a surprising result, however. The rustlers numbered eighteen men. Eleven of them were dead, the other seven wounded and taken prisoner.

None of them was Jack Rawson.

"What are you saying?" Sheriff Olsen demanded when Stovepipe informed him of that fact. "The ringleader of the whole damned bunch got away somehow?"

"Yeah," said Stovepipe as he patted his breast pocket where the folded telegram lay. "But I've got a pretty good hunch right where he's goin'."

CHAPTER FORTY-FIVE

The citizens of Hat Creek were startled that evening when shots broke out around the sheriff's office and jail. Two figures rushed out of the building and dashed toward saddled horses tied at the hitch rack in front. As Laura Dempsey swung up onto one of the mounts, Dan Hartford turned around and fired the gun he held at the jail, shattering one of the front windows and sending bullets screaming through the door he and Laura had left open behind them.

Then he jerked the reins of both horses loose from the rack, leaped into the saddle of the second animal, and hauled the horse around. Laura did likewise with her mount. Both of them leaned forward in the saddle as they kicked the horses into motion.

Sheriff Frank Olsen charged out of the jail and cursed sulfurously as he lifted his revolver and fired after the escaping prisoners. The shots boomed through the rapidly fading light and made people who were on the street scurry for cover. That seemed to be the only effect they had, though, because the fugitives didn't slow down at all.

The pounding of Dan's heart in his chest seemed almost as loud to him as those gunshots. He looked over at Laura's strained face and tried to summon up a reassuring smile, but he wasn't sure how well he succeeded. Worry filled him. He wasn't sure this jailbreak was a good idea, but it seemed to be their only real chance to escape the charges against them.

The settlement fell behind them. When Dan glanced back, he could see the scattered lights twinkling. He wasn't able to spot any pursuit. For now, it appeared that he and Laura had made a clean getaway. Dan kept his horse moving at a gallop, though, and Laura did likewise.

They didn't slow down until they had covered at least a mile.

As they pulled their mounts back to a walk, Laura said, "Dan, I'm so scared."

"So am I," Dan agreed. "I really think everything is going to work out, though."

"If it doesn't . . ."

"We're just not going to think about that," Dan said with a hard, bleak edge to his voice.

They rode north from Hat Creek. The Box D lay to the northwest, but there was nothing waiting for them there. Salvation, if there was going to be any, would come from the HS Bar, which was their destination at the moment. Once again, they were going to appeal to Laura's friend Jessica Stafford for help.

The sky darkened steadily until millions of stars were visible in the ebony canopy overhead. A three-quarter moon had poked over the Mogollon Rim, so between its silvery glow and that of the stars, there was plenty of light for the two riders to see where they were going.

Dan kept an eye on their back trail but didn't see anybody following them. That was good.

To keep the horses fresh, they alternated between a walk and a ground-eating lope. The miles fell behind them as the night wore on. The moon rose higher, marking the passage of time.

It was a long ride from Hat Creek to the headquarters of the HS Bar. The hour was close to midnight by the time Dan and Laura came in sight of the ranch house with its surrounding buildings. The barns, the corrals, the bunkhouse and cook shack and blacksmith shop all bulked darkly, with no lights showing. Everybody had turned in. The ranch was asleep for the night.

Dan wanted to keep it that way for the time being. He reined in and lifted his hand in a signal for Laura to stop as well.

"We'd better go the rest of the way on foot," he said. "Otherwise we'll have every dog on the place barking its fool head off. We don't want to rouse the crew, just Mrs. Stafford."

"All right," said Laura. "I understand."

She dismounted, as did Dan. They left the horses tied to some small trees, with enough play in the reins that the animals would be able to graze until someone came to fetch them. The two fugitives stole toward the house on foot, moving as quietly as possible.

Dan worried that the dogs still might scent them and raise a commotion, but luck was with them and he and Laura reached the side of the house without being discovered. They paused there, and Dan took advantage of this opportunity to draw Laura into his arms.

He hoped this wouldn't be the last chance he'd

ever have to kiss her, he thought as he brought his lips down on hers, but just in case it was . . .

She returned the kiss with the same sort of hungry urgency he felt. Both of them would have been content to have it go on forever.

But it couldn't. Dan drew back slightly and whispered, "Are you ready?"

Laura swallowed and nodded.

"Let's go," she whispered back.

Holding hands, they slid along the edge of the house to the front porch and climbed to it. They stopped at the door. Dan lifted his free hand and rapped softly but insistently on the panel. He kept it up until a step sounded on the other side and the door swung open a couple of inches.

"Who in the world is out there?" demanded Jessica Stafford. "I warn you, I have a gun—"

"Don't shoot, Jess!" Laura exclaimed. "It's me!"

"Laura?" asked Jessica as the door opened wider. "Good Lord, what— Is that Dan Hartford with you?"

Jessica didn't have a lamp or a candle with her, but the illumination from the moon and stars was enough for her to be able to make out the two figures on the ranch house's front porch.

"Yes, ma'am," said Dan, "it's me."

Jessica swung the screen door out and stepped onto the porch. As she had told them, she had a small pistol in her right hand. She said, "What are the two of you— Oh my God. You broke out of jail again, didn't you?"

"We had to," said Laura. "Sheriff Olsen found those rustlers and he and a posse wiped them out. But he still believes that Dan and I were working with them all along!" A shudder went through her. "Dan's still going on trial for murdering Abel and . . . and Henry."

"But surely, if the sheriff found the actual rustlers—"

"They were all killed," Dan said grimly. "There's nobody left to clear my name. That means I'm going to be convicted. They'll hang me for sure, unless Laura and I get out of this part of the country."

Laura put a hand on Jessica's arm.

"Can we stay here until we figure out what to do next, Jess? I know it's a lot to ask—"

"Nonsense," said Jessica briskly. Finding the two fugitives on her front porch seemed to have thrown her for a loop at first, but now she had recovered her usual cool aplomb. "Of course you can stay here. Come inside before anyone sees you. We don't want anybody else to know that you're here."

The three of them went into the house. Jessica continued, "Go into the parlor. I'll be back in just a minute, and we can talk about what we're going to do."

She was wearing just a nightdress. Dan figured she wanted to put on a robe. He and Laura stepped into the darkened parlor.

"Light the lamp on the table," Jessica said from the foyer. "There are matches next to it."

"I'll do it," offered Laura. "I've visited here enough that I know my way around."

"Be careful," Dan told her as he moved over toward a window that opened onto the front porch. He slid it open a few inches, slowly and cautiously so that it didn't make any sound. "Don't burn yourself."

"I think that's the least of our worries, don't you?"

"I don't want you to be hurt ever again," he said. "You've already been through enough."

"There won't be much more," said Laura as she found the box of matches on the table. She lit one, lifted the chimney on the lamp, and held the flame to the wick. When it caught, she lowered the chimney, and the soft yellow glow from the lamp welled out into the comfortably furnished parlor.

A step sounded from the open, arched doorway between the parlor and the foyer. Dan and Laura both turned in that direction, and despite being somewhat prepared for what they saw, Laura gasped.

A man neither of them had ever seen before stood there gripping a .45 revolver that he leveled at them. Just behind him and to the side stood Jessica Stafford. A cool smile curved her lips, and the small-caliber weapon in her hand was pointed at the two fugitives as well.

"Jess, what—" Laura began.

"Shut up," Jessica snapped. "There's nothing else to be said. Sheriff Olsen is probably already on his way out here. He found the two of you here before, after all."

"Yeah, but this time when he gets here, he'll just find bodies," the man said with an ugly grin. "The bodies of the man who murdered Henry Stafford and Abel Dempsey and the slut who planned the whole thing with him."

Dan started to take a step forward as his face twisted with anger. He said, "You son of a—"

"Hold it right there," rasped the man with the gun. "Unless you're in a big hurry to die. If you are, I'll be glad to accommodate you. Better remember, though, the lady dies a few seconds after you do."

"I can take care of that, Jack," said Jessica.

"Hell, baby, after the way you took care of Dempsey and Stafford, I never doubted that."

Laura forced out words, saying, "Jess, why . . . why are you doing this?"

"Because it wraps everything up all nice and neat. The whole ugly affair will be over. The two people who were behind everything will be dead, and so are all the men who worked for them."

"Yeah, the sheriff cost us some money when he and that posse raided our hideout this morning," said the man with the gun, "but in the long run it doesn't really matter that much. The real payoff was right here, and now we don't have to split it with anybody." He glanced at Jessica. "Isn't that right, Stella?"

"It's Jessica, damn it," she snapped. "You'd better get used to that, Jack."

"Yeah, sorry. I guess I'd better have a new name, too, when I show up in a few months to marry the Widow Stafford and help her run this fine big ranch."

"It'll be even bigger by then," Jessica said, "because I'll have bought the Box D and the other ranches we've nearly wiped out. This will be the biggest, wealthiest spread the Tonto Basin has ever seen."

"Yeah, and all that's left to make that come true is for these two to die," the man said as the gun in his hand came up toward Dan and his finger tightened on the trigger.

CHAPTER FORTY-SIX

"Drop it, Rawson!" Stovepipe shouted as he threw open the front door and charged into the foyer.

He had waited to announce his presence until Jack Rawson and the woman he now knew was really named Stella Bellamy had incriminated themselves good and proper. But that meant cutting it close and putting Dan and Laura in even more danger. It had to be done, though, so that Sheriff Frank Olsen could hear everything from the open window.

Now there was no time to lose. Rawson whirled toward Stovepipe. His mouth twisted in a hate-filled snarl. Stovepipe already had his gun out, but Rawson's reactions were rattler-quick. He got off a shot that burned past Stovepipe's ear before the range detective slammed two rounds into his body. Rawson reeled back under the impact and fell against Jessica. Blood from his wounds welled out onto her nightdress as he clutched at her shoulder with his free hand to keep himself from falling.

From the window, which he thrust up all the way

now, Sheriff Olsen shouted, "Get away from him, ma'am! Get out of the way!"

"Don't shoot!" Jessica cried. "Don't kill me! It was all Jack's idea, I swear! He forced me to go along with him—"

"You . . . lyin' . . . bitch!" Rawson grated. He still had his gun in his other hand. He brought it up, rammed the barrel against her belly, and said, "You know it was . . . all you!" as he pulled the trigger.

The muffled explosion threw Jessica back against the wall. As she hung there, her face twisted by pain and horror as a crimson stain flooded her midsection, Rawson staggered around in time for four more bullets—two each from Stovepipe and Olsen—to crash into his body. He jittered backward a couple of steps in a macabre dance and then collapsed, half in the foyer and half in the parlor. A couple of feet away, Jessica slid down the wall into a sitting position and died with her hands pressed to her stomach.

By now, Dan had Laura in his arms. He held her so tightly it seemed like he was never going to let her go.

Stovepipe looked over at the window and Olsen and said, "I reckon you heard enough, Sheriff?"

"More than enough," the lawman replied. "And it's going to be a while before it stops making me a little sick, too."

"That right there is what started me to thinkin'," said Stovepipe as he held up a red silk thread and placed it on the table in front of him. "I found it caught on one o' the rocks where the bushwhacker who killed Abel Dempsey was hidin' when she took that shot at Dan."

"She," Laura repeated.

"Yes'm. Miz Stafford—or Stella Bellamy, if you want to call her by her real name—never shied away from doin' her own killin' when she needed to. She killed your husband, and then she killed her own husband. Although I reckon she and poor Mr. Stafford weren't never legally married, since she'd already gotten hitched to Jack Rawson over in Kansas seven years ago."

They were all sitting around the table in the dining room of the Box D ranch house: Stovepipe, Wilbur, Dan, Laura, and Sheriff Olsen. Wilbur's left arm was in a black sling he would have to wear until the bullet wound in it healed, but the doctor had said it was all right for him to ride as long as he took it easy.

His old friend would have been here no matter what the doctor said, Stovepipe knew. Wilbur wasn't one for missing the wrap-up of a case.

Sheriff Olsen shook his head and said, "It's almost more than I can believe, if I hadn't heard it with my own ears. A lady like that, turning out to be a cold-blooded killer."

"Yeah, it's hard for a fella to wrap his brain around somethin' like that," agreed Stovepipe. "When I found that silk thread, I knew it looked like it came from somethin' a lady might wear, and then later on I saw Miz Stafford wearin' a silk shirt."

Laura nodded and said, "Yes, she did that a lot. She said she liked the way silk feels. Like . . . like money, she said."

"Her shirt got snagged that day, and that made me remember the thread I'd found," Stovepipe went on. "I recollected, too, hearin' Dan say he saw powder burns on the back o' Abel Dempsey's shirt. That meant whoever shot him got up close behind him. Dempsey was an old-timer who'd seen his share o' trouble over the years. He wouldn't let anybody get the drop on him like that unless it was somebody he trusted. Like, say, his wife's best friend."

Wilbur said, "So you knew she had killed Dempsey almost from the first, Stovepipe?"

"Let's say I had an inklin'. But I didn't have any real proof and didn't know for sure what was behind it. Then Stafford was killed, too, at a place where his wife knew he'd be, and I asked myself if maybe he was the real target all along. If Miz Stafford had her sights set on inheritin' the spread, then all the rustlin' and the mysterious deaths of those other ranchers would muddy the waters and keep suspicion from fallin' on her. Plus, they made some money off the stolen stock, too, which never hurts, and weakened the other spreads in the basin so she'd have an easier time takin' them over when she was ready. If all that was true, she had to be tied up with the rustlers . . . but I didn't know just how close that tie was until you gave me that reply to my telegram, Sheriff, and I found out that Rawson was married to a lady outlaw named Stella Bellamy who'd disappeared a few years ago. Didn't take much of a leap to figure out that Stella Bellamy was callin' herself Jessica Stafford these days. After that came together, it was just a matter of gettin' the proof."

"Which we did by staging that jailbreak and using these two as the bait for a trap," Olsen said with a solemn nod toward Dan and Laura. "That still bothers me. It was too much of a risk."

Dan said, "With our lives at stake, Sheriff, it was worth the risk. That's why we were willing to go along with Stovepipe's idea." He smiled across the table at Stovepipe and Wilbur. "I've got to say, you two don't look like any range detectives I've ever seen—not that I've run across that many of them."

"That's one reason we're good at our jobs," said Wilbur. "That, and Stovepipe's so blasted smart and stubborn."

"So what happens now?" asked Laura.

Olsen said, "The judge has already dropped the charges against the two of you, so I reckon you're free to go on about your business."

"But what *is* our business? My husband is dead, my neighbors are dead, the whole valley is in an uproar . . ."

"You've got a good foreman and a good crew here on the Box D," Stovepipe pointed out. "I figure with some work, you can put ever'thing right again." He smiled. "And I reckon Dan'd be glad to give you a hand."

"That's true," said Dan. "You know it is."

"That would look scandalous," Laura objected.

"Not to folks who know the truth," said Stovepipe. "I ain't sure I'd worry overmuch about anybody else."

"Anyway," added Wilbur, "some other scandal will come along, and before you know it people will have forgotten about all of this."

"I suppose you're right." Laura reached over and clasped Dan's hand. "I'm willing to risk it, if you are."

"You know the answer to that," he told her.

A short time later, Stovepipe, Wilbur, and Sheriff Frank Olsen stood on the front porch of the ranch house. They had left Dan and Laura inside, talking quietly about whatever it was they needed to talk about. For once, Stovepipe wasn't the least bit curious about what that might be. It was their business, not his.

"What are the two of you going to be doing now?" asked Olsen.

"Figured I'd send a telegram to our boss first thing in the mornin'," said Stovepipe. "I'll let him know how things here played out and tell him that Wilbur's shot up and needs some time to recuperate."

"Hey, I can ride," Wilbur protested. "The sawbones said I could."

"He also told you to take it easy," said Stovepipe, "so if there ain't no other urgent case that needs our attention, I reckon it won't hurt for us to rest and relax a mite."

Olsen suppressed a groan and said, "Does that mean the two of you are going to be hanging around Hat Creek for a while?"

"Looks like there's a good chance of it," drawled Stovepipe.

"You're not gonna sniff out some other mystery and wind up causing hell to start popping again, are you?"

"Sheriff," exclaimed Wilbur, "I sure wish you hadn't said that. Now you've gone and given him ideas!"

*Keep reading for a sepcial excerpt
of the new Johnstone adventure*

DIE BY THE GUN
A Chuckwagon Trail Western
by William W. Johnstone *and* J. A. Johnstone

*In this thrilling frontier saga, bestselling authors
William W. Johnstone and J. A. Johnstone celebrate an unsung
hero of the American West: a humble chuckwagon cook
searching for justice—and fighting for his life . . .*

DIE BY THE GUN
With one successful cattle drive under his belt,
Dewey "Mac" McKenzie is on a first-name basis with
danger. Marked for death for a crime he didn't commit
and eager to get far away from the territory, he signed
on as a cattle drive chuckwagon cook to save his own
skin—and learned how to serve up a tasty hot stew.
Turns out Mac has a talent for fixing good vittles.
He's also pretty handy with a gun. But Mac's enemies
are hungry for more—and they've hired a gang of
ruthless killers to turn up the heat . . .

Mac knows he's a dead man. His only hope is to join
another cattle drive on the Goodnight-Loving Trail,
deep in New Mexico Territory. The journey ahead is
even deadlier than the hired guns behind him.
His trail boss is an ornery cuss. His crew mate is the
owner's spoiled son. And the route is overrun with
kill-crazy rustlers and bloodthirsty Comanche. To make
matters worse, Mac's would-be killers are closing in fast.
But when the cattle owner's son is kidnapped,
the courageous young cook has no choice but to
jump out of the frying pan—and into the fire . . .

On sale now, where books are sold.

CHAPTER ONE

Dewey Mackenzie spun away from the bar, the finger of whiskey in his shot glass sloshing as he avoided a body flying through the air. He winced as a gun discharged not five feet away from his head. He hastily knocked back what remained of his drink, tossed the glass over his shoulder to land with a clatter on the bar, and reached for the Smith & Wesson Model 3 he carried thrust into his belt.

A heavy hand gripped his shoulder with painful intensity. The bartender rasped, "Don't go pullin' that smoke wagon, boy. You do and things will get rough."

Mac tried to shrug off the apron's grip and couldn't. Powerful fingers crushed into his shoulder so hard that his right arm began to go numb. He looked across the barroom and wondered why the hell he had ever come to Fort Worth, much less venturing into Hell's Half Acre, where anything, no matter how immoral or unhealthy, could be bought for two bits or a lying promise.

Two different fights were going on in this saloon, and they threatened to involve more than just the drunken cowboys swapping wild blows. The man with the six-gun in his hand continued to ventilate the ceiling with one bullet after another.

Blood spattered Mac's boots as one of the fistfights came tumbling in his direction. He lifted his left foot to keep it from getting stomped on by the brawlers. A steer had already done that a month earlier when he had been chuckwagon cook on a cattle drive from Waco up to Abilene.

He had taken his revenge on the annoying mountain of meat, singling it out for a week of meals for the Rolling J crew. Not only had the steer been clumsy where it stepped, it had been tough, and more than one cowboy had complained. Try as he might to tenderize the steaks, by beating, by marinating, by cursing, Mac had failed.

That hadn't been the only steer he had come to curse. The entire drive had been fraught with danger, and more than one of the crew had died.

"That's why," he said out loud.

"What's that?" The barkeep eased his grip and let Mac turn from the fight.

"After the drive, after the cattle got sold off and sent on their way to Chicago from the Abilene railroad yards, I decided to come back to Texas to pay tribute to a friend who died."

The bartender's expression said it all. He was in no mood to hear maudlin stories any more than he was to break up the fights or prevent a disgruntled cowboy from plugging a gambler he thought was cheating him at stud poker.

"Then you need another drink, in his memory." When Mac didn't argue the point, the barkeep poured an inch of rye in a new glass and made the two-bit coin Mac put down vanish. A nickel in change rolled across the bar.

"This is for you, Flagg. I just hope it's not too hot wherever you are." Mac lifted the glass and looked past it to the dirty mirror behind the bar. A medium-sized hombre with longish dark hair and a deeply tanned face gazed back at him. The man he saw reflected wasn't the boy who had been hired as a cook by a crusty old trail boss. He had Patrick Flagg to thank for making him grow up.

A quick toss emptied the glass.

The fiery liquor burned a path to his belly and kindled a blaze there. He belched and knew he had reached his limit. Mac had no idea why he had come to this particular gin mill, other than he was footloose and drifting after being paid off for the trail drive. The money burned a hole in his pocket, but Dewey Mackenzie had never been much of a spendthrift. Growing up on a farm in Missouri hadn't given him the chance to have two nickels to rub together, much less important money to waste.

With deft instinct, he stepped to the side as two brawling men crashed into the bar beside him, lost their footing, and sprawled on the sawdust-littered floor. Mac looked down at them, then let out a growl. He reached out and grabbed the man on top by the back of his coat. A hard heave lifted the fighter into the air until the fabric began to tear. Mac swung the man around, deposited him on his feet, and looked him squarely in the eye.

"What mess have you gotten yourself into now, Rattler?"

"Hey, as I live and breathe!" the cowboy exclaimed.

Howdy, Mac. Never thought our paths would cross again after Abilene."

Rattler ducked as his opponent surged to his feet and launched a wild swing. Mac leaned to one side, the bony fist passing harmlessly past his head. He batted the arm down to the bar and pounced on it, pinning the man.

"Whatever quarrel you've got with my friend, consider it settled," Mac told the man sternly.

"Ain't got a quarrel. I got a bone to pick!" The drunk wrenched free, reared back, and lost his balance, sitting hard amid the sawdust and vomit on the barroom floor.

"Come on, Rattler. Let's find somewhere else to do some drinking." Mac grabbed the front of the wiry man's vest and pulled him along into the street.

Mayhem filled Hell's Half Acre tonight. In either direction along Calhoun Street, saloons belched customers out to continue the battles that had begun inside. Others, done with their recreation outside, crowded to get back in for more liquor.

Mac brushed dirt off his threadbare clothes. Spending some of his pay on a new coat made sense. He whipped off his black, broad-brimmed hat and smacked it a couple times against his leg. Dust clouds rose. His hair had been plastered back by sweat. The lack of any wind down the Fort Worth street kept it glued down as if he had used bear grease. He wiped tears from his cat-green eyes and knew he had to get away from the dust and filth of the city. It was dangerous on the trail, tending a herd of cattle, but it was cleaner and wide-open prairie. He might get stomped on by a steer but never had to worry about being shot in the back.

He knew better than to ask Rattler what the fight had been over. Likely, it had started for no reason other than to blow off steam.

"I thought you were going to find a gunsmith and get some work there," Mac said to his companion. "You're a better tinkerer than most of them in this town."

Mac touched the Model 3 in his belt. Rattler had worked on it from Waco to Abilene during the drive and had turned his pappy's old sidearm into a deadly weapon that shot straight and true every time the trigger was pulled. For that, Mac thanked Rattler.

For teaching him how to draw fast and aim straight, he gave another silent nod to Patrick Flagg. More than teaching him how to draw faster than just about anyone, Flagg had also taught him when not to draw at all.

Rattler said, "And I thought you was headin' back to New Orleans to woo that filly of yours. What was her name? Evie?"

"Evangeline," Mac said.

"Yeah, you went on and on, even callin' out her name in your sleep. With enough money, you shoulda been able to win her over."

Mac knew better. He loved Evangeline Holdstock, and she had loved him until Pierre Leclerc had set his cap for her. Leclerc's plans included taking over Evie's father's bank after marrying her—probably inheriting it when he murdered Micah Holdstock.

Being framed for Micah's murder had been enough to convince Mac to leave New Orleans. Worse, the frame had also convinced Evie to have nothing to do with him other than to scratch out his eyes if he got close enough to the only woman he had ever loved.

His only hope of ever winning her back was to prove Leclerc had murdered Holdstock. Somehow, his determination to do that had faded after Leclerc had sent killers after him to Waco.

Mac smiled ruefully. If he hadn't been dodging them, he never would have signed on with the Rolling J crew and found he had a knack for cooking and cattle herding. The smile melted away when he realized Evie was lost forever to him, and returning to New Orleans meant his death, either from Leclerc's killers or at the end of a hangman's rope.

"There's other fish in the sea. Thass what they say," Rattler went on, slurring his morsel of advice. He braced himself against a hitching post to point at a three-story hotel across the street. "The House of Love, they call it. They got gals fer ever' man's taste there. Or so I been told. Less go find ourselves fillies and spend the night, Mac. We owe it to ourselves after all we been through."

"That's a mighty attractive idea, Rattler, but I want to dip my beak in some more whiskey. You can go and dip your, uh, other beak. Don't let me hold you back."

"They got plenny of ladies there. Soiled doves." Rattler laughed. "They got plenny of them to last the livelong night, but I worry this town's gonna run outta popskull."

With an expansive sweep of his arm, he indicated the dozen saloons within sight along Calhoun Street. It was past midnight and the drinking was beginning in earnest now. Every cowboy in Texas seemed to have crowded in with a powerful thirst demanding to be slaked by gallons of bad liquor and bitter beer.

"Which watering hole appeals to you, Rattler?" Mac saw each had a different attraction. Some dance halls had half-naked women willing to share a dance, rubbing up close, for a dime or until the piano player keeled over, too drunk to keep going. Others featured exotic animals or claimed imported food and booze from the four corners of the world.

Mac had become cynical enough to believe the whiskey and brandy they served came from bottles filled like all the others, from kegs and tanks brought into Hell's Half Acre just after sunrise. That's when most customers were passed out or too blind drunk to know the fancy French cognac they paid ten dollars a glass for was no different from the ten-cent tumbler filled with the same liquor at the drinking emporium next door. It was referred to as poor man's whiskey.

"Don't much matter. That one's close enough so I don't stagger too much gettin' to it." The man put his arm around Mac's shoulders for support, turned on unsteady feet, and took a step. He stopped short and looked up to a tall, dark man dressed in black. "'Scuse us, mister. We got some mighty hard drinkin' to do, and you're blockin' the way."

"Dewey Mackenzie," the man said in a hoarse whisper, almost drowned out by raucous music pouring from inside the saloon.

"Yeah, he's my friend," Rattler said, pulling away from Mac and stumbling to the side.

When he did so, he got in the way of the dark man's shot. Mac had never seen a man move faster. The Peacemaker cleared leather so swiftly the move was a blur. Fanning the hammer sent three slugs ripping out in a deadly rain that tore into Rattler's body. He threw up his arms, a look of surprise on his face as he collapsed backward into Mac's arms.

He died without saying another word.

"Damn it," the gunman growled, stepping to the side to get a better shot at Mac.

Shock disappeared as Mac realized he had to move or die. With a heave he lifted his dead friend up and tossed him into the shooter. The corpse knocked the gunman's aim off so his fourth bullet tore past Mac and sailed down Calhoun Street. Almost as an after-thought, someone farther away let out a yelp when the bullet found an unexpected target.

Mac had practiced for hours during the long cattle drive. His hand grabbed the wooden handles on the S&W. The pistol pulled free of his belt. He wasn't even aware of all he did, drawing back the hammer as he aimed, the pressure of the trigger against his finger, the recoil as the revolver barked out its single deadly reply.

The gunman caught the bullet smack in the middle of his chest. It staggered him. Propped against a hitching post, he looked down at a tiny red spot spreading on his gray-striped vest. His eyes came up and locked with Mac's.

"You shot me," he gasped. He used both hands to raise his six-gun. The barrel wobbled back and forth.

"Why'd you kill Rattler?" Mac held his gun in a curiously steady hand. The sights were lined on the gunman's heart.

He never got an answer. The man's pistol blasted another round, but this one tore into the ground between them. He let out a tiny gurgling sound and toppled straight forward, like an Army private at attention all the way down. A single twitch once he hit the ground was the only evidence of life fleeing.

"That's him!" a man shouted. "That's Mackenzie. He gunned down Jimmy!"

Another man said, "Willy's not gonna take kindly to this."

Mac looked up to see a pair of men pushing hurriedly through the saloon's batwing doors. It didn't take a genius to recognize the dead gunman's family. They might have been chiseled out of the same stone—broad shoulders, square heads, height within an inch of each other. Their coats were of the same fabric and color, and the Peacemakers slung at their hips might have been bought on the same day from the same gunsmith.

Even as they took in how the dead man had found the quarry Leclerc had put a bounty on, their hands went for their guns. Neither man was too quick on the draw, taking time to push away the long tails of their coats. This gave Mac the chance to swing his own gun around and get off a couple of shots.

Flying lead whined past both men and into the saloon they had just exited. Glass broke inside and men shouted angrily. Then all hell broke loose as the patrons became justifiably angry at being targeted. Several of them boiled out of the saloon with guns flashing and fists flying.

The two gunmen dodged Mac's slugs, but the rush of men from inside bowled them over, sending them stumbling out into the dusty street. Mac considered trying to dispatch them, then knew he had a tidal wave to hold back with only a couple of rounds.

"Sorry, Rattler," he said, taking a second to touch the brim of his hat in tribute to his trail companion. They had never been friends but had been friendly. That counted for something during a cattle drive.

He vaulted over Rattler's body, grabbed for the reins of a black stallion tethered to the side of the saloon, and jumped hard, landing in the saddle with a thud. The spirited animal tried to buck him off. Mac had learned how to handle even the proddiest cayuse in any remuda. He bent low, grabbed the horse around the neck, and hung on for dear life as the horse bolted into the street.

A new threat posed itself then—or one that had been delayed, anyway. Both of the dead gunman's partners—or brothers or whatever they were—opened fire on him. Mac stayed low, using the horse as a shield.

"Horse thief!" The strident cry came from one of the gunmen. This brought out cowboys from a half dozen more saloons. Getting beaten to a bloody pulp or even shot full of holes meant nothing to these men. But having a horse thief among them was a hanging offense.

"There he is!" Mac yelled as he sat up in the saddle and pointed down the street. "The thieving bastard just rounded the corner. After him!"

The misdirection worked long enough for him to send the mob off on a wild goose chase, but that still left two men intent on avenging their partner. Mac put his head down again, jerked the horse's reins, and let the horse gallop into a barroom, scattering the customers inside.

He looked around as he tried to control the horse in the middle of the sudden chaos he had created. Going back the way he came wouldn't be too smart. A quick glance in the mirror behind the bar showed both of the black-clad men crowding through the batwings and waving their guns around.

A savage roar caught his attention. In a corner crouched a black panther, snarling to reveal fierce fangs capable of ripping a man apart. No wonder the black stallion was going loco. He had to be able to smell the big cat.

The huge creature strained at a chain designed to hold a riverboat anchor. The clamor rose as the bartender shouted at Mac to get his horse out of the saloon. The apron-clad man reached under the bar and pulled out a sawed-off shotgun.

"Out, damn your eyes!" the bartender bellowed as he leveled the weapon.

Mac whirled around and began firing, not at the panther but at the wall holding the chain. The chain itself was too strong for a couple of bullets to break.

The wood splintered as Mac's revolver came up empty. When the panther lunged again, it pulled the chain staple free and dragged it into the room. The customer nearest the cat screeched as heavy claws raked at him.

Then the bartender fired his shotgun and Mac yelped as rock salt burned his face and arm. Worse, the rock salt spooked the horse even more than the attacking panther.

The stallion exploded like a Fourth of July rocket. Mac did all he could do to hang on as the horse leaped through a plate glass window. Glittering shards flew in all directions, but he was out of the saloon and once more in the street.

The sense of triumph faded fast when both gunmen who'd been pursuing him boiled out through the window he had just destroyed.

"That's him, Willy. Him's the one what killed Jimmy!"

Mac looked back at death stalking him. A tall,

broad man with a square head and the same dark coat pushed back the tails to reveal a double-gun rig. Peacemakers holstered at either hip quickly jumped into the man's grip. Using both hands, the man started firing. And he was a damned good shot.

CHAPTER TWO

Dewey Mackenzie jerked to the side and almost fell from the horse as a bullet tore a chunk from the brim of his hat. He glanced up and got a quick look at the moon through the hole. The bullets sailing around him motivated him to put his heels to the horse's flanks.

Again the horse bolted through the open door of a saloon. This one's crowd stared at a half-naked woman on stage gyrating to bad piano music. They were too preoccupied to be aware of the havoc being unleashed outside. Even a man riding through the back of the crowd hardly pulled their attention away from the lurid display.

Mac slid from the saddle and tugged on the reins to get the horse out of the saloon. He had to shoulder men aside, which drew a few curses and surly looks, but people tended to get out of the way of a horse.

Finally he worked his way through the press of men who smelled of sweat and lust and beer. He emerged into the alley behind the gin mill. Walking slowly, forcing himself to regain his composure, he left the Tivoli Saloon behind and went south on Throckmorton Street.

The city's layout was something of a mystery to him, but he remembered the wagon yard was between Main and Rusk, only a few streets over. He resisted the urge to mount and ride out of town. If he did that, the gang of cutthroats would be after him before dawn. His best chance of getting away was to fade into the woodwork and let the furor die down. Shooting his way out of Fort Worth was as unlikely to be successful as was galloping off.

Where would he go? He had a few dollars left in his pocket from his trail drive pay, but he knew no one, had no friends, no place to go to ground for a week or two. Mac decided being footloose was a benefit. Wherever he went would be fine, with the gunmen unable to track him because he sought friends' help. He had no friends in Fort Worth.

"Not going to get anybody else killed," he said bitterly, sorry for Rattler catching the lead intended for him.

He tugged on the stallion's reins and worked his way farther south along Rusk until he reached the wagon yard. He patted the horse's neck. It was a strong animal, one he would have loved to ride. But it was distinctive enough to draw attention he didn't need.

"Come on, partner," Mac told the stallion quietly. The horse neighed, tried to nuzzle him, and then trotted along into the wagon yard. A distant corral filled with a dozen horses began to come awake. By the time he reached the office, the hostler was pulling up his suspenders and rubbing sleep from his eyes. He was a scarecrow of a man with a bald head and prominent Adam's apple.

"You're up early, mister," the man said. "Been on the trail? Need a place to stable your horse while you're whooping it up?"

"I'm real down on my luck, sir," Mac said sincerely. "What would you give me for the horse?"

"This one?" The liveryman came over and began examining the horse. He rested his hand on the saddle and looked hard at Mac. "The tack, too?"

"Why not? I need some money, but I also need another horse and gear. Swap this one for a less spirited horse, maybe? And a simple saddle?"

"This is mighty fine workmanship." The man ran his fingers over the curlicues cut into the saddle. "Looks to be fine Mexican leatherwork. That goes for top dollar in these parts."

"The horse, too. That's the best horse I ever did ride, but I got expenses. . . ." Mac let the sentence trail off. The liveryman would come to his own conclusions. Whatever they might be would throw the gunmen off Mac's trail, if they bothered to even come to the wagon yard.

He reckoned they would figure out which was his horse staked out back of the first saloon he had entered and wait for him to return for both the horse and his gear. Losing the few belongings he had rankled like a burr under his saddle, but he had tangled before with bounty hunters Pierre Leclerc had set on his trail. The man didn't hire stupid killers. Mac's best—his only—way to keep breathing was to leave Fort Worth fast and cut all ties with both people and belongings.

A deep sigh escaped his lips. Rattler was likely the only one he knew in town. That hurt, seeing the man cut down the way he had been, but somehow, leaving behind his mare, saddle, and the rest of his tack tormented him even more.

"I know a gent who'd be willing to pay top dollar for such a fine horse, but you got to sell the saddle, too. It's mighty fine. The work that went into it shows a master leather smith at his peak, yes, sir." The livery-man cocked his head to one side and studied Mac as if he were a bug crawling up the wall.

"Give me a few bucks, another horse and saddle, and I'll be on my way."

"Can't rightly do that till I see if I can sell the stallion. I'm runnin' a bit shy on cash. You wait here, let me take the horse and see if the price is right. I might get you as much as a hundred dollars."

"That much?" Mac felt his hackles rise. "That and another horse and tack?"

"Don't see horses this spirited come along too often. And that saddle?" The man shook his head. "Once in a lifetime."

"Do tell. So what's to keep you from taking the horse and riding away?"

"I own the yard. I got a reputation to uphold for honesty. Ask around. You go find yourself some break-fast. Might be, I can get you as much as a hundred-fifty dollars."

"And that's after you take your cut?"

"Right after," the man assured him.

Mac knew he lied through his teeth.

"Is there a good restaurant around here? Not that it matters since I don't have money for even a fried egg and a cup of water." He waited to see what the man offered. The response assured him he was right.

"Here, take five dollars. An advance against what I'll make selling the horse. That means I'll take it out of your share."

"Thanks," Mac said, taking the five crumpled greenbacks. He stuffed them into his vest pocket. "How long do you think you'll be?"

"Not long. Not more 'n a half hour. That'll give you plenty of time to chow down and drink a second cup of coffee. Maggie over at the Bendix House boils up a right fine cup."

"Bendix House? That's it over there? Much obliged." Mac touched the brim of his hat, making sure not to show the hole shot through and through. He let the man lead the horse away, then started for the restaurant.

Only when the liveryman was out of sight did Mac spin around and run back to the yard. A quick vault over the fence took him to the barn. Rooting around, he found a serviceable saddle, threadbare blanket, bridle, and saddlebags. He pressed his hand against them. Empty. Right now, he didn't have time to search for food or anything more to put in them. He needed a slicker and a change of clothing.

Most of all he needed to leave. Now.

Picking a decent-looking mare from the corral took only a few seconds. The one who trotted over to him was the one he stole. Less than a minute later, saddle and bridle hastily put on, he rode out.

As he came out on Rusk Street, he caught sight of a small posse galloping in his direction. He couldn't make out the riders' faces, but they all wore black coats that might as well have been a uniform. Putting his heels to his horse's flanks, he galloped away, cut behind the wagon yard's buildings, and then faced a dilemma. Going south took him past the railroad and onto the prairie.

The flat, barren prairie where he could be seen riding for miles.

Mac rode back past Houston Street and immediately dismounted, leading his horse to the side of the Comique Saloon. He had to vanish, and losing himself among the late night—or early morning now—imbibers was the best way to do it. The wagon yard owner would be hard-pressed to identify which horse was missing from a corral with a couple dozen animals in it. Mac cursed himself for not leaving the gate open so all the horses escaped.

"Confusion to my enemies," he muttered. Two quick turns of the bridle through an iron ring secured his mount. He circled the building and started to go into the saloon.

"Door's locked," came the warning from a man sitting in a chair on the far side of the door. He had his hat pulled down to shield his eyes from the rising sun and the chair tilted back on its hind legs.

"Do tell." Mac nervously looked around, expecting to see the posse on his trail closing in. He took the chair next to the man, duplicated his pose, and pulled his hat down, more to hide his face than to keep the sunlight from blinding him. "When do they open?"

"John Leer's got quite a place here. But he don't keep real hours. It's open when it's needed most. Otherwise, he closes up."

"Catches some shut-eye?"

The man laughed.

"Hardly. He's got a half dozen floozies in as many bawdy houses, or so the rumor goes. Servicing all of them takes up his spare time."

"You figuring on waiting long for him to get back?"

The man pushed his hat back and looked over at Mac. He spat on the boardwalk, repositioned himself precariously in the chair, and crossed his arms over his chest before answering.

"Depends. I'm hunting for cowboys. The boss man sends me out to recruit for a drive. I come here to find who's drunkest. They're usually the most likely to agree to the lousy wages and a trip long enough to guarantee saddle sores on your butt."

"You might come here and make such an appealing pitch, but I suspect you offer top dollar." Mac tensed when a rider galloped past. The man wore a plaid shirt and jeans. He relaxed. Not a bounty hunter.

"You're the type I'm looking for. Real smart fellow, you are. My trail boss wouldn't want a drunk working for him, and the boss man was a teetotaler. His wife's one of them temperance women. More 'n that, she's one of them suffer-ay-jets, they call 'em. Can't say I cotton much to going without a snort now and then, and giving women the vote like up in Wyoming's just wrong but—"

"But out on the trail nobody drinks. The cook keeps the whiskey, for medicinal purposes only."

"You been on a drive?"

"Along the Shawnee Trail." Mac's mind raced. Losing himself among a new crew driving cattle would solve most of his problems.

"That's not the way the Circle Arrow herd's headed. We're pushing west along the Goodnight-Loving Trail."

"Don't know it," Mac admitted.

"Don't matter. Mister Flowers has been along it enough times that he can ride it blindfolded."

"Flowers?"

"Hiram Flowers, the best damned trail boss in Texas. Or so I'm told, since I've only worked for a half dozen in my day." The man rocked forward and thrust out his hand. "My name's Cletus Grant. I do the chores Mister Flowers don't like."

"Finding trail hands is one of them?" Mac asked as he clasped the man's hand.

"He doesn't stray far from the Circle Arrow."

"What's that mean?" Mac shifted so his hand rested on his gun when another rider came down the street. He went cold inside when he remembered he hadn't reloaded. Truth to tell, all his spare ammunition was in his saddlebags, on his horse left somewhere behind another saloon in Hell's Half Acre.

When the rider rode on after seeing the Comique was shuttered, Mac tried to mask his move by shifting in the chair. He almost toppled over.

He covered by asking, "You said the Circle Arrow owner was a teetotaler. He fall off the wagon?"

"His missus wouldn't ever allow that, no, sir. He upped and died six months back, in spite of his missus telling him not to catch that fever. Old Zeke Sullivan should have listened that time. About the only time he didn't do as she told him." Cletus spat again, wiped his mouth, and asked, "You looking for a job?"

"I'm a piss-poor cowboy, but there's no better chuck-wagon cook in all of Texas. Or so I'm told, since I've only worked for the Rolling J in my day."

Cletus Grant's expression turned blank for a moment, then he laughed.

"You got a sharp wit about you, son. I don't know that Mister Flowers is looking for a cook, but he does need trail hands. Why don't me and you mosey on out to the Circle Arrow and palaver a mite about the chance you'd ride with us to Santa Fe?"